THE VOID

By Greig Beck

momentum

First published 2018 in Momentum by Pan Macmillan Australia Pty Ltd
1 Market Street, Sydney, New South Wales, Australia 2000

A CIP record for this book is available at the National Library of Australia

The Void

EPUB format: 9781760559397
Print on Demand format: 9781760780050

Original cover design by Dean Samed,
adapted by Danielle Hurps
Edited by Samantha Sainsbury
Proofread by Laura Cook

Macmillan Digital Australia: www.macmillandigital.com.au

To report a typographical error, please visit www.panmacmillan.com.au/contact-us/

Visit www.panmacmillan.com.au/ to read more about all our books and to buy books online. You will also find features, author interviews and news of any author events.

Greig Beck grew up across the road from Bondi Beach in Sydney, Australia. His early days were spent surfing, sunbaking and reading science fiction on the sand. He then went on to study computer science, immerse himself in the financial-software industry and later received an MBA. Today, Greig spends his days writing, but still finds time to surf at his beloved Bondi Beach. He lives in Sydney, with his wife, son and an enormous German shepherd.

For NASA – the search for stardust continues.

We don't know what's really out there –
and maybe it's better it stays that way.

Colonel Jack Hammerson

PROLOGUE

Through the endless void, tumbling and spinning, crossing distances so vast that time becomes a meaningless concept.

And then ...

contact.

CHAPTER 1

Space Shuttle Orbiter Orlando, 330 miles above Texas

Commander Mitch Granger looked at the mission clock – 36.03 more hours to go, just a day and a half more. *Piece of cake.* They'd been up for a week now, and he was starting to feel the drag of home pulling him back harder than ever.

Homesick, he thought. *Hey, the homesick astronaut – not a bad title for a book.* He had always wanted to write one; after all, everyone was doing it these days and making a fortune.

Mitch leaned back in his seat and peered out the shuttle cockpit window. The glass was magnificently clear, even though the orbiter's portal windows were triple-paned, super-hardened optical-quality glass. He knew if he wasn't wearing the bulky suit gloves and pressed a hand against it, it would still feel numbingly cold and fragile. There were thirty-seven windowpanes in eleven different sizes and shapes on the shuttle, and all of them acknowledged as a point of possible engineering failure.

Just a few sheets of glass between me, a vacuum, and certain death, he sighed.

He reached up to tap the glass – safe as a bank. The shuttle orbiter technology was considered rock solid these days. On the Space Hazard Risk Identification Scale, where a low score equaled low risk, it rated 6.5 out of ten. Now human beings, they were a whole different kettle of onions. *We poor shaved apes rate up at 7.2* – there's your higher risk factors right there.

He inhaled a deep breath and then let it out slowly. They were a risk, the glass was a risk; up here every goddamn thing was a risk. Like it or not, they were in a metal shell, orbiting 333 miles above earth and hurtling along in orbit at 17,500 miles per hour.

He smiled dreamily; space was so vast, and everything looked frozen in place. There was nothing but pinpricks of light showing through to a blanket of black velvet.

At least with the windows they got to see out, which was some compensation. But still, everything was primarily run on autopilot or from NASA HQ, and in space nothing ever seemed to change, so really, their biggest challenge was fighting boredom.

Flight engineer Gerry Fifield floated back to his seat, pulling himself in and throwing a belt over his shoulder to stay in place. He started to press buttons, reading data from a screen. He spoke without turning.

"Beth is nearly finished back there, skipper."

"Thank god for that," said Mitch. "Wearing this suit is a bitch." He stretched, trying to get comfortable in the bright orange MACES suit, or Modified Advanced Crew Escape Suit. They were the new design and nothing like the silver or white Michelin Man suits of old. But the vacuum of space was a killer, and it needed to be kept out at all costs, and that meant wearing the modern equivalent of a suit of armor.

Mission specialist Beth Power was back in the bay area running some experiments that required the payload delivery doors to be open – and the bay doors being open meant spacesuits on everywhere in the ship.

Mitch turned. "How's Noah's Ark?"

Gerry smiled back. "Larry and Moe are running miles, Curly Joe is taking a nap, and Mustang Sally is just hangin' out as always. Plus, our creepy crawlies are doing their creepin' and crawlin' thing." Gerry raised his eyebrows. "All creatures great and small are all present and accounted for."

"Never work with animals or children – who was it said that?" Mitch grinned.

"Either WC Fields or Miley Cyrus – one of the greats, anyway," returned Gerry.

Noah's Ark was right. They had three mice, Larry, Moe and Curly Joe; a teenage sloth named Mustang Sally that may one day hold the key to long-term hibernation; and a panoply of ants, cockroaches, mantes, other bugs as well as giant earthworms in glass cases. Plus, thrown in for good measure, some plant and fungi stock.

Bottom line was the government's interest in space travel was waning, and to get a bird financially airborne these days, NASA needed to be a flying circus.

That and other more covert fund-raising activities. Mitch eyed one of his screens that held a small number count still increasing. Their biggest sponsor of this mission was the US military, and the screen count was of the images taken as they passed over Russia and Eastern Europe. Mitch looked away – he hadn't asked, and didn't want to know. It was well above his pay grade anyway.

Among the sea of lights on the console, a single one started to blink, demanding attention.

"*Whoa* there, Ripley just picked up something on the long-range scanner." Gerry straightened in his seat.

"Satellite or debris?" Mitch only partially listened; there was always *something* on the scanners. After all, space was a veritable junkyard these days.

"Ripley's checking now." Gerry listened to the computerized babble via a headset until a smooth feminine voice cut through.

The *Orlando* had five on-board computers that handled data processing and control critical flight systems. They talked to each other and even voted to settle arguments with RIPLE – the Relational Intelligent Processor and Logic Entity – known as Ripley, who was the head processor and mother hen, having the deciding vote.

Gerry held up a finger as he listened. "Ripley's got it now."

In a modern shuttle orbiter, pilots like Mitch and Gerry essentially flew the computers, which in turn flew the ship for them. In front of each man was a Multifunctional Electronic Display Subsystem, or MEDS, which was a full color, eleven-panel visual system the pilots called the 'glass cockpit'. Ripley was an upgraded AI, and probably the most advanced technology in the old shuttle design. She was the new brain in an old body, and her major task was to keep her eyes and ears on the ship and the universe, and then translate it back to the astronauts for any fine-tuning.

"What is it, and where's it from?" Mitch asked.

Gerry shook his head, frowning. "Not *from* anywhere." He turned to Mitch. "She says it's coming out of the void."

Mitch half turned – *the void*. It was a description for any area of space that was well outside of the solar system. It was deep space, uncharted and with nothing there for countless billions of miles.

"Not on any orbit?" He sat forward. "What size?"

"Not big, less than a dozen feet long." Gerry bobbed his head. "She says it'll pass close by us. Here, listen." He flicked the input to audio.

Mitch stared out through the thick glass of the cockpit window. "Talk to me, Ripley: what can you tell us?"

The calm feminine voice began. "Hello, Commander Granger. The unidentified object is in a non-elliptical orbit, traveling in a straight-line trajectory, and coming out of deep space quadrant ninety-five. It is traveling at 224.22 miles per second."

"Pretty slow." Mitch's eyes narrowed. "Size?"

Ripley didn't hesitate. "124.32 inches by 47.1 inches."

"Thanks, Ripley. Keep watching."

"Always, Commander."

Mitch exhaled. "So much for our guys on the ground always having our back – I'd better check with Russ; see what else he can tell us."

Mitch placed the headset on and switched to external. The computer would use NASA's DSN – Deep Space Network – to send signals back and forth between the *Orlando* and NASA. Luckily, they were close to home at 333 miles up, and would endure no time lag. He opened a channel.

"This is Commander Mitch Granger onboard the Space Shuttle Orbiter *Orlando*. Russ, are you there, over?"

Mitch only had to wait a few seconds. As he expected, Russell Burrows seemed to be there night and day, *every* day. When they were in space, Russ being on-deck was as dependable and regular as clockwork.

"Howdy Mitch, great looking morning. How's it look from up there?"

Mitch smiled, hearing his friend, engineer, and top dog at NASA Control. "Another beautiful day over the US of A, buddy, and not a cloud in the sky." He looked briefly over at Gerry's screen. "It'd probably look even better if we didn't have something in our front yard. What's going on, Russ? We got a small bogey in quadrant ninety-five, coming out of the void at about 224 miles per second."

"Hi, Mitch."

Her voice made Mitch smile. "Hi, back at you."

Anne's voice made him feel homesick all over again. Doctor Anne Peterson was one of the NASA ground technicians for the space program. She was also a trained biologist and medical doctor. She and Mitch had been dating for a year, and Russ had let her stay on-deck while Mitch was in orbit.

"Miss you," Anne said softly, and suddenly Mitch wanted to be home more than anything in the world.

"And me you, beautiful." He wanted to tell her he loved her, but knew the team would give him hell for weeks if he did. "Can't wait to see you again."

"You two love birds finished?" Russ had a smile in his voice.

"For now." Mitch grinned back.

"We can see your bogey, Mitch. Been tracking it since last night when it swung out from behind the moon. We originally expected it to pass you by with over 1,000 miles to spare, and no need to even mention it," Russ said. "Small, but heavy in trace metals and other composites that are unknown – could be meteorite, but doesn't seem on any sort of minor or major elliptical orbit. Maybe bumped out of the Kuiper Belt by an asteroid."

"*Originally* expected?" Mitch waited.

"Yeah, we received updated information just a few minutes back." Russ mumbled to someone in the background and then he whistled. "Looks like it'll come a little closer to you guys than we first estimated."

"How close? Ripley confirmed it'd miss us." Mitch stared out the cockpit windows to the quadrant from where he knew the object was approaching.

"Close, *real* close." There was a muffled conversation again before Russ came back. "Has Beth finished her work in the bay? Might be a good idea for her to pack it up and lock it down; just until this little guy has said goodbye to you."

There was a clicking sound and more muffled conversation, and Mitch could imagine Russ Burrows snapping his fingers and calling for more data, before he came back on the line.

"Our calculations are that it's still gonna pass by, but now within 120 miles of your position – give you guys a bit of a skinny." Russ turned serious. "Better strap in, just in case we have any more deviation and you need to give *Orlando* a little bit of a kick. Be skimming by your orbit in thirty-six minutes. Roger that, Mitch?"

"Roger that, Russ, over." Mitch shifted in his seat. He could read his friend like a book. The man came across as laid-back as you like, but underneath it Mitch could sense a little tension. Russ was worried about something – maybe the proximity, or maybe something else. And if Russ was worried, then *he* sure should be. Any *more* deviation, he had said. Since when do astral objects keep deviating?

Mitch started to open all the sensors, and spoke without turning. "Gerry, can you go help get Beth all squared away and back in her chair."

"You got it." Gerry unbuckled and floated backwards, pulling himself around on the chair edge, hitting the door-open button on the wall that separated the cockpit from the rear bulkhead door of the cockpit, and then torpedoing down the center of the cargo bay area to where Beth was working.

Mitch turned back to his screens. "Ripley, give me a constant data feed on our bogey."

"Presenting now, commander." Ripley sent the data directly to his MEDS screens and it scrolled up before his eyes. "Commander, I have detected an interesting anomaly."

"*Huh*?" Mitch's brows came together. "What is it?"

"There seems to be a rhythmic recurring emission from the object." Ripley's voice was objective as always.

"Feed it." Mitch listened as Ripley pushed and then boosted the sound to his headset. He closed his eyes and concentrated – there was a faint heartbeat-like pulse, and something else that could have been a low hum or buzz, like the sound a swarm of bees bedding down for the night.

He opened his eyes. "What do you make of it?"

"Unknown, Commander." Ripley paused.

"Hypothesize," he urged.

She complied. "High probability of background interference."

"Other probabilities?" He waited.

"Solar signal distortion, radio wave bounce, acceleration flow, other signal, type unknown," she intoned.

"Okay." He listened for a few more moments, feeling a small twist of unease in his gut. "Cut transmission."

Immediately the sound was shut off, and he breathed out. "High probability of background interference, *huh*?"

Curiosity got the better of him. "Let me hear it again, and amplify."

Ripley restarted the sound, and Mitch tilted his head, listening – clicks, weird scratching, and a dull, liquid throb, like a heartbeat. It gave him the freaking creeps.

"Hey."

"*Jesus.*" Mitch jumped in his seat.

"Easy there." Gerry grinned and floated back into his seat. "Beth will be done in five." He buckled in. "So what is it?"

"What it is, is just plain weird." Mitch switched the external sounds over to Gerry.

Gerry placed a hand to his earpiece and concentrated. "Holy hell. Interference maybe?" He frowned. "Or some sort of acceleration flow?"

"That's what Ripley suggested. But like I said, *weird.*" Mitch sat back. "The good news is it's small enough to totally burn up if it punches into the atmosphere."

"Commander Granger, come back."

Mitch touched his ear mic. "Go ahead, Russ."

"Look, *ah,* this might sound a little weird, but …"

"Weird, *huh*?" Mitch turned to roll his eyes at Gerry.

"Yeah, this little guy seems to have altered its trajectory." Russ responded, still cheery. "It's still just tumbling around up there, but now seems to be course correcting. Trajectory risk programs say it's now on collision course with you."

"Magnetic?" Mitch sat straighter.

"That's what we're thinking, iron-based composition and all. So we're gonna back you guys up a few hundred miles," Russ said. "Better get Beth in *right now*, and then we'll give you a little bump."

"Roger that." Mitch turned. "Go get her in, Gerry, pronto. And don't let her argue with you."

"You got it, boss." Gerry was already shooting back to the hatch door again.

Mitch looked out of the window, and for the first time he could make out a small dot of light that had appeared on his horizon. "Okay, Russ, I have visual now."

He watched it for several moments, and then looked down at his screen. Ripley couldn't tell him anything more than he already knew, other than to inform him that the object's internal pulse had elevated.

Getting excited, are we?

The thought made the hair on his neck prickle for some reason. He glanced at the countdown timer on one of the screens – time was vanishing way too fast. He touched his ear mic.

"Hurry up back there, you two. Bogey's gonna be on us in twenty-four minutes."

Almost immediately, Gerry came back into the cockpit with Beth now in tow. Both floated into their seats then buckled in.

"Sorry Mitch, but if we're gonna move the bus, I wanted to make sure there was nothing that's going to end up in our laps." She looked up and out through the window. "What have we got: debris?"

11

"Something like that," Mitch responded. "But its trajectory has altered – coming right at us now."

"Altered?" Beth turned back to him.

Mitch nodded. "Okay, ladies and gentlemen, let's run a skin check, and then prepare for a short and sharp controlled burn."

The skin check was a term for when they ran a fast diagnostic over the *Orlando*'s surface integrity. The onboard computers managed the hull's external health automatically, and even a pinprick would have had Ripley screaming at them. But protocol demanded a manual once-over prior to engaging thrusters. Besides, no one minded ensuring there weren't any swinging back doors or loose tiles when they were about to fire up a few thousand pounds of thrust.

"Okay, hull integrity is good and solid." Gerry ran eyes over a screen full of tiny green lights.

"Bay doors secure, seams are tight, and equipment locked down. All good here, boss," Beth added.

"Okay NASA, I'm waking up Ripley's engine security." He placed a hand on a screen that circled his fingertips, reading his prints, and giving him clearance. "And we are good to go." Mitch placed a hand on the joystick. "Initiating forward thrusters in, three, two, one ... *burn*." He pressed down with his thumb.

There was a sensation of added weight, a backward motion, and then a hint of blurring out of the cockpit window as if there was an oily dispersion from the nose cone of the shuttle as the thrusters burned fuel.

"First burn complete." Mitch shut the nose thrusters off as the *Orlando* slid backwards in space. His eyes were on the computer screen as he watched the seconds and distance count down. In a vacuum, even a tiny push one way would continue your progress in that direction until you hit something, or ...

"Ready on reverse thrust on, three, two, one ... *burn*."

... you got a little shove in the opposite direction.

Mitch engaged the rear thrusters for a minor burst to return the *Orlando* to the same orbital attitude. Almost immediately, Ripley gave him validation of his work.

"Back in new designated structural orbit and we have good spatial and attitude control. How do you read us, NASA?" Mitch sat back.

Russ came back immediately. "Roger that, *Orlando*, you are looking good. Checking your proximity relationship now."

Mitch waited, his eyes going from the MEDS screen to the view of space from the cockpit windows. He always enjoyed the interaction with the controls. Most of their missions were either so automated or controlled by a battalion of ground technicians that he felt sometimes he was only along for the ride.

"*Ah, Orlando ...*"

Mitch didn't like the tone in Russ' voice.

"... do you still have visual on our bogey?"

Mitch frowned, and then leaned forward. The small speck of light was still there. *But so what? He expected it to be.*

"Affirmative, Russ, we see it. What's our new proximity relationship?" Mitch continued to stare at the speck.

Mitch heard Russ click his tongue against his cheek. "Damndest thing, Mitch, when you course corrected, it did too. It, *ah*, kinda stayed with you."

Shit. Mitch felt his breath catch. "Say again, NASA. Confirm, bogey is *still* on intercept vector?" He felt both Gerry and Beth turn to look at him. There were several seconds of silence, and then ...

"That is affirmative, *Orlando*." Russ' demeanor had suddenly gone all business.

"How?" Mitch gritted his teeth.

Ripley responded smoothly. "The object seemed to project something akin to an electric charge that focused the direction and magnitude of the vector field. In effect, it created a magnetic field projection."

"Like a tractor beam." Mitch felt a prickle of perspiration under one of his arms as he tried to make sense of what that meant. "It projected it ... *at us*?"

"Unable to verify intent, Commander."

Fuck. He licked his lips. He'd seen what micrometeorites could do to the skin of a shuttle. Even a glancing impact could crack a single tile. Worst-case scenario was the computer didn't detect it until you were reentering the atmosphere. By that time, it would be too late to compensate, and the only option would be to toast marshmallows as you kissed your ass goodbye. He glanced at the timer; eighteen minutes, and it'd be on top of them.

"Okay, NASA, I'm going to burn again." Mitch turned to his crew who simply nodded. He felt his jaws tighten as he gripped the stick. "Engaging all pitch nozzles, in three, two, one ... *burn*."

This time *Orlando* pushed back, *hard*. Mitch heard Gerry grunt beside him, as the craft vented the burning fuel, pushing them backwards in its orbit. He watched the computer read down the numbers, and waited, waited, seconds seeming like an eternity.

He shut it down, relaxing his hand for a few seconds, before resetting their orbital attitude again. "Compensating burn on three, two, one ... *burn*."

Their orbital slide slowed and then stopped. Mitch looked up; the dot of light was still there, bigger if anything. It was like they had it on a piece of string.

"What the hell is that thing?" He suddenly felt cold fingers dancing up his spine, and swallowed down a lump of frustration rising in his gut.

"Control, *Russ*, this damn thing is still with us. Any ideas? Over."

"Yep, we see it, Mitch." Russ had a brief whispered conversation in the background before coming back on.

"Ripley says it's over ten feet, nose to tip; so if it sticks to us, we're never going to be able to compensate for its drag coming in," said Gerry.

Mitch nodded to his friend. "Russ, if the magnetic field on that thing is strong enough to track us, then it's damn well strong enough to stick to us; it'll fry our instruments."

"I hear you, Mitch. We're not going to let that happen – leave it with us guys, we're working on it."

Mitch exhaled through pressed lips. "We'll be here, over." He signed out.

Gerry turned in his seat, staring for a moment. "Mitch, we can't let that thing even kiss us."

"No, no, Gerry, we can't." Mitch stared at the proximity countdown. He felt like he had a lead ball in his gut.

CHAPTER 2

NASA's John F Kennedy Space Center, Florida –
Mission Control Room

"*Damn it!* Run it again." Russell Burrows ran both his hands up through his hair. "Come on, people. I got some of the best engineering, physics and mathematical brains in the country right here. So give me something." He began to pace.

"We could break it up." A technician sat straighter.

Russ stopped his pacing. "Go on."

"Well, if the object was fragmented enough, then even if the remaining pieces adhered to the skin, they might not cause undue distortion. They'd be small enough to simply burn away on reentry."

Russ turned and leaned across a desk. "What sized fragments?"

The technician turned back to his screen, typed for a few seconds, and then looked back to Russ. "Safest result would be fist-sized or smaller."

"Ooookay." Russ drummed his fingers on the desk. "This thing is basically a large lump of iron, and our astronauts have the equivalent of a telescopic hand-drill." He closed his eyes for a moment. "Exactly how long would that take to break it down to that sized debris? And I'm assuming it would be done via space-walk."

"Correct, sir. If they worked around the clock ..." The technician grimaced. "223 hours."

"Nine days." Russ sighed. "We've got twelve minutes until we are at intersection point." He looked skyward. "Anything else?" He waited in silence. Russ lowered his head. "Anything?" He looked at the faces of his brilliant technicians. There was nothing but anxiety, frustration, and a little fear.

It was time to update the *Orlando* on their progress. *Or lack of it,* he thought glumly, as he slowly pulled on his headset.

* * *

"NASA's got nothing." Mitch turned in his seat. "Beth, you're our science officer; any ideas?"

Beth looked up from her MEDS screen and rested on her elbows. "Well, we know it's a metallic-based composite. But Ripley tells me that it's only thirty-eight percent metallic. That leaves a lot of the mass that is unidentifiable. But even with only thirty-eight percent metallic weight, we estimate it'll be around 8,000 pounds. Small enough to vanish in the atmosphere ..." She grimaced. "... but if it hits us, I don't think it'll just *stick* to us."

Mitch nodded. "Yeah, that's what NASA figured. Okay, so we know the problem and possible outcome. I'm looking for answers now, people."

Beth shrugged. "Bottom line, don't let it run into us."

"Thank you, Beth; I wish I had of thought of that." Mitch's lips pressed together.

"That's why they pay me the big bucks." She jiggled her eyebrows.

"Can we get ahead of it?" Gerry asked. "Maybe reenter? Head for home before it gets to us. You said yourself this thing was small enough to burn up in the atmosphere. It won't be able to follow us."

"I thought about that, and no can do. We're well out of position and it'd probably put us over foreign territory or the Atlantic. *Orlando* is clever, but it isn't equipped for an ocean ditch, or to wind up in mainland China."

Mitch thought for a moment. "Okay, I'm keeping that option as our break-glass strategy. We only need a few more hours to get us over friendly territory, and then we can put it down on Route 66 if we need to. So, we need more time."

"What I wouldn't give for a photon blaster right now," said Gerry. "But seriously, I still think we can stay ahead of it until reentry – we're already on the countdown clock."

"I'll put that on the list as well." Mitch turned to Beth. "C'mon brains, what else you got?"

She grinned back.

"What?" Mitch asked, his mouth also hitching at the corners.

"We use the robotic arm," she said, still grinning. "We grab that sucker, and hold on. Means we'll lose the arm as we enter the upper atmosphere, but at least it'll all burn up while keeping it away from us."

Mitch sat back. "Not bad." Immediately his mind set to working on the plan.

"No, won't work. The arm might collapse back onto our tail as we generate reentry acceleration." Gerry grimaced. "Sorry, I liked the idea as well."

"It will work," Beth responded.

"No, he's right. It's too big a risk." Mitch sat back.

Beth continued to smile.

Mitch lifted his chin to her. "Okay, now what?"

"Okay, listen up, the payload bay is three times the size of our stalker, and can support ten times its weight." She held her hands wide. "We grab it and bring it into the hold. We retain the aerodynamics of the *Orlando*, and we get to take home a good-sized chunk of asteroid for the nerds to drool over. Bonus points all round." She winked.

Mitch sat thinking. "Hmm." He mentally tried to work through the risks, but there were too many to get his head around. The one thing he did know; doing nothing was not an option anymore. "Might be all we've got." He opened the link to ground control. "Russ, you there, buddy?"

"We read you, *Orlando*."

Mitch gave him a thumbnail overview and waited while Russ discussed it with an assembled team.

"We're gonna run a quick simulation – hold tight there, Mitch." Russ left the line open.

The crew waited, staring from their MEDS screens to the cockpit window. Russ came back within two seemingly eternal minutes.

"Computer simulation says it could work. Commander, we don't think it's an ideal option, but weighing it up against all the other non-ideal options, this one might just be best chance you've got to avoid a collision."

"Yes." Beth air pumped.

Mitch gave her a thumbs-up, and Russ went on.

"The way we see it, you've got an empty payload bay, the equipment to secure the debris, and the best robotic-arm operator on or off the planet sitting right next to you."

"Love you too, Russ." Beth grinned from ear to ear.

"Good enough for me," Mitch said. "Russ, while I'm going to work on getting us into position to take the catch, I'll need you to give me some new mass and speed calculations so we can plug in the new reentry math."

"Already working on the recalibrations now. We'll reset the timing and duration of your reentry burn from this end. You guys just concentrate on grabbing that asteroid before it comes in close enough for you to kiss."

Russ sounded like he sighed with relief. "Good luck, and let's get moving, you have five minutes until you intersect – we've all got work to do. Over."

"And out." Mitch turned. "Okay, helmets on. Both of you get back to the payload bay and make sure we're ready to put this thing to bed once you've grabbed it. Beth, you're on controls, and Gerry will assist in maneuvering it into a temporary cradle. I'm going to tilt the ship so our stalker should be right in front of you. Hopefully I can create a negligible speed differential so it should float right in."

"Sounds good to me, boss." Beth unstrapped herself, and floated to retrieve her helmet. Gerry did the same.

"And don't forget; this thing is magnetic," Mitch said. "So don't underestimate it moving erratically once it gets close to the hull." Mitch was about to turn back, but paused.

"Beth."

She turned.

"Don't let this thing touch us. If it sticks, well ..." He smiled. "... let's just not let it get that close." Mitch held her eyes until she nodded.

* * *

In the mission control room, Russell Burrows stood with legs planted and hands on his hips as he watched the data feed come back from his shuttle orbiter. The entire wall was made up of a bank of huge screens, but he focused on just one, its video feed showing the *Orlando*'s payload bay area. Two suited figures, Beth and Gerry, were both readying the controls for the robotic arm and the bay doors.

Russ paced; he had a headset on that plugged into one ear, but there could have been a brass band in the corridor and he wouldn't have paid it any attention.

He saw Anne Peterson standing silently off to his side, unblinking, and he bet holding her breath. She wasn't really part of the control team, but he cut her some slack since she and Mitch were an item. Besides, her medical knowledge of the crew and technical knowledge of the craft were always welcome.

Russ watched Mitch in the cockpit attempting to maintain course parity and speed with the object as it approached. He then switched to examine an external feed and saw the longish shape tumbling inexorably toward them – its approach puzzling, as it was inescapable.

Russ clicked his tongue. He'd be happy if the thing kept right on going past them and his astronauts didn't have to bring it in – *risk upon risk upon risk*. If there were any other way around it, he would never have agreed to them trying to catch it in space like some sort of second baser landing a fly ball. But the thing was homing in on their craft, so it was either grab it or wear it.

Russ rubbed his chin nervously and switched back to the payload area. The bay doors were slowly opening like long, oblong petals revealing the dark vacuum of space. Everything moved in slow motion – the doors, Beth and Gerry tethered to the inside of the bay, and now the telescoping robotic arm. He suddenly found he was chewing the corner of his nail, and dragged his hand away from his face as he watched the arm continue to gently extend. The multi-billion dollar, multi-purpose limb could pivot, pound or secure, and its tip could be fitted with everything from a screwdriver to a three-pronged claw. It was the world's most expensive Swiss army knife. The arm was now fully extended, three titanium composite fingers flexed open and closed a few times, and then waited, ready.

The bay-area camera showed the golden upturned face shields of the two astronauts as they watched the approaching object. Gerry stood well out of the way while Beth had both her hands on the arm controls, working the twin joysticks like a gaming-console player.

They all knew this was a one-time deal – if Beth missed, then there would be no reload. *Come on, Beth*, he prayed. *You can do it.*

Every proximity alert they had was blinking or bleeping at them, warning about the fragment bearing down on the shuttle's body – the inevitable proximity junction was upon them.

The feed switched back to the object – so close now Russ could see the pocks, ridges, and what could be blotchy areas of discoloration. The thing looked solid and heavy, and given it was only thirty-eight percent ferrous material, with the rest unknown, he wondered if they had underestimated its true weight and mass. He hoped Beth would be able to hold on to it if it turned out to be heavier than their analytics software had extrapolated.

It bore down on them. He switched to the bay-area camera. Beth was moving the robotic arm. He waited, feeling his gut churn. The object was filling the screen – purple-gray, strangely not tumbling anymore, but simply floating toward them as though it was slowing down – *coming in for a soft landing or had its magnetic field somehow stopped its roll?*

Small puffs from the jets angled the *Orlando* into an ever so slightly better position, and Russ held his breath as it neared – 500 feet, 400, 300, 200, 100. Now down to yards. He heard Beth's voice, talking to herself, or maybe the fragment, as she coaxed it into the claw.

Then she had it.

The object was caught by one end in the pincers. Applause broke out in the NASA control room, but the cool and controlled language in the orbiter didn't match it.

"Bringing it in," Beth said as the arm slowly retracted. She carefully folded the arm back in on itself and laid the object gently into a cradle on the payload bay floor, keeping the pincers engaged.

The cameras zoomed in on the object and Russ squinted. There was glinting coming off some sort of crystalline structure on its surface, and the discoloration he had seen now almost looked like some sort of fluid leakage – impossible in space.

Gerry immediately started the overhead door closing routines and then rushed to lock the object in place.

* * *

Commander Mitch Granger smiled and nodded at the cargo bay screen. "Atta girl."

The darkness of space was shut out as the bay doors gently closed. He then swiveled one of the cameras toward the object and enlarged the frame. It was longer and squatter than he expected – more pod-shaped, rather than a shard of something that had broken off. He saw the discoloration on its surface – *perhaps some sort of ancient oxidation?*

A small pain began behind his eyes followed by a sound, or rather sensation, in his head akin to a soft buzz or thrumming. *Stress,* Mitch concluded.

"Talk to me, Beth."

The mission specialist floated over to it, and held up a scanner. "It's hot."

Mitch groaned. "What's the count?" If it was too hot, they'd have to keep their damn suits on from now until they got home.

"No, not radiation, that's bang-on the astral background count, but I mean it's *physically* hot." She held up a hand just hovering over the object. "I can feel it right through my glove. It's got to be 120 degrees, maybe more."

"Is it a stable or fluctuating heat?" Mitch's eyes narrowed.

He waited.

"*Huuuh*? Oh, stable, for now I ... I guess" Beth responded. "But, *strange*." Her voice sounded dreamy, and she continued to hold her hand up before the fragment.

Mitch leaned a little more toward his screen. "Okay, that's close enough."

Gerry joined her, but just stood silently staring at the rock.

"If the object is secure, please return to the cockpit." Mitch cleared his throat and waited. "Gerry, Beth, can you hear me?"

The pair ignored him; worse, he could see Beth's hand began to move closer to the space rock.

"Mission specialist Bethany Power, do not touch that object. Do you read?"

There was a skittering sound from behind him and he looked over his shoulder to see the three mice going crazy in their glass tank. But that only drew his eyes to the next container, and caused his brow to deeply furrow – the giant earthworms were all up from the soil and had piled up on one side of their glass container. Also, the ants had created a mesh-like structure with their bodies. They weren't moving, but instead were lumped against their wall that was closest to the rear hatch. It was if they were frozen, watching and waiting for something.

Mitch turned back and licked dry lips. "Beth, this is a direct order – *do not – touch – that goddamn ...*"

"I just ... can't ... oh-*oooh, wait.*" Beth seemed to crane forward.

"Magnify Beth's hand, times ten," Mitch ordered. Ripley immediately complied and zeroed on Beth's gloved hand. He saw Beth's fingers inching closer to the sparkling fragment of asteroid.

Mitch cursed. "Magnify, times twenty." The screen images increased in size again. "What the ...?" There seemed to be a tendril coming from a small fissure in the rock. It wavered for a moment as if testing the air, before becoming rigid as Beth's hand approached.

"*Beth, watch out!*"

The tendril sprung forward like a piece of elastic, striking her fingertip. She screamed and pulled, back, but amazingly the tendril stuck, and then thickened, spread and continued to hang on.

"Hey!" Gerry sprinted toward her.

Beth screamed again, as a pulse passed through the *Orlando* and the cameras whited-out.

"Shit." Mitch unbuckled and pushed from his chair, heading fast for the rear door.

* * *

"*What the hell?*"

Russell's mouth dropped open as the feed from the orbiter whited out. "What just happened, people?" He swung one way then the other.

"Lost comms, sir." Scotty McIntyre was his right-hand man and one of his most senior ground technicians, and he, like the rest of his team, were already working furiously on communication diagnostics.

"*I can see that!*" Russ backed up, looking over the banks of engineers, technicians, and programmers – all the computer screens were up, but there was no data. *None at all.* One after another his people sounded off – *no communications* – *no telemetry* – *no topography*, and then, exactly what he didn't want to hear – *Ripley's gone dark.* He ground his teeth; Ripley *never* went dark as she had her own isolated power source to protect against exactly this sort of thing.

"*Goddamn, talk to me people.*"

A hand gripped his forearm, and he looked down to see Anne's ashen face. He had no answers for her.

"*Orlando*'s still there." Scott had brought up the radar image, and sure enough, it showed the elliptical lines of the shuttle still in its orbit. Russ breathed a sigh of relief. At least the orbiter was still in one piece.

He finally breathed. "What happened, Scotty?" He looked back at the screen. "Did that damn thing we picked up just EMP us?"

"High probability, boss." Scotty McIntyre was running simulations, and then shook his head. "But we won't know until the crew or Ripley tells us." He turned in his chair. "They'll need to reboot to bring everything back online."

Russ groaned. He knew even an automatic rapid reboot still took thirty minutes. *We've just been struck deaf, dumb and blind,* he thought, as he felt his stomach start to cramp. He looked at his watch – and there's still twenty-eight minutes to go.

CHAPTER 3

The Cockpit, Space Shuttle Orbiter Orlando

The images were reflected back hundreds of times in the multi-faceted compound eyes of the ant as it stared into the bay area through the door's porthole-like window. It was the highest insect of the pyramid of tiny bodies, and its antenna twitched as it sensed for vibrations.

Though no sound emanated through the hermetically sealed door, it could see the mouths of all three beings were open, and the tiny insect felt the vibrations from the screams right throughout the craft.

The *Orlando* went dark then, and cold. The ant pyramid collapsed, and the tangled mass of bodies froze, waiting, as they drifted in space.

CHAPTER 4

NASA Control – Space Shuttle Orbiter Main Monitoring Room

"Crossing into friendly airspace in three, two, one ... *now*."

Scott McIntyre, senior NASA technician, continued to watch the screen before him as the blip passed over a red line indicating the *Orlando* space shuttle had moved out of Russian astro-territory.

"We're now over the Chukchee Sea, crossing the Bering Strait and coming up on Point Hope, Alaska. Co-ords are: 68°20′49″N, 166°45′47″W. We are looking good, people."

"Thank god. How long until reboot complete?" Russell Burrows paced, chewing his nails, sipping coffee and generally feeling like the last few hairs on his head were raining down around him like a cat shedding on furniture.

Scott bobbed his head. "Well, if boot-up started when we suspected, then we've only got ... fifty-eight seconds remaining, and counting down."

"Under a minute, *Jezuz*." Russ clenched his fists and stopped before the largest of the wall data screens that was still dark. He felt it was now like a window onto the vacuum of space giving him back an empty nothingness. He unclenched his sweaty hands but then folded them under his arms, tight, and watched from under lowered brows.

Russ glanced at Anne Peterson, who stood a dozen feet away, her hands clasped before her, and he swore he could see her lips moving in silent prayer as she, too, watched and waited.

Though Russ wasn't much of a believer in the big head honcho in the sky, he decided, *what the hell*, he'd say a few words for luck as well.

"Ten seconds," Scott yelled without turning from his screen.

Come on, Orlando, give me something. Russ used his teeth to nip off another corner of thumbnail.

The room fell to tomb silence as every one of the people in the room stopped what they were doing and stared up at the large screen.

"*Three, two, one …*" Scott took his hands off his keyboard and sat back. His eyes were wide as he stared.

The panel fizzed for a few seconds, and then began to stabilize.

"*Yes!* Ladies and gentlemen, we are *back* online." Scott raised both fists, but then froze, his mouth hanging open.

It was like a portal to hell – screaming, darting movement as if bodies were running blindly, knocking into things, jerking away and running again. The vision was blurred, or rather greasy, as if the camera lens was coated in something glutinous.

Sticky string-like fibers seemed to reach for them, and were followed by more panicked screams – not just those of men and woman in fear or confusion, but rather like that of tortured souls, yelling in pain and horror from the pits of Hades itself.

"Oh god." Russ gulped; he couldn't tell which of his astronauts was screaming, or even if it was a man or woman.

He spun to look at Anne who went to her knees, mouth working and eyes wide and wet. He spun back to Scott.

"Turn that down. Non-essential personnel clear the room, *now.*" He waved to his security detail, and then pointed back at Anne. "Help her out."

Russ then sprinted to the console next to Scott, as Anne straightened and brushed off any help. Anne glared, first at him, and then back at the wall screen. *Tough woman,* he thought as he sat down and opened communications with the *Orlando.*

"Commander Mitch Granger, do you read?" Russ waited for a few more seconds, trying to hear through the hellish sounds on the shuttle cockpit. "Commander Mitch Granger, do you read me, over?"

Russ waited a few more seconds. "Commander Mitch Granger, flight engineer Gerry Fifield, mission specialist Beth Power, *do – you – read me*, over?"

The screaming continued for several more seconds before it lapsed into sobbing, then moaning, and then nothing.

"Have we lost them?" Russ turned to Scott.

Scott shook his head. "Comm link is strong and holding." He eased back in his chair, and half turned to the room full of technicians. "Larry, what have you got on their PLSs?"

Russ lifted – their Personal Life Sign should tell them something about their underlying physical state. From across the room, a brush-cut young man named Larry cleared his throat.

"Well, we've still got all their signatures, but they're ..." The man looked pained. "... I dunno, different."

Scott's forehead creased, and then both he and Russ turned to the technician. "What do you mean, *different?*"

Larry shook his head. "Looks like they're unconscious or maybe something even deeper; like a comatose state. Fading in and out. Doesn't look huma—"

"All of them?" Russ asked, feeling a knot tighten in his gut. "Have they still got atmospheric integrity?"

"Yep, all good there." Larry looked confused. "Even though their life signs are weak, Ripley says there's still movement onboard."

"Least that's something." Russ got to his feet. He paced one way for a few steps and then the other. "What the hell is going on up there?" He walked closer to the large central screen, and put his hand to the microphone at his mouth. He swallowed dryly.

"To all and any member of the *Orlando* crew, please come in. Over." Russ licked his lips. "Please send a sign that you can read us, urgent. Over." Russ knew there was a dozen ways they could communicate. Even if all the standard comms went down, they could use the cabin lights to blink out a Morse code message. He stared at the empty screen as the seconds stretched.

"*Fuck, fuck, fuck.*" Russ paced again for a few moments. "We can't wait." He spun. "Bring them down, *bring them down, right now.*"

"You got it, boss." Scott started to type furiously, and yelled commands over one shoulder then the other. "All right people, by the books, we are going to initiate auto control." He turned to a line of technicians behind him. "What are we over now?"

"Nothing good right now, but we've got a couple of emergency drop sites in Canada, nearest being CFB Edmonton coming up – it's a Canadian military forces base located in Sturgeon County."

"I know it, in Alberta," Russ said. "I'll alert them, and we can start a long reentry to glide on in to it." He clapped his hands. "Ladies and gentlemen, let's bring our astronauts home."

The babble of voices rose in the command center as every scientist, technician, and administrator worked rapidly at their controls. They quickly overrode *Orlando*'s cockpit control system and then began working directly with Ripley to initiate several gentle burns to angle the shuttle orbiter's nose down toward the Canadian base at CFB Edmonton.

On the large screen, there was an inbound trajectory plotted as a solid black line. The angle of descent meant that the shuttle would glide for thousands of miles, reaching speeds of Mach 2.5 on its way to the Edmonton emergency runway. It would still take hours to finally make touchdown, but Russ felt his confidence build as they had the shuttle in their control and his team had trained for this so many times he bet they could do it in their sleep.

"Walk in the park," Scott said.

Russ straightened, feeling better ... until the alarms started blaring.

"*What the hell, now?*" Russ sprinted to Scott's terminal.

Scott was shaking his head. "Something's gone wrong."

"You think?" Russ leaned over him, and briefly looked up at the large screen. "Hey ..."

"I know, I know, they're *way* off course." Scott grimaced. "I don't know how, but Ripley is being overridden. *Orlando* has put herself into a dive – she's going down, I mean, *straight down.*"

"No, no, no, at that speed she'll end up bug shit on a windscreen." Russ wiped his mouth with a hand and felt nauseous.

"*Hooold* it ... she's slowing." Scott's brow was now permanently furrowed.

"Slowing?" Russ straightened. "*Jesus Christ,* there's someone still alive in there." Russ couldn't think straight as the floor of the control room exploded into a chaotic melee of shouted voices and rushing people as information was sought, used, and sent. He pulled the headset back over his head, and switched it on, blanking everything else out.

"Commander, *Mitch*, I don't know if you can hear me, but you've got to relinquish manual control. Mitch, anyone, *please*, if you can hear me but can't respond, just switch the orbiter back to auto-pilot, so we and Ripley can bring you in safely … *please*."

What the fuck is going on up there? Russ felt panic rising in his chest again. He looked back up at the screen. There was another directional line now branching away from the trajectory they had plotted into the Edmonton runway. They were pulling out of their death dive, but they were still far too steep on reentry.

It was weird; if he had to guess, he'd say it looked like someone had detected NASA's intrusion, and decided to break its control, and then, what? *First, put the* Orlando *into a nosedive and destroy it and themselves?* Russ wiped his brow with a sleeve, and tried to make sense of it.

It was if they'd changed their minds and were now trying to glide the shuttle in. It didn't make sense – it was like there was a war going on up there. He watched as the *Orlando* leveled out a little more.

"*Jesus.*" Russ spun. "Scott, give me a destination, ASAP. Put it up on screen."

His friend's hands flew, and then up went an extrapolated vector represented as a dotted line. It ended at a point on the map way up in Alaska.

"*Hooooly* shit." Russ put a hand to his forehead and blinked for a few moments allowing his mind to catch up. "We, we need to be there." Russ snatched up a phone, and held it away from his mouth for a moment. "I'm taking charge of this personally. "

Scott stood. "Count me in."

Russ nodded. "We need a rescue and recovery plan. And we need to leave, like, *now*."

CHAPTER 5

Senate Building, Kremlin, Russia

"An American space shuttle has crashed." Viktor Dubkin allowed himself a small smile as he sat before the Russian president.

President Volkov, known as the 'Little Wolf' but never to his face, remained impassive, his unnaturally cold blue eyes didn't waver or blink as he sat staring back.

After another moment, one eyebrow rose a fraction and he grunted. "The shuttle that was photographing the nuclear missile sites across the globe, *da*?

Dubkin nodded slowly. "The very same, my president." He spread his hands. "Normally we could not care any less. We know that they know, approximately, where our missile fields are – just as we know where theirs are – these are no secret to any good spy agency." He pursed his lips for a moment. "But where this becomes problematic is we now know that they were using the new ground-penetrating technology developed by their military. It has the ability to see inside the silos and identify the specific kiloton profile of each missile." He paused. "It can also tell which are real or just decoys."

"Hmm, a little *too much* information." Volkov's eyes swiveled. "But the shuttle is crashed, so the problem is now solved?"

"Perhaps not," Dubkin said. "It broke its normal orbit, but we don't believe it was a catastrophic crash. It came down hard in the Revelation Mountains in Alaska, and may still be intact." His brows went up. "And that means the data could be still intact."

Volkov shrugged. "Destroy it. Before any rescue and retrieval mission can be organized. Who will be able to say it wasn't obliterated when it hit the ground."

Dubkin bobbed his head. "I would have recommended this option myself, except for one thing." His smile widened. "The Americans weren't just filming us. They were photographing every nuclear missile site in the world – every potential adversary and ally … and even their own sites. This film is invaluable, and I think critically important to Russia." He leaned forward. "It is a gift, Comrade President, just waiting to be plucked from them."

Volkov's eyes narrowed. "And I suspect a potential gift also to China, Iran, and North Korea." He made a grumbling sound of assent deep in his chest. "Invaluable to us, and also worth billons if sold." Unbelievably for Dubkin, he saw the corner of Volkov's mouth lift microscopically.

Dubkin clasped his hands together over his stomach. "Best case scenario for NASA is at least forty-eight hours before they are there." He grinned. "And we are just across the strait. We can be there long before the Americans."

Volkov pointed. "Mister Dubkin, I hereby order you to retrieve this film."

"Yes, sir." Dubkin gripped his armrests, ready to stand, but waited a moment. "I think we must send our best team, a small one, but one that can endure hardship and still retain speed, stamina, and strike capability. After all, they might encounter strong resistance, maybe even from American Special Forces."

"Yes, maybe even HAWCs," Volkov said. He raised a finger and waved it in the air. "Our team must strike like a hurricane and then vanish like the wind. I think it is finally time for us to give the Kurgan a field test. Take charge."

Dubkin smiled as he stood. "Perfect, comrade president, it shall be as you direct." He bowed and left, having gotten everything he needed.

CHAPTER 6

Pacific Ocean, twenty miles west of Monterey, California

The super yacht *Manhattan* sliced through the warm, azure water off the continental shelf. She was 121 feet from bow to stern, sleek and sporty and from the highly sought after 3700 Fly Series range – there was a waiting list, that is, if you could come up with a spare 80 million and change.

The yacht could accommodate nine guests with four full-sized luxury cabins. She had a salon and dining area with open-plan architecture creating a sensation of endless space. Added to that, large windows on port and starboard allowed all the rooms to be bathed in natural light. She was a little slice of heaven on the high sea.

The retired senator, Robert A. Anderson, owned this particular boat. He and his wife, Gillian, had taken the *Manhattan* out for a spin, planning to head down to a little restaurant they knew at Coronado in San Diego. They'd stayed in radio contact, up until an hour earlier, when the boat had suddenly gone silent.

Casey Franks' eyes were unblinking and her mouth set in a grim line as she watched the yacht begin to slow. She stopped rowing the small boat and lifted an arm to wave as the ship's bow turned toward her. Excitement began to build in her chest.

She felt perspiration run from her scalp down her neck and then form a river along her spine from the weight of the thick wig she wore. In her ear was a small communication plug that also touched her tympanum nerve allowing it to both send and receive covert communications.

She waved as she spoke through her grin. "Two on deck, multiple movement signatures below, numbers unknown. No sign of the senator or his wife." A device at her feet clicked madly and she reached down to read some figures and then switched it off.

"Rad count is well above background normal – the package has got to be onboard. I am locked and loaded and ready to roll, boss."

Casey waved again. The CIA, as well as numerous other global intelligence agencies, had been monitoring the movement of the dirty bomb for the last few weeks as it made its way out of Libya and across Italy. But then it had vanished. The USA was one of the few countries that had a radiation net over its borders and coastline, whereby nothing nuclear could be snuck into the country – that was unless it was heavily shielded, as they suspected was the case here.

The Orbiting Space-Based Infrared System, SBIRS, or *Sabers*, to those who knew about it, could sniff a high radiation signature, but if the bomb was in a lead-lined casing, then you had to be up real close to detect it. Problem with that was, once you eyeballed it, you showed your hand, and had to be prepared for the assholes to detonate it.

All the involved countries were on a heightened alert, and when the senator's boat went dark, it was suspected a hijacking had taken place. When looking for a large bomb delivery mechanism, air, rail, and sea are top of the list. The *Manhattan* would make the perfect delivery system.

Casey momentarily glanced toward the invisible shoreline, and thought about the ramifications of the weapon. A dirty bomb detonation at sea, with prevailing winds, would send a cloud of radioactive dust over a coastal city and potentially contaminate a million people.

Combined American intelligence agencies had formulated plans for recovering or neutralizing the bomb, but none could guarantee safe takedown without triggering the device. Added to that, there was no scenario where the senator and his wife came out alive.

In the blink of an eye, Intelligence handballed it to the military, who immediately speared it toward Colonel Jack Hammerson. The commander of the Special Forces arm of the secretive Hotzone All-Warfare Commandos, designate HAWCs, had a mission plan in progress in less than five minutes.

"They're coming in nice and close to take a look, boss." Casey flicked strands of blond hair from her eyes, and continued to wave.

Into Lieutenant Casey Frank's ear came a deep, authoritative voice. "I can see them now. Keep them interested for a few more minutes – mission is *go*."

A figure in the water, lying on the sheltered side of her boat sunk down and disappeared into the depths. Casey focused her attention on the approaching vessel. Alex Hunter, the Arcadian, would sink for another twenty feet, and then use long strokes to power toward the *Manhattan* – he had no air tanks as these would give a telltale bubble trail. It didn't matter; she knew he would stay down for as long as it took.

Casey grabbed the oars and began to row gently out in front of the luxury yacht, forcing it to stop, and keeping their eyes on her. Her muscular arms and shoulders flexed and rolled with each pull, but were hidden by a cotton shirt. Also hidden was a multitude of tattoos, burns and bullet wounds, plus a ripped frame that was all bulges and sinew. Like all the HAWCs, Casey had honed herself to be a living weapon.

The *Manhattan* was still over a hundred feet away, and she knew that somewhere between them, Alex Hunter, her HAWC team leader and possibly the greatest soldier she had ever known, was already closing the distance.

Casey's grin widened as she looked up at the leering faces, and she whispered through her smile.

"Wouldn't wanna be you assholes in the next few minutes."

Several men crowded the deck and waved, whistled and called her over.

She nodded, smiling sunnily. "Yeah, sure, I'll join the party." She began to row again, flicking the wig's long hair forward and letting it fall over her face, especially on the side with the deep scar that ran from jaw to cheek and twisted her mouth into a permanent sneer.

* * *

Twenty feet down, Alex swum smoothly, reaching forward and pulling the water back along his sides. He only needed a facemask as the distance wasn't great, and he wanted to be unencumbered when he boarded the *Manhattan*.

He had memorized the vessel's schematics, as he knew he needed to move quickly and surely, because the moment he was onboard he'd have mere seconds to make the difference between death of the hostages and perhaps detonation of a dirty nuclear bomb.

Above him the water was a magnificent blue, with the golden sun almost directly overhead. But below, the rays of sunshine penetrated down another few dozen feet before the depths swallowed all light.

Alex's neck tingled from a sense of danger before he felt the surge of water from below. The fifteen-foot great white shark rolled slightly as it passed underneath him, checking him out with one soulless black eye.

Oh shit. Not now.

The creature was more than twice as long as Alex, and outweighed him by many hundreds of pounds. And down here in its element it was a dagger-toothed torpedo. The only weapons Alex had were a range of knives fastened to his belt, but the last thing he wanted was a pool of blood – his or the sharks – spreading in the water.

He kicked harder, increasing his speed, still feeling the huge presence circling him down in the depths. He knew how big sharks attacked, diving and then coming up fast like freight trains in an ambush. He was quick in the water, but he wouldn't stand a chance of being able to get out of the way of the massive creature rushing up from below with gaping mouth and row after row of serrated blades ready. Once it had him, then the best he could hope for was being spat out – if not, he'd lose limbs or be bitten in half.

His neck and spine tingled, and he could make out the hull of the *Manhattan* no more than twenty feet ahead. He'd make it to the craft, only if the shark left him alone. He used both arms and legs now to pull hard through the water, angling slightly to head for the huge transom at the boat's rear.

He started to come up through the clear water, and he prayed that onboard the only thing that was of interest to the watching men was a small dinghy out front with a blonde woman seemingly lost at sea.

His initial plan was to ease himself up and over the transom, but right about now, he didn't like the idea of waiting in the water with a shark closing in. He felt another surge, closer, and he looked down to see the shark turn on its side again, the eye, like black glass, fixed on him for a second or two before the giant predator flicked its tail and angled down into a dive. It had decided he could be eaten and was going to take a run at him – his time was up.

Alex tore furiously through the water coming up at the end of the transom and not stopping, but instead launching himself to land and roll along the six-foot flat diving platform until he was tucked behind the stern gunwale. There was a thud from below, probably the shark's tail as it turned, pissed off because its meal had escaped.

Alex sucked in a few huge breaths, and turned back to the water. A gray lump surfaced. The shark had lifted its head about three feet from the water and hung there watching him.

"Sorry buddy, not today."

The shark slowly sank beneath the surface, and Alex pulled off his mask and lay still, just letting a hand rest on the stern and allowing his senses to reach out to see if there was anyone close by. He couldn't detect anyone, but with the throb of the idling engines so close, hearing anything was out of the question.

He rose slowly, just letting his eyes come up over the gunwale. The deck was empty so he slid over. Normally, his training dictated he move to take over the control room on the upper deck, but the nuclear bomb changed everything. He needed to seek it out. Once neutralized, the terrorists were just flesh and blood killers, and not potential mass-murderers with a weapon of mass destruction at their disposal. He made his way to the cabin doors.

Beneath his feet he felt the engines rev slightly as they'd obviously decided to move in closer to Casey. The extra noise would conceal his approach, but also mask the movement of the terrorists. He moved quickly to the galley door, and when he was just three feet from it, it opened.

A huge man pushed outside, his hands cupped around a tiny flame that he held to the tip of a dark cigarette. He froze and stared. Alex was tall at 6'2" but this guy was half a head taller.

The man reacted quickly, his coal-dark eyes going from surprise to confidence in a blink. One ham-sized fist flicked out with a straight-arm lunge punch aimed toward Alex's throat. Alex recognized the stance and the training. This guy was *Hezar-Jihadi*, the Party of a Thousand Martyrs, combat-hardened fanatics whose hatred for the West was only matched by their determination to see a world governed by their laws, their religion and their leaders – anything else was a blasphemy.

Normally, the rapid punch would have crushed an opponent's larynx, and with oxygen shut off, even if Alex stayed on his feet, suffocation would be minutes away. But the fatal mistake the terrorist made was that the confidence he had in his own abilities meant he attacked first instead of calling for backup.

To the man's shock, Alex caught the log-like arm, yanked and twisted it, dragging the terrorist toward him. He then used the v-shape between his thumb and forefinger of his other hand to strike at the man's neck – doing to the terrorist what he had planned for Alex.

The big guy's cigarette shot out of his mouth like a bullet followed by an extended tongue, but then nothing else, not words, shouts, or even a breath. Alex had shut down his respiratory system. With his windpipe collapsed, only a tracheotomy would save him from strangling to death. He turned, clawing at his throat, and heading fast for the refuge of the cabins. Alex grabbed his collar, lifted the man from his feet, walked him to the side of the boat, and then flung him out over the gunwale.

Alex was about to turn away from the railing when an eruption of bloody water told him that the great white shark had been waiting just below the surface. He smiled grimly at the man's fate.

"Welcome to America."

The boat's engines stopped, and Alex paused for a moment. He heard some laughing from the upper deck, and he grinned. It could only mean that Casey had convinced them to take her onboard. He hoped they liked surprises, because things were about to get *real* interesting for them.

Alex went through the galley doors, and his eyes immediately adjusted to the lower light. The *Manhattan's* galley was open-plan, and the huge room had a bar, viewing deck, computer hub and couches all stylishly laid out. It also had blood splatter and two bodies, belly down and naked, rope looped around their necks and then tied to their wrists and ankles, forcing them both up into painful curves.

Alex crossed to them and kneeled. He already knew it was the senator and his wife, and guessed how the torture had unfolded. The wife, Gillian, had her throat cut, her face calm, almost serene as her life had leaked away. But trussed and facing her was the senator, his face monstrously beaten to be almost unrecognizable.

Alex looked from the woman to the man – Gillian would then have had her throat sliced open in front of her husband. Where the woman had accepted her fate, the senator's battered face was twisted in agony. But Alex knew that it wasn't the physical pain that the senator had found intolerable, but being forced to watch the destruction of everything he had loved that had broken him.

Whether the terrorists were trying to extract some sort of concession or confession from the man was unknown. But the senator had voted for increased raids on terrorist strongholds in the Middle East, so perhaps they just wished to both physically and psychologically torment him to death as payback.

Evil is real. Alex reached out to lay a hand gently on the man's forehead. He almost recoiled as he immediately felt a shock run through him. The man's last experiences still ricocheted around inside him like tormented wraiths shrieking in anguish and anger.

He stared down at the battered face. "Rest easy, for I am your vengeance." Alex's teeth ground together as he gently closed the man's eyes.

Alex drew his hand back from the dead senator, noticed it shook slightly, and made a fist to calm it. Behind his eyes he felt a pressure building that soon began to burn.

Let me free, a small urgent voice whispered from a cage he kept locked deep in his mind. He ignored it and slowly rose to his feet and drew two of the knives that sat on his belt – long and short tanto-tipped Ka-Bar blades. The night-black hardened steel blades were laser-honed to scalpel sharpness, and didn't lose their edge even when called upon to cut bone. He headed for the lower-deck door. His hands gripped the blades so hard the rubberized grip began to pop and protest as it was compressed.

The fury grew inside him, and so too did his senses. He could feel everything now. Several men crowded together inside working feverishly on something – *the bomb* – getting it ready, excited about the prospect of the death and destruction they were about to rain down on the heads of the innocent.

Not this day. He breathed through gritted teeth. *And not any day.*

* * *

Casey's small boat bumped up against the huge yacht and she looked up the twenty feet to where the men hung over the edge looking down at her.

"Aren't you boys a sight for sore eyes!" Casey called coquettishly. "Heroes come to rescue a damsel in distress!" They stared flat-eyed for a moment.

"How's the fishing?" Casey flashed the men the biggest, flirtiest smile she could muster.

One with jug ears shook his head and then took a thick cigarette from his mouth for a moment. "No fish."

"Haven't you got a fish finder?" Casey looked along the length of the boat, trying to see if there were any other inquisitive eyes on her. Satisfied she looked back up at the men.

Jug-ears smirked. "I have a woman finder. And it's pointing at you."

"*Ooh*, I'd love to see it. Is it a big one?" Casey winked.

The two men conferred for a moment, guffawed and then slapped each other's shoulders, perhaps not believing their luck. They seemed to make a decision then grinned widely down at Casey.

"We drop a ladder."

"Yay!" Casey clapped her hands and then quickly dropped them, not wanting the men to see the gnarled knuckles and blunt fingers.

As the pair went to find a ladder, Casey hummed softly and pulled on a pair of gloves. These were no ordinary gloves, but HAWC Special Forces issue with armor plating across the knuckles and backs.

To the men it would have looked like she didn't want to get her hands abraded from the coming ladder climb. She flexed them, smiling as her excitement peaked. Casey had been a HAWC for several years now, and though she wasn't as tall as the male operatives of her Special Forces unit, she made up for it with a mix of ferociousness and expertise in hand-to-hand combat that made her one of the Arcadian's first choices as backup on many missions.

"Party time," she whispered as a ladder unfurled beside her.

Casey went up the rungs quickly, and one of the men reached down to grip one of her upper arms and pulled her over the side.

The man held on tight and frowned. Perhaps expecting to feel soft flesh, but instead finding rock-hard muscle. The jug-eared one got behind her and grabbed at her long hair planning to pull her head back. He would have exposed her throat and had her immediately in a position of submission.

But the long hair came off in his hand, and he stood staring at it for a few confused seconds as if he'd just caught a strange and disgusting species of animal.

Casey started to laugh at their expressions, and imagined the disappointment and surprise at instead of having some sort of lost bimbo woman, the person that stood before them had a white flat top, scarred face and a neck that was corded with veins and swirling with tattoos.

"*Ack.*" Jug-ears threw the wig to the deck. "This is no woman." He drew a hunting knife.

The other terrorist, still holding her upper arm, went to spin her around to face him, and Casey went with it, using the momentum to come in fast. She brought the point of her elbow back hard into his eye socket. There was a wet sensation on her skin, and also the satisfying crunch of orbital bone.

Before she let him go, she jerked his arm straight, and then brought the same elbow point down on the back of his elbow, crunching the joint.

"Ouch." She grinned. "You like that?"

He howled and backed up, one arm hanging useless and the other hand over his eye. Before he was out of range, Casey shot out a roundhouse kick, knocking him over the side to the water.

She turned toward Jug-ears, her face pulled into a smirk. He lunged with the blade, and it shot forward toward her stomach. Casey used a flat strike to deflect the thrust, and then grabbed his wrist and twisted it, hard and fast. She held him, his arm at an odd angle, so she could simply reach down to yank the knife from his hand.

"Should have gone fishing, asshole."

She wanted to take the blade and bury it into one of his jug ears, but her primary orders were to secure the wheelhouse – and she still had questions for them.

"It's your lucky day."

She curled one hand into a fist, and smashed it down on the bridge of his nose. The armor plated HAWC glove was like a house-brick and her arm a pile driver. Jug-ears was smashed to the deck and Casey crouched beside him. She put a hand over his mouth, raised the man's knife and then slammed it down on his hand, spearing it to the wooden deck.

She ignored the muffled scream, and in Arabic, she whispered through a terrifying smile.

"Listen and live; are there any others like you in the wheelhouse?" She took her hand away from his mouth.

The man looked up, blood running thickly down his chin from his shattered nose. He gritted bloody teeth and began to curse in Arabic.

"I see."

Casey grabbed his skewed nose and twisted, crunching the already broken cartilage. He began to howl and she clamped her other hand over his mouth.

"*Shush, shush,* there." She leaned closer. "Now, you want to try that again?"

She began to twist once more, but he shook his head.

"No one there," he hissed.

"Good boy." She stood, looking down. "Hey, you forgot to show me your woman finder." She chuckled for a second or two, before smashing her armor-plated fist down like a sledgehammer onto the back of his skull.

The base of his head dented inwards, and the man started to convulse.

"Oops." She shrugged. "Oh well."

She shoved the body over the side, and then sprinted up the steps to the upper-deck wheelhouse, saw it was empty, and pressed the stud at her ear.

"Wheelhouse is ours."

* * *

After hearing Casey tell him the boat wasn't going anywhere, stage one was now complete, and Alex placed a hand against the woodwork. He could sense the men inside – six of them – one would be a technician, the other five would be the heavy hitters, men prepared to brutally kill or die in the name of what they believed.

He inhaled slowly through his nose, smelling the faint trace of ozone in the air – he didn't need a Geiger counter to tell him there was high-grade enriched plutonium and an initiator being assembled behind the door.

Alex knew the components were safe to transport when kept separated. But once they were put together as a single device, the risk of detonation went up exponentially. You only constructed a tactical device when detonation was imminent. That told him the terrorist cell believed they were geographically in place and just about ready.

The other thing he knew was that the amount of leakage he could sense meant the men inside were as good as dead, and they probably couldn't care less, as the *Manhattan* would be vaporized anyway. In a way, they would be the lucky ones, as a dirty bomb wasn't designed to contain the initial uranium collision that triggered the nuclear explosion. Instead it was meant to break apart immediately and disperse its toxic particles.

The impact blast would be a lower intensity, but the high lethality factor came from the rapidly outward-spreading cloud of deadly radioactive material. Once it touched the skin, or was embedded in the respiratory system, then depending on dose, it either killed quickly or slowly and agonizingly over a few weeks. It would even corrupt waterways and the ground soil for generations.

Alex heard the excitement and good humor in their voices. Perhaps at the thought of hundreds of thousands dead, untold billions in clean-up costs, and the only casualties for the terrorists would be this one boatload of fanatics. It would be a massive strategic and propaganda win.

He counted down, feeling his heart rate rise as everything around him seemed to slow. He visualized what he needed to do. Bottom line, it all boiled down to one thing – keep them away from the detonation switch.

He sucked in a breath, gripped his blades, and charged the door, exploding it open. There was that split second of frozen shock, like a flashbulb going off but it broke quickly.

The men were professionals, and weren't stunned to inaction by the sudden appearance of the near naked intruder. Instead, they all leaped into action. Some dove for cover, most reached for weapons. For Alex, the scenario confirmed what he had sensed – six men, five big and hard-looking, and one down kneeling beside a device that looked like a huge misshapen gas cylinder.

They came fast, two trusting their bare hands and the others waiting their turn with guns or perhaps hesitant to fire near the device. One screamed for Khaled, obviously the technician, to continue his work. The smaller man turned back to his bomb, his hands working furiously as he tried to shut everything else out.

The first man swung a big, looping right cross, and Alex allowed the arm to pass over his shoulder so he could swing back with his fist to embed the short Ka-Bar into his temple with a wet crunch. He let the fast-moving body continue past him to crumple against the wall.

Alex had already decided there would be no prisoners, no surrender, there would only be death – the ghosts of the senator and his wife demanded it. *Those who made fear will know real fear this day*, he thought as he increased his speed.

Like an engine moving to higher revolutions, Alex's mind and body worked many times faster than his opponent's. A hand came down on one shoulder, trying to turn him around, he shrugged it off, ducked under a knife and then came back up with an uppercut to his attacker's jaw, not pulling his punch, driving the man's mandible bone back and up into his skull. The dead body flew up to strike the low ceiling.

Then the gunfire began. Bullets flew, striking metal and wood, ricocheting or punching holes through the walls, floor, and ceiling. The overhead light exploded, and only beams of sunlight remained from the porthole-sized windows. The smell of cordite and dust, woodchip and gunsmoke filled the crowded room with a blue haze.

For Alex, the darkness moved the odds even more in his favor, and he dove, rolled, and came up in front of one of the shooters to immediately bury his longer blade into the man's forehead.

Bullets flew indiscriminately and there came a sting of pain across his cheekbone, and then the meat of his shoulder felt like a horse had just kicked it. He twisted away, scooping up the fallen terrorist's body with his blade still extruding from the face, and flung it back to where tiny gouts of flame indicated the shots were coming from.

There was a grunt and the shooter was knocked down. Alex dove at him, just as he was pushing his comrade's dead body from himself. Alex's weapons were gone, but like most in the Special Forces, his body was a weapon, and he could use what he had – in this instance, the top of his head.

Alex used his momentum to ram his forehead into the front of the man's face, flattening it between him and the wall.

The terrorist's arms dropped, and Alex snatched a long and heavy hunting knife from the man's belt.

The remaining terrorist had given up on a direct attack on Alex and instead lurched for the bomb. The device initiators were simple on homemade tactical weapons – you just needed to fire a pellet into a larger ball of high-grade fissionable material, like plutonium. The high-speed collision generated a reaction that would continue until detonation. The effect was inevitable and devastating. A homemade high-velocity mechanism – similar to a gun – would do it. It only needed one thing – a trigger.

Alex saw the red, thumb-sized button on top, and the huge man closing in on it while the technician kneeled back, his work done, and his eyes wide.

"*Stop!*"

The force of Alex's voice made the man pause. His eyes locked with Alex's; his hand outstretched and only feet from the trigger.

Alex, just a yard away, pointed with his blade, and spoke slowly and clearly. "First I'll take the hand." He dropped his arm, keeping the knife down at his side but blade side pointed up.

The man stared for another moment before his lips begin to curl up at the corners.

"*Allah Akhbar!*" he screamed and then lunged at the button.

Alex swept the blade upwards faster than the eye could follow. The hand and forearm separated just below the elbow, with the hand spinning in the air like a wet glove. Blood spurted, covering the cowering technician who still kneeled before the bomb.

The terrorist's eyes went wide as he looked at the spurting stump for a moment, before he gripped it and stared to yell. Insanely, his eyes went back to the trigger.

"And then I'll take the rest." The next sweep of Alex's blade and the man's yell was also cut off as his head fell back on the remaining skin flap of his near-severed neck.

Alex dropped the now sticky blade to the side. The room was now silent save for the occasional drip of blood, the settling of last breaths in collapsing bodies, and the groan of splintered decking wood.

Alex looked down at the technician who had his hands up, eyes round as silver dollars.

Kill him too.

Alex frowned. "*No.*"

"Say again, boss?" Casey's query came back immediately into his ear comm.

"Where are you?"

"Top deck, doing some housekeeping," she said casually.

"Good; device secured, coming up in a second or two." Alex looked back down at the technician.

"I surrender," the man said softly.

Kill him – remember the senator.

Alex recognized who it was, or *what* it was. It was from his Id, the one he called *The Other*, the creature that lurked there and fed on violence. He had carried it ever since his *cure* – the Arcadian treatment, the experimental formulae administered to him had given him back his mind and body following a catastrophic battlefield injury. But it had released something from his deep subconscious. Something near primordial in its lust for brutality and blood.

He stared down at the small man as the thing in his mind exerted pressure on his will. He'd mostly learned how to cage and control *The Other*. But violence freed it and once escaped, all it wanted was blood and more blood.

The technician lowered his hands slowly, and let them rest on the edge of the device.

Alex touched the communication pellet at his ear again. "Franks, call in immediate evac."

He looked back at the man, who smiled up nervously. His eyes shifted, and Alex could see the bloom of heat on his cheeks as his blood pressure rose.

The technician licked his lips. "I will tell you everything."

"I know you will," Alex said.

The man's eyes dilated. His hands were mere inches from the trigger. He licked his lips again.

"Please." The man shook his head, but his hands seemed to move a fraction closer to the trigger.

Or did they move? Alex couldn't tell if they really moved, or he only *wished* they had.

You see? Take your eyes off him, and he'll detonate it.

Alex crushed his eyes shut, and reopened them, trying to blink away the devil inside.

He's laughing at you, just like he was laughing when they tortured her, the senator's wife, and then butchered him.

Did the technician's hand edge closer again?

Of course it did, the voice whispered urgently. *They trussed the senator and his wife up, and then made him watch her bleed out. Oh, how they laughed as he begged for her life.*

Alex's hand bunched into a fist.

* * *

Two minutes later Alex bounded up to the control deck. Franks turned. "Captain on the bridge." She grinned.

"What have we got?" Alex asked as he wiped bloody hands on a towel he had picked up.

"Two choppers inbound; one HAWC and one Coast Guard. The CG guys also have a containment team and will take control of the vessel once the bomb is removed. And then we both get to spend hours in decontamination and debrief."

He nodded. "Perks of management."

"I'm in management?" Casey's grin dropped as she saw the ripped skin on Alex's face and red-ragged hole in his shoulder. "Trouble?"

"Nothing I couldn't deal with." He shrugged. "No survivors."

She grunted. "They were dead the moment we boarded."

Alex threw the towel into the corner and stared out at the horizon. "No, they were dead the moment *they* boarded."

* * *

Captain Geoff Jackson and his containment team were dropped onto the *Manhattan*'s deck. He had been told to expect two waiting Special Forces operatives. One was a tall male, in bathing trunks, looking like he was carved from stone and with eyes that went through him like lasers. The other a stocky woman, he guessed, with a scarred face and more muscles than he had.

He saluted. "All threats neutralized?"

"Confirmed; the *Manhattan* is yours." The tall man returned the salute, and then he and the woman turned to jog toward a black – and insignia-free – waiting helo.

Another larger, heavy duty H-53 US Marine Sea Stallion chopper hovered close by, waiting to lift off the disarmed nuclear package when Jackson's team had secured it.

Jackson stood with hands on hips as the Special Forces chopper left. The guy never introduced himself, but he'd heard the stories. He heard that the operatives sent in were a group called the HAWCs and when they were called in, the only thing left to do was cart out the bodies.

But there was one HAWC who was near legendary, and it was the eyes that gave the guy away. They were said to be like twin windows to hell. And after standing before the man, he'd looked into them, and known it was true.

So that was him, the Arcadian. He'd heard about him, but like most didn't even think he was real, instead some sort of made-up story about a soldier that couldn't be killed to bolster support in the ranks.

The guy was a one-man weapon of mass destruction. Before joining the Coast Guard, Jackson had faced enemy fire over Afghanistan, and dropped into some real wild shit in his military days. But something behind Hunter's eyes unsettled him. *Maybe all the weird stories were true*, he exhaled. *Just glad he's on our side.* He turned to his team and circled a finger in the air.

Jackson followed his team as they lugged a huge lead-lined box down to the lower deck where Hunter said he had left the device. Their own disposal technician went through the galley doors first.

"*Jesus Christ.*" The man recoiled back out the door, now with an arm up over his lower face.

"What?" Jackson unclipped his sidearm and pushed past him. He froze in the doorway as waves of revulsion swept over him. The smell was the first thing – wood chips, cordite, blood and other body fluids. Then the visuals kicked in. Dead and broken bodies were everywhere – five, six, seven, he had no idea how many corpses at this point. Some were missing limbs, another lay back with eyes open and a knife protruding from his forehead, and in one case, a skull near squashed flat.

"What the fuck did this?" his technician whispered. He looked at Jackson, his eyes now haunted. "Did those two HAWCs do this?"

Jackson shook his head slowly. "Nope, I'm betting just one of them. These assholes just pissed off the wrong guy." Jackson tried to only breathe through his mouth. "Forget about it. We need to secure the device and get the fuck out of here. The mess is someone else's problem." He turned. "Do your job, people."

The technicians carefully entered the room followed by the box carriers.

"Little help here, boss." The technician pointed.

Jackson swallowed down some bile, and crossed to the device. There was a body slumped over it, its hands lying on either side of the trigger, but with the top of its head caved in to nose level. It looked like someone had pounded down on it with a sledgehammer.

Jackson lifted a leg to kick the dead body back off the device. He thumbed toward the bomb. "Now hurry the fuck up."

Jackson looked slowly around the room; a cordite fog still hung in the tight space, and rods of bright sunlight cut through it. There were bullet holes in the ceiling, floor and every single wall.

Just how the fuck do you stand in here and survive that? He shook his head. *Easy; you send in a soldier they say couldn't be killed.*

CHAPTER 7

Senate Building, Kremlin, Russia

Viktor Dubkin stepped from the elevator on sub-basement 12. The underground levels below the Kremlin senate building continued on down another three floors, but below him there was nothing other than the interrogation rooms, and with them, the smell of blood, fear, and death. They made him feel physically ill. He had no problem with ordering death, and even torture. He just didn't like to be close to it when it happened.

This floor, and the few above it, were far more interesting; they contained the research and development laboratories, and he was confident this one in particular was going to make a difference to Russia's future on the field of combat. Though all the major countries were investing heavily in cyber warfare, pulse, magnetic and microwave weapons, Russia had learned significantly from the urban battlefields of Chechnya, and its lesson had been that asymmetrical warfare always demanded close-order contact – hand-to-hand, face-to-face, and where the biggest fist, boot, tooth and claw, won the day.

He hummed to himself. Dubkin knew that if his pet project was a success, then the rewards would be immense – glory, favors, and wealth. He nodded to the two lab-coated scientists, who buzzed around him like miniature satellites, deferring to his seniority, and also well aware he was one of the chief sponsors of their program. They showed him to one of the largest rooms and as they approached, the doors slid back. Entering, the three men found themselves behind a heavy glass partition looking into a hall-like space where six men trained with weapons, in hand-to-hand combat, and lifted weights with heavy gauge iron bars bending like bows.

Once again, Dubkin felt an odd sensation in his chest – he wasn't sure if it was pride, awe or maybe a little revulsion. These men were the experimental 'Kurgan', the code name for the Russian combat troops of the future. The road to success had been long. Decades of grotesqueries were buried in unmarked graves, but eventually the breakthroughs came after they managed to extract information from a captured American scientist who had worked on the Arcadian program.

Each man was a giant, nearly seven feet tall, and hugely muscled. One of the scientists stood beside Dubkin, hands in lab-coat pockets and nodded toward them.

"The genetic treatment has given them enormous advantages. The skeletal framework is heavier and far more dense, and the musculature striations are longer." He snorted. "The ministry of sport would kill for just one of them at the next Olympics."

Dubkin turned, his mouth turned down. "You think we spent billions on these subjects to turn them into sporting toys?"

"No, no." The scientist blanched. "I just meant that they are physically superior to any other human being on the planet. They are a marvel; that was all I meant, comrade Dubkin."

Dubkin stared for a moment more, making the smaller man squirm before he grunted and turned back to the glass in time to see one of the men punch a heavy bag so hard, his fist penetrated the leather, spilling sand to the ground. The scientists brightened again.

"That one is Zlatan; he's the natural leader and superior to the rest in intelligence, strength, and aggression. He really is something else entirely."

The huge man turned pale eyes on the window and stared straight at Dubkin.

"He can see us?" The Russian politician had a sudden urge to take a step backwards.

"No, not possible." The scientist raised small, neat eyebrows. "Even though their senses are heightened to be well above average, the glass is one-way mirrored and soundproofed."

Dubkin nodded, unconvinced. He watched as a woman came into the room and had Zlatan sit down, and she began checking his hands, perhaps for injuries. She smiled, and the man's large features melted momentarily as he looked up into her face.

The scientist watched the pair for a moment. "Their *handlers*, the women, are with them constantly, and have formed intimate bonds with the men. It keeps them interested and docile." The scientist nodded, either agreeing or congratulating himself. "We have them psychologically imprinted for loyalty. But the Kurgan are strong-willed, so we added a little fail-safe."

The scientist smiled dreamily as he watched Zlatan and the woman together. "After all, a man in love will do anything, yes?"

"The women know to do this?" Dubkin tilted his head.

"Oh yes, each man has his own, um, special lady." The scientist turned back to the glass. "The sweetest fruit is dangled, but never actually eaten."

"Good, good." Dubkin liked what he saw ... until one of the men stripped off a sweat soaked shirt, revealing what seemed a deformity.

"What is *that?* What's wrong with him?" He squinted, seeing bands or lumps underneath the man's skin, across his chest and lower back, and even extending up his neck to the base of his skull.

The scientist grinned with pride. "What is wrong with him? Nothing as far as our treatment is concerned. We just subjected them to more and more trauma while putting them through our gene-manipulation programs. Their DNA was tricked into thinking they needed to be more physically robust to survive, and it obliged by rewriting itself to better protect them.

Dubkin grimaced at the misshapen shape of the man's torso. "Deformed."

"Well, yes, there *are* observable changes." The smaller man nodded. "His skeletal architecture has rewritten itself – his ribcage is now almost a solid mass of interlocking plates. Cartilage extends down over his softer organs, and within his thighs, calves, arms, and neck, there are strips of cartilage, more like that seen in a cuttlefish, that give extra scaffolding support, strength, and stability. Added to that their skin is more like toughened leather than the soft stuff covering us weaker beings." He smiled, lovingly. "In a way, the men have grown their own personal suit of armor; it just happens to be inside them."

The scientist titled his chin. "Just a few years back, in Texas, a man by the name of Tiny Meeker set a record when he bench-pressed over 1,100 pounds – a phenomenal weight." He raised his eyebrows momentarily before turning back to the glass. He nodded to one of the Kurgan at the bench. "That man there, Stroyev, is lifting 2,000 pounds. Zlatan could lift even more."

Dubkin was impressed and looked down as another scientist stepped closer to him. He nodded deferentially, and also beamed with pride. "The Kurgan heal quickly, don't get sick, and we have built-in loyalty conditioning – basically, they are perfect."

Dubkin grunted. "On paper." He rubbed his chin for a moment. "I want to see one of them in action. See what they can *really* do."

The scientist bobbed his head. "What did you have in mind … and when?"

"A little field testing in the old district. If this Zlatan is the best, then let's see the best in action." Dubkin looked at his watch; it was just 9 pm. He smiled. "Now is a good time … and I know the perfect place."

* * *

Zlatan stared in at the patrons through a small mesh-covered window in a door that was thick enough to deter a bomb blast.

The bar, 'Glebs', was in Kupchino, the Frunzensky district of St Petersburg, and an area even the locals knew to avoid at night. After dark it became a place inhabited by drug dealers, street gangs, and general down and outs. The police never bothered going there – even if there was a murder – until the sun came up.

Zlatan's near colorless eyes missed nothing as they took in the single room filled with thick, blue tobacco smoke. Even from outside he could smell the stale beer and body odor. There were about thirty occupants, mostly big brutish men with broad Slavic features, and dark, stained teeth. A few slatternly women laughed too loudly and were dragged onto laps, where they cooed and ground down hard onto waiting groins.

Zlatan forced the grin from his face, pushed the door open, and headed straight for the bar. He stumbled once as though intoxicated, all eyes were on him, taking in his expensive clothing, gold watch, diamond ring and chain around his neck. Perhaps they thought he was some sort of high-paid sports star who was on a bender and had wandered into the wrong place. Or maybe he had come to satisfy his urge for a rougher trade. Regardless, even though he was a big man, he knew his inebriation and trappings made him impossible to ignore – and for some, impossible to resist.

He sat on a stool, ordered a beer, and pulled out a wad of cash, peeling off a 5,000 ruble note – the salmon-colored banknote was a rarity and worth more than most of the bar occupants earned in a year.

The barkeep frowned, refusing the denomination and leaned in closer to the stranger.

"I think you are in the wrong place here. Take your money and go, quickly."

The huge man just grunted then pulled out a smaller 500 ruble note from the stack and slapped it down, telling the barkeep the change was his. The man froze in confusion for a moment – no one tipped in his establishment, and certainly not that much. After another moment, he shook his head, cursed the man's stupidity and took the money.

Zlatan smiled, feeling the interest and tension rise in the room. They would come at him soon; he could feel their hunger now, coming off them in waves. They stared and licked fleshy lips like a pack of wolves encircling a lone animal in the forest.

He reached into a pocket and pulled a cigarette-pack sized device free and placed it on the booze-stained bar. It had a dark dome on top, and inside a bank of cameras sprang to life taking in a 360-degree image of the room, and transmitted it back to Dubkin, the scientists and, Zlatan hoped, also to his beautiful Rahda. She had told him to make her proud – she could count on it.

"You looking for a woman, drugs, weapons?" A rat-faced man sidled up to him. He looked like a cross between a ferret and human being. His eyes never stopped moving, darting around in a pocked face, but always coming back to alight on the massive Rolex on Zlatan's wrist. "Something else? I have everything." He turned and snapped his fingers twice. "Albina, come."

The barely conscious woman stumbled closer and did her best to look seductive, but her bloodshot eyes kept rolling back in her head, and there were crusted sores at the corner of her mouth and one nostril.

"Albina likes you. Do anything you want."

Zlatan turned to the pair, and raised his voice to a slurring shout. "Fuck off, *shlyukha!*"

The woman shrunk back at the old Russian word for whore, and Weasel-face showed a row of small, dark teeth as he backed away a few steps. His eyes never left Zlatan's watch. Behind them, groups of men whispered, sizing him up, planning.

The Kurgan lifted his beer, sipped and spat it out on the floor. "Dog's piss."

An empty bottle slammed into the back of his head, causing Zlatan to lean forward momentarily, and then turn to the small device on the bar to nod. When his head came up he was totally devoid of expression. He got to his feet, and headed for the door. Catcalls, whistles, and more projectiles followed. Other men also got to their feet, intent on following him outside.

But he didn't leave. When he got to the door, instead of exiting, he slid the deadbolt across, locking it, and then turned. The first men to come at him were big, raw-boned, covered in gulag tattoos, and their faces carried broken noses and numerous scars from lives lived fighting.

One swung a wooden chair down on Zlatan's head and shoulders so hard it shattered, but before the man had even finished on his follow-through, the Kurgan had caught a chair leg out of the air and used it like a dagger embedding the splintered end deep into the eye socket of one of the men. He shot out a tree trunk-like arm and caught the other man by the throat, and then grabbed his waist, lifted him above his head, and slammed him down across one knee. The sound of his spine cracking was like a rifle shot.

The women fled and the room exploded in shouted curses, frantic movement, and a rush of bodies as they all came at him at once with knuckle-dusters, knives, and guns.

The small device on the bar top caught it all.

* * *

Back at the laboratory Viktor Dubkin blanched as he watched blood spurt, bones break, and limbs pulled from sockets. Never had he witnessed such methodical brutality inflicted on other human beings.

One big man with a face like a potato swung a long blade into Zlatan's ribs. He struck hard, but the knife barely penetrated. The man probably thought the giant wore body armor, but the reality was his armor was grown internally. Zlatan merely pulled the knife from the man who tried to turn away, and swung the blade back at him so hard, the shaft passed through the back of his neck, coming out his mouth to then nail him to the wall, so he hung there like a coat on a rack.

Dubkin blew air softly through pursed lips. The other thing that amazed him was even with the bestial ferocity the massive Kurgan displayed, his face remained impassive, not even breathing hard.

In another few minutes it was all over, with just two men left – the barman, ashen-faced and holding his hands up, and another man on the ground attempting to rise.

Zlatan looked down briefly at the struggling man, and casually lifted one size-fifteen boot before bringing it down on the face of the man so hard his skull caved in.

Slowly he lifted his gaze to the barman. Dubkin pressed the communication button, and his voice transmitted directly to a small pellet in the Kurgan's ear.

"No mercy, no survivors."

Zlatan reached down, picked up a discarded gun, pointed it and fired twice – both bullets hitting the barman between the eyes.

Dubkin nodded, satisfied. He checked his watch. "Three minutes and seven seconds; very good." He turned to the scientist. "I have a mission; I will need them."

The scientist's eyebrows rose. "How many? Several are ready for ..."

"All of them." Dubkin turned away. "Get them ready for immediate departure. I will brief them as soon as Zlatan returns."

CHAPTER 8

US Strategic Command (USSTRATCOM), Offutt Air Force Base, Nebraska

"A tragedy." Colonel Jack Hammerson, 'Hammer' to his friends and enemies, had the phone on speaker and leaned back in his chair as five-star General Marcus Chilton related the events of the *Orlando* space shuttle orbiter crash.

"Revelation Mountains, Jack, bad news for recovery; almost inaccessible, and this time of year, even an airdrop is suicide for any normal rescue team – nothing but white-outs, blasting winds, and rock faces that make the Matterhorn look like a playground slide."

"I know the area, Marcus; we've done some training work there. It's a little bit of hell, right here on Earth."

He turned to the large window overlooking the parade grounds, and waited for the general to get to the point. Hammerson was the head of the elite Special Forces group known as the HAWCs. They went in when everyone else wouldn't or couldn't, and did jobs the other security and military agencies didn't even want to know about. And just as well, because his team made their own rules, and when they were done, there was blood and broken bodies – always the other guys'.

Chilton's voice lowered. "Okay, Jack, that was the above-the-line speech, and now for the ears-only upload."

Hammerson took the phone off speaker, and plugged the pellet into his ear. He sat forward, his large fingers clasped together on the desk. "Go, sir."

"Jack, the *Orlando* was using one of our latest model deep-ground penetrating imagers. As the orbiter was going to be circling the world 300-plus miles up, we decided to make use of its altitude to take a few pictures – in fact *loads* of pictures. We set it to capture images and then let it run."

Hammerson knew all about the capabilities of the DPIs. "Oh, good lord." Hammerson tilted his head back and shut his eyes momentarily. "We mapped ourselves, didn't we?"

"Oh yeah," Chilton replied. "Problem was, we couldn't transmit the images back to base – the probability of them being hacked and intercepted was too great. We needed to physically accept that device back into our hands." He grunted. "Jack, that film is as lethal as it is invaluable."

"Who else knows about it?" Hammerson had a sinking feeling.

"We know the Russians and probably the Chinese know about it, but they couldn't do a damn thing about the *Orlando* when it was in orbit. Now that it has fallen out of the sky, they can."

Chilton drew a deep breath and let it out in a low rumble. "That was the bad news. Now for the worse news – the Russians now have the jump on us. Our intel tells us they're about to dispatch a team or already have. Jack, we can't have an unarmed NASA recovery team running into a few Russian torpedoes up on those cliffs now, can we?"

"No sir, that we *cannot*." Hammerson smiled grimly. "You want us to ride shotgun?"

"NASA is calling the shots on this as they know their bird. Normally, we'd send a standard Spec Ops team, but this has complications. We understand that Russia is putting a top team in for a fast snatch. They intend to blitz the site. These guys are displaying a distinct lack of respect; Jack, we, and by that I mean *you*, need to remind them who they're dealing with."

"Be a pleasure, sir." Hammerson smiled grimly.

"One more thing, there's a quarantine order over the entire site, and it's not just for show. Where the *Orlando* went down we managed to get some initial satellite images before the cloud cover closed it all in. Looks like some sort of contamination dispersion. I'm sending you the Sabers images and initial report ... now."

A second later Hammerson's computer pinged.

"Got 'em." He immediately opened it and went to the first set of the satellite images. His brow furrowed. The *Orlando* had come down in among a set of massive jagged mountaintops that formed a sort of tooth cavity about two miles wide. He could tell by the way there were clouds hanging at its shoulders that it was high, and some numbers printed down the side confirmed it – 10,100 feet up.

It was high, cold, and virtually inaccessible. On this day it was calm, but Hammerson had been in the territory and knew it normally would have been a freezing hell of hurricane winds and chill factor of a hundred below in unsheltered areas. The only other place he could think of to make a fast extraction any more difficult might be the bottom of the ocean.

"Long way up," Hammerson observed.

"Sure is, and a long way from home," Chilton responded. "Average altitude where *Orlando* came down is 10,000 feet, and it's close to absolutely nothing."

Hammerson enlarged one of the images. He could easily make out the impact skid-line of the craft as it obviously came in at a hard angle. There was a debris plume, but the craft seemed to be primarily intact. The several pictures he looked at were time-stamped only minutes apart but as each image progressed in time they showed what looked to be a growing stain around the craft. The first was a dozen feet, and the last, hundreds. In addition, the last picture seemed to be blurred, but only over the spreading stain.

"What am I looking at here? Is that some sort of chemical leak, or fuel burn?" Hammerson squinted at the images.

"Unknown, but something sure is spreading, Jack, and it's not a burn. Our tech teams believe something is growing down there." He exhaled. "And that weird distortion of the image – well, we *think* that whatever that stuff is that's spreading on that mountaintop, it's giving off some sort of gas."

"That's a pretty damned hostile environment to be growing in; extremophile, maybe?" Hammerson asked. He knew that only a few creatures could live in a place that was deadly to anything else. Extremophiles, named after their extreme environments, could thrive in hot vents at the bottom of the ocean, sulfur pools, or underneath permanent ice sheets.

"What else could it be?" Chilton replied. "But what sort?"

"Nothing I've heard of." Hammerson stared at the images. "Especially something with that speed of spread ..." He checked the time stamps. "... this is happening over a matter of minutes."

"Indeed," Chilton said. "But it gets even weirder – we got movement as well."

"Holy shit – *survivors?*" Hammerson began thinking through the rescue implications.

"Could be, but how? There's some audio from the cockpit; it's not encouraging."

"Sir?" Hammerson's brow's knitted.

"Best if you hear it yourself, Jack. Anyways, Sabers has lost sight now, and we can't improve resolution any better than what we've got. But before we went over the horizon, we picked up some thermal signatures before it whited-out completely. The signs definitely showed objects – life forms – moving away from the downed craft."

"Well, if it is our people, those guys won't stay warm for long," Hammerson observed.

"I know. Make a plan, Jack, ASAP. Work with NASA. Find out what happened. First prize is you bring back that film, and locate any survivors. Second prize is no one else gets it. Anyone tries to stop you, well, you know what to do."

Hammerson's mouth pressed into a grim smile. "Yes sir, that's what we do."

"Okay, that's it for now. You come up with anything else, feel free to share your observations with me. Good luck, God's speed and strength to you and your team." The general disconnected.

Jack Hammerson quickly read through the remaining briefing papers, and went to the bios of the missing astronauts – all quality pilots, technicians and scientists themselves. Not one of them looked prone to making mistakes, or freaking out.

He read the mission report and saw that the crew had been attempting to evade some space debris, and eventually had brought it onboard ... and then everything went to shit. Two possibilities: it was all a coincidence, which as far as he was concerned, never happened. Or whatever they dragged into their hold made everything go bad, real quick.

Hammerson rubbed his chin and opened the attached audio and visual files from the shuttle orbiter's last moments that Chilton had mentioned.

"Jes-*uuus Christ*." He sat back – the screaming, moaning and other sounds of pain, utter desperation and hopelessness made the hair on his neck prickle.

"What the hell happened up there?" He narrowed his eyes and then ran the recording forward and back a few more times. The voice analyzer couldn't determine which astronaut's voice was which, or for that matter, even which was male or female. When Hammerson closed his eyes then ran the recording again, he wasn't sure the screams even sounded human.

He checked the cargo manifest. There were lab animals onboard. *Maybe*, he thought. The visuals were even more inconclusive as something greasy looking seemed to have been smeared or splattered over the internal camera, and the cabin became indistinct as it filled with something like smoke or fog.

Could have been an onboard fire. He sat back, thinking. There were other possibilities, of course – one was sabotage. After all, the Russians were a little too quick off the mark for his liking. And the *Orlando* going down in Alaska, separated from Russian territory by around fifty miles of Bering Sea, was also a little too convenient.

He hated the thought of having to work with civs, but at least he'd worked with NASA before and found them competent. Sending them up there without HAWCs might be a death sentence if the Russians decided they wanted to play hardball. He imagined what was likely to happen if a Russian team of torpedoes came across a wounded astronaut or unarmed civilian. If the Russians wanted to remain invisible, they'd eradicate all evidence of having been there. Basically, if anyone saw them, they didn't live to tell.

Well, if the Russians were sending torpedoes, then he'd send nukes. "And that's why they call me *the Hammer*." He smiled as he brought up his active HAWC list.

CHAPTER 9

Los Angeles Times, *Major News Desk*

Morag O'Sullivan pushed her shock of thick, red hair back up off her forehead as she scanned the NASA news feed. Her brows drew together.

"Hey …" She leaned back in her chair. "… the news feed about the *Orlando* space shuttle has been removed." She tapped her lips with a pencil for a moment. "Weird." She remembered the last time NASA's news feeds went dark on their space program, and that was during the horrific *Challenger* disaster. She rested her chin on a hand. "Does anyone care?"

"Nope." Phil Bellows, her older colleague, could not have sounded more disinterested.

"Well, I *do*." Morag leaned forward to look at a tiny picture on her desk of a smiling woman dressed in an astronaut's space suit. It was Eileen Marie Collins, now retired, but in her day she had been an air-force colonel, test pilot, first female commander of a space shuttle, and was awarded medals for her work. Collins was also born in County Cork, Ireland, where Morag was born. To Morag, and all of Cork, the woman was a hero. Her exploits in the space program had made Morag a fan of NASA since she was a little girl.

"Yeah, I definitely do."

At 32 years of age, Morag already knew that few were like her and she reflected on changing tastes and the attention span of the space-watching public these days. There was a time when the shuttle simply taking off was big news. Today, a few people floating around up in the darkness, deploying a multimillion dollar satellite or doing tumble-turns in zero gravity, was about as exciting as having your tax done.

Just give me more Lady Gaga hair care tips. She snorted as she tried to find anything on the deep web about the *Orlando*.

As Fred Benson, her editor, often said, "If *you're* interested, then your job is to *make* the public interested. But first give them something to be interested about."

And that's where the 'ol O'Sullivan magic came in. She smiled as she scrolled through more data, looking for something, *anything*, on the *Orlando*. After another ten minutes, she gave up – there was nothing.

Odd. Shit always went wrong in space flight – human error, equipment failure, and the unforeseen weird stuff were always happening. NASA, to its credit, managed to work through most problems, big and small, before they even got reported. But they still got reported – NASA kept up a constant stream of media-friendly babble.

A shuttle landing might get a few lines toward the middle of the paper. But a shuttle crash was still front-page news. Their news feed had gone dark and that made her investigative journalist's antennae quiver.

The news business these days was so competitive that sometimes it seemed like a cross between dog fighting and a race track. You had to be first in with a story, and then be prepared to fight for it, and even rip it right out of someone else's mouth if it came down to it. She had a feeling about this missing shuttle, there was a story there, and knew it could be the break she desperately needed.

Her fingers now flew over the keyboard, and she quickly found an image of the *Orlando*'s crew and studied their faces: flight engineer Gerry Fifield, mission specialist Beth Power, and Commander Mitch Granger. She snorted, the commander looked straight from central casting – strong jaw; thick, dark hair and a piercing gaze that radiated intelligence and good humor. They shouldn't have been able to shut NASA up about them. So where were they?

She twisted in her chair. "Hey Phil, where was the *Orlando* shuttle supposed to land?"

The older reporter kept scowling at information on his screen. "Earth probably." He looked up and winked. "But seriously, who even cares anymore?"

"Yeah, thanks Phil; that's why they pay you the big bucks." Morag put her hand on the phone. "As my mother always used to say – *fly free, girl*." She grinned. "I'll find out myself."

"Wise mother." Phil nodded. "Go ahead and call them. But I wouldn't." He glanced at her. "Because, if there *is* something going on, as soon as you, a reporter, asks them a question, you'll be telling them you're onto them."

Morag paused, phone in midair. He was right; if there was anything of interest being kept from the public, any leads would disappear like smoke as soon as she poked her head up.

"Fuck." She slammed the phone down.

"And *that's* why they pay me the big bucks." He went back to scowling at his own screen.

Morag eased back into her seat, her fingers steepled at her chin. The shuttle had gone missing as soon as it entered western airspace, and the deep web indicated it had been somewhere over Alaska. She knew there were several emergency runways up around that area long enough to accommodate the bulk of a shuttle orbiter landing if something had gone wrong. So what had happened then?

If it's crashed, then tell us – what's the big goddamn secret?

She lunged at her keyboard to dive back into the deep web, this time trying foreign data sources. Sure enough, one in Chinese looked like it had extrapolated a descent trajectory for the craft.

She hit the translation app on her screen. "*Bingo.*" She leaned forward, enlarging the area where it came down. *Freaking Alaska* – about as remote as you could get ... and that was a good thing, as there'd be no one else checking it out.

Morag tapped her lips with a knuckle. If she went, it'd mean dropping everything and going, like *right now*. Possible, as all she had waiting at home was a half tub of yoghurt in the refrigerator, a few pot plants, and a cat ... that liked the neighbors more anyway. It was doable.

So much to do. Her fingers flew again over the keyboard as she entered some travel queries. It was around five hours to get to Anchorage in Alaska from Los Angeles. She could then hire a chopper out to the NASA test base or hitch a ride or stowaway or whatever it took. She sat back, thinking. She'd need a camera guy, one who was a climber. That narrowed it down to one. She'd worked with Calvin Renner before, and knew he was just off assignment, had climbing experience and was big and tough enough to scale the Matterhorn, while lugging fifty pounds of equipment.

She tried to calm her surging excitement. If she was the gun reporter, then money, time, and materials were no object. But as she was still making her bones, it meant begging for scraps. She bit her lip. And this job was way above her expense allowance.

Her hands slowly moved to the keyboard, and she opened her email. Morag began to type carefully, crafting every word as she prepared a meeting request with her editor. She included all the hot buttons she could think of: government cover-up, potential death in space, exclusivity, breaking now. She read it back three times before she was satisfied with the few lines.

Show time. She hit 'send'.

The corners of her mouth turned up. Once she had her budget, NASA wouldn't dare turn her away or refuse to answer a major media organization's questions. Sure, she'd have to bluff and double bluff, but, *NASA*. She felt a warm flutter in her stomach, just thinking the name.

Morag's email pinged – Fred Benson, calling her up for a meeting. She swiveled in her seat. "Gotta date, Phil. Don't wait up."

"Never do," he said without turning away from his screen.

* * *

Benson was a big guy, the color of dark coffee and with a shaved head. He smelled of cigars and overwork. He had an infectious belly laugh but could strike fear and crush dreams with a yell that just about burst eardrums. To say he didn't suffer fools was an understatement.

Morag put her hand on the door handle, paused, collecting herself. She pasted on a smile, pushed the door inwards, but just poked her head around it.

"Morning, Mister Benson." Her smile widened.

He waved her in. "Mister Benson, *huh*? Must want something, Morag." He continued to sort through a pile of papers several inches thick.

Morag took a seat. "Nope, but got something for you."

His eyes flicked up at her. "I read your email; impress me."

"The *Orlando* Space Shuttle has vanished from the space-monitoring feeds. Now NASA has gone dark on it. Last time they did that was during the *Challenger* disaster."

"So a shuttle has tech problems. What else you got?" Benson went back to his papers.

"I think there's more to it. It looks like it's come down in Alaska. Even the Chinese are confused; and they seem to know more about what we do, than even we do."

He bobbed his head. "Yeah, okay; write up a few lines on it, and keep watching for anything that eventuates. We might get a few grabs out of it."

Morag licked her lips. This was getting away on her. "Like I said, there's more to it." *Time to bluff*, she thought. "NASA is scrambling a secret team to head up there now. Something big is happening ... and I can join them."

He looked up slowly. "Really? How the hell would you know that, let alone be able to join them?"

She held his eyes, her own unwavering even though her heart was racing. *Here goes nothing.* "Because I know Eileen Marie Collins, the retired NASA astronaut and first female commander of a space shuttle."

His eyebrows went up. "You got an in?"

"You bet. I can join their team, and be first on the ground – we're talking first breakers." She nodded, trying to radiate confidence.

"I'm listening; what would you need?" Benson sat back.

She shrugged. "Not much really; a cameraman with high-altitude experience, travel expenses, plus my exclusive byline. It's *my* story."

She sat frozen, waiting as she saw him ruminating.

"When?" he asked, still holding her gaze.

"Gotta go right now if I'm going to catch that NASA team."

Benson continued to stare, and time seemed to stand still. And then ...

"Go."

"*Yes*." Her face split with a grin as she got to her feet.

"And Morag."

She paused.

"You better bring me something hot."

"Count on it." She headed for the door.

CHAPTER 10

Jack Hammerson reread the summary of the report before him, titled: *BREAKOUT*. It was the result of several years' observational analysis, interviews and conversations with Captain Alex Hunter, Hammerson's HAWC team leader.

Alex Hunter was the first, and probably the last of their AWP, or Advanced Warrior Program, soldiers. The Arcadian program, from which he had drawn his codename, had literally caused him to rise from the ashes of a living death. Science had given him gifts and curses, but it was looking more likely they were in unequal measure.

He rubbed a hand across his face, his focus still on just a few paragraphs as if his mind had become a wheel stuck in sand, ever spinning, but not able to escape.

The military psychologists; Hammerson; Alex's partner, Aimee Weir; and even Alex Hunter himself had worked hard to suppress the psychopathic urges of *The Other* that inhabited the deep, dark places in his mind. Alex had been given techniques to calm himself, and usually they worked, or at least he said they did.

Early diagnosis of a dissociative identity, or in layman's terms, a split personality disorder, were far from satisfactory, and in fact, the detection of a neocortical mass in the center of his head led to theories that there was a physical aspect to the aberrant personality that haunted him. What they had at first thought to be a benign knot of scar tissue that surrounded an old bullet fragment in his brain was suspected of being something far more sinister.

Under MRI analysis, the mass was neuro-architecturally determined to be a bundle of synapses that had its own blood flow and was even triggering independent electrical coupling and neuronal synchronization, just like his brain did. But when they tried to investigate it more thoroughly, Alex's body and mind had reacted – it was if the mass, the source of *The Other*, was defending itself.

"*Hmm.*" Hammerson scratched his chin. *Yeah, that's you, isn't it?* He thought. *That's where you live; the monster from his Id.*

The HAWC commander turned the page, feeling his heart sink even further as he read on. There was the potential for total takeover of his personality. Alex Hunter, the person they knew, loved, and respected was currently the dominant personality pattern. And *The Other* was the rogue pattern he kept locked away. But the report's author suggested that this psychological entity was becoming stronger not weaker, and perhaps it wasn't Alex who freed it at will, but *The Other* that let itself out, whenever it chose.

The author also suggested they needed to prepare for the possibility of this darker personality not just asserting itself to become the dominant one, but one day becoming the *only* one.

Jack Hammerson knew that when that manifestation occurred, Alex Hunter wouldn't be Alex Hunter anymore; he'd be a near unstoppable killing machine. The implications were horrifying – for Aimee; his son, Joshua; and Alex himself. And then there were the implications to Hammerson and his HAWCs.

What do you do with mad dogs? Hammerson already knew the answer to that. His eyes moved to the icon on his screen labeled 'SWP' – *Synthetic Warrior Program*. There was an old saying about hoping for the best, but preparing for the worst. To that end, he had prepared a contingency plan to defend them all against a rogue Alex Hunter. He hoped the day would never come, but if it did, then they were ready to fight fire with fire.

Create a monster to kill a monster, Hammerson thought glumly. *I hope, never.* He sat staring at the report for several more seconds, not seeing the words anymore as his mind had turned inwards. The knock at the door gave him a start.

"*Jesus.*" Hammerson closed the report and pushed back from his desk. "Come."

He already knew who it would be, so he cleared his mind and smiled as he stood. Alex Hunter paused to briefly salute, then he crossed to his superior officer with hand outstretched.

"Sir."

Hammerson gripped the hand, examining his protégé. Alex had gray-green eyes that could project warmth, like now, or radiate a cold ruthlessness with an unblinking stare.

"Good job on the *Manhattan*." Hammerson pointed to the chair opposite his own at the huge mahogany desk. "We recovered the device, all terrorists down, and Joe Public gets to sleep easy."

"Except we lost the senator and his wife," Alex said.

"True." Hammerson sighed. "Gillian and Robert Anderson were dead the moment they boarded. Sometimes fate has plans for people and nothing or no one can change it. You saved millions of lives that day, but bottom line, we *can't* protect everyone, everywhere."

Alex stared into space. "We are the sword and shield."

"Damn right." Hammerson nodded. "Let's move on. Are you rested?"

Alex turned. "Sure, if you call being decontaminated and debriefed for hours resting. I'm still waiting for that leave you promised me."

"I promised you leave? Must be slipping." Hammerson chuckled. "Anyway; I promised *Aimee* I'd give you leave – there's a difference." Hammerson raised his eyebrows. "How are she and Joshua by the way?" He watched Alex closely.

"Good, no, *great*. Having us all together, like a real family, it's changed my life." Alex seemed to relax further into the chair.

"And the headaches?" Hammerson smiled, watching.

Alex waved it away. "No, none."

"Anger flare ups, conflict, or ... voices?" Hammerson's eyes narrowed. "*That* one voice."

Alex's eyes slowly lifted, the gaze direct. "No, no, and no." He opened his hands, arms wide. "No change, I'm fine, Jack. So there's probably no need to watch them, *us*, anymore, right?"

"Probably not." Hammerson just left it there, committing to nothing. The techniques they were using seemed to work while he was conscious. But even Alex knew that when dreaming, the monster ran free.

But while under control, that monster was very useful. Hammerson tilted his head. "You'll have to bring Aimee and Josh in for a hello. I miss them both." He sat back. "In fact, I've got something for Josh."

The corner of Alex's mouth lifted. "Please tell me it's not a weapon."

Hammerson smirked. "In the wrong hands, it might be." He folded his arms. "I've got a friend that works out at the Fermilab National Accelerator Laboratory."

"The Tevatron particle collider at Illinois?" Alex's brows went up. "I've heard of it. They're doing some interesting particle-collision work."

Hammerson nodded. "That's them; they also run some interesting breeding programs for guard dogs. They're designed to be big, strong, and with intelligence that's well above average. The boss of the pack, Fenrir, has just sired another litter; I think I can get Josh a pup."

"Jack, Joshua has been after a dog for years. But I think I'd like him to pick one out himself." Alex said.

"I know, I know," said Hammerson. "But he won't find one like this. And besides, he gets to pick it … sort of. These dogs are part of their Wolfen Guardian Program, and they're called that for a reason. They can almost understand human speech. The dog will protect Joshua and Aimee with his life, and will mortally bond with them." Hammerson shrugged. "For when you're away."

Alex sat thinking for a moment. "I guess it wouldn't hurt for him to have a look." He stared from under his brows. "But no strings attached, *huh?*"

Hammerson smiled. "No strings. In fact, I'll run them out there myself. There's a male pup, three months old; I think its name is Torben."

"Torben, *Tor*, I like it. Okay." He looked up. "Hey, did you just say, *for when I'm away?*"

Hammerson opened his arms. "Got a little job for you."

Alex's grin faded. "One day, you calling me in here will be just to shoot the breeze." A line appeared between Alex's brows. "What have you got?"

Hammerson clasped his fingers together. "It's a retrieval – the *Orlando* Space Shuttle Orbiter has come down. We need to search for survivors, and retrieve a package, top priority. Little more than twenty-four hours, in and out."

Alex nodded. "Please tell me it doesn't involve a cave, or at least it's somewhere warm."

Hammerson's mouth hiked at one corner. "Well, I can tell you it's certainly above ground – *well* above ground. Good enough?"

"No caves?" Alex cocked his head.

"Nope; no Antarctic labyrinths, and no going beneath any dark ice." Hammerson smiled grimly. "But as for the *somewhere warm*, well, save that for your holidays." He sat down, hit a few keys and pushed the image feed on his computer up onto a wall screen. "Revelation Mountains."

"Alaska." Alex whistled. "Yeah, *well* above ground is right."

The ten-by-eight-foot screen showed the satellite view from several hundred miles up. The geography was a gray-blue and white-capped rumpled sheet. Hammerson zoomed in and they flew down from space as the HAWC leader selected a grid and enlarged.

The clarity blurred for a moment before the resolution software cleaned it up. He stopped at about a thousand feet up.

"A lot of what we are seeing here is computer extrapolation. What it can't see it's interpreting based on best-guess algorithms, because it's dealing with some weird cloud formations that are distorting the image over the site."

Alex frowned, stood and walked closer to the screen. "Looks like a giant volcano."

"It does, but it isn't." Hammerson gestured to the screen. "That cusp is around 10,000 feet up, and created by three mountains being wedged up against each other, making a giant floating crater about two miles wide."

"Like a molar with a bad cavity," Alex observed. "But there's something missing; snow. All the other peaks close by are covered, but this crater is ice-free. Did the *Orlando* suffer a fuel burn on impact?"

In response, Hammerson highlighted the area and further increased magnification. There were the remains of *Orlando*, its skid line, and its broken, battered shell plus the familiar cone-shaped spray pattern of debris dispersal.

"There she is, the *Orlando*, busted up real bad, but the cabin and bay area came down primarily intact. What that angle of descent and its fuselage positioning tells me is that it obviously came in under some sort of control, otherwise it'd be in a million pieces with nothing larger than a matchbox." He turned to Alex. "Then there wouldn't be anything for us to do."

Hammerson joined Alex at the large screen. He pointed. "But that smudge you see is growing larger, and science division does not believe its chemical, heat, or debris scatter. What they *do* think is it's something organic, and it's growing." He turned, arms folded. "Something that spilled out of the *Orlando*."

"What the hell were they working on up there?" Alex asked.

Hammerson shrugged. "Just your basic low gravity experiments. They also had some lab animals, some mold and fungi spores, insect specimens, but nothing that could conceivably cause what we've seen on that mountaintop. But …" He held a finger in the air. "… the outlier in all this, is that they took onboard a fragment of space debris."

Alex turned. "We talking space junk?"

"No," Hammerson said. "Part of an asteroid, NASA tells us. Came out of the void – deep space." He went back to his computer and then split the image – the first remained as the mountaintop, but the second now showed the video feed from inside the *Orlando* cockpit just before it went down. He started it playing.

Once again Hammerson gritted his teeth at the sound of panic, fear and madness. The rushed movement was blurred, but no matter how many times he heard it, it still wavered between being vaguely human vocalizations to something that was bizarrely unidentifiable.

"That was the last contact from the *Orlando* before it dropped out of orbit." Hammerson turned to Alex.

Alex continued to stare hard at the screen. "Play it again." He then asked Hammerson to play it over and over, each time the creases in his forehead grew deeper.

"If you ask me, sounds like someone sent us a recording straight from hell." Hammerson grimaced. "After that, they went dark." He returned to his seat and leaned back in his chair. "And then they came down hard in the mountains."

Alex was still frowning. "Three voices, two men and one woman – I've never heard such fear in a human voice. Screaming for their lives." Alex looked back at the mountains. "And now, something is growing up there, when nothing should have even survived the crash."

"Something did; we got movement as well. We just don't know from what."

"The last image is blurred," Alex observed.

"That's right, those weird low clouds; our Sabers satellite has detected a range of gases that are being held over the crater in high concentrations. It seems a pretty primordial mix. Our science teams think it might have a high fungal, bacterial or viral load, causing some sort of xeno change. Whatever is growing down there seems to be off-gassing."

"Well, can't be all that lethal if we've picked up movement, so there's someone or something alive down there." Alex retook his seat. "So why us?"

Hammerson expected the question. "That's what I said. Normally, I'd kick this type job straight back upstairs. We've got enough potential firestorms going on in the world that we can be poking our noses into. But then the general told me two things – one is that there's a data chip that contains the images of every missile silo in the globe. He wants it retrieved from that crash site at all costs."

Alex whistled.

Hammerson nodded. "And the second thing is, we've intercepted a Russian communication – seems they're going to make a play for it as well. They'll be there before us, and we expect they'll send some heavy hitters. They'll want to get in quick, steamroll anyone that gets in their way, and then vanish." He looked into Alex's eyes. "And you know what that means?"

Alex nodded. "I do, they'll clean the site." He snorted softly. "So now it's a race."

"It's always a race, son." Hammerson gave him a crooked smile.

"I choose my team?" Alex raised his chin.

"The HAWC team, sure. But be advised this is a NASA mission, we're just riding shotgun." He held up a hand as he saw the protest building. "I don't like it either, but this one is not in my control."

Alex's eyes narrowed. "NASA controlled until I determine a hotzone. Then I own it."

Hammerson smiled. "Works for me." He slid a computer tablet toward Alex. "Here's your available mission stock; pull a team together. The NASA techs you're going to be chaperoning are already inbound. Say your goodbyes, pick your team, and get down to the armory." He sat back. "Six hours, you're airborne."

Alex grimaced. "Jesus, Jack, Aimee will ..."

Hammerson held up a hand. "I've taken the liberty of flying them in." He checked his watch. "And by now they should be both out on the far training grounds, having a picnic."

"Pretty confident, huh?' Alex shook his head, but grinned.

Hammerson shrugged. "Been meaning to catch up with them. And besides, later I can organise for Josh to see the dog. Give them both a hug for me." His face became serious. "Then be ready to brief your team, prior to dustoff."

Alex grabbed the tablet, stood, saluted and went to turn toward the door when he paused. "Where's the big guy up to?"

"Sam?" Hammerson smiled. "Oh, he's got all the new kit built in."

"Built in?" Alex raised his eyebrows.

"Oh yeah." Hammerson returned the smile. "Been out of surgery for weeks. He's down in the armory now. About time we put the big guy back to work." Hammerson saluted and Alex pushed out through the door.

Jack Hammerson lifted his coffee and toasted the screen. "Here's to you, Mother Russia. You didn't really think it was going to be that easy, did you?" He picked up the phone. "Put me through to General Chilton."

CHAPTER 11

Alex couldn't help the grin spreading across his face as he headed to the secure elevator that would take him down to the secret armory of USSTRATCOM's research and development weapons division. It was situated deep below the base, and accessible only to a handful of people.

R&D weapons division, or as the HAWCs referred to it the 'toy store', gave the HAWCs special access to new weaponry. They acted as guinea pigs for the new weapon tech, and in return they got it before anyone else. Ninety-nine out of a hundred times it worked, and rarely did anyone get vaporized anymore.

Alex stood before the featureless silver doors, and waited for them to scan his facial features and sniff his DNA.

As he waited he used the technical note pad to call up the bios of the HAWCs he had available. He'd take a large team, eight players, including himself. He knew each HAWC would be the equivalent of half a dozen standard Spec Forces operatives from anywhere in the world.

He smiled grimly. With that many HAWCs at his back, he could take down a city if he needed to.

"Captain Hunter."

Alex looked up to see a solid looking young soldier, whose face he recognized. He quickly looked down at the pad, and saw the same features staring back from the new HAWC inductees list.

"2nd Lieutenant Steven Knight." Alex said and the soldier came to a rod straight attention.

"Yes sir." He had shortcropped blond hair, slight sun damage to his nose and cheeks, telling of either days on the beach or the farm – the Midwestern accent told him of the latter.

"I just want to say, it's an honor to meet you, sir, I've been wanting to …"

"Says here, you're ex-Ranger stock." Alex glanced again at his bio.

"Sir, yes sir." He stared straight ahead. "Best shot in my squad."

Alex nodded. "Peak fitness, high pain threshold, excel at hand-to-hand combat, weapons tech expertise …" Alex nodded as he read. "… and climbing experience."

The man's lips curled up slightly at the corners. "Free climb down at Devil's Lake in Wisconsin, every chance I can, sir."

"Devil's Lake is for weekend hikers." Alex stared hard at the young soldier, and his smile dropped. "And you've no HAWC mission experience."

Knight's jaw firmed. "I'm ready, waiting and mission fit, Captain Hunter. Just say the word, sir."

Alex leaned in real close, and gave the man *the stare*. Knight continued to look straight ahead, not blinking, not moving a muscle. Alex knew his glare could reduce grown men to puddles of nerves; Knight didn't budge.

"2nd Lieutenant Knight, then consider you've just had *the word*. Authorization will be sent, you will communicate to no one and you will be ready and waiting down at rallying center five for kit-out and mission briefing in two hours."

Knight's lips compressed as he tried to hold in the grin. He saluted and Alex did the same. He looked about to say something else.

"Go!" Alex yelled and then chuckled as the man spun and raced back down the corridor.

He turned back to the elevator and the scanners checked him again. Satisfied, the two-feet thick doors slid back slowly. Both the doors and shaft were constructed of almost solid titanium, and if through some miracle they were breached, then the shaft itself would be immediately sealed with a plug of solid steel, ten feet thick.

Stepping inside, Alex felt the momentary claustrophobia of being shut in an iron box, but he set the feeling aside as he reopened the technical note pad. Alex brought up the first bio – Casey Franks. The brutal-looking woman stared hard back at the camera lens. She was tougher than many of the bigger men she worked with, and in a firestorm, she wasn't afraid to be the first through a door. He'd just finished a job with her, and he couldn't ask for a better agent to have at his back.

Alex pushed her profile into the mission folder and slid to the next. He couldn't help grinning. Why take a few armored vehicles when he could take a bulldozer? Sam Reid's image filled the frame, and not just because it was a close-up; the man was physically huge. Sam was a few years older than Alex was, and probably the closest thing Alex had to a friend in the HAWCs. They'd been on many missions together, and it was on one of them, in the jungles of South America, that Sam had his spine crushed, rendering him a paraplegic.

But Sam wasn't finished with the HAWCs, and they weren't finished with him either. Sam had enthusiastically volunteered to try out the new MECH technology. The Military Exoskeleton Combat Harness was the next generation heavy combat armor. On Sam, the synaptic electronics were a molded framework that was built on, and into, his body – light, flexible and a hundred times tougher than steel. Sam was as good as new, except now, the big man could run faster than a horse and kick a hole in a steel door.

Sam also possessed an intellect that made him one of the best military tacticians they had. He was an unbelievable asset to have on a team. But much as Alex would have put him on the mission list immediately, he had been concerned that the weight of the MECH suit would render him far too goddamn heavy and cumbersome for the high-altitude mission.

Rather than reject him, he'd wait. The Hammer had said he was getting an upgrade – Alex would find out soon enough exactly what that meant.

He scrolled to the next group of HAWCs. There were several others he had worked with before: Drake Monroe, Anita Erikson, and the big Aussie, Max Dunsen. Dunsen, or Dundee to the other HAWCs, was big and as tough as boot leather. If Alex could keep him and Casey Franks from killing each other, then they made a formidable team.

He looked over the others, some new blood that Hammerson himself had rated well off the scale – Andy Garcia – and he then added in Steve Knight. He slid all the profiles to the mission folder that would automatically send a call up alert to them no matter where they were in the world.

With barely any sensation of slowing, the elevator eased to a stop several hundred feet below ground. The entire subterranean complex was encased in sealed titanium and lead shielding that made the basement levels impregnable to a nuclear blast and impervious to electromagnetic pulse attack.

The design was like an upside-down wedding cake, with the larger test facilities at the top and moving down to the smaller R&D laboratories, and then onto the lower level containment cells for biological specimen testing and hazardous materials work.

The doors slid open, and a huge figure lunged in at him so fast, Alex only had time to raise arms to stop being pushed off his feet.

"Jesus Christ." Alex pushed the big bear of a figure off him and back out of the massively thick doors before they closed again.

"I remember when soldiers used to have respect for their senior officers." Alex grinned and looked the man up and down. "So, the new and improved Samuel Jefferson Reid." He cocked his head. "They couldn't do anything about the face, *huh?*"

Sam threw his head back and laughed. "Hey, I earned every lump, crease and scar on this ugly mug." He saluted and stood at attention.

"At ease, soldier." Alex walked around him. Sam was six-five and about two axe handles wide at the shoulders. He had arms that were straining the sleeves of his all-black HAWC uniform, and where once before he had an external exoskeleton MECH suit covering his legs and lower back, now he just looked normal.

"So, where is it?" Alex asked.

Sam held his arms wide and turned in a circle. "All new and improved."

Alex's enhanced senses picked it up then, the small whine of hydraulics as Sam turned. He also felt the small tingle in his head he always got when he was close to a source of radiation.

"Surgical implants?" Alex raised his brows.

Sam nodded. "Tungsten chromium blend; it's lighter than bone, and the tungsten blending gives it a tensile strength of 1,510 megapascals – titanium only has 434."

"And the chromium would give it flexibility." Alex tilted his chin up at Sam. "Your legs were the problem, so why am I picking up a residual trace from your upper body?"

Sam grinned. "Why do you think I was able to push you off your feet? First time ever." He held up an arm, turning it over, and then making a fist. "They inserted the full-body kit while they had me on the table. I'm the first to trial the internally bonded advanced MECH endoskeleton. The next generation of combat suits will be internal. I can armor up if needed, but now the core infrastructure is inside me and powered by a miniature shard of radioactive material – my own nuclear power plant. I have the mobility of a normal soldier, plus the added speed and strength of a horse."

"Good, because you can never have too many pack horses on a mission." Alex held out a hand. "Welcome aboard."

Sam reached forward to take his hand and Alex turned his large mitt over, looking at it. He could just make out the tiny lines running over the back of his fingers, hand, and wrist before disappearing under his uniform.

"Long surgery?"

"Tag-team of fourteen doctors and thirty-six hours. They had to weave the nano-mesh over every bone, integrate them into my muscle fibers to act like nerve endings, and finally link them to each other – over a million micro-stitches. The final bit was making sure I had control of everything. And for that, they needed me conscious."

"Sounds painful," Alex observed.

"Pain just lets you know you're still alive. It was a small price." Sam began to squeeze Alex's hand.

Alex grinned. "How could I not know you were going to do that?" He squeezed back.

Both men stared into each other's eyes, both just smiled as if they were doing little more than taking in the scenery, but both was exerting enough pressure to pulverize stone. Sam's hand was now more like a flesh-covered vice. But Alex was no ordinary human being either. Where Sam's hand was a vice, Alex's was an industrial press.

Pain to Alex was nothing more than a supercharger that he felt, absorbed, and then used. The more Sam squeezed, the harder Alex was able to squeeze back.

Alex watched his friend's face, seeing the temperature change on his forehead and his cheeks begin to redden. Perspiration broke out on his brow and an almost imperceptible grinding noise came from their hands.

Sam tried to maintain his grin, but Alex could see the pain behind his eyes now. He pressed a little more, prepared to stop soon if he thought he might damage Sam's hand. He didn't need to.

"Uncle!" Sam gasped and let go. "Okay, I've still got some catching up to do." He smiled ruefully and shook his probably throbbing hand.

"I'm impressed. If only I had someone like you on a mission I'm putting together." Alex punched his large friend's shoulder. "But I guess you'll be busy opening all the stuck jelly-jar lids up in the mess hall."

"Oh, I'm mission-ready. Maybe you'd like to go again, double or nothing?" Sam stuck his still very red hand out again.

"You want to prove yourself, big guy? Well then, consider yourself off the wait-list as of two minutes ago." Sam beamed. "I'm taking a large team – seven HAWCs."

Sam's brows went up. "That's a lot of muscle."

"Yep, and it's for a retrieval, from about ten thousand feet up in the Revelation Mountains." It was Alex's turn to grin. "Just to make it interesting."

Sam whistled. "Climb or drop?"

"Depends on weather conditions. Mission profile has been sent down to Grey," Alex continued. "We need to review the toolkit, and then link up with our NASA people. We're in the air in …" Alex checked his watch. "… five hours."

"Got everything I need right here," Sam said pointed with his chin. "Heads up; our favorite geek."

A small man bustled down the surgically white corridor, hands jammed in lab coat pockets. He lifted one free to throw them a small wave that turned into a sort of salute when he spotted Alex.

Chief research scientist Walter Grey came to a stop. "Captain Hunter, Lieutenant Reid." A nervous smile flickered on his lips before fading.

"Grey," Alex said and thrust out a hand. "Good to see you again."

The smaller man took it. "Yes, yes, likewise, Captain."

Alex tried hard not to smile. Grey looked anything but pleased to see them. Simple reason was Alex and the HAWCs scared him. They were like a different species – big, aggressive, and with an intelligence that pushed the boffins hard. They also had a bad habit of destroying his 'toys'.

He let his hand slip from Alex's. "I've seen the mission profile – extreme cold, significant altitude, and possible toxic air. Also, not very conducive to optimum firearms performance, so best leave the HKs home this time."

"Makes sense," Alex responded. "But I'll still take the full Ka-Bar set."

"Fine." Grey shrugged.

The trio headed along the corridor. Grey's voice rose as he talked faster, nervously pointing to different sealed doors as they passed: *laser technology, biologicals, handguns, rifles, combat body armor, sensory enhancement.* Alex nodded, but stayed silent. He knew all these weapons labs intimately as he'd trialed many of their tech in the field.

Grey slowed as they approached the ASU – the Armored Soldier Unit – the center for all physical shielding for the field operative. A soldier's combat fatigues of old had been replaced by new materials that were more a mix of body armor and computer system. The new lowest level infiltration suits had active camouflage with micro-panels capable of altering their appearance, color, and reflective properties, enabling the wearer to blend into their surroundings. The next level up for a front-line solider was full confrontation gear with hyper-strong body armor that came in various levels of defense – lower level micro-mesh that could stop a 9mm slug and be worn under normal clothing, moving up to full ceramic or biological plating, able to defray direct hits from a shotgun or assault rifle.

"I understand from Colonel Hammerson there's a risk of contamination," Grey said. "We've been developing an armored HAZMAT suit. Might be ideal for this mission."

"Cool." Sam rubbed his hands together in anticipation.

Grey stopped before a silver door that looked like a sheet of solid steel. He laid a palm on a glass panel, the outline of his hand was briefly illuminated and then the door soundlessly slid back into the wall. He led them into the cavernous space and the lights automatically came on around them.

There was a mannequin wearing an all-black compression suit with biological plating over the chest, biceps and thighs, and with smaller armadillo-like scales over the stomach and neck.

Alex had worn similar suits, and had found them both tough and pliable. For colder environments, they even had warming cells built in. This one was new in that the stand-out feature was that it covered the head and face. The flexible scale-like plating extended up the neck, each plate overlaying the one below it, but stopped at the forehead and chin where there was a clear oval panel acting as a full-face visor.

"What do you think?" Grey beamed.

"I think it looks a little stifling," Alex said, frowning.

"Ah, but just wait." Grey stepped toward it and touched a small stud beside the faceplate; it fully retracted up and away. He touched it again to bring it back down and then adjusted something that made four lenses protrude from the visor, making the face look totally alien.

"Whoa, quad vision," Sam said, grinning. "Like the Warrior system?"

"Oh yes." Grey nodded enthusiastically. "But where that had four separate tubes for light enhancement, this image intensifier can be adjusted to amplify thermal, light, and also deliver macroscopic vision."

"I like it," Alex said. The quad vision looked weird, the four tubes making it seem that the wearer had four eyes, but in fact the image kit had a computer application that overlapped the images, giving the wearer vastly superior peripheral sight with an almost wrap-around 98 percent field of vision.

Grey reached up to tap the faceplate. "Impact resistant polymer; you could take a direct hit from a shotgun blast, and still walk away with a face."

"But will the face still be on the neck?" Sam winked at Grey.

"Of course." Grey looked indignant. He turned the model around, indicating what looked like two pads between the shoulder blades. "Compressed oxygen cylinders can give you breathable air for forty-eight hours. Pumps and heating cells all work off a miniaturized nuclear chip." He pointed at Sam. "Similar to the one powering your internal MECH Suit, Lieutenant.

Sam nodded. "No complaints."

Alex stepped forward and lifted the dummy's arm. The gloves over the hands had ribbed fingers for grip, and plating over the knuckles and back of hand. *Good.* If they needed to get physical, using the suits was like having built-in brass knuckles; they tended to finish arguments real quick.

Sam walked around it, his brow creasing. "One question: how the hell does someone, *ah*, take a leak in that thing?"

Grey looked bemused. "Inside; where else?" He swung the model around on its plinth and showed them the back. There was a barely perceptible rise in the rear armor plating.

"Waste conversion system – filtered and converted to drinking water. Body temperature, of course."

"Nice one," Sam said. "And if I need to …"

Grey shook his head. "For that, you'll need to peel yourself out of the suit in the cold, I'm afraid. Solid waste presents a contamination and storage problem."

Sam grunted and looked skeptical.

Alex scoffed. "For Christsake, Reid, just go before you get into it." He grinned. "And no vindaloo curry before dust off."

"No promises." Sam grinned back.

Alex turned to Grey. "Good work. There'll be seven HAWCs including myself, and we're out of here in a few hours."

"No problem, send the bios. I've got all your measurements so we can engineer them right now. Be ready in an hour." He made some notes.

Grey clapped his hands. "And now. Let's go and look at some sub-zero environment weapon tech." He headed toward an adjoining door that linked them to the next R & D lab.

Alex and Sam followed him in. The new room was longer than it was wide, and at one end there was a target set up – a half torso. The hangar-sized room also sported multiple firearm racks.

Sam spotted some of the newer light-emitting weaponry. "Lasers?"

"No can do," Grey threw back. "Our analysis indicates an environment high in methane and hydrogen. You fire a laser in that, and it's liable to ignite the entire mountaintop."

"*Ouch.* What else you got?" Sam pulled a gun from a rack and checked it over.

Grey came and took it from the HAWC. "Well, we can't use anything that has either ignition-based initiators, propulsion or impact detonation devices, so that rules out a lot of the standard weapon tech."

"What about compressed air or EMP?" Alex folded his arms.

Grey snorted. "Old tech. I've got something even better. Magnetics."

Alex raised his eyebrows. "Rail design?"

Grey held up a finger and waggled it. "Well, we're still trialing rail-gun tech in our airforce and naval assets. We know we can get much greater muzzle velocities from lower energy than weapons powered by conventional propellants – means we can deliver bigger payloads faster and with greater accuracy."

"Faster is right," Sam said. "I've heard using electro-magnetics to achieve a high velocity can make the projectile near invisible," he said. "But my understanding is that the tech is freaking huge, like *tank-sized* huge."

"Oh yes, the heavy conflict weaponry still requires a good-sized hardware footprint," Grey agreed. "Our rail guns can deliver tungsten armor-piercing shells with kinetic energies of nine megajoules at two miles per second – at that velocity a tungsten rod projectile could penetrate down to a bunker buried beneath a mountain. But you're right, the big power systems are still truck sized."

"So, no rail gun." Sam's mouth turned down.

"I didn't say that." Grey showed a row of neat little white teeth.

"You've miniaturized it?" Alex smiled.

"Yes, we did. We lose some delivery speed, and they're only down to rifle size, but even then, we still managed to achieve muzzle velocities of 1.1 miles per second, and with enough kinetic energy to punch a tiny hole through six inches of solid steel." He shrugged. "If that's *all* you wanted it to do." He held his smile, waiting.

Sam chortled. "Okay, I'll bite. What else can it do?"

"I'm glad you asked." Grey rubbed his hands together. "You might not want to achieve a surgical-sized pinhole in your target. Instead, you might want something a little more

... *meaningful*." He lifted his chin. "I believe in the past, there have been a few of your adversaries that fit into that category, *hmm*, Captain Hunter?"

Alex just grunted, remembering his last mission – the creature he had encountered beneath the Antarctic ice was something that had evolved separately from the surface world. Maybe once it had been some sort of cephalopod, but it had developed into something massive, horrifying, and with a cold intelligence that had cost them a lot of lives. Back then, he'd wished he had a howitzer.

Grey went to one of the gun racks, and lifted something that looked more like a flattened box than a gun. The object had a shortened barrel and bottle shape molded into the square design.

Grey telescoped it out to a length of about three feet, turned it on its side and held it out.

"I present the RG3 – Generation-3 Rail Gun – field of combat ready."

Alex took it from the diminutive scientist. It was heavier than it looked. He turned it over in his hand. There was a front grip, rear handle, standard trigger and guard, but with several studs on its side plus a small round dial.

"It's got some weight." Alex ejected a magazine that was about the size of a packet of cigarettes; this was where the bulk of the weight came from. He looked inside at the rounds – there seemed to be many hundreds, all packed in tight, like needles.

He also saw that they weren't smooth but were more like tiny machines than solid material. He jammed the clip back in.

"How many?" he asked.

"Standard clip has a thousand rounds." Grey beamed. "Some operatives may find they don't have to reload for an entire mission."

"We'll take some spare clips. We might go duck hunting on the way home." Sam held out his hand and Alex handed him the gun. Sam hefted it.

"The weight you feel is from the ammunition pack, but also in the lead casing for the radioisotope thermoelectric chip. It powers up the twin parallel conductor rails." Grey leaned closer to point along the gun's body. "Along here we have a sliding armature that would be accelerated by the electromagnetic effects of a current flowing along the rails, and—"

"Hey, aren't electromagnetics susceptible to EMP weapon attack?" Alex knew the Russians were working on several devices to knock out battlefield electronics. "Be a pain in the ass to be caught in a firefight with a dead box in my hands."

"Of course it would. You were paying attention when I mentioned the lead casing for the radioisotope, weren't you? It has a nuclear power source, and is impervious to electromagnetic pulse. It only charges the rails for .003 seconds before firing. Even if the pulse wave knocks out that charge, it's ready to fire again in under a second."

Sam pointed to one of the target dummies. "Well?"

"Go ahead," Grey said. "It's currently set to single shot, but it can be ramped up to full metal storm if needed."

"What about the heat?" Alex asked. "A thousand rounds, and using it on rapid fire, should generate enough friction heat to melt the casing."

"Very good." Grey waggled a finger again. "And it did with the earliest versions. But ..." He grinned. "... that's why we now use ceramics in the conductor rails."

Alex nodded, satisfied.

"Only one thing left to do then." Sam pointed and fired, only holding the weapon in one hand. He kept his finger down on the trigger. There was barely anything above a whisper. Alex detected the dummy moving fractionally, so he knew there'd been a strike.

"Did I hit it? What happened?" Sam looked at the gun. "I felt a little recoil, but …"

"Let's see." Grey went to a panel and pressed a few buttons, causing a small screen to lift. "I'm going to rewind." He hummed for a moment. "Okay, now watch."

Sam and Alex looked over his shoulder. The target dummy filled the screen, and just when Alex was losing patience he saw a tiny hole appear in the center of the head – even in slow motion the projectile was moving too fast to capture. All that was revealed was a small puncture in the dummy's face, and then another indicating where the projectile had exited out the back.

"Oh yeah, in and out, I hit it good." Sam nodded. "But you're right, these pinpricks will have low stopping power. Some big badass might think he's only been stung by a bee."

"Hold that thought." Grey grabbed the gun from Sam's hands and moved the dial up to half way. "Now try."

Sam walked back into position, raised the RG3 and fired. Almost magically a golf ball sized section of the impact gel vanished from the center of the head, splattering down to the end of the room.

"Whoa." Sam grinned.

"Still think they'll feel like they've been stung by a bee?" Grey cocked an eyebrow.

"Maybe a giant one." Sam went to fire again, but Alex took the gun from him.

"My turn." He set the dial to its highest setting, aimed and fired. The entire head of the dummy disappeared in an explosion of gel.

Grey folded his arms. "You can thread a needle, or put a hole the size of a softball through anything you aim at."

Alex fired again, blowing away another section of the dummy. He looked at the weapon. "Oh yeah, this'll do." He smiled grimly. "And don't forget our spare mags."

"Really?" Grey looked unimpressed. "Just make sure you take it off maximum setting before hitting any ducks, won't you?"

"Hey, I hear they're pretty big ducks up there." Sam took the RG3 back from Alex, and fired again at the remains of the dummy, obliterating the bottom half completely. *Boom*, he mouthed through his smile.

"I'll have your weapons, spare ammunition and armor ready for you." Grey scowled at Sam and took the weapon from him. "Now, I understand this will more than likely be an adversarial engagement, yes?"

"We hope to avoid it," Alex said. "But they send HAWCs for a reason."

"I know, *expected confrontation*," Grey agreed. "So, now, something for defense I think you'll both like." He pressed a small stud in the wall and a drawer slid out. In it was what looked like gauntlets that fit over the lower arm. Grey took one out and slid it up his forearm.

"*Um* ..." The scientist opened another drawer and selected a 9 mm pistol. He handed it to Alex. "Take this."

Alex took it – a SIG Sauer SP2022 – he drew the slide back, but already knew it was fully loaded from the weight in his hand. He paused.

Grey adjusted something on the gauntlet, walked twenty feet down the shooting range and turned to face the two men. "Fire at will."

Alex looked briefly at Sam, shrugged, and pointed the gun. Grey brought his forearm up and a faint whirring sound began. In front of him a three-foot disc shaped area began to become less distinct.

Alex fired twice directly at the man, and the bullets were pushed away – not ricocheted, but more like they hit something that absorbed their energy and then discarded them. Alex fired three more times – same result.

"Hold fire," Grey yelled from behind the disc.

"Impressive." Alex lowered his gun arm. "What the hell is it?"

Grey dropped his arm, the whirring stopped and the air in front of him cleared. He lifted his chin. "Personal combat shield – it's basically ionized air trapped in a circling compression wave." He grinned. "We accelerate the molecules in the air to near speed of light, and actually create an artificial gravity field using the centripetal force to keep it in a confined area." He looked down at the gauntlet and patted it. "So far, we can only do it on a small scale, but we hope one day to be able to use it as a city-wide missile shield. Just think of that." His eyes lit up.

"What can it stop?" Alex asked.

"The personal shield can stop multiple caliber projectiles from 9 mm up to a 7.62 mm battle rifle rounds."

"*Hoooly* shit." Sam clapped. "Let me see that." He held his hands out.

Grey removed the gauntlet and adjusted it to fit on the much larger man's forearm. He gave Sam a few seconds of instruction and then stepped back.

Sam switched it on and moved it about. "No weight."

Grey shrugged. "Why would there be? It's just using the surrounding air, but reorganizing the molecules into a rotating lattice formation."

Sam backed up several steps. "Okay, boss, let me have it." Alex aimed and fired off three quick rounds. Every single one struck and dropped away.

"Nothing – didn't even feel the impacts." Sam lowered his arm. "It's a shield, but near see-through."

Alex stepped forward and reached out a hand toward the circle of compressed air. He felt solid matter beneath his fingers. Even though the circle of air was slightly oily in appearance, like swirling water, his mind still told him that he should have been able to reach through it. However, his hand told a different story.

Sam turned it off and handed him the gauntlet. Alex slid it on, and repeated what Sam had done, and initiated the shield. Alex also backed up a few steps.

"Okay, big guy; charge."

Sam grinned and lowered his brow. He was a large man, at 250 pounds easy. He was also assisted by the internal MECH suit technology that gave him the power of a battering ram. He dropped his shoulder and sprinted at Alex.

Alex raised the shield and widened his stance. Though Alex was stronger than Sam, mass and velocity were on the bigger HAWC's side. Sam crashed into Alex and the shield, and Alex skidded backwards from the massive impact. But it was Sam that was flung aside.

Sam sprang to his feet. "That shit is tough – combination shield and battering ram."

Alex nodded to the scientist. "Well done; add them to my shopping cart."

"Good. Been wanting them to get a run in the field – and no one tests out our stuff like you guys. I want a full report on all the new tech when you get back." Grey waved them on and then led them out through a different set of vault-like rooms.

Alex felt the presence as soon as he entered one of the darkened chambers. He pulled up hard, his head turning.

"What the hell is that?"

Grey looked sheepish. "Yes, I wanted you to see her."

"Her?" Alex frowned. He could sense he was being watched even more strongly now that he was inside – or a better description might have been that he was being *scanned*.

"Lights up," Grey said. "Spot." Immediately more lighting came on and a single stronger beam came down directly over a lone, seated figure.

Alex couldn't help his mouth dropping open. "You have got to be kidding me." He crossed to the figure. "It's a robot." He bent to look into the blank face.

Sam joined him. "Pretty ugly."

Grey went and stood beside it, placing a hand on its slim shoulder. "Oh, it's more than a robot. She's part of our Synthetic Warrior Program." He glared at Sam. "And she's a thing of beauty, as well as being the ultimate in autonomous mobile computing and communication packages." He smiled. "And much more."

The slim human shaped figure sat wired into a chair-type capsule. It shone dull silver as if made of pewter or brushed steel. Except for a slight slimness to the frame, it looked in proportion to someone approximately five feet nine or ten.

Grey then jogged to a console in the far corner and spoke over his shoulder. "Go ahead, touch it; it's not powered up just yet. Just give me a minute here."

Alex placed his hand against the cheek. The smooth silver skin of the face was featureless with just some bumps and depressions giving a hint to facial features. The synthetic skin was smooth and just below body temperature, but still warm. Alex dropped his hand to the shoulder and squeezed. The material gave slightly and he could feel a definite hardness beneath, like scaffolding or bones.

"It feels like skin, and it's warm." He laid a hand flat against the chest. "And by the way it's already on; I can feel it."

"No, not yet; maybe just some residual energy release or heat diffusion from the power plant," said Grey. "It's experimental HiPER fusion – High Power Energy Release through fusion reaction – stable, clean, and allows miniaturization without energy sacrifice or even degradation."

"Nuclear powered." Alex felt the chest again, sensing the slight buzz of enormous energy residing just under the synthetic skin.

"Oh, yes." Grey worked at the console for a moment before looking back at Alex. "The power plant fuses the lighter nuclei together and releases enormous amounts of energy. Thanks to a little help from our Canadian cousins we were able to package it in a reactor the size of a human heart – the only real difference is the human heart outputs about five watts of power, but Sophia's here will give her nearly a megawatt of energy and beat for a thousand years ... or for as long as the casing stays intact, anyway."

"Sophia, huh?" Alex ran his hand over the arm. "I can't feel any seals; no joins on the surface at all."

"There are seals, but they're internal folds and can only be opened on command."

"Yours or hers?" Sam asked.

"Both." Grey shot back. "What you're seeing is the result of ten years work, and many billions of dollars in investment."

Alex lifted one of the arms, turning it over to look at the hand and palm. "Feels like steel, but soft; I'm assuming some sort of synthetic woven alloy."

"Correct," Grey responded. "Twenty times tougher than Kevlar and more akin to spider silk for its pound-for-pound tensile strength. In effect, it's molecular chainmail covering advanced technology and hydraulics, and don't be misled by the slim design. Due to the advancements in microtechnology, size does not mean strength. Sophia is probably stronger and faster than both of you combined."

The scientist fiddled behind a console and immediately two glowing, almond-shaped orbs appeared where eyes should be on the almost blank face. The figure turned to Alex, and he could feel an examination taking place. And more, he felt a tingling in the center of his head.

"She's scanning me." Alex returned the analysis, and detected a level of complexity that was astounding before he was suddenly cut off, like a steel door slamming shut to block him. "I can feel her in my head."

"She undoubtedly finds you interesting. She can link and target, *uh,* I mean, *find* anyone we designate." Grey smiled as he fiddled at the console. "Vocalize please, Sophia."

"Good morning, Captain Alexander Hunter and Lieutenant Samuel Reid; nice to meet both of you."

"It knows us?" Sam asked.

"Sophia has access to our military personnel database, so knows your basic details from there. That's all."

There was a slight tingling in Alex's head before the figure spoke again.

"Captain Hunter, I detect you have a different neural architecture, possibly resulting from the penetration by a small caliber bullet fragment lodged within the core of your cerebellum at the mid-point between the hypothalamus and thalamus." Sophia's head titled as though to examine him further. "Your brain has compensated for the trauma by developing a benign internal mass, but ... there is also some foreign material still there – that is unidentifiable. You are now *different.*"

Alex rubbed the small scar above his eye, and Grey chortled. "No secrets from Sophia, I'm afraid." He came around from behind the console. "Well, shake her hand, captain."

The silver figure silently rose from its seated position in front of Alex, and offered him its slim hand. The being stood shorter than he and its slight body made it look significantly less powerful than his broad frame as he loomed over it. Alex reached out, took hold of the hand and squeezed slightly. The android squeezed back with equal pressure.

"Don't be shy, you can't hurt her; go on, squeeze harder." Grey watched them both closely.

"Take it to school, boss. And don't hold back." Sam grinned and looked at Grey. "Hey, how much do those hands cost? Hope you got spares."

"I'll try not to break it – like I nearly did with you." Alex grinned at Sam, and then looked briefly at the science officer. "Remember, this was your idea."

The slim hand compressed slightly like normal flesh and bone, but didn't buckle.

The head titled again. "Three hundred psi – you are an extraordinarily powerful human being, Captain Hunter." With that, Sophia squeezed his hand back, *harder*.

Alex applied all the force he could bring to bear. Enough to pulverize bones, and even compress steel tubing if he so wished. It was impossible to tell what the effects were as Sophia didn't flinch and there were no facial features to gauge an expression of pain or even irritation.

Alex then felt the bones in his own hand start to bend and the veins in his arm stood out like thick chords. He ground his teeth together. *Shit.* Pain began to flare in his hand. Immediately the pressure stopped. Alex's hand now throbbed mercilessly.

"Phew." Alex nodded at Grey. "Thanks, that was getting nasty."

Grey shrugged. "Don't thank me; it was Sophia that decided to desist. She has a lot more hydraulic power than your enhanced physical strength. She read that you were at the limit of your physical capabilities. She could sense your physical pain and she shut it off."

Sophia still held Alex's hand, her blank face turned toward him. "You are different."

"He sure is," Sam said. "Careful, boss, Aimee better not find out you're down here flirting with the new weapon tech."

Sophia released Alex's hand. "Aimee?" She turned to Sam.

Grey went back to the console, worked for a moment, and then Sophia sat back down. The soft glow in her face dimmed, as though the eyes had gently shut.

"The power I felt there; unbelievable." Alex continued to rub his hand and then turned to Sam. "Looks like we're out of a job, big guy."

Sam just scowled down at Sophia.

Grey laughed softly. "Not quite; physical power is nothing; anyone can build a bigger battering ram. Our first prototypes were as powerful as all hell, but couldn't tell the difference between friend and foe, and the dozens of distinctions in between." Grey pointed at the android. "Sophia's conscious decision to release you rather than do you harm is where the bulk of our investment went. The hyper-tough chassis was easy. But what we wanted was something that could be auto-dependent, could make life or death decisions in differing environments, and could learn and adapt. In effect it needed a brain, with human-like deterministic logic. We wanted it to make the *right* decisions."

Alex stared at it. "I'm still feeling redundant."

"Not quite yet." Grey smiled down at Sophia like a proud parent. "The original problem was no matter how many human psychological applications we tried, it continued to make flawed decisions based on a *save thyself first* self-preservation model. Also, in battle situations, it sometimes wanted to compete. But, it wouldn't stop competing. Sometimes it seemed to get ..."

Alex scoffed and looked at Grey from under lowered brows. "She got angry, didn't she?"

"Maybe some would call it that." He smiled flatly. "Then we had a stroke of luck when we came across the brilliant work by the German scientist called Frans Knopper on 'machine learning and the female brain' – groundbreaking, and just what we were looking for. She wrote a paper on neurological gender differences, and how females have more white matter dedicated to communication, problem-solving and connecting information, which gave them an inbuilt species cooperation trait."

He placed his hand on the android's shoulder. "We just needed an appropriate logic model. And we found one. It's called ALP – Applied Logic Patterning. But one that could handle stress, and women can do that five times better than men."

Alex folded his arms. "We want our technology to be like us, yet we humans have some deep psychological baggage – little things called emotions." He walked around the android. "Who wants a robot that feels envy, greed, hate, and ... vengeance, right? Some emotions can be deadly."

"Yes." Grey's eyes locked momentarily on the HAWC leader's, and Alex suddenly wondered how much the scientist knew about his own psychological storms.

The scientist's eyes slid away. "Anyway, Knopper's ideas provided the seed for our software teams, and became the genesis of a new line of thinking. The female traits were ideal to include in a being that would be required to work as both an individual and as a member of a team. It needs protective instincts – maternal instincts, if you like. Remember, it is more than just a mobile military logistics computer or weapon, it's a guardian." His mouth quirked up. "A guardian angel, in fact."

Alex smiled. "And we need all the help from the angels we can get."

"And who guards the guardians?" Sam stared hard at the seated android. "It can learn, *huh*?"

"Oh yes," Grey said.

"So, *Sophia*," Alex said softly.

Grey nodded proudly. "Sentient OPerational Heuristic Interactive Android – *Sophia*. The key thing being *heuristic*; it means she learns by trial and error, just like we do."

"Sophia was the Greek goddess of wisdom," Sam said.

"Correct; it kinda fit." Grey beamed. "Eventually, she'll make better and better decisions, and even make best-guess judgments. She'll be our guardian against, *uh* ..."

The man paused, and Alex felt evasion. "Against what?"

"Threats," the scientist said, keeping his eyes on the android.

Alex continued to watch him, and suddenly felt there was a reason Grey had wanted him to meet Sophia. Or perhaps he more wanted Sophia to meet him. "From threats, huh?"

"*Hmm, hm.*" Grey gave him a crooked smile. "Shall we?" He motioned to the exit.

They headed for the silver door and Alex stopped briefly as Grey turned out the lights. He stared back at the seated figure. He frowned. *Did it just move?* He had the distinct sensation he was being watched again. He went to turn away from the darkened room, and for a split second, he thought he saw two small lights slowly come on as though eyes had gently opened in the dark.

CHAPTER 12

Once back at base, Zlatan could see the outline of the stranger behind the one-way glass window. They thought they were invisible, but they weren't, not to him, and he could also hear every word they uttered.

They were finally getting an assignment outside of the training camps – *good*. He and his men were eager to test themselves. What use was it to be told you were a superior soldier if you were never really benchmarked against an enemy soldier?

The huge Kurgan was excited by the prospect, but there was a downside of leaving. He looked up into Rahda's face as she checked his blood pressure, and then wrote on a chart. He felt his heart swell. From the moment they had begun working together he had fallen in love with her, and he hoped, no, *he knew*, she with him.

She was the first person to see him as something other than a lump of flesh and bone designed to fight and kill. They had stolen moments together where the cameras and eyes of the administration managers could not find them.

She had called him her *solnishko*, her sunshine, and then she had let him kiss her, deeply. Zlatan had felt her body beneath her clothing, running large hands over her breasts and buttocks, and he had become rock hard. Her small hand had slid between them to grasp him through his trousers, squeezing and tugging at him, until he had exploded too quickly. He had apologized through his light-headedness, but she just smiled and pulled his ear closer to her mouth.

"Soon, soon, my *solnishko*," she had whispered.

"Yes," he had promised her in return. "Soon."

Now she dabbed iodine on the abraded knuckles of one of his hands. Already he was healing, but she did it anyway with her encouraging words and usual shy smile. When she finished she raised a hand to his face, running small soft fingers from his temple to his jutting jaw. Compared to her, he was an ogre, but she didn't see that. He knew she saw beneath the hardened flesh, jutting bone and bunched muscle.

She held out the small photograph, and he took it, looking down and seeing the image of her face. He turned it over, and his smile broadened as he read the words. Zlatan looked up into her eyes, feeling his heart flying in his chest.

"Yes, yes, I will."

She was his beauty, and he her beast, and he would do *anything* for her. Zlatan drew her to him. One day they would make a life together. He smiled, showing large spade-like teeth.

Maybe when this mission was done, his dream would come true.

* * *

Nunman Iqua, Alaska – Western-most entrance to the Yukon River

Ivan Zlatan lifted his near colorless eyes to look at his squad. The five huge men, near bursting from their cold-climate suits, sat in the hold of the compact submarine in silence, eyes unblinking and ignoring all external stimulation. They were like human-shaped machines just awaiting activation.

Their St Petersburg class submarine glided into the mouth of the river at a depth of just ten feet below the surface. The sub was the smallest in the Russian fleet and had been upgraded for coastal stealth with the introduction of fourth generation diesel-electric turbines that produced much quieter air-independent propulsion.

While nuclear-powered submarines dominated in submergence times and deep-ocean performance, their reactors must constantly pump coolant, generating a heat bloom and detectable acoustic signature that was easily picked up by orbiting military satellites when they ran shallow. But the smaller, high-tech non-nuclear attack submarines were virtually invisible to the eyes in the sky.

The submarine's captain had been in these waters before, and knew every bend, twist and shallow along the river. He knew that this time of year it was cold, and though not frozen, the low temperature reduced melt runoff and so meant that the river shallowed out in many areas, with some stretches demanding they came to the surface – but only ever after dark.

Zlatan shifted, feeling enormous energy run through him, and feeling constrained by his inaction as well as his clothing.

He surreptitiously reached into a slot in his vest and eased out the tiny photograph. He cupped it in his hand and first read the words written on the back and then turned it over to gaze upon the face of his beautiful Rahda. His thick lips curved into a smile. When this mission was over, he would ask, no, no, not *ask*; he would *demand* they release him from the facility.

And then he would be free with Rahda. He smiled down at the image. He hadn't asked her yet, but he planned to make her his wife. His smile widened momentarily before his eyes flicked left and right. He exhaled, none of his men were watching. *Good.* He slipped the picture back into his vest.

He needed to focus now. Their destination was the small town of Mission, an old mining post founded by Russians and many of the locals still had close ties to the Motherland.

The submarine would glide up the Yukon River just below the surface. Anyone standing on the bank might make out the silent shadow passing beneath its surface, but think it a whale. It was not unheard of for the large cetaceans to travel up the river.

An airplane would be waiting to drop them close to the mountain, but not too close. They knew the Americans would be watching the peak. They would maintain the element of surprise, but it would be traded off against speed and safety, as they would need to climb to the downed space shuttle wreckage.

Zlatan smiled; it mattered not. They could walk, hike, run, or climb for weeks without breaking stride. Strength and energy was not their problem, impatience was.

Ivan Zlatan felt the coiling sensation of urgency in his gut and pushed it back down. They needed to be there first, and they were on schedule. He looked along his men and saw the curled fists and set jaws, and knew each and every one of them would be feeling the same thing he was – mission success was everything, failure was unthinkable. They were unbeatable and they were ready.

He was about to turn away when he saw one of his men looking at something cupped in his hands; the man's cruel lips curled into an unnatural smile. Zlatan wondered who was in the picture.

CHAPTER 13

USSTRATCOM Base, Far Training Grounds,
NEBRASKA

"He beats one, he beat the other ... the score line is wide
open." Alex pretended to sidestep while holding the ball
under one arm as he jogged toward a place between two trees.

Coming at him fast were Joshua and Aimee. The boy's face
a mix of delirious happiness and determination.

"Sack time," he yelled, and came in low at Alex, grabbing
one of his thighs.

"Defenders pile on, but the quarterback is still gonna make
it." He held the ball up as the imaginary line approached.
"Gonna spike."

"Mom, go high," Joshua yelled trying unsuccessfully to
upend Alex by holding onto the trunk-like thigh muscle.

Aimee, watching with hands on hips, groaned. "*Ooookay.*"
She began to run at Alex and then grabbed his shoulders.

"*Arrghh*, defenders pile on." Alex fell backwards, but
turned over onto his belly and pretended to crawl to the line,
trying not to laugh. "Must ... make it."

"Never." Joshua leaped on his back, climbed up his body and wrenched the ball free. He ran to his own line, spiking the ball down and doing his victory dance.

Alex rolled over, laughing, and Aimee snuggled in beside him. He put his arm under her head. Both lay there with the soft grass beneath them and the sunshine on their faces.

"Another mission," Aimee said flatly. "But this is what we should be doing. This is where you belong now."

Alex opened his eyes, breathing deeply. He knew she was right; Josh had changed everything. He lifted his head and watched the boy kicking the ball in the air and racing to catch it.

"Hey, remember, I met you on one of those missions." He rolled toward her, resting his head on his propped arm. "It's only a couple of days; little more than a babysitting run."

She stared back up at him, her dazzling eyes like blue fire. "It's always just a couple of days. And every time you come back with a few more scars, a little more haunted, and a little more ..." she leaned away, staring up at the sky.

He could guess what she was going to say: more brutal, less human, maybe even, more like *The Other*.

"Beneath the ice, last time, we both nearly died." She turned, and her eyes bored into him. "You stretch luck too far. We don't want to lose *you* ... and don't *you* lose us."

He reached across to brush strands of dark hair from her forehead. "I do what I do for you and Joshua, and the millions of other you and Joshuas in the world. Some things in this world are dangerous and need to be faced. You know that; you've seen them."

"They do." She grabbed his hand. "But not always by you."

"No, not always by me." He lay back down. "Not always."

"*Oof!*" He folded in half as Joshua landed on his belly and knocked the wind out of him. The boy laughed hysterically. Alex grabbed him, pulling him down between them.

"Thanks, buddy. A little warning next time, *huh?*"

"Wish you didn't have to go, Dad." Josh looked at the ball as he spoke, and his small forehead creased.

Alex looked at Aimee. "Did you ...?"

Aimee shook her head. "He knows; he always knows."

Alex sighed and turned back. Yeah, he already knew that – he had felt the boy inside his head many times. The bond of love was strong between them, but he felt Josh could drop in whenever he liked now.

Hammerson had said it was a trickle down effect of the Arcadian treatment Alex had undergone. Josh seemed to have inherited some things from Alex that went well beyond his looks; the mental connection between them being only one of them. He'd need to be more guarded in the future as the link might reveal things that might terrify the boy.

He faced his son. "I wish I could take you," Alex said to him. "But I need someone here to look after your mom ... and the puppy."

Joshua's head snapped around. "*What?* What puppy?"

"Oh, hey, didn't we tell you?" He looked across to Aimee, whose eyebrows were up. Alex grinned and turned back. "Yeah, sure, I meant to mention that we're getting you a puppy. But I need you to pick it out, and get it settled in while I'm away. It's a big responsibility."

Joshua's mouth hung open.

"Can you do that for me, buddy?" Alex shrugged. "Because we can leave it for a day or ..."

"*Yes!*" Joshua threw the ball in the air, and kneeled up. He placed both hands on Alex's chest. "*Yes, yes, yes!*" His eyes were so wide they looked about to pop. "When!"

"I know Uncle Jack said he could take you out anytime. But it's really up to your mom." Alex grinned and turned slowly to Aimee.

Joshua's eyes homed in on her. "Mom?"

Aimee chuckled. "*Ooh*, ambush." She made her face serious. "Well, we do have a few things to do before ..."

"Mo-*oooom*." Joshua's brow furrowed with alarm.

"Oh, good grief." She elbowed Alex who just grinned. "Well, maybe tomorrow." She leaned up on an elbow. "Go and kick the ball some more. Dad and I are going to have a little talk."

"Ye*ssss!*" Joshua screamed away, picking up the ball in one hand and punting it high, and then sprinting after it.

Alex looked at Aimee's beautiful but now angry face. He grinned sheepishly. "Surprise."

* * *

Surprise, he smiled as his mind took him back to his family moment. That *surprise* was going to cost him three dinners out and a week of foot rubs. *Worth it.*

Alex continued to stare out the window of the Twin Otter turboprop plane, but he was still mentally back on the park's soft grass. He remembered Aimee's stern look as the sunlight made her hair shine like a raven's wing, and her eyes were luminous with sparks of fire. He could still hear Joshua roaring with excitement.

He missed them both already. He closed his eyes as he replayed what she had said to him: *this is where you need to be now.* She was right. After a life led fighting, always fighting, he finally had something to come home to – an oasis of calm in a turbulent world.

His eyes flicked open as reality intruded. But there were horrors in this world, things that waited in dark caves, or fell from skies, or lurked in impenetrable jungles waiting to attack and bring misery and death to innocent people. Alex fought for them, for Aimee and Joshua. *They* were who he fought to keep safe.

The plane juddered in the air and his reverie began to dissolve. But maybe, just maybe, it *was* time someone else did the fighting.

The Twin Otter jerked again. Though the boxy-looking, cobalt-blue airplane seemed ungainly, its combination wheels, floats, and skids meant it could take off and land on water, snow, grass, or gravel on even the shortest of runways. It was uncomfortable, but practical.

As they were entering foreign territory, to avoid suspicion they'd needed to take civilian craft. Not ideal, but speed and secrecy needed to be balanced, for now. Onboard there were the eight HAWCs plus the three NASA science and engineering team members. Though on paper, there was room for more people in the plane, the size and bulk of the HAWCs made it feel enormously overburdened.

Alex knew they were already over the Alaskan airspace, and though inside it was warm, outside it was well below freezing. He turned away from the window – lined up across from him was his second in charge, Sam Reid; then Casey Franks; Max Dunsen; and Andy Garcia.

Next to him were Drake Monroe, Steve Knight, who looked like he thought being here with the seasoned HAWCs was too good to be true, and lastly, the statuesque and formidable Anita Erikson. Most were all sprawled legs and shut eyes. The mission was supposed to be a quick snatch, in and out in a matter of hours. But Alex knew reality wasn't like that. Shit always happened, and they were the ones who either got dropped in it or had to clean it up.

Alex let his eyes move to the NASA tech crew. Leading them was Russell Burrows. Up front he seemed a likeable guy, but Alex sensed something below the surface, fear maybe. Russ was only concerned about the remote possibility of finding survivors, probably his friends, from the downed *Orlando* shuttle, and couldn't care less about the military tech onboard. That was fine by Alex. Next to him was Scott McIntyre, Russ' senior technician, young and serious, but seemed a little twitchy. And then came Doctor Anne Petersen; she was a scientist and also had a medical background, and for Alex that made her value go up. He also detected something when she asked about the astronauts that made him think she had a personal attachment to someone on the shuttle orbiter. There was a level of concern in her voice that exceeded NASA loyalty or team camaraderie.

All three looked nervous and uncomfortable in their cold-weather gear with breathing apparatus hanging over their backs. They were also as intimidated as hell by the huge HAWCs. Alex didn't bother trying to break the ice; after all, people tended to do their jobs more efficiently when the adrenaline was pumping or they felt eyes on them. And Alex would be watching every one of them.

The closest runway they could get to the peaks of the Revelation Mountains was Lime village, population twenty-nine, and only eighty miles from their destination. The upside was it had a hard-packed runway they could drop in on. They would then rendezvous with a chopper, which would take them up to the mountaintop basin.

Alex heard the pilot's laconic drawl in his ear, *"Ten minutes out."*

"Heads up, people, going down," Alex addressed the group.

The HAWCs sat forward, immediately alert, and started to run through a final weapons check. The NASA team looked wide-eyed, with Scott McIntyre suddenly going a few shades paler.

"Captain." Russell Burrows leaned forward. *"Uh,* how long until we get to the actual mountaintop?"

Alex shrugged. "Getting *to* the mountain, maybe only three to four hours. But getting to the cusp where the *Orlando* went down might all depend on you. I'm not going to sugarcoat it; it's gonna be tough."

As if in response, the pilot turned down the cabin heating to acclimatize the group. Russ Burrows pulled his collar up. "We'll keep up."

Alex nodded. "Good, because my primary mission is retrieval; your safety is secondary."

Burrows snorted. "Well, that's great; to protect and serve, *huh?*"

Casey Franks leaned forward. "Nah, that's the other guys."

Burrows muttered something as he sat back.

"Captain Hunter, just how close can they get us … to the cusp, I mean?" Anne Petersen's brow creased as she stared up into his face.

"Unfortunately, we might not be able to drop at the mountaintop or into it. The visibility is now down to zero due to irregular fog formations up there. Also, the prevailing winds this time of year blast down from the northwest, so we'll be coming in on the sheltered, eastern side. As a backup plan, we have identified a shelf of stone a few hundred feet from the rim that's about twenty feet wide that our pilot could drop us onto … with luck."

Alex saw her mouth tighten with anxiety. It didn't matter; they all needed to be ready. "I expect it to be a fast and hard drop." He smiled grimly. "As a medic, you may have some work to do."

Her jaw set as she collected herself. "Okay, then what?"

Good for her. "Then, doctor, we have to scale a few hundred feet to the peak and drop into the cusp."

Steve Knight whooped. "Straight up a sheer rock face, in subzero temperatures, with swirling wind. Hell yeah."

Casey Franks winked at Anne. "Walk in the park, lady."

"For us, she means," Max Dunsen brayed, and Drake Monroe high-fived Casey.

"We'll all be fine," Alex said. "In fact, to make sure of that, Franks and Dunsen just volunteered to be your shock absorbers on the way down."

Casey shook her head, mumbling: "Well, that's just fuc—"

"*What*, soldier?" Alex glared.

Casey jerked upright. "Nothing, sir, just saying, *that's just fine*. Looking forward to it, boss."

Sam Reid looked up and grinned momentarily before reading more information from a small computer screen strapped to his inner forearm. He leaned in closer to Alex.

"There's no further intel on our Russian gatecrashers. Is it too much to hope they fell into a chasm?"

Alex grunted. "We're never that lucky. They're ahead of us so we assume they're already on the ground, somewhere, waiting." He looked up. "Soon as we set down, I want a perimeter."

"You got it." Sam leaned back to relay instructions to the HAWCs, who listened intently. The HAWCs concentrated, their eyes focused and intense, looking like a pack of hungry wolves waiting to be unleashed.

Alex felt his own wrist computer vibrate. It was Hammerson with an update on their landing site. They were in radio silence, except for secured send-and-receive. They also used the non-vocal communications when civilians were in earshot.

Sabers still has zero visuals on drop zone.

Alex entered his response. *Thermals?*

Nada; everything is warm down there. Go to backup plan. Hammerson out.

Alex sighed; *always the hard way*. He sat back, looking across at the NASA crew. The windchill up that high in Alaska could drive temperatures down to a hundred degrees below. However, today he only expected around forty to fifty below. And then, once they entered the crater, it'd rise to around fifty above – still cool, but nearly a one hundred-degree swing. Their suits and bodies would have to work overtime to adapt.

Then there was the melt runoff. All that heat would melt snow and ice. The rock faces would be slippery as hell and might still be running with water, sending rivers down on top of them, especially if the heat bloom was spreading.

Hammerson had said the gases emanating from inside the crater were staying over the basin, a little like a blister. Whatever was down there was keeping the strange air close and not letting it escape. *Weird.* The winds up there tended to scream over the mountaintops and should have scraped out and dispersed any gases long ago.

Maybe a good thing. Given the possibility of the gases being toxic, having them contained was probably a gift.

The airplane started to descend and he noticed Anne Peterson looking at him again. Her face was pale. He nodded to her, and she returned the gesture. That was all he had for her.

She came and sat next to him. "Captain, I meant to ask you …" She pressed her lips together for a moment before going on. "Do you think they, the astronauts, could still be alive?"

"No."

She looked taken aback. "Uh, wow, thanks for that."

He continued to watch her face for another few seconds. "I wish I thought different, but I don't. Though it's warm in the crater, if anyone survived the impact, our scientists tell us that there are toxic gases in there."

"But I thought they detected movement, that might have been …" She slumped.

"Unlikely." He kept watching her. "Someone on that craft means something to you, right?"

Anne stared at the ground for a moment before looking up at him. "Commander Mitchell Granger. *Mitch.*" She gave him a watery smile. "We talked about getting married after this mission." Her eyes glistened.

"You shouldn't be here; emotions lead to mistakes." Alex felt the air density shift, as they got closer to the ground. He looked over his shoulder out the porthole window and saw the long dirt track coming up.

Anne bristled. "Hey, listen—"

"We're just here to do our jobs, Doctor Peterson. If not, people die." He turned and nodded to Sam.

Sam swung to the HAWCs. "Immediate perimeter deployment as soon as that damn door opens. *Clear?*"

"*HUA!*"

The wheels bounced and they swung sideways a few degrees before the Twin Otter settled on the runway. Sam was already standing in the center of the plane holding onto some overhead rails, his huge frame like the Colossus of Rhodes.

They rolled to a stop, and Sam pulled open the door. Casey Franks went through it first, followed by the other soldiers, with the group immediately fanning out.

Sam then jumped down, looked one way, then the other, before pointing at several buildings, causing the HAWCs to sprint toward them. He then lifted a scope to his eye, turning slowly as he scanned the far perimeter, Alex knew, looking for snipers.

"Let's go, people." Alex waved the NASA crew out. They needed to get the Twin Otter up and gone quickly so their chopper had a clean landing pad.

Behind them a few locals came out to stare. Sam Reid lifted his hand to them, but the other HAWCs scrutinized the gawpers closely. Sam then grabbed the NASA gear and dumped it on the ground as the three technicians leaped down.

"Over there." Alex yelled the words loud enough to be heard over the still spinning propellers and pointed to a place beside the runway.

He checked his watch – time was good, and everything on schedule. He leaned into the plane and gave the pilot a thumbs-up before he shut the door. In another few moments, the Twin Otter was leaping down the track, gathering speed before bouncing once and then lifting off.

He watched it for a moment and then shifted his vision to a dot that had appeared in the sky – their inbound chopper.

He nodded. "I like it when things go to plan."

They'd secured a big bad Chinook helicopter from a private operator, an ex-military guy. The large, muscular craft was a twin-engine, tandem rotor heavy-lift helo with a wide loading ramp at the rear of the fuselage and rapid rappelling capabilities. It was also fast at nearly 200 mph, and they'd loaded extra fuel for the air-work that needed to be done. Another payoff was the craft's size and strength meant it had good stability in high winds – they'd need that – and a truckload of luck.

The final bonus was securing a pilot who was mad enough to take risks, and being a Vet was smart enough to keep his mouth shut. If it were just his HAWCs, it'd just be another day at the office. But Alex knew with the NASA crew with them, it was going to be something else entirely.

He watched the powerful helicopter get bigger in the sky. On the rappel, they'd be like worms on the end of a fishing line, dropping from the craft, and then relying on the skill of the pilot to dangle them over where they needed to be – a twenty-foot-wide ledge. If everyone did their job, kept their nerve, the Chinook held it together, and the winds behaved, then they might just be plonked down where they wanted. If not, then instead, they'd be slammed into the side of the granite rock face at about a hundred miles per hour.

Alex grinned, feeling his blood already pumping hard; he couldn't wait.

The Chinook touched down and Alex waved Drake and Casey forward. Both HAWCs ran for the doors, pulling them open and then standing back, watching the terrain.

Alex turned to the NASA crew. "Move it, we are on the clock, people."

"*Contact!*"

Alex's head snapped around at Casey's voice.

The HAWCs were like machines – their rifles came up as one to draw a bead on the two figures that sprinted from one of the dwellings toward the open door of the helicopter.

"Hold fire." Alex yelled. He saw that neither was armored up, or looked anything like combat professionals. They got to the chopper without turning once and dove inside.

Casey Franks ran for the door and poked her head inside. Sam Reid immediately spread the HAWCs in a defensive position, and sent two to cover the NASA crew. He then jogged to join Alex at the helicopter door.

Casey pushed her RG3 rifle up over her shoulder to its carrying slot and thumbed toward the interior of the craft.

"Fucking hitchhikers."

Alex stuck his head inside, and Sam loomed up behind him. The chopper was as he expected – big, roomy, and good tech. But what shouldn't have been there was two people seated inside. The red-headed woman had her arms folded and defiance was set hard on her features. The young bearded man seated next to her looked less confident as his eyes went from Alex to the huge form of Sam.

"Get 'em out." Alex turned away.

Sam leaned back in. "Saying this just once: exit the craft, *now.*"

The woman's eyes were steady. "I don't know who you are, but I bet you're not with NASA, and I know they're the only guys supposed to be heading up on that mountain to where the *Orlando* Space Shuttle Orbiter went down."

Alex turned back slowly. She was probably bluffing, but he didn't like what he was hearing. The woman went on.

"The *Orlando* crashed up there, and no one knows why, and very few people even know it's not in space anymore. So listen, big fella, we're going up there. We might as well go together."

Sam growled. "Let's be clear, you don't exist. Exit the craft, or we will be forced to … assist you."

Casey leered in at them, her scar making her face appear even more terrifying.

"Oh, fuck no," the bearded guy whispered as he went a shade paler. "This is going too far, Mags."

The woman didn't flinch as she stared back at Sam. "Then what, tough guy?" She thrust her chin forward, and lifted a smart phone and threatened to take a picture of him. "I don't know who you are, yet, but how about I splash your picture all over the front page and we find out that way, *huh*?"

Alex had heard enough. "Franks, please assist these two *citizens* from our helicopter."

"Yes, sir."

Casey launched herself into the rear of the helicopter and grabbed the woman. She lashed out, but was no match for Casey's brute force, and ended up on her ass on the ground screaming obscenities. The man jumped out quickly before Casey could get to him, and cowered as if expecting the female HAWC to beat down on him for her own enjoyment.

The red-headed woman leaped to her feet, not seeming to be intimated by the fearsome Casey in the least. She came at her, teeth bared.

"I could sue you back to the fucking Stone Age for that." The woman moved in even closer and stabbed a finger right in Casey's face. "And ..."

Casey grabbed the hand and twisted. The woman howled and went to one knee, whereby Casey pushed a hand onto the back of her shoulder. The woman went down onto both knees and screamed some more.

The man with her momentarily looked like he was going to intervene, but must have seen the expressions on the HAWCs' faces and changed his mind.

He settled for holding up both hands, and dancing on the spot. "Easy there, we're cool, we're cool."

Casey just pushed harder.

"That's enough." Scott McIntyre rushed in and grabbed at Casey. He used both hands to yank hard on the brawny woman. "I said ... *that's enough*."

Casey continued to keep one hand on the woman's shoulder, but wrenched an arm back, catching McIntyre on the chin with the point of her elbow. His head shot up, and she then used a leg to sweep him off his feet. McIntyre fell hard beside her, and Casey stuck a boot on his neck.

"Let him go; *that's an order*!" Russell Burrows yelled as he rushed to his colleague's side. "As the senior NASA official, I am the authority on this mission."

Casey just seemed to press down harder, her sneer growing.

Burrows turned to Alex. "Let. Him. Go. *Now*, or your superiors will hear about this."

Casey turned and grinned up at him as she now held both the red-headed woman and McIntyre down. "The fuck we care."

People started to edge out from the low buildings to watch.

"Shut it, Franks." Sam Reid edged forward, but Casey looked to Alex.

Alex's eyes were hard as he stared, his mouth twisted in a small smile.

"Boss." Sam laid a huge hand on Alex's shoulder.

"*Huh?*" Alex felt a small fire go out inside him. "Franks, let 'em up."

Casey took her boot off McIntyre, who quickly rolled away, holding his throat and hacking like he was choking. Casey then shoved the woman onto the cold gravel. She was immediately on her feet massaging her shoulder and hand, her eyes blazing.

She dusted herself down, and then grinned. "So ..." It was as if she flicked a switch as a change came over her. "Now that we're all friends; my name is Morag O'Sullivan, *Los Angeles Times*, major news desk." She thumbed over her shoulder to the man. "My brave partner in crime is famous cameraman Calvin Renner." She turned to him and grimaced. "Oh, put your hands down, you putz."

Renner slowly lowered his hands as if he suddenly remembered he still held them up. Morag turned back to Sam, and then Alex. She stuck out a hand and waited. No one moved. After several awkward moments, Morag lowered her hand, and shrugged. "Anyway, I was serious when I said we're going up the mountain with or without you."

Alex turned away. "Ready the equipment; we're leaving."

"We're going," she said defiantly.

"Ain't happening," Sam said in a growl and followed Alex.

"Yeah, how are you going to do that, Paul Bunyan, tie us up?" She folded her arms.

"Works for me," Casey said and turned to Alex. "Want me to get the zip-cuffs?"

Morag scoffed. "Sure, you could do that, *and* smash our gear as well. But then you'd have to shut up the locals. We made a few friends here." She waved to a few people who had come out of some flat-topped houses to watch the group. Her mouth curled into a smile. "All you'd do is slow us down a little, but confirm there's a real story to chase. In a few hours, we'd have a press chopper here before you even made it to the top."

She turned and started to nod to her cameraman. "You know what? Go ahead. You'd make this a bigger story than it might be. Make my news day; I might even win an award." She grinned at Russell. "I'll make NASA famous again."

"We can't have this leaking out; not until we're ready," Russell blurted out.

"It won't," Casey leered. "We have facilities where we can keep these two nice and quiet, until we're done."

"Oh, fuck off," Morag snarled at the female HAWC. "What, are you North Korean now?"

Casey had her hands on her hips. "Say the word, boss, and they won't be talking to anyone, ever."

133

Morag kicked some gravel at her. "Try it."

Russell grabbed Alex's upper arm and tried to turn him, but found it impossible. Instead, he moved in front of him.

"Captain, this mission is the highest-level security and secrecy. We cannot have these people loose, but also I will not see them harmed or incarcerated." He looked at his wristwatch. "Fact is I can probably use them. We take them with us, control them; that's my recommendation, *no*, my order."

Alex groaned as he listened.

"Here's the plan," Casey said. "We throw them out of the chopper. Accidents happen." She looked like she was enjoying herself.

Renner audibly gulped and backed up, but the female journalist was unbowed. "We're experienced climbers, and set to go, right here, right now. And if we do go, at least you can keep a lid on whatever it is going on up there ... for now." She came closer to Russell, staying out of Casey and Alex's reach. "We can certainly help you ... be happy to. Just tell me how."

Russell shrugged. "I need this documented."

"Can do that," Morag agreed.

"But the footage stays with us," he added.

"Ah." Morag pinched her lip for a moment, and then tilted her head. "We share it."

"No can do, until it's cleared by NASA." He folded his arms. "Last chance."

Morag's eyes became crafty. "You strike a hard bargain, sir. But I accept." She turned to smile sweetly at Casey.

Alex knew that the woman would try to secrete the footage somehow. There was no way any journalist worth their salt would wait for a government agency to release sensitive and unique footage to them. He also knew that there was no way he would let them leave with anything that contained any recordings – images, sound, or data – of a HAWC mission.

"Then we've got a deal," said Russell.

"Not until the boss says so." Casey remained stone-faced.

Alex rubbed a hand up through freezing hair and felt every one of his HAWCs watching him. He walked a few paces and stopped, looking up at the granite peaks where they needed to be in the next few hours. It looked freezing, inhospitable, and deadly as all hell.

He snorted. *What the fuck do I care if these guys want to commit suicide?* He turned slowly. "You have no idea what you're asking for."

"Yes, I do; we'll be fine." Morag stepped forward.

Alex stared for a moment more, and then smiled grimly. "If you're slow, we will leave you. If you ask for help, we will ignore you. And if you fall, then it will be into your graves. Got it?"

"Very dramatic." She nodded with mock conviction. She turned momentarily to Renner and raised her eyebrows. "We're in."

Alex turned to Russell Burrows. "You wanted this; they're your problem. You own it." He went to turn away but paused. "One more thing; have you got breathing equipment?"

Morag tilted her head. "Sort of; we've got oxygen masks for the altitude."

Casey chuckled. "You're dead."

Anne walked forward. "We brought a couple of spare suits."

Scott McIntyre glowered. "Hey, hang on, they're for us if we need them."

Anne frowned. "Scott, you know it's very unlikely we'll need them. Be civil please."

"And what if we *do* need them?" He growled as he stormed away.

Anne turned back to Morag and hiked her shoulders. "Of course you can have them."

"Thank you." Morag held out her hand. "It's Morag."

"Anne, Anne Peterson." Anne shook her hand.

"NASA, right?" Morag smiled as the woman nodded.

Alex grunted. "Once we enter the crater; you'll need those suits." He then clapped once, the sound like a rifle shot. "Okay, let's load 'em up, we're out of here."

Morag turned to Renner and made a small circling motion in the air. Renner lifted a small handheld action camera that fit in his palm and started to film the HAWCs.

Alex spun. "*Hey!*" His voice froze the man to the spot, and his eyes became round. In two strides, Alex was up in the man's face, and ripped the small tube from Renner's hand. He held it up.

"If you film any one of my team, we will destroy every piece of equipment you have, understood?" Alex made a fist, and the metal casing on the camera crushed. He dropped the shards to the ground.

Renner watched it fall with wide eyes. He nodded once, mouthed *okay*, with no actual words coming. Morag O'Sullivan folded her arms, her mouth tight.

Alex glared a moment longer and then turned to the NASA crew. "Let's go."

Sam yelled instructions, and in another two minutes the chopper was in the air.

CHAPTER 14

Revelation Mountain Peaks, Orlando *Crash Site*

Ivan Zlatan was first over the rim of the mountaintop and stared down into the massive crater formation.

It had taken them an entire day to climb to the peak, without a single break, and it had not been without cost. He had started with five Kurgan, five of the top engineered combat soldiers in all of Russia, and perhaps the world. But he had lost one good man. Divinov had been big, strong, and unlucky. The shelf of rock he had clung to had simply fallen away like the skin of an onion. He dropped around 500 feet to the first rock shelf where he had bounced once then vanished from sight. No one would bother going looking for his body, and Zlatan only cared about his team's reduced strike capability.

Like his remaining comrades, Zlatan's fingers were near frozen, and his muscles ached and joints screamed, but they would mend with the rapid healing their metabolisms would undertake in the next few hours.

He had received his last update from Moscow just minutes before. A large helicopter was on its way to the plains spread out before the mountains – *good*. It meant the Americans had not yet arrived on the mountain, and his team was first in.

It didn't matter. Even if the Americans *were* already here, and had retrieved the camera data, his orders were to bring it back it to the Motherland at all costs. The Americans would hand it over, or he'd take it from their cold, dead hands. It didn't matter if they had Special Forces assets – in fact he hoped for it. Zlatan smiled grimly. He wanted them to put up a fight as he would like nothing more than to test his Kurgan against the best America had to throw at them.

He looked again into the crater. It was enormous, miles across, and strangely devoid of ice now he was at the top. He still felt the bitter cold at his neck as he perched above it, but on his face, he could feel the warmth emanating from below. No doubt it would be warm once they were under the blanket of the strange, thick fog. He stared. It swirled and moved like a sea that had eddies, currents, and whirlpools all just below the surface.

Visibility would be impeded, and he had been told to expect a communication blackout once they descended. But still, Zlatan had the advantage, and he needed to use it. He felt a moment of uncertainty and calmed himself by thinking of Rahda. *For you, my love.*

He looked out over the massive smoke-filled crater that looked like a titan's boiling cauldron then waved his men on. Together they descended the several hundred feet down the side of the mountain and entered the smog layer – well before they had even found the bottom.

Zlatan held up a hand, watching the fog swirl past it. Looking closely, the fog wasn't actually a mist, but instead countless small dust-like particles. The closer to the ground, the more there was. He could just make out a soft whining sound, like the noise the wind makes when it sneaks in through a gap. *Strange.*

It was like entering the atmosphere of an alien planet. The Russian grimaced as the particle gases stung his nose and throat – he had been told by his superiors to expect a significant moisture suspension, possibly from ice melt. But this stuff had a tang of something different, something *organic*. The Kurgan bodies would be able to fight off most contaminants and toxic substances, and he hoped this wouldn't prove debilitating.

In a few more seconds he adjusted, and was at least thankful for the blanket of warm air allowing his fingers to thaw and the ice on his body to melt. He rubbed at his dripping nose. It was only around fifty degrees Fahrenheit within the mist layer, but compared to above it, it was a luxury.

After several hundred feet of scaling down, the Kurgan reached bottom. Zlatan slowly turned; the mist layer here was so thick, it created a twilight gloom, and underfoot he felt something that was akin to slimy moss.

He held up a hand and his team froze. Zlatan stood silent, listening – had he heard something? Movement? He let his eyes slide slowly around them and strained to hear.

Nothing now but the background whine. After another moment, he gave up and turned to his team. "Virinov, use the tracker."

The man close to him nodded, and removed a cigarette-pack sized device from a pouch, turned it on and held it out. Immediately a pulse emanated from the device and he watched it for a few seconds before lifting his head and pointing off into the distance.

"That way; 4,400 feet."

Zlatan looked in the direction Virinov had pointed – just like all around them, there was nothing but a wall of thick cloud. He blew hard, making the speckled fog in front of his face swirl away into tiny spinning eddies.

His tongue was coated with the strange sweet taste of the mist. He spat on the ground. It came out like a paste.

Zlatan waved his men forward. "Move out."

CHAPTER 15

Morag took off a glove and placed a finger against the helicopter window – even through the double-layer insulated glass it was so cold it stung her fingertip. She pulled it back and blew on it before jamming it back into her glove.

She looked down at the plains of dry, brown grasses. Some caribou meandered about as they flew over, a few patches of snow were like blinding white oases, and from time to time a wind flurry would lift some flakes that danced madly across the uninviting scrubby landscape.

Upon departure she had maintained her furious indignation at Alex Hunter and his team, but when they turned away she had winked at Calvin, and nodded at his camera. Calvin had raised his eyebrows and shook his head, but she mouthed with her teeth clenched, *start fucking filming* with all the silent force as she could muster. The cameraman had looked pained, but surrendered. He snuck out another spycam and held it rolled in his fist. He began to record some film in the chopper, panning it over the faces of the HAWCs. He then carefully lifted it to capture the NASA crew as well.

Morag felt extremely confident. She'd worked with military types before; a few *yes sirs, no sirs,* and the occasional smile, and you could wrap them around your little finger in no time. She hoped.

She looked again at the group in the massive chopper's hold. All the men could have been cut from the same block of cold, hard iron: rock-like stubbled jaws, multiple scars, and eyes that were so alert, they looked like birds of prey. The one called Garcia looked Spanish, had the thickest hair she had ever seen on a human being, and was missing a small piece of his left eyebrow.

The two female HAWCs, Casey Franks and Anita Erikson, looked like they could easily hold their own with the tough-looking men. For one, Casey was probably just as heavily muscled, and Morag noticed that the guys gave her due respect, as there was a ferociousness about her that was intimidating, even to them. She reminded Morag of a spring-loaded bear trap – keep clear or lose an arm. Adding in a scarred face did nothing to humanize her in any way. She looked tailor-made for the job.

The other Special Forces woman, Erikson, was taller and leaner, with brown hair pulled back tight and Nordic-sharp cheekbones. Her voice carried a hint of a Germanic accent and Morag noticed that from time to time the woman's eyes went to Alex Hunter. Morag smiled; there was some interest there. *An old flame maybe or just hopeful.*

She followed the woman's gaze to the HAWC leader. She knew what Erikson was looking at – Morag also liked the look of him. Alex Hunter was big, brutally handsome, and definitely a take-charge kinda guy. If she could win him over, she'd have them all saying *"cheese"* before they knew it.

Casey Franks turned in her seat and leaned a forearm on its back to stare for a few seconds.

"So, news-chick, what's your story?"

"I'll show you mine if you show me yours," Morag shot back with a grin.

The HAWC woman sneered, or maybe smiled. It was hard to tell as up close Morag could clearly see the scar running from chin to up past her eye that pulled her cheek into a sneer.

"Deal – you first," Casey said.

"Okay." Morag nodded. "Well, I'm Morag O'Sullivan, and I'm a journalist who works the major news desk at the *Los Angeles Times*. Calvin there is our gun cameraman."

Casey never even looked at him, and didn't seem interested in him or his story in any way.

"Your turn."

"Casey Franks, soldier and stone-cold killer." She grinned, meaning it.

Morag raised her eyebrows. "Must look good on a resume."

"Does on the ones that count." Casey motioned with her head to the peaks looming up in the distance. "So, climbed before?" she raised her chin. "And I'm not talking about in some swanky gym where you play on colored lumps of plaster stuck on a wall."

Morag snorted. "Listen GI Jane; I've been up Mount Rainer, 14,411 feet. Higher than where we're going now."

Casey nodded. "That's just a fucking steep hill for tourists. What else you got?"

Morag leaned forward. "And for fun, I climbed *the wall* of the El Capitan in Yosemite – the hard one." Morag sat back. "What about you?"

Casey grinned. "I know that El Capitan face – I free-climbed it."

Morag grunted. Free-climbing was where you went up with nothing but fingertips, toes, and a heart as big as Texas. It was obvious this was one pissing contest she was not going to win.

Morag smiled. "Not going to give an inch, are you?"

Casey shook her head slowly. "Got to tell you, girl; you act pretty ballsy. But out here you're nothing. You shoulda stayed at home this time." Casey turned back around.

Morag eased back in her seat. "Yeah, well, my mom always said, 'fly free, girl'. That's what I'm doing." Morag felt like shooting back something else more cutting, witty, or brutal, but had nothing. She gave the back of Casey's head the finger and turned to the window again to silently fume.

Outside, she saw that they were now rising over the peaks, and felt the helicopter skid in the air as a particularly heavy gust blew them sideways a few dozen feet. The pilot corrected quickly, but she knew he was contending with wind spurts of around 100 miles per hour, and updrafts, side drafts, and downdrafts blasting up and around the fiercely uneven geology.

Looking at the formidable peaks, she could almost hear the tectonic plates crashing and grinding together, continuing to form the mighty up-thrusts that were like monstrous sharpened teeth rising thousands of feet into the sky. Morag shivered and not from the cold this time.

In no time, dark featureless granite gave way to blinding white snow, and then they lifted higher, and into the clouds. Morag's mind drifted back to her hectic news desk, then to warm cocktail bars and sandy beaches.

"Five minutes, people."

Alex Hunter's voice made her jump, and she turned to watch some of the HAWCs prepare the drop ropes.

The drop ropes.

A small voice in her head finally agreed with Casey Franks, and she knew this might just be the dumbest thing she'd ever done.

* * *

Alex went and sat up next to the pilot. Outside, the snow mercilessly spattered against the cockpit's Plexiglas. He saw the retrieval spike extending out before the nose of the chopper – a fifty-foot rod that ended in a y-shaped fork – it would be used to grab the samples from the air that Anne Peterson would be collecting and sending up. That was unless the wind blew them all the way to the Arctic Circle.

He didn't like the chances of recovering the samples. But NASA and the military were interested in whatever it was down there that seemed to be transforming an environment as hostile as this one. If it was something benign and manageable, it could mean a solution to reclaiming deserts, or even future planetary terraforming.

He watched the pilot wrestle with the stick as the helicopter jumped and bucked around them. Alex realized he didn't even know the pilot's name. He leaned forward. "Hunter."

The pilot nodded, but continued to stare dead ahead. "Vincenzo – beer and football lover, pilot, and certified lunatic."

Alex smiled and looked out at the maelstrom around them. "Lunacy helps in places like this."

"Oh yeah." Vincenzo grinned. "Coming at us from every direction. I correct one way, and then we get pounded from the other way." He bared his teeth for a moment as the chopper dropped about fifty feet. He turned to look briefly at Alex. "We get clobbered by one of those super-gusts close to the face, and we're bugs on a windshield."

Alex grunted, feeling for the guy. Pilots tended to be as cold as ice, so for him to even mention his concern meant he was worried to all hell.

"Hopefully we'll be in a wind shadow closer in. And if not …" Vincenzo shrugged.

Alex understood. "The ropes we've got will get us down eighty feet. We can drop all at once – you just need to hold us in place for a single minute. Can you do it?"

"Hell or high water I'll do it." His eyes flicked to Alex again. "But might not be me that determines how long you've got."

"Yeah, I get it." Alex then pointed. "There."

Vincenzo turned back. The peak still rose hundreds of feet above their heads, but on the wall of the mountainside, there was a ledge of stone about twenty feet wide.

"Jesus. *That's* where you want me to drop you?" The pilot whistled. "One minute hang time, right?"

"All we'll need." Alex got to his feet. He laid a hand on the young pilot's shoulder. "Good luck."

Vincenzo smirked. "Hey, you get the hard job. Once you send up the samples, I get to go home." His face became serious. "Drop and release; I hang around for the package until I've used my fuel budget, then I'm outta here."

Alex nodded, and headed back to the rear cabin. He held up five fingers, and his HAWCs immediately went into action. There were eight drop ropes, three each side, and two from the huge ramp-like rear door. They had a tension strength of over 1,000 pounds, and their winches could lift a small car if need be. Weight wasn't the problem, but speed was, so for the civilians it meant doubling up as the only way to get down quick.

Alex planted his legs in the bucking chopper and faced the civilians. "Our drop lines are eighty feet *only*, and our pilot is going to have a devil of a time keeping us steady and in place. We have sixty seconds to drop to the ledge and disengage."

He looked at their faces. All sat with wide eyes and he bet, racing hearts – *good* – adrenaline improved alertness and reaction times.

"We will be doubling up – you will all be coming down strapped to one of my soldiers. This is—"

"I can drop by myself if ..." Morag had her hand up.

Alex's voice rose. "This is *not* negotiable." He glared for a moment and Morag just shrugged. "NASA team: Russell Burrows with Mister Monroe. Scott McIntyre with Mister Dunsen. Anne Peterson with Ms. Franks. Morag O'Sullivan with me, and Calvin Renner with Mister Knight. Mister Samuel

Reid will take all your gear – anything you forget to give him, stays on the chopper."

Sam loomed up behind him like a huge wall, and nodded once.

"Any questions?" Alex looked along their faces again. They probably had hundreds, but kept them behind their teeth. He checked his watch; it was time.

* * *

In moments, the HAWCs had attached their drop lines and lashed their respective civilians to themselves. Morag was strapped to the front of Alex and tried to adjust the tight cords, but failed.

"Hard to breathe." She winced and looked up and over her shoulder at him. "I hope this isn't where I get accidently dropped off."

"Don't give me any ideas." Alex's mouth might have just lifted a little at the corner. "All you need to do is follow my instructions." He looked over her head to his team. "Visors down and hook in."

Morag watched as Alex touched his neck and like magic, a dark scale-like hood telescoped from somewhere on his neck up and over his head and was then followed by a shield moving down over his face. He suddenly looked artificial, assembled almost, like a robot.

"*Um*, do I need my facemask to breathe?"

"Just your goggles; save your oxygen for when we're in the crater. We just need vision for the drop and landing – you'll see why." He reached up, and with a solid *clank*, hooked his drop-line to an overhead winch and turned to look over his HAWCs. She felt his chest swell.

"HAWCs, we are *go*."

Sam Reid bellowed in response. "*Muscle up!*"

Alex turned back to the rear of the bucking chopper. *"I can't hear you!"*

"HUA!" roared the group, and formed into lines.

Jesus Christ, what have I got myself into? Morag wondered.

Alex punched a large button on the wall, and the rear and side doors whined open. Morag immediately threw her hand up as a hurricane of wind and snow particles were flung in at them like stinging white shrapnel – this is what Alex had meant by protecting their vision on the way down. Without eye cover, they'd be blinded.

She turned again to look up at Alex's face. She could just make it out behind the visor and saw that the granite-hard jawline looked to carry a small smile. Where she was shitting herself, she bet he was looking forward to it. She saw him speak softly behind his visor, possibly to the pilot one last time. He held up a hand and slowly lowered the fingers one by one.

Morag's heart smashed in her chest as he went from three down to one, and then he was running for the ramp, taking her with him. His HAWCs followed. She screamed as Alex leaped into space.

Morag shut off her scream and snapped her mouth shut as the cold stung her teeth and hard bits of ice and snow hurt her mouth. She was blinded and deafened by the screaming wind – *and this was supposed to be the sheltered side of the mountain.* The combined weight of each HAWC and passenger was probably between 400 and 450 pounds but still the wind tossed them around like corks.

She felt Alex twisting and trying to maintain his position as they dropped rapidly toward what she expected was the rock ledge. But they surely had no hope of seeing it among the flying snow. Every now and then the helicopter would jerk them, like a fly fisherman trying to sink the hook in a trout, and they'd swing wildly one way then the next.

She didn't know how far they'd dropped or how long they'd been dropping, as her fear made every atom of her being become tunnel-focused on their landing. In another second, the huge face of the cliff loomed right in front of them and she saw the ledge, but horrifyingly, they were nowhere near where they needed to be and were fast coming to the end of their rope.

Alex locked off their drop line to stop their descent, and she wondered whether he was in communication with the pilot, trying to get him to swing them closer. She could dimly make out other bodies hanging like fruit from slender threads waiting for the right time to cut loose.

Then it came, the chopper yawed toward the cliff face as the wind slowed by a few dozen miles per hour. They swung at the ledge and Alex got ready to release them – fifty feet, forty, thirty, twenty. Momentum was with them when suddenly the chopper started to pull back. But it was too late now; they were committed.

'Fly free, girl,' she heard her mom whisper. It gave her strength.

Alex punched the release on his tether and let gravity and momentum do the rest. They flew the last twenty feet toward the rock ledge, but way too fast. She knew at this speed, she'd be obliterated against the stone. Unlike the soldiers, she wasn't built like a tank or wearing an armored suit.

Fuck, she screamed in her own head, bracing herself, as Alex's left arm tightened around her. Morag raised an arm, knowing it would be the first thing smashed, and also knowing that a broken arm, ten thousand feet up a freezing mountain could probably be a death sentence.

I'll leave you behind, she remembered the HAWC leader saying.

She gritted her teeth as they hurtled toward the rock wall and ledge. Alex raised his free arm in front of her, and suddenly a three-foot disc of air swirled before them. They struck hard and Alex rolled them both, the shield taking most of the hard impact instead of their bodies. They continued to roll, and then Alex used the momentum to spring back to his feet and run hard at the cliff wall to move out of the way of the other soldiers who were coming in fast.

Every single one of them made it, using their shields, hitting hard, rolling and coming back upright. Morag still wore a grimace of fear and her heart was hammering. She exhaled in disbelief. *She didn't even feel like she was the same species as these super humans.*

Alex disengaged his shield, unhooked Morag and then retracted his hood. "All right?"

She grinned up at him, still shaking. "*That* was intense."

"This party has only just started." He turned away to look to his team, probably counting them off. He then walked back a few steps to edge of the ledge and craned his neck to look up at the peak still a few hundred feet above them. To Morag it looked a sheer face of dark granite, but after a few seconds, Alex nodded.

"No problem." He called his HAWCs in. "Erikson, Dunsen, Knight, you're up. Let's go, people."

Morag noticed that the three HAWCs had somehow retained their drop lines, and like gymnasts, each ran at the wall, leaped, and clung on. Like spider monkeys, the three Special Forces soldiers started to climb and fast.

"*Whoa.*" Morag shook her head in awe. When she said she'd climbed before, she didn't mean anything like this.

The HAWCs stuck carabiners in crevices, and hammered in pitons where they had to, and then threaded their rope through them as they went. In no time they were a hundred feet up, and Alex turned and shouted over the wind.

"Next up! Let's go! Let's go!" He turned to stare up into the swirling snow.

Morag followed his gaze, but could see nothing. But she suspected he was looking for their chopper which was waiting somewhere up in that mad blizzard. She didn't envy the pilot for a second.

It was her turn next and she started up. The cold had already caused a thin layer of ice to form on the rope, making the soft elastic fibers slippery, and she had to concentrate every inch to stop from sliding back down.

Behind her on the rope, Alex was last in line and coming quickly, scaling easily, as if he was just climbing a ladder to change a light bulb. The wind still buffeted them, but at least in close to the cliff face it was less ferocious. She glanced up. Above her, she guessed, the lead climbers must be near or at the summit by now, and she turned back to the wall, focusing on the rope, on each grip-release-grip over and over again, edging upwards a few feet each time.

Morag didn't want to look behind or down. Even though she had climbed peaks before and didn't regard herself as having a problem with heights, if she saw even for a second the dizzying void below her, she might lock up. She simply could not let that happen while Alex Hunter was right behind her – she didn't want his help. She was no damsel in distress – never was, never would be. She gripped, hard, cursed under her breath, and yanked herself up another few feet.

Minutes later, a hand grabbed the back of her jacket and roughly dragged her up and over the rim. She skidded forward on her belly, and then rolled over to suck in air. Her fingers were curled into painful claws and she blinked several times to make the flaring stars of exhaustion go away.

Steve Knight crouched beside her. "Okay?"

Morag sat up, still dizzy. "Yeah, yeah."

The young HAWC slapped her shoulder. "You did well."

He headed back to his group, where they stood on the peak's edge, helping the last few climbers, while some stared down over the other side. She watched as Alex Hunter came up and over the rim, his face mask still up, and not even breathing hard. She looked around and saw that the only ones sitting or lying flat were the NASA team and Calvin Renner.

She struggled to her feet, and wobbled for a moment. All the HAWCs stood ready, and a few had strange-looking weapons drawn – *odd, why?* She joined them at the edge and stared down into the massive formation created by three mountains that had collided together in some distant primordial past to create a massive crater basin many miles across.

Beside her Sam Reid stood rock still and as she watched four lenses lumped the visor over his face. It gave the appearance of some sort of giant alien being staring down on the puny Earthlings below it.

Morag turned back to the mist-filled basin. The more she stared, the more the hair on the back of her neck rose. "Well, that's not creepy at all," she whispered. *Like the boiling sea of another world.* Suddenly she wished that Alex Hunter *had* tied her up and left her behind.

CHAPTER 16

Alex stared down into the thick mist. It was impossible to see anything through it, and it hung in a layer over the crater floor that extended for miles. Whatever had come out of the *Orlando* had massively spread.

He exhaled slowly; he had a bad feeling about this one. With any luck, they'd be gone within another eight to twelve hours. Without luck, they had breathable air for two days – one day, if it was high activity. He set a timer on his wrist that would begin counting down when he engaged his oxygen.

Alex then quickly sent off a message to Hammerson: *Reached peak, zero casualties, commencing search, over.* The message screen on his forearm screen rotated for a few seconds, before giving him back a single word – *failed.*

Shit, must be the effects of the atmosphere blister already. He'd expected it, and they'd planned for it. He'd have to send up communication bullets as they went. This meant he could get brief messages out, but nothing could get in – one-way comms only – as good as it got.

They were above the strange mist layer, and with his visor still up, he couldn't smell any unusual odors, but he could feel the warmth against his face. He'd give the team another few minutes to acclimatize before dropping down. The temperature differential would be too extreme for the civilians, so better to ease them into it.

As Alex watched something seemed to lump in the center of the sea of cloud like a whale coming to the surface but not quite breaching. The huge dark shape traveled for several hundred feet before sinking from sight.

"I hope that was a trick of the light." Sam had appeared beside him.

"You and me both," Alex said, continuing to watch. "Hammerson said they detected movement, so …"

"Can't see a goddamn thing." Sam retracted his quad lenses, held up an arm using his wrist scanner, and moved it over the crater. He read some data and whistled. "The actual floor of the crater is still another 500 feet down, and given the mist only starts about half way, we still got some climbing to do."

"At least it's all downhill." Alex grinned up at his friend.

Sam nodded. "Yep, there is that." He lowered his arm. "What the hell is keeping it from blowing away?"

"Good question … and next one is, where is it all coming from?" He checked his wrist communicator again. "Comms are down. So its electromagnetic influence is reaching us even up here. I can't smell anything, but we'll need to permanently hood up as soon as we start to descend."

Sam grunted. "Can you see anything?"

Alex knew what he was asking, and turned back to the smog. His vision was far superior to anyone else's, and could even see changes in thermal radiation. He stared, concentrating, and saw that further out over the mist, there was the occasional swirl and eddy, as if whatever he thought he saw before was still swimming just beneath its surface.

"There's certainly movement down there. But I can't tell what it is, or whether it's a single signature or multiple objects moving together."

"Our Russian friends … or maybe survivors?" Sam raised his eyebrows.

Alex continued to stare. "Don't think so."

Sam sighed. "Why do I get the feeling that this was never going to be a simple rescue and recovery mission?"

Alex snorted. "If that's all it was, they wouldn't have needed us. So let's find the *Orlando*, and get the hell out of here." He turned. "Knight."

The young HAWC joined them. "Boss?"

Alex nodded toward the crater. "Give me a direction on the *Orlando*."

Steve Knight held up a tracker, the screen showing a 3D representation of the crater basin, cutting it up into a grid, and then identifying a quadrant where the main shuttle fragments rested. He pointed with a flat hand.

"North, northeast, 4,569.3 feet. Terrain is … wait a minute." He frowned as he looked at the formations. "Hard to get an accurate geographic reading; there's plenty of weird formations down there, maybe rock, but …" His frown deepened.

"What is it?" Alex watched him.

"System must be screwy. Formations that were there a few seconds ago are now gone." He turned slightly, angling the scanner. "No, not gone … just somewhere else."

"Could it be that the magnetic disturbance is giving us some distortion?" Sam's brows rose slightly.

Alex looked at Sam whose face said he didn't believe it for a second. Alex nodded and looked back out over the murky air. "Okay, that's enough sightseeing. Let's find us some holiday snaps and maybe a few dead astronauts."

The group shed a lot of their clothing. The HAWCs now stood at the cliff edge, gazing out over the crater basin in their armored suits, hoods up and looking like a group of heavily muscled black-clad robots. The NASA crew donned a modern version of lightweight HAZMAT suits and breathing equipment, and Morag and Calvin wore the borrowed same. Piles of cold weather clothing lay at their feet. It wouldn't be needed down lower where the temperatures reached fifty degrees and well above that in humidity.

Alex watched the group begin to scale down and then paused to briefly look up at the clouds above. He could just make out the thrum of a helicopter he knew was up there somewhere. He didn't like the odds of being able to grab the sample from the sky, but if Vincenzo said he could do it, then Alex had to believe him.

He turned to his team. "Franks, Dundee, take us down."

"Yo." Casey leaped over the side, followed by the Aussie, and then the rest of the group.

Scaling down, even with his insulated suit, Alex felt the warmth embrace him. The air was thick, and he knew it wasn't just the humidity, but the mix of strange gases being given off by something the *Orlando* might have brought down with it. He paused to look at his gloved hand – it glistened, like it was coated in oil. And the mist seemed to be small particles rather than a gas.

Alex let go of the rope and dropped the last dozen feet, and on landing his feet squelched. He looked down, seeing the green-gray sludge.

Nice. "Knight, give me an LF check."

The young HAWC pointed his forearm reader at their surroundings and turned slowly. "Holy shit. Life forms off the chart." He shook his head. "Hard to get any sort of clear reading. I'm overloading the sensor."

Alex grunted. "Probably the free-floating bacteria – basically this fog is a living thing." He looked down at the muck he stood in. "As well as this stuff." He frowned, listening. "Anyone else hear that?"

"Yeah," Sam said. "Like some sort of whine, like when you got a goddamn mosquito in your room. Where's it coming from?"

Alex shook his head, turning slowly. It seemed to be coming from all around them. Everywhere.

"This mist ... it's not a gas," Anne Peterson said, waving a hand slowly in front of her face. "This is suspended particular matter. Bacterial clumps, maybe algae, or maybe something else entirely." She waved her hand in front of her face again making the mist swirl. "It has weight, so the lighter form is suspended, and after a while it sinks, clumps, and becomes this slime matter."

"Could this have been here before?" Alex moved some of it with the toe of his boot. It lumped up, and stayed that way. "Under the snow and ice, I mean?"

"Maybe, or maybe it came from the shuttle and has been growing. We've all seen the bloom spread after the crash." Anne also pushed at it with her toe. "It's like a lichen, but ..." she lifted her foot and some stuck. "But a bit more like a slime mold." She turned about. "And it's everywhere – could be the basis for a food chain, anyway. I'll take a sample. At least we can get this back to the lab."

She took out a canister from her pack and crouched. Anne went to scoop the jar across the organic matter.

Russell Burrows lunged. "*Wait.*" He held up a hand. "Careful, Anne, don't get any on you." She froze and he straightened. "Sorry, we don't know exactly what happened to our astronauts, but we *do* know that it occurred after they took the space debris onboard. And if this stuff has anything to do with the space debris ..."

She grimaced. "Right, right, sorry, could be some sort of contaminant."

"And we're fucking standing right in it." Dundee bristled.

"Shut it, soldier," Sam shot back.

"Don't worry, I believe it's too large to get in through our sealed suits." Anne took out a small spatula and used it to scoop some into her jar. She screwed the lid closed, held it up and shook it. The sample settled for a moment, before sliding up one side of the canister. She peered at the sample and shook it again. "Strange. Doesn't look like anything I've ever seen before. Don't know if it's plant, eukaryote, or animal. Almost like mucus."

Anne shook her head. "I can't really tell whether it starts as particles that eventually sink to clump into the slime. Or it starts as the slime, and then separates to become the free-floating particles. What state comes first?"

Russell crouched beside her and squinted. "Is that stuff moving?"

Anne jiggled it. "Doubt it."

"Gross." Casey Franks bent to stare into the glass jar. "Looks like snot."

"Thank you, Professor Franks." Alex stared at the greenish gloop. "So this mold or fungus might be responsible for giving off the gas?"

Anne shrugged. "Sure, why not? Plants and fungi can give off everything from methane and oxygen to microscopic spores. We won't know for sure until we get it back to the lab." She held up the container and jiggled it again. "And even if it isn't off-gassing, it will be saturated with it."

Alex looked up at the cliff face. "Seems to like warmth. As soon as it gets closer to where the atmosphere bubble ends, it stops growing."

"Most life on Earth prefers warmth and moisture." Anne looked around. "This is a perfect bio-environment for life. I should probably try and collect more samples." She held out the small specimen jar.

Alex reached toward it, but then paused – he was sure the small whine had become louder.

"What is it?" Anne asked.

Alex moved his hand away, and then back toward the jar. The whine increased and decreased as if the substance inside was reacting to his hand.

Anne scoffed. "Don't be scared."

He lowered his hand. "I don't think I'm the one who's scared." He knew only he could hear or sense the reaction. But he also knew that *it* knew he was here. He turned slowly; it probably accounted for the feeling he had that they were being watched – maybe by a billion eyes, for all he knew.

No. He straightened; there was something else out there. Something bigger.

Anne stared in at the glob, turning it slowly in her gloved hand. There was a small smile on her lips.

"Let's hurry this up." Alex turned to stare out into the curtains of biological brume. He caught Sam's eye, who nodded and also began to scan the near-impenetrable living fog.

"Hey, Dundee." Casey was grinning at Dunsen. "There's something on your boot."

Dunsen curled a lip. "Yeah, right; I'm not falling for that one, Franks."

"Okay, sure." She nodded toward his boot. "But maybe you should *toss it on the barbie.*"

Monroe chuckled. "She's right. You got a passenger there, buddy."

Dunsen cursed under his breath and was about to turn away, when he must have felt something. He looked down.

He started to kick his leg. "What the *fuck* is that?"

There was something making its way up his leg. It looked like some sort of glossy-green, muscled crustacean, with long spindly legs.

Dunsen drew a long, outback hunting knife, and in a single swift motion sliced the thing free. He growled, closing in on it.

"Don't." Anne held up a hand.

Dunsen's huge boot came down on the critter with a satisfying crunch. "Fuck you, prawn," he said, and ground his boot for a second. When he lifted it, only shell and goo remained.

Anne scowled. "I could have collected that."

"You still can. I caught it for you." He grinned. "And now it won't bite."

Monroe smirked. "Dundee making friends with the locals."

Dunsen resheathed his huge knife. "Yeah, and I *don't* come in peace."

"Idiots; we need more samples." Anne placed hands on her hips.

"Sorry, no time for more," Alex said. "Your existing sample has some of the particle gas as well as the biological material. Everything else you need should be locked in its cells. Send the package up, doctor, and let's get your labs looking at it."

Anne looked about to protest but Alex held firm. "If you don't do it now, the chopper is likely to leave and then we'll get nothing back." He waited.

Anne sighed. "Damn it. So, it's this or nothing, huh?"

Alex just held out a hand.

She tsked, and then handed the canister to him. Alex looked in at the sludge for a few seconds before tossing it to Sam. The HAWC opened his pack and took out a squat gun, which he telescoped open. He then put the small vial in a large bullet-shaped plug, snapped the barrel closed and pointed it skyward.

"Fire in the hole." Sam pulled the trigger.

Alex watched as the small projectile sped away. He tracked it for only a short while before it vanished in the cloud.

"That's it?" Anne asked.

"Yep. The rest is up to Vincenzo and his butterfly net." He faced her.

"How do we even know if he got it?" She tilted her head, her brow furrowed.

"We don't." Alex looked back to the sky. "We trust him to do his job."

* * *

The small canister burst from the cloud cover, heading straight up. As soon as it passed out of the interference zone the chopper's instruments were alerted and Vincenzo swung back hard and accelerated.

The pilot knew he had less than half a minute to grab the speeding capsule while it was on its upward velocity. At its zenith, it would deploy a small aluminum balloon, but given the wind speed, this would act more like a sail than a parachute. Instead of the sample capsule hanging in the air before floating slowly back to the ground, and giving him many more minutes to line up his snatch, the wind would grab it and blow it all the way to the damn Arctic.

Vincenzo leaned forward, pushing the big helo to its limits. From the front of the chopper the twenty-foot pole extended with a v-shaped clasp, ready. The small canister reached about 500 feet in the air at the peak of its arc, hung there for a second or two, and then as programmed, a silver balloon burst open.

Several things happened: the canister didn't drop but now floated, and then as expected, the wind caught it and it accelerated away, with Vincenzo in determined pursuit.

He leaned forward in his seat, his lips pulled back and teeth bared as he bore down on the speeding dot in front of him.

"Don't you try and side-step me now, baby."

Yards, feet, inches, and then he caught the small rope between the balloon and the canister, and the clasp locked down on it.

"*Got ya!*"

He sat back and exhaled. "Walk in the park." Vincenzo grinned, and then spoke into his mic.

"Sample package recovered; coming home." He banked hard and looked down into the weird boiling fog that filled the crater basin.

"See you on the flip side, Hunter. Good luck."

In another minute, he was gone.

* * *

Alex quickly entered a message into his forearm screen. *Arrived, no casualties, no sign of hostiles, search commencing.* He added information about the environment, the weird slime that seemed to move, and the mist. He then sent it to a numbered communication bullet, and pointed his arm upward. A small tube appeared on the back of his wrist unit – he flexed, and the bullet was fired.

The communication gun was a similar design to Sam's, but it was miniaturized and used only for compacted data squirts. Alex stared upward, but already the projectile would have risen approximately 4,000 feet, and in a microsecond, sent an encrypted packet of information that would be bounced off secure satellites all the way back to his boss, Colonel Jack Hammerson.

The small projectile would have one more task – as it came to the end of its upward velocity, and its compressed data was well away, the explosives would be triggered, obliterating it. Nothing above dust-sized fragments would fall back to earth.

Alex lowered his arm, and the small tube retracted back into the forearm unit. He continued to watch for a moment more before sighing and beginning to pivot back to his team. He suddenly spun to the wall of mist.

He could sense something big. Close by, but just out of sight. And there was something else. Beneath his feet, he felt a slight tremor or vibration. He closed his eyes and tried to concentrate to get an image of what it might be, but whatever it was, it had either stopped or moved away.

It was too big; had to be some sort of tremor. Alex opened his eyes and turned slowly. Around him the haze was swirling slightly. The back of his neck tingled and every fiber of his being told him there was danger ahead. At this point they couldn't see anything, and nothing showed on their instruments – if they could even still be trusted. He then saw Calvin Renner trying to film, but cursing at the lack of clear vision.

He knew his HAWCs were watching him. They could sense his unease and were on edge. The group was exposed and vulnerable. "Armor up, DVP – Franks at point."

"*Yo!*" Casey fist pumped.

The HAWCs responded by pulling their RG3s and spreading into formation. DVP stood for Defensive 'V' Pattern – like an arrowhead, and Casey Franks would be its tip.

Sam Reid organized them, his huge body pushing, glaring, and overseeing Alex's orders. He pointed to the NASA crew. "Civilians to the center of the group, *now*. We expect hostiles, people, so stay alert." He walked around them, and once satisfied turned to Alex. "On your orders, boss."

Alex grunted. "Knight, find me that shuttle."

"Boss." Knight fell in at Casey's shoulder. The stocky female HAWC would cover him, as he would be partially distracted by the tracker.

Knight looked up momentarily and then pointed with a flat hand. "This way, 448 feet."

"And counting down," Casey said, and led them in.

CHAPTER 17

Alex checked his watch. They'd already been on the basin floor for an hour – they were burning time ... and precious oxygen.

Their original plan was to find the shuttle, retrieve the image disc, and then be on their way out within ten hours. If things proved more complicated, then they were prepared to hunker down overnight. But that was worst case.

He turned to the civilians. "Let's move it up, people."

They headed into the gloom, trying to remain silent, but failing as the slime squelched beneath their boots.

"Captain?" Russell Burrows waved to him. "A word?"

Alex turned to nod at Sam, who let him fall out from the center of the group to catch up to Alex.

"This is weird," the NASA scientist whispered.

"No shit." Alex continued to watch the mist.

Burrows cleared his throat. "You, *ah*, guys been in this type of thing before?"

"No," Alex said. "Not exactly like this."

"So, we're flying blind then?" Burrows asked.

"We adapt, we do our jobs, and then hopefully, we all go home in one piece." Alex glanced at the man, seeing the hint of fear in his eyes. "You'll be fine, as long as you and your group follow instructions."

Casey Franks raised her hand, and the HAWCs froze. Alex threw an arm out in front of the NASA engineer. "*Stop. Quiet.*"

Scott McIntyre and Anne Peterson crowded in close to each other, and Morag O'Sullivan and Calvin Renner also froze, eyes wide, but listening intently.

After a moment, Morag whispered to Alex. "What are we listening for?"

"My nerves to snap." Renner said back under his breath.

Alex ignored them, concentrating as he tried to locate the sound, but it seemed to be everywhere.

"I hear it," Anne said softly. "It's like ... insects buzzing."

Alex rotated slowly – it *did* sound like insects. There was a soft hum coming from all around them that definitely wasn't artificial, and reminded him of a parkland on a summer afternoon – a low background *zumm*, not unpleasant, but steady.

"Like some sort of locust or cicada, but ... not quite the same," he said.

"There's nothing indigenous like that up here," said Anne.

"Motion sensors say nothing is out there," Sam said.

"What if it doesn't show up on the sensors?" Calvin Renner said. "What if it's like some sort of ... entity? All around us."

"Like a ghost?" Garcia grinned. "*Boo.*"

Renner's face twisted. "No, smartass, I meant—"

"*Quiet.*" Alex glared, closing them down. "Something's there."

Renner raised his head. "What is it? There's nothing—"

"Shut it," Casey snarled. "Boss senses something; means there's something out there. Now shut the fuck up and stay alive."

"Stay alive?" Morag stiffened.

"Jesus, lighten up, will you?" Renner snorted and turned to sneer at Morag.

Max Dunsen eased up next to the cameraman. "Hey, asshole."

Renner turned to look up at him.

Dunsen grinned like a death's head. "Listen, mate, take a look around – does this place look like Bondi Beach to you?"

Renner stared for a moment. "*Uh*, where?"

Casey Franks scoffed. "Jesus, Dundee, like who the fuck knows where that is?"

Dunsen spun to her. "Shut up, Franks." He turned back to Renner, edging even closer. "Fucking Waikiki, then. *Well, does it?*"

"No, sir, it doesn't." Renner held up his hands and backed a few paces away from the towering HAWC. "Look, I'm just the pictures guy." He turned away to Morag and rolled his eyes. "Fucking GI Joes," he whispered.

Alex blocked them out and tried to open his senses and push out into the mist. Just when an image started to form in his mind, the buzzing stopped.

The sound wasn't right. In fact, now he wasn't sure the buzzing was occurring externally at all. It felt like it was everywhere but nowhere, like the tiny whine still singing around them, but the more he concentrated, the more he thought the sound had been inside their heads. And he sensed a constant presence, everywhere.

He continued to search. His neck still prickled and a gentle pain began behind his eyes, adding to his frustration. It was like the feeling you had in a pitch-dark room, when you held out a hand, seeing nothing, but knowing that something was probably there in the dark, seeing you without you seeing it.

The pressure in his head increased slightly as if something was reaching back at him. He sealed it off. *What the hell is in here with us?* He exhaled. *We'll find out soon enough.* He turned to his team. "Garcia, double-point with Franks."

The swarthy HAWC nodded and joined Casey Franks, who bumped fists with the man, their knuckles making a clacking sound from the armor-plating cover.

"Stay alert, people." Alex turned, as Sam joined him.

"What is it?" Sam kept staring directly ahead.

"I don't know; it's weird. I get the feeling we're being watched. And it's pissing me off that I can't tell from where or by what."

"The bug sounds?" Sam asked.

"If they *were* bugs," Alex said. "We need to stay sharp. This is not our turf anymore, and I get the feeling that who or whatever it is can see us a lot better than we can see them."

"Why am I hoping it *is* just a bunch of Russian torpedoes?" Sam snorted.

Alex just let his eyes move over the haze. Around the group it swirled and billowed. The civilians began to bunch up in the center like a herd of animals sensing circling predators.

There were some rock extrusions like islands in the muck, but also waist high mounds that could have been nothing more than great lumps of the slime. He had an urge to fire a few rounds into one.

The HAWCs, perhaps picking up on Alex's unease, tightened their grips on their guns. Already, the heavy, opaque atmosphere made it a ghostly twilight. But Alex knew once the sun went down, there'd be no moon, no stars, and the darkness would be absolute. The HAWC visors had quad vision equipped with thermal and night vision, but the fog would probably even reduce those applications' usefulness.

Alex suddenly felt the buzz again in his head, but this time ramped up, accelerating; he whipped his gun up.

"*HAWCs!*"

The first attack came fast.

* * *

Something came out of the gloom in a blur, larger than a man, and so damn fast it was impossible to make out. Several guns made sputtering sounds as projectiles flew toward it, but even though the HAWCs had reaction times much faster than normal people, they were still too slow and the thing had already sped past where they had put their darts.

Max Dunsen took the hit and grunted with pain as he went down hard. Casey Franks leaped to stand in front of him to give him cover.

"I got ya, big guy."

Dunsen rolled and came back to his feet. "Owe you, mate." He immediately pulled his RG3 rifle from over his shoulder.

"*Form up!*" Alex yelled the words as he saw that amazingly, Dunsen's tough armor-plated suit was slashed across the forearm and thick, red blood was running down his sleeve. "*Halo ring.*"

The HAWCs drew into a tight circle, facing outwards and pushing the civilians in behind them.

"What did you see?" Sam Reid asked the injured Dunsen.

Dunsen shook his head. "Was too bloody fast, but I damn well felt it – hit me like a fucking train." He looked down at his bleeding arm. "*Shit.* A train with teeth."

The heavy mist swirled, agitated, as something moved around them. Alex could hear heavy breathing like that of a large animal.

"We're being circled," Alex said. "On my ready ..."

The thing had vanished, but then it, or another one like it, came at them from their other side. Only Alex was fast enough to react and fire. The resulting unearthly squeal made Morag shrink down and cover her head.

The creature darted across their field of vision before

vanishing again into the haze.

"It's testing our defenses," Sam said.

Morag grabbed Sam's back, as if trying to keep him close. "It's testing us? It knows to do that?"

"There's more than one." Alex's head turned as he sensed something invisible to everyone else circle around them.

Morag turned to her cameraman. "Renner, hope you're getting this."

The man grimaced behind the small camera he held up to his face. "I'm trying. But everything's happening too fast. Autofocus can't keep up."

Something darted out, staying just far enough back to be indistinct, and hung there for a moment. Its huge misshapen form remained for a few seconds and Alex had an impression of large, glossy-black lidless eyes in an elongated bulbous head. The HAWCs wasted no time concentrating their fire on the apparition. The squeals of pain brought delight from the squad.

"Yeah, eat that shit." Garcia fired again, and every HAWC watched the shadow pass in and out of the curtains of cloud.

The thing roared, vanished for a moment and then reappeared. The HAWCs now sent hundreds of rounds per second at it, and knew they must have hit it, but still couldn't bring it down. It appeared again, and again, as if it was taunting them.

Alex tracked it with his fire, sure he was hitting the thing, but it refused to go down. It was then that from the opposite side of the group another of the creatures launched itself at them. It grabbed Anne, and Alex felt time slow around them. He turned to see it, the thing, holding the female NASA scientist, and looking down at her, and her back up at it. Time froze as the pair, one human and one abomination from hell, locked gazes.

Anne's eyes rolled back in her head and she fell to the ground, unconscious. The thing looked like it was bending to lift her. Alex bared his teeth, preparing to charge through the group when the HAWCs standing either side of the stricken woman went to close ranks. Even her NASA colleague, Scott McIntyre overcame his fear to push at the thing, but all he managed to do was get in the way of the HAWCs' RG3s and stopped them from getting off clear shots.

In the blink of an eye, the creature gave up on Anne, and flicked out one long limb, taking hold of HAWC Steve Knight and yanking him off his feet. Scott McIntyre was pushed aside, but not before getting ripped by one of the spikes extruding from the thing's arm like a row of huge thorns.

Alex pushed though the group then, but the creature spun away and then like a shadow vanished into the opaque walls, taking Knight with it.

"*Man down, man down!*" Sam roared orders and guns swung back and forth as the swirling fog closed around them.

Morag was crouched beside Anne Peterson and for a few seconds there was confused chaos around them, until Alex Hunter strode forward, and the group parted like a biblical sea. He began to run.

"*Stay on guard,*" Alex yelled over his shoulder as he went after his soldier.

CHAPTER 18

Ivan Zlatan halted his men for a break. Though none were fatigued, he needed to get his bearings as he felt they were going in circles. Their tracking equipment was only working sporadically now, and coupled with the heavy snow-like mist, it made navigating by landmarks impossible – it had strained even *his* iron nerves.

His men milled around, none talking, all impatient and sullen. All had bleeding noses and gums, headaches and a few of them also exhibited strange, lumpy rashes. But there was nothing he saw that would impede their combat readiness.

He couldn't tell if it was the altitude, the strange-smelling air that coated the inside of their noses and mouths, or a combination of both. But at least his lungs didn't feel hot and tight like they had when they first entered the mountaintop basin. *Perhaps we're acclimatizing now.*

He inhaled, smelling the high-methane content. It added further frustration, as the gas was extremely flammable and even explosive in high concentrations. It meant it would be too risky to use anything incendiary or even small arms. He cursed that bureaucrat Viktor Dubkin for not anticipating this when he sent them on the mission with standard weaponry.

But he remembered the initial briefing and images displayed – the fog just wasn't there when the shuttle first came down.

It's spreading. What will it be like in another hour, a day? They needed to complete their mission and get out.

He joined his men, who all stood, none sitting or lying down. He could understand why; everywhere you looked was coated in a greasy slime that stuck to their boots, and seemed to work its way up their lower legs. His men could deal with any hardships, but why lie in stinking mud if you didn't have to.

Zlatan looked at each of them – four remaining – they had lost Valentin on the climb, but he still had Naryshkin, Russlin, Stroyev, and Torshin, all with eyes still burning with military obedience and a desire to fight. None would even think of complaining.

He drew in a deep breath, filling his lungs, before letting it out slowly. There was no discomfort this time; yes, they were acclimatizing, he knew it. Zlatan turned slowly; looming from the mist were strange growths rising to about twenty feet in the air, and some with what could have been trunks ten feet around. It was if they pushed up until they came to the limits of the atmosphere bubble and stopped, knowing that beyond that meant death.

Though it reminded him of some sort of macabre, dead land, he knew there was life out there. They had grown used to the constant background sound that could have been an insect's thrumming coupled with an underlying soft whine, and he was sure there were other larger movements obscured by the shadows and hanging fog. It was strange, either the things that were making the noise were experts at camouflage, or they were invisible. When he stared at where he thought the noises were coming from, they stopped, and then began again somewhere else.

Zlatan was about to lead his team onward, when suddenly all surrounding sounds fell away. He held his hand up slowly, pointed at his eyes then ears, and then motioned to the bank of gloom. His Kurgan drew their daggers, alert and waiting.

They stayed frozen for many minutes in the absolute silence that was like the vacuum of space. Zlatan finally waved them on, and in just a few more seconds he heard it again, the heavy sliding, as if someone was dragging a wet sack over the ground – *slide, stop, slide, stop* – always keeping pace with them, moving when they did, stopping when they stopped.

Zlatan felt the ground gently vibrate beneath his feet. He was sure it was coming closer. And then, it stopped again.

"*Ach.*" Behind him, Naryshkin stumbled.

Zlatan turned, about to curse his man's clumsiness, when he saw that his soldier had been stopped dead, one foot in the front of the other, and the rear one snagged by something.

Naryshkin went to lift it free but couldn't. "Is stuck." He tugged on his foot, and then looked back at it. He recoiled.

"*Po'shyol!*" His voice became more urgent. "*Something on it.*"

Zlatan clicked his fingers and pointed. Russlin and Stroyev nodded and jogged toward the stuck man and gripped his arms.

Russlin looked up. "Looks like, maybe a snare."

Zlatan crossed quickly to Naryshkin who was now tugging on his leg even harder without being able to set it free. Closer now, Zlatan could see that there was what looked like glistening, dark cables over the toe of his boot. At first, he thought it might have been metallic, perhaps even space debris, but as he watched the cables climbed higher up past his ankle.

He felt it then, the grinding slide again, and he realized why he could never see it – it was underneath them the whole time, burrowing and sliding along.

He spun, looking at the ground at their feet. The thing had been listening to their footsteps, following them, and just waiting for an opportunity to shoot up to snatch at them when it was ready. Like it had with Naryshkin.

"It's below us." Zlatan dove toward his trapped man, and reached down to tug at the cords around Naryshkin's boot. As he did, even more of the glossy cables burst from the greasy mud, and encircled more and more of his soldier's leg.

"It hurts." Naryshkin groaned and threw his head back.

Zlatan pulled with all his strength, but he couldn't lift free from what was below them. Whatever held the man was either enormously strong or much bigger than he expected.

The slimy soil around Naryshkin's boots began to churn, and the Kurgan quickly pulled his blade and hacked at the cables that were now around his leg to the thighs. But for every strand he severed another two seemed to take their place.

The soil started to erupt around Naryshkin. Whatever was below the ground was beginning to surface, undoubtedly to claim its prize. Naryshkin began to panic, and pulled his gun, but Zlatan grabbed his arm and ripped it free, and then ordered his men to attack the ground. All of them started to hack and stab at the cords, the ground, and anything that looked to be surfacing.

In a five-foot circle around the stricken man, the ground boiled like water and then up rose a ring of tusks. Naryshkin's curses became incendiary in their intensity and it was then that Zlatan realized that they weren't tusks at all, but teeth.

The creature started to appear, a bulbous giant worm, with the cable things that had enmeshed his soldier's legs extending from its end like a thick beard of tentacles. What held him was the feeding end, open now like a colossal lamprey; a deep-sea creature that had a circular mouth lined with rasp-like teeth for gripping onto flesh and bone.

Naryshkin was dragged down at the same time as the circle of foot-long teeth began to close.

Zlatan and his men fell upon the monstrous worm, stabbing and hacking, but it was like trying to do damage to an armored truck, and their blades refused to penetrate the scaling.

Naryshkin had sunk now to his waist, his arms flailing, and he reached out, holding onto his comrades, Torshin grabbed an arm, but the sleeve came away in his hands just as the massive teeth came together.

Zlatan gritted his teeth at the sound of crunching bones. The Kurgan warriors' bodies were a wonder of massive armor-plated bone growths, but they stood little chance against something that was the size of a killer whale, and whose ocean was the slick mud below them.

His soldier's screams turned wet as dark blood spewed from his lips. In a couple of mighty tugs, his body vanished below the greasy surface.

For several minutes afterwards, they heard dragging and sliding beneath them as the monstrous creature slid back to its lair to enjoy its meal in peace.

Zlatan got to his feet, and wiped hands, slick with greasy slime and blood, on his trouser legs, leaving long streaks in their wake.

None spoke, but just stared at the churned ground that quickly seemed to knit together, the weird mud sliding and meshing like a wound closing over.

"What was that thing?" Torshin asked.

Zlatan shook his head. "Who knows; but from now on, I suggest we watch where we walk."

Torshin balled Naryshkin's sleeve up and tossed it to the ground where the man had disappeared. "It seems hell reaches up to us even on the mountaintops."

"Have you not heard?" Zlatan turned back to stare briefly at the ground. "When you are going through hell, there is only one thing to do." He looked up to smile grimly at Torshin. "Keep going."

Zlatan waved his men on, and they vanished in the swirling mist.

CHAPTER 19

Shit! Sam bared his teeth as he stared out into the soupy air, trunk-like legs planted, and hands so tight on his gun, they started to ache. Whatever those things had been they were no dumb animals. They had used a frontal attack as a diversion, so they could then come at them from the rear – a simple and effective tactic.

With all their tech, they were still nearly blind ... and he didn't like it. He turned and let his voice boom over the group. "*HAWCs, armor-up – two-tier.*"

The HAWCs edged back, forcing the civilians into a tight bunch – some went to one knee and the others stood at their shoulders. Then with an almost imperceptible whirring sound, the air began to swirl and condense in front of each of them as they deployed their shields. Over the top of each of these, the HAWCs had their guns pointed out at the surrounding mist, creating a double layer of gun barrels and shields. If anything came at them, they couldn't help but hit it.

Sam's teeth remained grit – they'd underestimated the things, and they just damn well paid for it. He waited, watching, and straining to hear anything over the small and insistent background whine. He turned to look over the group

– the HAWCs were like a single interlocked machine. *Good.*
Behind them, the civilians huddled. The camera guy, Renner,
tried to film, but his hand shook so violently that after a
moment Morag reached up to ease it down.

"It's okay." She smiled, lopsidedly. "It'd just be Bigfoot
shots with that shaky hand, right?"

Renner nodded and tried to smile, but his fear made the
attempt look more like a frightened chimpanzee.

Sam turned back to the alien landscape. The mist swirled and they all became statue-still, their focus intense.
Behind him, he felt Morag get slowly to her feet behind the
ring of warriors.

"Have they gone?" she asked him softly.

After a moment Sam nodded. "I think so; after the captain, I
bet." He half turned, seeing his man losing blood. "Dundee, put
a damn patch on that wound and seal your suit." He looked to
the NASA man, Scott McIntyre, nursing a hand that was also
showing red through his biohazard synthetic material.

"Bad?" he asked.

McIntyre shook his head. "Nah, just spiked on something."

"Good, then for now, just patch the hole, put pressure on
it, and we'll worry about blood loss later."

"Yeah, yeah." McIntyre pressed the wound, and Russell
Burrows pulled some plastic tape from his pack and helped
him seal the rip, binding the arm tightly.

Sam saw Dunsen still watching the mist. "*Now*, Dunsen."

"*Yo.*" Max Dunsen looked down, seeming to finally
remember that his arm was dripping thick blood to the
ground. Sam saw that, oddly, where it fell, the blood quickly
vanished as the slime closed over it, or worse, consumed it.

Sam shook his head. This place gave him the creeps. He
watched as in a practiced motion Dunsen pushed his gun up
over his shoulder, and opened the forearm sleeve, exposing
the wound. It was a ragged rip that welled blood. He then

reached into a kit and took out an adhesive patch, which he slapped over the wound.

Dunsen saw Morag watching and he grinned. "Med patch, got all the antibiotics, adrenalin and steroids to kill anything nasty and promote rapid healing." The wound immediately stopped bleeding. "See, better already, darlin'." He winked at her and rolled down his sleeve, affixed the suit to his glove, and flexed his fingers.

"Kills anything nasty, huh?" Morag pulled in a cheek. "Anything nasty, that we know about," she said.

He looked up sharply, but then snorted. "Yeah, well, the rest is up to the angels then, right?" Bravado and body intact, he fell back into the HAWC line.

"What now?" Russell Burrows asked Sam.

"We wait," the HAWC said evenly.

"How long?" McIntyre asked.

Morag scowled. "Jesus, you guys, give Alex a—"

Russell spun at her. "I wasn't asking the press gallery."

"Asshole," Morag spat back.

Russell's lip curled. "Should have let them leave you beh—"

"Shut it," Sam growled as he looked out at the fog from under lowered brows. "We wait until the captain comes back in. End of story."

"We're running out of time." Russell made a hissing sound between his teeth. "Do you know why we're here, Lieutenant?"

Sam's head came up slowly but he didn't turn. Russell put his hands on his hips, and turned to Morag.

"We are both here to find the *Orlando* Space Shuttle Orbiter module. Accepted it's for different reasons, but still, that is both our priorities. Please remember, you are here because of us, we are *not* here because of *you*."

Max Dunsen began to chuckle. Sam Reid turned fully toward Russell then, who looked up at him. Though Sam didn't step out of the line, he straightened to his full height and loomed high over the NASA engineer. His voice was measured.

"Without us, you'd all be dead in an hour." He lowered his head to look the man in the eye. "We will stay until I say so. Clear?"

Russell stared.

"*CLEAR?*"

The roar even made Morag jump. Russell nodded quickly and turned away, suddenly finding something else to do. Sam glared for a moment longer and then went back to watching the impenetrable speckled clouds pressing in on them. Sam knew his job right now was to keep everyone alive, and everyone under control ... and he'd damn well do it.

He couldn't tell how much time passed, as each and every second seemed an eternity of held breath and jagged nerves. But then, just as he felt he might need a new plan, a solitary figure walked out of the mist.

"Shields down," Sam said, relief washing over him.

* * *

The circle of discs vanished and their group parted as Alex Hunter strode into their center. He threw something to the ground, and they all stared.

"Knight?' Sam asked.

"Gone." Alex shook his head. "They're too quick. I followed but the tracks just seemed to vanish."

"What – *the fuck* – is that?" Casey Franks' scarred lips managed to curl even more in disgust.

The something was a claw, four fingered, or three and a thumb. The digits were thick, brutish and mottled green, and each ended in a cruel-looking talon.

"Well, Dundee, now you know what slashed you," Sam said.

Dunsen crouched, and drew his long hunting blade, lifting the claw slightly. He whistled. "It looks like it's from a big, bad ass bird."

Russell Burrows and Anne Peterson also crouched beside it. "May I?" Russell took Dunsen's knife and poked at it. "It's certainly not from a bird, Mister Dunsen; this thing has got an opposable thumb." He looked up. "And you say this came from the thing that attacked us?"

"One of them." Alex nodded and turned to Sam. "It was big, a biped, and at least seven and a half feet tall, and probably around 500 pounds. One came at me, so I cut that off it."

"Good, means we can hurt them." Sam squared his shoulders.

"Looks like a hairless bear claw," Monroe said. "Except for the number of claws or fingers or whatever they are. Maybe it's a mutation."

"Bears don't have opposable thumbs. In fact, *trapezio-metacarpal articulation* is primarily confined to higher-order creatures like primates and us." Anne looked up momentarily, but her vision seemed turned inwards. "*Us,*" she repeated softly.

Russell rested his forearms on his knees as he crouched. "I would have said simian morphology for sure, but it seems to have a type of scaling, like a reptile." He tapped it with the knife. "Weird, maybe not scales, more like a hard shell like the chitin you see on crustaceans. What do you think, Anne?"

The woman just stared down at the thing.

Russell leaned closer. "Anne?"

"*I don't know.*" She looked up, and her face was bleached white behind her visor. "I don't know."

Alex stared at the women, confused. He felt she was hiding something. "Anything you can tell us will help, Anne."

"He's right. Come on, this is more your field," Russell said. "Up close, it does look more like crustacean segments." He angled his head. "But I can see there are bones inside *as well* as the endoskeletal protection." He sat back. "This must be one tough sonofabitch." He turned to raise his eyebrows at her. "Anne, c'mon, tell me what you're thinking."

"I, I just don't know anymore," she stuttered and looked distracted.

"Then just guess," Russell pressed.

She grimaced behind her visor. "*Uh*, obviously some sort of resident mutated organism of unknown definition."

Casey's lips pulled back in disgust. "Mutated organisms, yeah, *Morgs* for short. *Perfect.*"

"Works for me," Dunsen added.

"But resident?" Scott McIntyre scoffed. "There's nothing like these creatures, resident or otherwise, anywhere that I know of."

"He's right." Russell looked skeptically at Anne.

"We don't know that." The female NASA agent stood quickly and walked away a few paces.

"Jesus," Scott said, watching her.

"Hidden all the way up here in the mountains, it could be like a Yeti thing," Dunsen said.

"A Yeti?" Monroe snorted.

"I'm just thinking out loud here, okay?" Dunsen snarled back.

"Yep, I've seen one – about six-four and speaks with an Aussie accent." Casey reached out to punch Dunsen's shoulder with the back of her hand. "Just messin' with ya, big guy."

Alex stared at it. "I also don't buy that these things are resident. This creature looked like it had evolved to adapt to this type of environment – it could see in the mist, breathed the gases, moved fast in this damn slippery mud, and was strong as hell."

"This thing, this *Morg*, looks more hatched than born." Sam looked down at the talon. "If they can be hurt, they can be killed. We take 'em down."

"Always my plan," Casey said.

"*No*, we don't know they meant to kill us." Anne spun back at them. "For all we know, they think we're attacking *them*."

Alex saw the woman's eyes go wide, showing real fear, but for what and who?

"Whatever," Casey said. "They're fucking dead."

"They coordinated their attack on us, even though we outnumbered them," Alex said. "Out there, they tried to encircle me. They're not dumb animals – we can't afford to underestimate them again."

"Jesus, Alex," Morag said. She turned back to the claw, disgust and fear twisting her features. "I've reported on some strange stuff, but I've never seen anything like this in my life."

"No one has. That thing isn't indigenous ... and I mean *earthly* indigenous." Sam straightened, gripping his gun even tighter.

"Wait, what?" Calvin Renner scoffed. "You mean that thing might have come down in the fucking space shuttle?" He gave Morag a hard look. "Jesus Mags, we're out of our depth here. We need to call this off, and just get the fuck out of here."

"Settle down. It didn't come down in the shuttle. It's probably like Monroe said, some sort of deformed ..." Morag shrugged. "I don't know what."

Casey nudged it with her boot. The claws clacked together. "This high up, and so remote; maybe Dundee is right ... for once."

Dunsen snorted. She glared at him for a moment before turning at Alex. "Remember those things up at Black Mountain?"

"I remember." Alex shook his head. "But I don't think that's what it was."

"There's something else that's weird." Russell used his probe to turn it over. The huge clawed fingers curled, and he pressed one out flat. "I think this thing has fingerprints."

"What?" Anne immediately pulled a small smart phone from her pocket and photographed the claw tips.

"Seriously?" Renner pointed. "What are you going to do, see if it's got any outstanding warrants when you get home?" He looked on the verge of panic.

Morag shrugged. "Take your pussy hat off and put your news one back on, Calvin. This thing is the find of a century." She looked at Alex. "Can we take it with us?"

Alex looked back down at it for the moment. "No. No excess weight. Also, these things are meat eaters."

"How do you know that?" Anne demanded.

"I just … know it," Alex responded, still staring at the claw. He had seen the jaws and teeth; they were used for ripping and tearing flesh. And he had felt the hunger coming off the things in waves – they wanted him for the meat on his bones, he could sense it.

He straightened. "I don't want anything catching the scent of that piece of bleeding meat and come looking for it." He turned again out at the mist. "Speed is the key … now we know there's more than just Russians out there."

Anita Erikson nudged Max Dunsen. "Bleeding meat, that'd be you."

"Yeah, and I'm all beef." He winked at her.

"Knight?" Sam asked.

Alex turned back to the ominous fog. "Yeah, we need to track and find him."

"How?" Russell Burrows asked. "You said yourself, there's no trail."

Alex kept his back turned.

Anne walked closer. "I'm so sorry for your loss, Captain, but we should leave these things alone. You *know* our priority is the downed *Orlando* shuttle. It's vitally important now."

"She's right." Scott McIntyre shrugged. "You and your men knew the risks, and we can't afford diversions. Leave him; time is critical."

Faster than Morag could even comprehend, Alex Hunter was in front of the man, his hand around his throat and lifting. McIntyre was not a small man, but his feet left the ground, and amazingly the HAWC leader didn't even seem to be straining.

The things were meat eaters, and they had taken his HAWC. And then this guy wanted to cut him loose in a blink. Alex pulled McIntyre real close, visor-to-visor, so close McIntyre would be able to see every spot, line and scar on the HAWC leader's face.

Alex teeth were grit. "And if it was you snatched by one of those creatures?" Alex pointed the man's face toward the huge claw. "Would you want us to leave you alone with that?"

"No." McIntyre's voice was little more than a squeak.

Alex let him go, dropping him to the slime, and turned away. "Form up."

The HAWCs fell in around him, and Morag noticed that the civilians crowded in closer; even Scott McIntyre.

Alex's head turned, looking along his team. "We *find* our HAWC."

"HUA!"

He raised a clenched fist. "And we show them who the real killers are."

"*HUA!*"

CHAPTER 20

NASA Astrobiology Laboratory, Greenbelt, Maryland

Chief science officer Jim Teacher read the plaque on the wall as he waited for his delivery.

NASA Astrobiology; dedicated to the study of organic compounds derived from stardust and future sample return missions, meteorites, lab simulations of Mars, interstellar, proto-planetary travel.

Quite a mouthful, but it made him beam with pride. The bit about *stardust* always got him right in the heart muscle. It conjured up images of shooting stars, sparkling magic dust, and kids sitting cross-legged in wide-eyed wonder.

The phone buzzed, and he snatched it to his ear, grinning as he heard the news.

"Excellent. Take it directly to lab-45, we're all set." He watched on the monitor as the helicopter touched down and his technicians raced to meet it.

He replaced the phone. "Aren't we, Harry?" Jim looked toward his ever-morose colleague, Harry McManus, who was standing beside him also watching the monitor.

"Sure, ready as we'll ever be … with what we've got."

"Yeah, well, we'd all like more funding, Harry." Jim sighed. "But we aren't going to get it, are we? And with a downed shuttle, it's going to be even tighter to get budget approval next year."

Harry groaned, grumbled to himself and folded his arms, his eyes still on the monitor as technicians took the sealed container from the helicopter pilot. "Strange business." Jim turned. "But was it there under the ice, or did it come down in the shuttle?" He turned back to the screen. "Or, is it finally our stardust?"

Harry shrugged. "According to the *Orlando*'s mission manifest, there were plenty of plant and animal specimens onboard."

"Blasted by radiation, yeah maybe," Jim stood. "We'll do this one by the numbers, right?"

"Always do," Harry mumbled.

* * *

Harry McManus cursed the primitive conditions that he and fellow astro-biology scientist Sarah Mantudo had to work in as he perspired into his heavy polyurethane suit. He shifted and rubbed an arm against his side, trying to wipe away a tickling river of sweat running down to further soak his underwear.

The private sector had so much more money, he cursed, and therefore top of the line facilities, staff, and rates of pay he could only dream about. Government agencies had to fight for every scrap. And Jim was right, a multi-billion-dollar shuttle orbiter going down didn't exactly scream *money well spent*.

He could only grimace and put up with his slicked hair and hot, red face behind his splatter mask and bio-filter.

He snorted; they didn't even have full HAZMATS or negative-air-pressure labs. They sort of faked it and usually that was enough. But today, he didn't think it was, and that made him nervous as hell.

He blinked and tried to focus on his work. Initial analysis showed the *Orlando* sample contained two things: the first was the greenish-brown blob of biological matter. The second thing was some of the gases that had collected in the mountain-crater basin.

The spectroscopic analysis hadn't been conclusive, answering a few questions, but raising dozens more.

Harry read the chart again and shook his head as he looked at the elemental breakdown of the atmospheric gas. The thing was, today's atmosphere contained approximately seventy-eight percent nitrogen, twenty-one percent oxygen, one percent argon, and 0.4 percent carbon dioxide, plus small amounts of other gases and water vapor, depending where you were on the planet.

But the gases from the *Orlando* sample were extremely high in methane, carbon dioxide and thirty-two percent oxygen – eleven percent higher than in the current global atmosphere. This stuff was thick and heavy, the greenhouse gas from hell, and was one possible reason for why the gases were creating a sort of heavy environmental bubble over the Alaskan mountaintop.

But he knew there was a precedent for this type of atmospheric structure. Harry let his mind wander – hundreds of millions of years ago the sun was only about seventy percent as bright as it is today. Earth should have frozen over, but it didn't because heavy gases in the atmosphere trapped enough of the sun's heat to keep it warm.

And he also had a suspect. Harry looked at the pictures the scanning microscope had taken moments before. He had also run a biological filtration over the mixture, and the results both intrigued and alarmed him – there were significant amounts of a free-floating spores, sub-microscopic, and some little bigger than a virus. They would have easily been missed if he hadn't run them through the micron filters.

He enlarged one of them, looking closely at the spiky ball with a whip-like tail. There were also small holes all over the spore that seemed to quiver, or vibrate, as if ... he frowned, looking across to the collected matter in the filter.

Harry grabbed a small microphone and set it up over the mass of spores, and recorded for a few minutes before transferring it to the computer. He ran it back, and his screen showed the vibrations as a constant sound, so he turned it up. There it was. A sort of whine, like wind whistling in through window cracks of an old house.

There were plenty of precedents – after all, *Urnula Craterium* was a species of mushroom that hissed as it released its spores. But this had more of a musical note texture. Harry chuckled softly. Maybe these guys are all singing to us. *Or screaming ...*

That's enough of that, he thought

He went back to his scope, peering down at the microscopic entities. They were similar to the bluish-green microscopic organisms called cyanobacteria that lived in Earth's oceans. They absorbed carbon dioxide, water, and sunlight via a process of photosynthesis, and then they gave back oxygen. But these little guys from the mountaintop were also giving off a whole range of gas mixes and were airborne, and nothing like their water-based cousins – if they were even related.

As Harry watched several of the microbes used their spikes to join together, then more of them, until they had formed a clump that settled on the floor of the container, creating a tiny speck. *Like the slime.* But then they broke apart and dissipated into a gas again that was an atmospheric primordial soup.

Harry looked over at his colleague, Sarah. "Have you got a sec?" he asked.

Sarah lifted her head from her microscope, and listened as Harry told her what he'd just learned about the microbes and the heavy gases.

"Gigantism," she said distractedly.

He straightened. "Go on." He concentrated, deciphering the mushy words coming through her bio-filter.

Sarah continued to work on the biological sample for a few more moments. "Remember the insects during the Carboniferous period?" She looked up from her microscope. "They grew large in the air, some as big as condors, and on the ground, to horse size. Insects don't have lungs, but instead a tracheal breathing system, which limits how big they can get because they can't absorb the necessary oxygen. But millions of years ago when oxygen levels were higher, then those upper limits didn't apply."

"*Meganeura*," Harry said softly, referring to an ancient, extinct dragonfly as big as an eagle.

"Yep, plus spiders the size of a small dog and even a freaking millipede nearly nine feet – would not have been a fun time to be a soft-bodied mammal." She went back to looking down her scope.

"Interesting," Harry said. The weird thing was that he had just read a paper that postulated that early forms of bacteria had been a factor in the first instances of evolution in organisms – they had triggered cellular and even DNA changes. And the most abundant bacteria on a primordial Earth could have been like the ones he was seeing. It had always been suspected that life on the planet was kick-started by microorganisms that arrived from somewhere else in the universe.

Harry stared off into the distance and let his mind work. What effect would they have on life now, if they arrived again?

Perhaps another catalyst for the evolutionary process – to both man and beast?

Gigantism, Sarah had said. He mulled the word over as he sifted through the implications. He shook his head to clear away some frightening thoughts.

"Anyway, how're your tests going? Anything interesting?"

"Well ..." She nodded slowly into her microscope eyepiece. "This substance has switched on, become activated, probably because of the higher temperatures in the laboratory." She looked sideways at him. "In a freezing environment, it's inactive. In a moderately warm environment like on the mountaintop, it'd start to grow, but primarily stay benign. But here, like in this lab where it's seventy-two degrees, its metabolism is accelerating." She looked back down. "It seems highly caustic and looks to be converting organic matter. A little like some sort of digestion process."

"Caustic – an acid? Is it excreting it?" Harry asked. "You need to—"

"Yes and no, and more like coated in it, *now*," she responded. "And yes, Harry, I have checked the data, three times. It's coated in a substance that's suspiciously like a digestive enzyme."

"It's certainly unique. In the atmospheric sample, I can see spore-like microbes free floating. I would expect that if this embeds in an organism it might influence the DNA." He turned to her. "Perhaps even making mutagenic changes there."

Sarah snorted. "More likely just give you a nasty burn."

Harry sighed. "Jesus Christ, you know what? We shouldn't be working on this stuff here. It requires much greater scientific scrutiny, better equipment, and a truckload more damned biosecurity."

"Harry, we work with what we've got. That's what makes us great." Sarah turned and winked before looking back down into her microscope eyepiece, and moving the sample a little under the lens. She reached up to adjust the scope at her eye a tad.

"Yeah, great." He was about to turn away when he noticed that she had her visor up again.

He sighed. "Jesus, Sarah, will you at least please put your face mask down?"

She made a guttural sound in her throat. "I can't see a damn thing. And the vents are working full blast anyway."

Their benchtops had vents that sucked the air down to the filters, scrubbers and incinerators. Nothing should float free at all. Sarah pointed at them, and then turned, looking angry, and slapped the mask down over her face.

"Thank you." Harry sighed again, louder and longer this time. He should have refused to work on the samples unless he and Sarah had biosafety level-4 facilities.

He snorted. *Like bullshit he'd refuse.* If he'd said no, then NASA would have called up that weasel, Bernie Hillstrop, to come in and do the analysis; he was dying to take over Harry's department. He clicked his tongue. Still, the risk of contamination was extreme.

All biologists and especially astrobiologists knew that human life, in fact *all* life on Earth, was precariously balanced and therefore fragile. One of the reasons for its survival was a thin skin surrounding the planet – the ozone layer – that acted as a solar blanket, and a shield against anything trying to enter. Only the largest objects could make it through, but were usually then obliterated on impact. But anything else ended up being vaporized before it could touch down on the planet's surface.

Nothing could get through – Harry straightened – unless you brought it through inside your space shuttle and transported it all the way to the ground.

"Harry, come and give me your opinion here." Sarah stood beside the microscope, and fiddled with her mask again.

"Something interesting happening with your mold?" he asked.

"Mold? This thing is to mold as a Neanderthal is to modern man." She pointed a finger at his chest. "You know, that might just be it. If you took some mold and let it evolve for a few million years, you might get something like this."

"That's a bit of a stretch," he said as he leaned over her scope. He placed his eye over it, and adjusted the resolution. Sarah was right; it was damn hard to see while wearing the Plexiglas splatter mask as it distorted the image.

Sarah crouched down next to him. "Rapid cell division, and looks like they're differentiating."

"So? We knew it was still viable."

"Yeah, I *know* that, but once I added in a simple sugar solution, these cells immediately consumed it – and I mean, *quick*. I think this stuff will eat *anything*. But that's not all; then it started budding – and I mean massive sporogenesis."

"Damn, wish we had the instruments to weigh the molecular weight of the samples before and after, but ..." he shrugged.

"Yeah, yeah, blah, blah, no budget." Sarah grinned and looked skyward for a moment.

Harry looked back into the lens. "*Hmm*, you're right, definitely bigger though." He watched as the material divided, bubbled and slid, converting the last of the sugars into more of ... *itself*.

"Like a Trojan Horse," he whispered.

"Huh?" Sarah leaned closer.

"The *Orlando* ... it was like a Trojan horse, bringing this *stuff* in past our safe walls, our atmospheric shield." He turned to look at Sarah who had her visor up yet again.

"Sarah, will you please *drop that visor*. We're exposing ourselves to enough damn risk as it is."

"Can't work with this stupid thing, Harry." She snapped it down, cursing under her breath, and then folded her arms.

"Anyway, if you want my opinion, this mold reminds me a little of a polyphyletic organism."

"Polyphyletic?" Harry frowned. "You mean like a slime mold?"

"Yeah, sort of, but much more advanced. And those spores that're free floating in the atmosphere, well, this stuff is saturated with them." She laid a hand on the base of the microscope. "It's acting like a cellular entity now, like a *protist* slime mold. But when I first started to examine it, it was more like a *plasmodial* slime mold, in that it was enclosed within a single membrane without walls and as one large cell – a super cell."

"Syncytium." Harry came closer.

"Yes. Essentially nothing more than a bag of cytoplasm containing thousands of individual nuclei."

"I saw it; the spores clumped together, and then broke apart – almost at will. But what does that tell us?" Harry asked. "You're the expert."

"Well, it tells me it likes the warmth. It triggers its metabolism, switches it on, makes it get *hungry*, and then it sprays spores and goes looking for food." She tilted her head. "It decides when it wants to be a single cell, or individual cells – it can coalesce at will."

"From *protist* to *plasmodia*? That's a neat trick. It decides if it wants to be big or small. Hey, you think it's doing this consciously?" Harry waved that thought away. "That's dumb, forget I said that."

"No, no, not dumb at all," she said. "But if not consciously, then surely instinctively. After all, ants can operate as individuals, but also form colonies and act as a single hive mind."

Harry nodded.

"There's nothing like it, Harry. *Nothing.*" Sarah had her hands on her hips, and her eyebrows were way up. She grinned. "Understand?"

"What?" He tilted his head.

"There's nothing like it, *on Earth.*" She beamed.

He scoffed. "Let's not get ahead of ourselves."

"Why not?" She grabbed his arm. "Life from space; this could be it." She grinned. "Here's NASA's damned stardust, Doctor Harry H. McManus."

He laughed. "Well, let's hope not, or they might ..." his face dropped, and he stared.

"What?" She frowned back at him.

There was a speck in the white of one of Sarah's eyes. He frowned and craned his neck forward to see a little better through their visor shields.

"*What?*" She took a step back.

Harry peered at her. "Did you touch the slide and then your microscope lens?"

"Maybe, I don't know." Her brows snapped together. "What the fuck, Harry?"

"When your visor was up, did you ... *did you let the lens touch your face?*"

"I don't ..." She raised a gloved hand, the fingers hovering inches from her cheek. She looked like she desperately wanted to touch it. Her head whipped from one side to the other, perhaps searching for something reflective to look into.

"Hold still." Harry raced to the benchtop and got a swab; a long, thin stick with cotton fibers wound around one end.

She flipped up her splatter mask. "Is there something there? Is it on me? Please tell me it's not on me."

Harry saw panic on her face, and he grabbed her arm.

"It's corrosive, but ..." Sarah tugged back. "We don't know what it can do to mammalian tissue. *We don't know what it can do!* Get it off me."

Harry grabbed her again. "Just hold still." He held up the swab, preparing to wipe away the biological speck. Sarah's eyes widened in fright. "*Hoooold* it right there." He eased the swab toward the speck.

It moved.

Harry jerked back, and immediately regretted it. Sarah gulped air in horror, like a drowning swimmer going down for the last time. Harry also felt a bolt of fear run through his gut. The thing had moved away from the swab, he was *sure* of it.

Behind his visor it was becoming stifling. He tried to blink away the rivulets of sweat running down his face.

"Sorry, Sarah, *ah*, missed it. Stay still."

His hand shook when he reached out again. But this time when he neared it, the tiny speck of matter darted away across her eyeball. He jabbed at it but missed, and the blob vanished into the corner of Sarah's eye.

"*Fuck!*"

Sarah's expression turned to outright terror and she backed up, her hands up and fingers curled into claws. "*What*, Harry?"

"I, I missed it." He swallowed in a dry throat and his mind felt like it was short-circuiting from fear.

"You missed it – *twice?* What the fuck does that mean?" She tore off her visor and flung it across the room and then spun back. "How did you miss it? *How?*" She suddenly jerked a hand up toward her face, and he grabbed it holding it away. Her arm was trembling. Or was that his?

"Sarah, please, just hold still, dammit, and sit down." He pushed her back into a seat, and ripped his own visor off, dropping it; to hell with his own safety.

He searched for the tripod magnifying glass, grabbed it and stood it on the desk next to her. He switched on its ring of halogen lights and angled it toward her.

"Open your eyes wide, and look to your right." Sarah shivered and the color had drained from her face, but to her credit, she kept still and did as he asked.

Harry looked deep into the outer corner of her eye. The orb itself looked normal, if not a little red from a spray of fine spidery veins. He was sure his own eye looked the same – lack of sleep, too much coffee, and eyestrain from staring down too many microscope lenses.

"*Eeeasy*, just hold it there." He tried to keep his voice soothing, as she had gripped his wrists, *tight*.

"Look away." The pupil stayed where it was. "Sarah, look away please." He insisted.

"I am."

Harry frowned, pulling back a moment, and noticing that her other orb had shifted the pupil away into the corner as he instructed. But the one he was examining stayed fixed – on him.

"Are you sure y—"

The errant pupil finally slid away from him – but in the opposite direction of its twin.

He frowned. "*Uh*, are *you* doing that?"

"Doing what?" Her grip on his wrist got tighter. "What are you talking about?" She pushed at him. "Hand me a mirror ... or the specimen tray."

Harry glanced at the silver tray. "Not yet." He hung onto her. "Keep looking away."

Sarah's eye turned to fix on him, but only the one he was examining.

"It stings, Harry." She whimpered, and a tear ran down her cheek. "And I'm getting a headache."

"Don't worry, I'm just going to rinse it out." Harry felt a hard knot tighten in his stomach. The eye was a gateway to the human body, and a direct path to the brain.

Harry lifted a small vial of sterile saline solution, and let some drip into the eye. The fluid didn't stay on the eye's surface, but seemed to be immediately absorbed.

This stuff will eat anything, Sarah had said.

He put a few more drops in, then a lot more. It all just seemed to drain inwards.

Then, to his horror the pupil just melted away to leave a totally white orb. Then the entire eye shriveled like a deflating balloon, and then collapsed back into an empty socket.

Gas escaped from the gaping hole – horrifyingly, he smelled it through his bio-filter – methane, CO_2, nitrogen, just like from the *Orlando* sample. He wasn't wearing his visor and he quickly held his breath, and went to pull back, but Sarah's hand on his arm tightened.

Her mouth dropped open. "*Gah.*"

"Let go, Sarah," He let the empty water vial fall to the floor, and used his spare hand to try and dislodge her fingers. "*Please – let go – now.*"

"*Gah, gah.*" Her mouth swung wider as it worked, as if she was suddenly unable to speak the language.

"*Gah, ga-aaah.*"

Her other eye shrunk into the socket.

"Oh god, Sarah." Harry's head whipped around to the phone on the wall. He needed help – he snatched at her hand that was pressing so hard on his forearm now that his fingers were beginning to throb.

"*Gaaa-aaaaaaaaaaa ...*"

Harry felt his colleague begin to vibrate, and there came a small moan, but it was his own voice. He gave up trying to dislodge her hand and instead used his greater mass to drag himself and her with him toward the phone on the wall.

Sarah came slowly, but she was strangely heavy. Not fighting against him, but more a dead weight, like he was dragging a sack of wet sand.

"*Help!*" His yell did little but echo in the sealed laboratory. Harry continued to drag at Sarah, and the pain in his forearm was so acute now, that his hand was swelling and his fingers wouldn't bend anymore. It felt as if someone had looped steel cables around his arm and yanked it tight.

He looked down at her upturned face; the empty sockets were dark moist holes, and her mouth hung slack. However, her jaws still worked as though she was desperately trying to speak.

"Ga-*aaaaaaacgghhhkkk.*"

Her gag became a wet, ragged sound, and then insanely he saw within her open mouth that her tongue had crumpled back into her throat. Her head looked tiny, as the collar on her suit swamped her.

Harry felt sanity leaving him. "*Heeeeeelp!*" He screamed even harder and yanked at her, pulling furiously.

Contaminated, was all he could think. *The sample infected her.*

Harry finally tugged them both to the wall phone, but in his panic he couldn't dial, or even speak. To his left he spotted the fire alarm.

He leaned across and punched the huge, red button on the wall, and then turned to lean against it as the klaxon horn sounded and a red light began to spin slowly over his head. Sarah was still hanging on to his arm, but had slid to the ground. He looked down at her and saw her body looked strangely misshapen.

Harry was now hyperventilating, but froze in confusion when he saw a long smear of greenish-brown emanating from the legs of her suit as though she was leaking something. He knew that in death, and even in extreme trauma, the bowels and bladder can void, but this stuff looked horrifyingly like the material that had been sent to them in the sample Sarah had been investigating. What had Sarah told him? That it was converting matter.

Looking back at her, he couldn't see her face anymore. It was as if her head had retreated into her suit.

His arm was numb from her grip before, but now it stung like fire. He looked down and saw that Sarah's fingers had somehow penetrated the thick rubberized polymer material of his suit sleeve. She had managed to rip open the tough fabric and worm her fingers inside to be against his flesh.

"God no, no, no." His head throbbed and he began to taste something unpleasant at the back of his throat that was obviously welling up from his stomach.

He turned. "*Hurry-yyyyyyy!*" His scream was futile but all he had left.

Harry began to weep as he watched what was once his friend and coworker's suit writhe and palpitate on the floor as though there were small animals fighting within it. The revolting wriggling moved up her arm toward his.

"*Stardust,*" he whispered, and started to cry.

* * *

"*Jesus!*" Chief science officer Jim Teacher jumped about a foot out of his seat as the klaxon horn sounded.

"Fire drill ... *now?*" he asked his empty office. He grabbed at his phone, calling through to security. He sniffed, not smelling smoke. There'd still be an evacuation, he bet.

Security came back to him quickly.

"Where is it?" Jim asked.

"Alarm initiation point is lab-45, sir." Jim overheard them conducting a background discussion for a few moments before they came back on the line. "Doesn't seem to be any thermal warnings, so maybe it's chemical spill. We're still calling an evacuation to be safe and heading down now. The fire department has been notified."

"Okay, I'm on my way." Jim hung up. *Lab-45 – that was where Harry and Sarah were working.* He headed for the door.

Under the relentless, blaring alarms, people were filing out to their designated assembly areas, and Jim worked his way back through the tide of people. Lab-45 was an underground unit and in a module separated by several hundred yards of white corridor – good for security and for fighting fires, but bad if you needed to get to it in a hurry.

Jim sprinted now, the horn obliterating all other background noises. He shouldered open the double white doors to the laboratory complex and entered the outer offices. It was now deserted and he slowed to a jog as he counted down the labs getting to 45. Finding it, he entered the outer control room and walked toward the large double-layered, toughened glass of the window. Jim stepped up close.

There was smoke but no fire, nor was there any sign of Harry or Sarah. The once pristine and sterile white room was putrid. He stepped closer and squinted. What he had assumed was smoke seemed to be some sort of speckled, particulate gas, heavier near the floor.

Jim grimaced; revoltingly, there did look to have been some sort of explosion within the hermetically sealed room. The floor and walls were lumped with a greenish-brown matter, and there were even strands of it hanging from the ceiling. He quickly checked a live CCTV feed from the airlock between the rooms and finding that also empty, he pressed the intercom.

"Harry? Sarah?"

He frowned, trying to see around the streaks running down the window and let his eyes run over the room's interior. He pressed the open mic again.

"Harry, where the hell are you, buddy?"

He pressed himself up closer to the window spotting something. "There you are."

On the floor in the corner, there were two tangled hazardous material suits but strangely deflated looking. *They took 'em off? Why?*

Jim moved along the edge of the window, trying to see into every nook and cranny. There was really nowhere for anyone to hide, unless they had forced themselves into one of the small cabinets, which would be impossible for someone like Harry, who was stick-thin but six-three.

Both the inner and outer airlock doors were still sealed, and he damn well didn't pass them on the way down here. He turned as two security guards entered carrying fire extinguishers.

"Stay back." He held a hand up in their faces.

"Chem-spill?" One asked and looked past Jim. His lips curled. "Jesus, it's a freaking mess in there. Is everyone out?"

"I ... don't know." Jim continued to stare in at the suits, and as he watched, the larger of the two, wriggled slightly.

"Wait." Jim stared.

The suit's arm began to move. His brows drew together just as something that looked like a mouse-sized blob of green-brown mud squeezed out. It left the end of the sleeve and continued to slide across the white floor until it came to another mound of the same material, where it promptly merged with it. The larger mass quivered momentarily.

"Oh god, *Harry*." Jim's mouth hung open.

"Harry McManus and Sarah Mantudo." One of the security guards checked a digital pad. "According to this, they're still on the base. They must have got past us."

"No, no they didn't," Jim said and put a hand over his mouth feeling his gorge rise. "They never left the room - they're still in there."

"What? Where?" The guard turned and squinted.

Jim pointed. "I think, *there*."

"That ... *shit*? What the fuck happened to them?"

"Maybe contamination, or some sort of infection." It was crazy, but Jim knew it was true even as he said it. It was something NASA had war-gamed for decades.

The security man looked disgusted. His face then became smooth. "Protocols, sir."

Jim took a step back. The room was a fully sealed germ and fungal containment unit. It didn't have all the modern facilities from the private sector, but there was one thing they didn't scrimp on.

"I'm recommending *immediate* sterilization, sir." The guard's voice became hard.

"I ... I was ..." Jim shook his head to clear it. "Yes." He crossed to a heavy box on the wall, keyed in a code and waited for it to pop open. Inside there was a small pad with a tiny green light and a single button clearly marked: *Lab-45 Room Sterilization.*

"Goodbye, my friends," he whispered. He didn't hesitate and pressed the button.

The room was flooded with gas, momentarily clouding his vision, and then it was ignited. Everything turned a brilliant red, as in seconds temperatures in the room blasted to 1,600 degrees.

"*What – the fuck – was that?*" the guard said softly, his face shining red from the glow of the window.

Jim turned back, feeling the heat right through the toughened glass. "I don't know," Jim said and sat down before he fell down. "But everything that occurred in that lab would have been recorded. So, we goddamn better find out fast."

"Fucking nightmare," the other guard said, and wiped a hand up over his forehead.

"Yeah, and it gets worse," Jim said. "We have people right in the middle of where that stuff came from."

CHAPTER 21

Fermi National Accelerator Laboratory, Batavia, Illinois

Jack Hammerson's eyes flicked to the rearview mirror. Aimee Weir sat in the back of the black SUV with her arm looped around Joshua's shoulders.

"How's school, Josh?"

Joshua shrugged. "Dumb, boring."

Hammerson smothered a smile as Aimee nudged the boy. "It's not boring." She looked up. "He just finds the pace a little slow."

Hammerson nodded. "Well, we've got some special classes in at the base ready for him if he'd like to take a look." He raised his eyebrows. "They'll be far from boring."

Aimee's eyes narrowed. "I don't think so."

Hammerson shrugged. "Self-defense, strategic thinking and analysis ... and I hear they need smart young people who have puppy dogs."

"*Huh?* That'll be me." Joshua turned, grinning widely.

"No," Aimee said.

Joshua scowled. "Mom, I want to do it."

"We'll talk about it later." Aimee turned away.

Hammerson smiled. He'd wanted to get Joshua in for special testing for years. This was his opportunity.

If anything ever happened to Alex Hunter, or the man went rogue, it'd be good for his special military team to have a close relationship with the boy. In the future, his talents may be able to be exploited.

Joshua sat up straighter as they approached the security gates. "Uncle Jack?"

Hammerson grinned at hearing the boy refer to him like that. "Yeah, Josh?"

"Is that one of the Guardians?"

Hammerson looked back to the gates where a tall security guard had a dog sitting beside him. It was an enormous German shepherd that came to his waist, and must have weighed in at 140 pounds if it was an ounce.

"I bet it is," he responded cheerily.

"Jesus, Jack, will ours get that big?" Aimee's voice was awed.

Hammerson chuckled. "Only if you overfeed it." He slowed at the gates and let the window down. He turned in his seat. "So not too many treats, okay, Josh?"

"Not *too* many." Josh grinned. "Just some."

Aimee groaned, but still smiled down at him.

Hammerson handed over his ID and the guard looked at each of them briefly. He stood back and the dog got up on its hind legs and peered in at each of them, inhaling deeply, doing its own security check.

It fixed its eyes on Joshua and stared. After another few seconds, it backed away and dropped back down.

"Creepy," Aimee said.

"Cool. I felt it in my head," Joshua quickly added.

For some reason Hammerson thought the dog had been standing up on its hind legs without needing to lean on the car. The guard waved them on, and he looked in the rearview mirror at the boy.

"In your head, huh? And can you *feel* inside other people's heads, Josh? Like mine?" His eyes flicked from the road to the boy.

"No." The boy smiled.

Hammerson felt relieved, but then ...

"Unless I try." His honest smile widened.

Hammerson cleared his mind. "Best if you don't *read* other people, Josh. It can be intrusive. But we can talk more on that later."

"Or not." Aimee added.

They next headed toward the main building, the huge white edifice that looked like two slices of toast leaning up against each other.

Hammerson branched off on a side road, heading toward a smaller white domed building. "We're meeting Doctor Albert Harper, the chief physicist at the animal facility."

Aimee wound down her window. "Jack, these animals, they're safe, right? You wouldn't be putting some sort of experimental animal in with my family, would you?"

Hammerson saw concern in her eyes as he glanced into his rear view. The thing was they *were* experimental. But the Guardians were into the fourth-generational iteration of breeding stock, and Harper had developed a pure strain. He knew Aimee would never buy that answer – she didn't trust him, and probably never would.

So he lied. "You have my word on it."

They pulled off the drive to where a short, balding man waited for them with his arms clasped behind his back. He lifted one to wave.

"Here he is, the man himself, Doctor Albert Harper." Hammerson stepped out and quickly opened the rear door for Aimee and Joshua. The boy nearly flew out, obviously expecting Harper to produce a puppy from under his lab coat.

"Albert." Hammerson waved.

"Jack." Harper gave him a small salute followed by a smile.

Hammerson stood aside. "May I present Doctor Aimee Weir, and a young man looking for a puppy dog."

Aimee strode forward, hand out. Harper shook it firmly. He then shook Joshua's hand.

"Looking for a puppy, huh? Well, you came to the right place. You're a lucky boy, Joshua; these dogs are very special."

"So is he," Hammerson said, meaning it.

"That's what I hear," Harper said.

Hammerson felt Aimee's eyes on him, as she was probably wondering what he had divulged about Alex Hunter's son.

"Lead on," he said to Harper.

Harper led them into the animal facility, and they passed through some administration offices with a few guards monitoring cameras and other equipment. Harper turned to Joshua.

"Have you ever had a dog before?"

Joshua shook his head, his eyes on the pens. "No sir, but I've read everything about them and I like them a lot. And I *always* wanted one."

Harper nodded. "Well, that's good enough for me."

Aimee was tight-lipped. "A small one would have been a good start."

Harper smiled. "Well. they all start small, right? And these guys don't yap all the time, and in fact can grow to anticipate what you want. They're smart."

Then they entered the main animal pen area, and Aimee winced at the cacophonous sound of howls, yelps, and barks.

She snorted. "They sound pretty noisy to me."

There came a single loud grunt from the rear of the room and it immediately quietened.

Harper turned to Hammerson. "Fen knows we're here."

"Who?" Aimee frowned.

"Big Fen, the sire," said Harper. "He's the pack leader, and the first of our new breed of Guardians. He's perfect, and has an IQ that ..."

Hammerson cleared his throat, and Harper shut down. He smiled, adding: "He's their leader, *ah*, pack leader."

Joshua nodded. "I can't wait to own one."

Hammerson turned to Joshua. "You don't own these dogs, Joshua, you adopt them as a family member."

"That's right," Harper said. "But first you'll need to meet Fenrir, or Big Fen as we call him in here. Okay?"

Joshua eyes were wide. "But what if he says no?"

"Then you'll just have to convince him to say *yes*." He slowed. "Here we are."

Harper had Hammerson, Aimee and Joshua stop before a large pen. Hammerson saw it was more a room than an animal cage, and seated in the middle of it was the largest damn German shepherd he had ever seen in his life. His mind immediately screamed: *wolf*, but he kept it behind his teeth.

"Oh, my, *god*." Aimee's mouth hung open.

The dog had a blanket over its shoulders, and its unnatural blue eyes stared into each human's momentarily, lingering on Hammerson and narrowing for a moment or two, before then fixing on Joshua. There they stayed.

"Holy *cow*." The boy stared back, unblinking.

Hammerson noticed the blanket over the dog's shoulders looked weirdly lumped as if there were real shoulder joints there, and it was broad, and not the usual narrow, slim slope of a canine's front half. He also had the impression it wasn't sitting on its haunches, but resting like a person.

"Fenrir." Harper nodded, but to the dog.

There was silence for a few moments, as the group took the large dog in. It was Joshua who broke it.

"Yes," Joshua said, his eyes on the dog. "Yes, I will. I promise."

"What, honey?" Aimee looked down, and then crouched beside the boy.

Joshua ignored her, never turning away from Fen. "I promise he'll be my friend forever. No, my *brother*." He nodded. "Yes, with honor, nobility, and strength, I promise."

The dog grunted and closed its luminous eyes. Joshua turned, beaming. "He said yes."

Harper nodded. "I knew Big Fen would. He can sense a good heart."

Aimee scoffed. "You're kidding, right?"

Harper shrugged, about to respond, when Hammerson silenced him with a look.

"*Hmm.*" Aimee raised an eyebrow.

Joshua led the way, his grin splitting his face. "Fenrir wanted him brought up with honor, nobility, and strength. I promised I'd do it." He looked up at Aimee. "Torben is the firstborn of Fenrir and Morgana."

They came to a larger area that housed eight tumbling puppies, all wrestling, rolling, and playing. All except one that sat at the gate. Joshua ran and then crouched before it.

"Torben."

The puppy put its paw up at the wire, and Joshua did the same as they stared into each other's blue eyes.

Aimee looked incredulous. "We have to ask its father for his permission to adopt, and then here it is with its travel bag all packed and ready to go – where's its toothbrush and pajamas?"

Hammerson laughed. "I guess sometimes things were just meant to happen."

On the way back out to the SUV, Joshua had the dog in his arms, and talked softly to it as it dozed. The trio had to wait as a school bus came through the front gate and pulled up, disgorging a group of boisterous teenage students.

One of the students, a tall young man, stood looking up at Fermilab for a moment, and Hammerson saw he looked to have Native American features. He turned to them and spotted the puppy in Joshua's arms.

"Hey, nice pup – Shepherd, *huh*? I've got one at home." He went to walk on, but Joshua spoke up.

"Yep, and he's mine." Joshua looked up at him. "His name's Torben, but I'll call him Tor."

"Okay, cool." He nodded, and stuck out a hand. "I'm Arn."

"Joshua." He shook Arn's hand, his smile immediately dropping. "You're going on a trip."

Arn shrugged, and looked less than enthused. "Yeah, school excursion – to this place."

Joshua shook his head slowly. "No, a lot further than that."

"What?" Arn frowned, letting Josh's hand go.

"Joshua?" Aimee stepped toward him, but the boy continued to stare up at the youth. Arn backed away. "A bit freaky, dude."

Hammerson's phone beeped and he pulled it from his pocket to check the message. "Excuse me." He turned away as he read. There had been a significant incident at NASA's astrobiology labs where the samples from the mountaintop had been taken. He felt a knot of unease coil in his gut.

Jack Hammerson put the phone back in his pocket and turned. He pasted on a smile and laid his hand on Joshua's shoulder.

"Time to go, Josh. Let's get your new pal home."

* * *

Hammerson tapped his chin with a knuckle as he read the reports from NASA's astrobiology labs. It was a fucking nightmare.

He gritted his teeth as he stared; give him armed combat, give him terrorists, or something tangible to fight against, and he'd prevail every damn time. But this was something that scared the shit out of him.

He replayed the footage from inside lab-45, seeing the two scientists first become infected, corrupted, and then, literally dissolve into lumps of mud, and just like Alex had said in his data squirt, *mud that goddamn moved.*

Whether it was some sort of aggressive mutation-causing pathogen in the atmospheric gas sample, or making contact with that creepy slime shit, the agreed prognosis from the NASA science teams was that as the temperature increased the biological matter became triggered, and its growth, aggression, and appetite accelerated. Bottom line: avoid physical contact at all cost.

The only upside he could take away was that the laboratory flash burn NASA initiated for full sterilization had totally eradicated everything. Significant heat left nothing but ash.

Hammerson then looked at the last of his related reports, the one that contained satellite data images of the *Orlando* crash site, viewed as a time-stamped progression map. The atmosphere bubble and the weird mist in the mountaintop crater continued to enlarge. Within hours, a few days at most, it would spill over the crater lip and begin to advance along the Alaskan Revelation Mountain valleyways.

He had ordered the retrieval, read *confiscation*, of the final samples that were in the NASA HAZMAT vaults and had them transferred to one of their military biology research centers. USSTRATCOM had their own specialized biohazard facilities that dealt with biological warfare defense and design and it was superior even to those of the CDC.

They'd done additional testing on the biomaterial from the mountaintop and the results were alarming, and, so far, a long way from illuminating. They found the gases were loaded with free-floating spores that seemed to seek out cells, inserting themselves into them, like sperm into the ova.

For one experiment, they introduced the material to two different laboratory rats in identical sealed capsules. In a few hours, one of the rats was nothing but a pile of gray sludge – that moved – just like what happened to the two scientists in NASA's lab-45.

But the next capsule's occupant had also been changed, but not in the same way. As the rat's body became saturated with the spores, it had grown bigger, stronger, and had shed its fur. It then developed what looked like a carapace of armor plating and a face that made Jack's hair stand on end. The rodent grew more eyes, larger teeth, and also a taste for flesh – it became an abomination from hell.

His scientists had told him the atmospheric gas sample had a unique biological content. The free-floating spores acted on an organism's genetic material triggering changes at the cellular and DNA level. Basically, it was a rapid-acting mutagen unlike anything they had ever seen.

The scientists had postulated that it probably didn't know it was causing problems, in fact, what it was doing was triggering massive changes – evolutionary – to cope with potential new surroundings. Anything inhaling, ingesting or even coming into contact with this stuff was going to be ... *altered*, one way or another.

Hammerson ran one large hand up through his iron-gray crew cut. How did it choose? Why did one rat become a monster and the other absorbed? He read on.

They assessed that the biological material could have begun as a single spore, and then started to grow the more it ingested. They surmised that the spores acted on a creature's DNA in different ways – some organisms it would bond with and accelerate their evolutionary changes to become a grotesquery. And others it would use to grow *itself*. This is what it had done with the NASA scientists – fed on them and converted them into itself.

He looked again at the before pictures of the rats – they seemed identical. But something in one of them had caused it to become a nightmare. Perhaps the spores had determined that one was strong enough to take the changes. And the other was fit only to serve as protein to be assimilated as a spore factory.

One became a warrior, and one became seeds – defense and reproduction, he thought. *Perfect infiltrate, spread, and advance strategy.*

Hammerson sat back; he still had so many questions. What would have happened to the scientists if it had found them worthwhile to be advanced to a new form of evolutionary state? And what would have happened next if the gray slime hadn't been incinerated? And had there been any fragment of Harry and Sarah's consciousness still existing in the new formless state? He blanched at the idea. *Bad shit.*

He then changed documents to reread Alex Hunter's brief information delivery from the top of the mountain. They were in the hot zone, and commencing their search. All was progressing to schedule.

Hammerson steepled his fingers. The temperature in that mountain basin was still fairly low at between forty and fifty degrees. According to NASA this was just enough warmth to switch the stuff on, but not enough for it to go bat-shit crazy like in lab-45.

It seemed to be still contained within the crater basin … for now.

But if it got out? His lips pressed into a tight line. *It had better not.*

Jack Hammerson looked again at the final images of Harry McManus and Sarah Mantudo, and then at his mission countdown clock.

He sighed as he picked up the phone. He had to tell the boss. And he bet he already knew what he'd recommend.

"Get me General Chilton."

CHAPTER 22

Alex took the lead with Casey Franks. They moved in a double line, jogging this time. Sam was close to the civilians, and even though Morag felt safer having the huge warrior so close to them, she still felt a shiver run from the base of her spine up to her scalp. The mountain crater top had moved from just being weird and creepy to now goddamn deadly.

The HAWCs had their shields facing the greasy looking forest, and to Morag it felt like she was inside a locomotive, with the swirling discs of compressed air as the wheels, and the walls of armored HAWC muscle their carriage.

The ground squelched beneath their feet, and several times Morag slid as they weaved in and around the huge columns that loomed from the mist. She couldn't determine if they were mutated trees, mud-coated rock formations, or the actual mud itself, trying to grow up and out of the crater. But the strange thing was there were more and more of them. And when she looked closer, she thought she could see movement inside them, like crustaceans and worms squirming in the soft mud of a riverbank at low tide.

After a while Alex called a halt and bent to pick something up. The soldiers immediately went into a defensive ring around him while his attention was diverted.

Morag marveled at how these Special Forces soldiers worked like a machine, every one of them knowing what was expected before it was even asked. Looking past them, she saw the muscles in Alex's shoulders bunch for a moment as if he was straining against what it was he held, or maybe against something inside him. After another moment, the HAWC leader tossed the thing aside.

"Double time." He waved them on, picking up his pace.

As Morag passed by the object she saw it was the missing HAWC's helmet, torn off and cracked open, like the skin of a watermelon. She glimpsed something moist inside it, but didn't want to look too closely because she already knew it was going to be blood.

Alex pushed his gun up over his shoulder and held up a hand. The group stopped.

"Sam."

The HAWC jogged forward, and Morag waved Calvin with her and muscled through the group so they could hear.

Alex and Sam stared at something on the ground, and Casey Franks faced the haze, her back to them, and gun up to cover them.

"Ah, shit." Sam's massive shoulder's fell.

Morag continued to watch Alex Hunter. She frowned. Oddly, his body looked like it was beginning to vibrate. On one arm, he held the swirling shield and over his back his gun. But his free fist was clenched and it shook as though he was under extreme pressure.

She inched forward to see what they had found – then wished she hadn't. Bones. All of them stripped of meat but still streaked with red strands of gristle and sinew. The larger ones were cracked to get at the marrow. Beside them was a shredded HAWC armored suit. The super-tough plating and Kevlar weave was no match for whatever had peeled the man out of it to get to the soft flesh beneath.

Steve Knight, she remembered him – he'd been a nice guy. Her breath caught in her throat. Knight was as tough as they come – but never stood a chance against whatever had taken him.

"Oh god." She turned away, and she heard Calvin gag. The final insult was the skull, sitting upright in the greasy mud. It, too, having anything edible – inside and out – ripped or scooped from it.

She heard a growl, deep and menacing. Morag turned back, made fearful by its proximity. Her first impulse was to back away, as she expected them to be confronted by the thing that had devoured the young HAWC. But she quickly found where the sound was coming from – *Alex Hunter*.

"Boss?" Sam reached out a hand toward his leader, and quickly turned to Casey Franks.

"Get 'em back."

The female HAWC immediately spun, pushing at the civilians and HAWCs alike. She elbowed Morag, but the journalist dodged around her and continued to watch.

Sam held Alex's shoulder, but Morag could see he was actually keeping him at a distance. He also brought his shield around to be between them.

"Pull it back, boss … *fight it,*" Sam urged softly.

Alex Hunter's two armored fists came up, still vibrating for a second or two before his rage exploded.

Sam stepped well back as Alex swung the arm that held the shield into an outcrop of rock, the granite protrusion blew apart into a thousand fragments with a noise the journalist even felt up through the soles of her feet. But he wasn't finished, with his free hand he swung back at the rock, punching it, and blasting out another huge piece of stone, which flung away into the shadowy mist.

Then, with a continuing roar, he battered the rock until the outcrop was rubble.

She knew that the HAWC gloves were armor plated, but she had to assume his hand was smashed to smithereens.

"*Stop that!*" she yelled. What good was he going to be to the group with just one hand?

Sam kept his distance as though waiting for the hurricane to blow itself out. Morag crossed to him, grabbing his hefty forearm.

"Lieutenant, aren't you going to stop him? He'll cripple himself."

Sam looked down, staring for a few seconds, before pushing her back behind him to shield her ... from Alex.

"No, he'll be fine. He's ... different to us." He looked back to where Alex was finishing demolishing the boulders, and whispered more to himself than to her. "He just needs to let him out."

She looked up at him. The way he said 'him', made her think it wasn't some sort of episode where he was just blowing off steam, but more like something – *someone* – that needed to escape. Her journalistic instincts immediately kicked in.

"Who ... *what*, is he *letting out?*"

"What?" Sam said distractedly, and then quickly looked back at her. "Nothing. He's just pissed. We all are."

"Nothing, *huh?*" She repeated and looked back at Alex. *More like something*, she bet.

After a moment more, Alex went to his knees, and placed one hand on the severed skull of Steve Knight for a moment as though saying farewell. He let his damaged right hand dangle at his side. He rose slowly.

"I fucking knew it," she whispered. Morag saw that his right hand was deformed from the impacts, as she expected it to be. In his gloves, she saw that the small bones of the fingers, the knuckles and the metacarpal bones in the hand were probably obliterated, and now more like splintered wood.

Idiot. Now you're fucking useless when we need you most.

She was about to give Sam Reid a piece of her mind, when she saw Alex Hunter straighten and roll his shoulders. He held up his smashed hand, and while she watched, the bones within the gloves seemed to pop back into place, the knuckles sliding and moving, and the fingers straightening.

"*What the …?*" Her mouth hung open.

"Like I said, he's different," said Sam.

Alex took in a deep breath and rejoined them. Sam Reid placed one hand on his shoulder.

"He's gone, boss, there's nothing more we can do."

Alex's eyes were still blazing. "We can be ready next time. These things are not indigenous, and whatever came down in that shuttle is a direct threat." He turned to the mist. "To be eliminated with extreme prejudice."

"I hear that," Sam said. He turned to Morag. "Let's go."

She let him direct her back to the group, but she turned a question gnawing at her. "Hey, I know one of the things you guys were supposed to do was search for survivors. If there was even the remote chance anyone made it down alive in that shuttle, how could they survive with those things down here?"

"They couldn't," Alex said.

Anne Peterson's arms were folded tight, as she overheard. "If the fuselage was intact, they could seal themselves in."

"Maybe, but unlikely," Alex said. "These things seem strong enough to peel the skin of the *Orlando* open. Better for the astronauts if they were dead when they arrived."

"Don't say that." Anne said something else, but it was unintelligible.

"It's okay, Anne," Scott McIntyre said, and reached out to put an arm around her, their suits chafing against each other. "We gotta keep some hope, right?" He looked from Alex to Sam.

Both had grim expressions.

"Let's find that shuttle, and get the hell out of here," Sam said.

Morag turned and saw Scott rub his wounded arm and grimace.

CHAPTER 23

Zlatan waved his men to a crouch. He momentarily ground his teeth from the pain behind his eyes – the headaches were still there, worse. And he was hungry all the time; not for the shitty protein bars they had all been given to last them the mission, but for something more … *substantial.*

He looked to his man closest to him – Stroyev – he looked different now. His brow seemed heavier, his entire head elongated. The man had never been handsome, in fact quite ugly. But now his features made him look grotesque. Even his eyes seemed – no, *were* – larger, and the pupils were glossy black and dominating the entire orb.

He faced away. *Maybe I'm seeing things in this damned dust-fog. Or maybe seeing things clearer.* He reached up and felt his forehead. There were strange bumps there and the brow was just as heavy as Stroyev's. *Oh Rahda, I wish I'd stayed with you.* But he was determined to finish his mission quickly and escape this hellish place. Once home, he knew his fantastic metabolism could heal anything. They'd all be good as new in no time.

Zlatan pivoted, realizing his vision was sharper now and he could see further into the mist. Now he could make out shapes, and his mind formed mental pictures, impressions, without even seeing them.

He peered around one of the slime trunks that seemed to be growing larger by the minute. He knew now their mission was nearly complete as he watched the remains of the downed space shuttle orbiter appear out of the mist.

Getting close, it was bigger than he expected. The craft was 122 feet in length, fifty-nine feet high, and with a wingspan of nearly eighty feet. Both stubby wings had been sheared off, and there was fragment debris everywhere. He could see the long skid line disappearing back into the smog where the shuttle had come in and slid to a halt. Surprisingly, the ship was mainly intact, and looked to have come in on its belly in the semblance of a controlled landing.

Zlatan was impressed. He doubted even the best pilots in Russia could have achieved that landing on a low-visibility mountaintop *and* inside a crater basin.

The *Orlando* was mostly buried in the revolting mud, and now it looked as if the slime was trying to claim the fuselage by growing up and over it. Strange fans, nobs, and growths like mushrooms seemed to undulate back and forth across the skin of the craft as though deep underwater and moving in a soft current.

There was a tear in the metal skin of the craft at the bay area, but unexpectedly, the front cockpit hatch was open. Zlatan had been briefed on the American shuttle design, and knew the door could only be opened from the outside with a unique NASA key, or from the inside by the astronauts.

He had no instructions as to what to do if he encountered American astronauts. They didn't concern him, and as long as they didn't interfere with his primary objective, they were of no consequence. But if they tried to intervene, then they would be terminated. It would be their choice.

Zlatan motioned for his men to advance. In a line, they moved forward. He and Torshin toward the open cockpit hatch, and Russlin and Stroyev toward the rear.

He shook his head, hard, and scowled – the damned humming or buzzing was becoming more insistent. It even overshadowed the incessant whine within the particle mist. But now the noise was almost understandable as if it was a language. He tried to block it out.

The slime was thickening as they neared the craft, ankle deep, and Zlatan could see it actually spilled from every opening and rent in the skin of the shuttle.

He and Torshin were first to arrive, and they eased along the side toward the open door. His hand went to a pouch at his belt that held a small flashlight, but changed his mind – he didn't need it anymore, as his eyes seemed perfectly comfortable in the low-light conditions. Zlatan nodded to Torshin and together they slipped inside, knives drawn.

There were no astronauts, alive or dead. As expected, the cockpit was in disarray, but amazingly a few of the tiny lights still glowed indicating that some power and possibly some applications were still running throughout the craft.

At the rear of the cockpit, there were some smashed glass specimen tanks, their contents gone. Torshin squinted at the remaining names still on the broken receptacles, and read in halting English: "*Bradypodidae* – three-toed sloth. *Theraphosidae Arachnida* – tarantula spider. *Driloleirus* – giant earthworm. *Orthoptera* – crickets. *Linepithema humile* – Argentinean ant colony." He snorted. "Maybe the bugs were the ones in charge of the craft."

Zlatan grunted. "Yes, funny; now find the camera data."

Torshin straightened and began looking over the control panels. The data should have been stored somewhere transportable so it could be rapidly recovered once the shuttle had landed. This meant the US military could get their hands on their prize before waiting on NASA to release it. Zlatan knew this also meant they probably wouldn't need to dismantle much of the equipment. All they'd need to do is find the media the images were stored on and eject it.

"Sir."

The call came from the doorway, and he turned to see Stroyev leaning in through the cockpit cabin hatch.

"What is it?"

"There is something you should see."

Zlatan turned to Torshin. "Find me that data." He followed Stroyev outside again and into the broken rear-bay area of the craft. Immediately he was assailed by the smell – rotting plant and animal matter, and something else he couldn't identify. The particle mist was even thicker inside.

"Look." Stroyev pointed.

In a cradle was a long piece of jagged stone. It had cracked open, showing a glowing green interior, and looked to be cooling as it gave off smoke-like vapor. Zlatan stared and saw that the vapor was actually the particle mist, and it came in waves, is if from exhalations. There was also a gray sludge seeping from it and plopping to the ground.

"So, this is where our strange mist and slime is coming from." Zlatan felt an odd attraction to the thing.

The mass inside the rock seemed to throb and drip the ooze. But closer to it, the odor was the most powerful.

"Stinks," Zlatan said.

Russlin seemed transfixed. "No, I think it smells ... *glorious*."

"Why would they carry this with them?" Stroyev held a hand up. "I can feel it; it's warm." He went to approach.

"Don't touch that," Zlatan said sharply. "Maybe they didn't take it with them, but collected it from space."

He snorted. "It's just a rock ... filled with hot mud."

Zlatan went to step closer, just as Russlin's voice turned his head.

"And these ..." Russlin used his knife to lift something orange from the ground. "They're everywhere, shredded uniforms." He squinted at the material. "Ripped to pieces." He looked up. "They tore them off?"

Stroyev snorted. "So, we have some naked American astronauts running around, *da*?" he bobbed his head, leering. "Was any female?"

Russlin crouched. "Bones." He gathered a few in his large hands. "And fresh." He straightened. "These look chewed." He lifted the two halves of a skull, cracked down the middle. "I think it used to be some type of ugly monkey."

The skull had huge teeth, more akin to that of a bear or wolf. But the cranium was oddly enlarged, deformed, and with way too many eyeholes.

Zlatan remembered the manifest. "They had live specimens onboard."

Russlin nodded. "Well, I think maybe someone got hungry." He grinned momentarily, and then brought it closer to his face and sniffed. He then shut his eyes and inhaled deeply, looking like he was enjoying the perfume. His mouth slowly opened, and his tongue eased out toward it.

"*What are you doing?*" Zlatan frowned.

"*Uh?*" Russlin shook his head, and looked confused. "Nothing, it just smelled ..." He dropped the skull portions. "*... nothing.*"

Zlatan looked around. The rear of the shuttle reminded him of something – the remnants of a meal, the balled packing materials, and torn cloth ... Then it hit him. A *nest*. Something was living here. Could it be the astronauts?

He turned, and tried to remember what Torshin had told him about the specimen list. There was nothing larger than a sloth or monkey.

But that skull Stroyev held up looked like neither. Had it changed somehow? Zlatan also remembered the monstrous thing that had attacked them and dragged Naryshkin down below the slime. It slid beneath the ground and burrowed up to get them – like a giant worm. He glanced at the worm specimen tank. Could it be the same thing? A creature that had somehow changed or been changed? By what?

Zlatan looked again at his men. All now seemed bulkier, misshapen. He looked at his hand and saw the fingers looked longer and thicker, and the end two now didn't separate until nearly the first knuckle. Plus, the nails were darkening and growing more round and sharp like talons.

What would Rahda think?

He turned to the rock fragment. *The gas.* The smell inside the bay area was overpowering. It was sweet and corrupt like decomposing vegetable matter. He walked toward the fragment of rock in its cradle, feeling the warmth against his face as he approached.

Zlatan stood before it, peering in past the glow and squinting to get a better view. He waved away some of the mist and saw the repulsive blob, like a ball of tangled spaghetti that throbbed and wrestled with itself. Tendrils emanating from a central mass undulated softly and it reminded him of some sort of giant amoeba. His head now thumped mercilessly as he bent forward.

Zlatan was transfixed, and watched as a one of the tendrils reached out and encircled his wrist. He recoiled, cursing, and was about to lash out at it but his mind scrambled and fizzed like static.

"*Kapitin.*"

"*Huh?*" He turned, confused. What had he been doing? He couldn't remember. His memories had been whited out, and there was a small ache in his wrist that made no sense.

Torshin held up a small disc, marked with the serial numbers they'd been told to look for. "Got it."

Zlatan nodded, relieved. "Good news. We go." He turned to leave, but his legs momentarily disobeyed him. He wanted to stay. More than anything in his life, he wanted to stay, with the rock, within the ship. He inhaled the gas, the scent was so strong inside the bay area, and its bouquet suddenly seemed intoxicating.

He pushed back; his mission was complete and home was where Rahda was. He shook his head, and then led his three Kurgan out.

He stopped dead, holding up his hand. Zlatan tilted his head, listening. "We have company."

He squinted, seeing the faint images of the approaching people. "The Americans." He reached behind him and pulled a four-foot steel rib from the skeleton of the *Orlando*.

His men did the same, and then spread out into the gloom.

CHAPTER 24

Drake Monroe held up his tracker and turned to Alex. "Shuttle, 300 feet, dead ahead."

"Got it." Alex slowed them from a jog to walking pace. He didn't need to see the slow-moving bodies to know there were living beings out there, waiting for them.

At first, he thought it might have been the monstrous attackers that had taken Steve Knight, but as he reached out and concentrated on them, he noticed something strange. He wasn't detecting the bestial sensations he had from the Morg. And he knew what human patterns felt like – the heartbeat, the breathing, and body warmth – but this was different again. Something in-between.

Everything is messed up in this damned place. Had to be the strange atmosphere; it was still making it difficult to identify anything accurately. Alex slowed again, and this time spread his team.

"What is it?" Russell Burrows asked.

Alex ignored him, and turned to the HAWCs. "Erikson, keep 'em all back, and keep 'em quiet."

"Sir." She slid away to the civilians pushing them away from the soldiers.

"The rest of you, eyes out. We're not alone." Alex turned back to the shuttle. Casey, Sam, Dunsen, Monroe, and Garcia had all drawn their RG3s and were moving like ghosts.

The HAWCs deployed their quad scopes with the four lenses lumping the front of their visors making them look like alien robots. Alex knew the HAWCs would be switching between thermal, light enhance and motion sensors trying to get an idea of what awaited them out there, but he knew nothing was fully penetrating the biological fog.

Alex didn't like leaving the civilians so far back, but he had no choice. If there was going to be an ambush, it'd be here, and he didn't want them put at risk any more than they were already.

When he saw the outline of the *Orlando* take shape in the mist, Alex waved the HAWCs down, and walked forward by himself. He then stopped and waited. There was something else there, inside the craft, he knew it, and it was trying to invade his mind. The more he tried to probe it, the more it pushed back. His neck prickled with the danger, and he expected an attack from anywhere and everywhere at any second.

He saw the door of the *Orlando* hatch was open, and the fuselage had a huge rip in it. Sam came and stood at his shoulder.

"What do you see?" Sam whispered.

Alex kept his eyes on the *Orlando*. "Nothing, but it's weird. I can sense there's someone or something in there. Maybe it's the goddamn mist making it hard for me to pinpoint exactly what it is." He turned. "But it's not human."

The bowling ball-sized rock struck Sam, mid chest, and smashed him off his feet. Then they came. Fast. Emerging from the furiously agitated haze holding metal rods, knives, and hands hooked into claws.

Alex spun to meet them. "*Engage.*"

Alex's arm came up, and his shield whirred to life, deflecting the initial charge. But the impact was like being struck by a battering ram. Who, or what, had struck him had the strength of several men. Alex rolled away, shield up, and ready for the next attack.

The Russians. Had to be. The huge men came out of the mist, a few with guns raised. The last thing Alex wanted was a firefight. The HAWCs weapons were safe in the explosive atmosphere, but he bet the Russian weaponry, if discharged, was liable to turn the entire mountaintop into a giant fireball that'd consume them all. He knew that if the HAWCs fired, they'd provoke return fire.

"No shooting," Alex yelled, and rolled as an iron bar struck the ground again and again, trying to hammer him.

The HAWCs shelved their weapons over their backs and entered the fray against their bigger opponents.

Alex saw Sam rise back to his feet. Casey Franks roared as she dove, her shield engaged on her forearm and a Ka-bar knife in each hand. She had the blades pointed backwards so she could still use her armored knuckles to punch, and then bring in backward thrusts of her knives to slash at her foe.

Max Dunsen and Andy Garcia grappled with another of the Russians. Spetsnaz, GRU, or any other Special Forces that Russia could pit against them should have fallen like wheat before the scythe, but to Alex's amazement, his HAWCs were being beaten back.

No, not just beaten back, but obliterated. One massive arm swung out, striking Dunsen and knocking him twenty feet back into the mist. Then Garcia was grabbed around the throat, lifted off his feet, and shaken like a rabbit in a hound's mouth before being slammed down into the mud.

Garcia was groggy, but drew his longest blade, and stabbed upwards, but the laser-honed tip refused to penetrate the ribs of his opponent. In return, the Russian holding him down kept one large hand on Garcia's throat, pinning him in place as he drew his other arm back, lined the HAWC up, and then with a sickening crunch, he punched down with all his strength into the HAWC's helmet.

Astonishingly, the fist passed through the armored face-shield and on into Garcia's face and skull.

"Noooo!" Alex was up and charging. He dropped his shoulder and cannonballed into the figure, knocking it off his man. He pulled Garcia up, but there was nothing he could do; the HAWC's head was destroyed.

He stared into the ruined face of his dead soldier, as time fell away. It was impossible, the helmets were near unbreakable, and the human skull could withstand over 500 pounds of pressure before crushing. Alex let Garcia's body slide back to the ground.

The Russian had crushed Garcia's skull with one fist.

Alex turned slowly, teeth bared. So could he.

Sam Reid was trading blows with a being larger than he was. Even though Sam had internal MECH technology, it was he who was struggling with his opponent. Dunsen rejoined the fight. He, Casey, and Monroe faced an opponent together, but against the Russian they seemed to be taking turns being flung around like rag dolls.

Alex felt the movement in the air before he saw it, and raised his shielded arm in time to stop the metal bar coming down across his neck. Even though the super-compressed air defrayed the massive blow, he still grunted from the force of it, and his feet sunk a few inches further into the ooze.

He spun and came up with his knife, the metal blade horizontal, and he stabbed in hard at the Russian's ribcage. The razor-sharp edge, with Alex's force behind it, should have penetrated the ribs, and found the heart or at least the lungs – either should have meant immediate death or incapacitation.

But the blade barely entered the skin, and then struck something that felt like solid bone where none should have existed. Alex looked up into the face for the first time – the man didn't wear any breathing apparatus, and his features were a grotesque mask of elongated jaws, heavy brow, and large, black soulless eyes like those of a shark. The man grinned, showing teeth that were strong and inward curving.

The Russian lunged, but he underestimated Alex who pivoted and brought the knife back around, roaring and swinging with all his strength into the meat of the Russian's shoulder. There was no bone or armor plating there and his eight-inch knife sank to the hilt, delivering a devastating injury, and one that should have rendered the Russian's arm useless.

This time the Russian howled with pain as he dropped his iron bar, and he quickly reached up to catch the hilt of the blade and Alex's hand in his own. Alex saw that the giant hand only seemed to have three large blunt fingers and it completely wrapped around his own.

The Russian tried to crush Alex's hand but couldn't, and instead Alex pushed the blade further into the mottled flesh.

"It hurts, *da*?" It was Alex's turn to grin.

The Russian growled and Alex stared into the black discs of eyes. *What's happening to these men?*

Unexpectedly, the Russian straightened then jerked back, lifting Alex up off his feet while still gripping his hand. He pulled it from the knife and used Alex's arm to swing his body around and whip him hard to the ground. Alex grunted in pain as his head thumped down and he felt the impact jar every bone in his body. His vision swam, and his mind began to wander away.

His adversary ripped the knife from his shoulder and flung it away and then bent to pick up the fallen steel bar.

Look. The voice in his head was urgent but disdainful. *I said, look!*

Alex's blurred vision focused on hurricane of violence around him. Without the ability to use modern weaponry, it reminded him of movie scenes of age-old gladiator battles – huge warriors in armor battled each other with swords, clubs, and shields, as well as the most basic of weapons; hands, fists, elbows, and heads.

He saw Sam Reid lifted from the ground by one of the most grotesque men he had ever seen in his life. The HAWC was held aloft for a few seconds before being slammed down to the mud. His adversary then went to stomp down on him, but Sam caught the huge boot and hung on tight.

Three other HAWCs battled another of the men. Alex's confused state making it impossible for him to tell who was who in their robotic-looking suits. Alex knew his HAWCs were an indomitable force and near-indestructible human beings, but the Russians were even more super-charged and bestial. They not only held their own with the American Special Forces soldiers, but their strength seemed to far surpass them.

Look at your loyal soldiers now. The voice chuckled cruelly. *They follow you, and see where have you brought them? To hell, of course.*

He turned his head, seeing the fallen body of Garcia.

Once you're dead, they're all dead. Close your eyes, and just let it all go. The cruel laugh again. *After all, that's how a coward would die.*

The metal bar then came down across his chest, and Alex felt the ultra-tough biological armor-plating crack. The suit held, but it wouldn't for long.

That's how a coward would die.

Alex's stupor made him feel like he was tied down. He tried to roll away, but too slowly, and the next strike of the bar was across his lower back. Lightning bolts of pain shot through him.

"I'm not a coward." Alex strained.

Then get the fuck up. On your feet, soldier ... or let me take over!

The voice was now a roar as the bar came down again and again.

Fight or die – choose! The cruel voice goaded, urged, and tormented him. Alex knew who it was – *The Other*, drawing power from the conflict, wanting to be released, and thirsty for blood.

Alex whipped the shield around in time to stop the bar striking his head. Through the shield, the Russian, or whatever he had now become, became a blur as he used the metal bar and one huge fist to pummel down on Alex.

Alex held the shield aloft to take impact after impact. He weathered the vicious blows as each became ever more furious.

The Other wanted blood, and gave him a choice – *fight or die*. Anger as well as adrenaline and steroids surged through him. He pushed to his feet. "I choose to fight."

The metal bar swung down, but instead of it striking the shield again, Alex turned his arm, and caught the bar, and held it even though the Russian tried with all his might to jerk it free.

For what seemed an age, but would have been only a second or two, the adversaries stared into each other's eyes. Alex's would have seemed to burn with an intensity and fury that made other men shrink back. But the HAWC saw in those inky, soulless depths something the Russian didn't want him to see – doubt.

Alex gritted his teeth, and jerked back hard, ripping the bar free. Faster than the Russian could react, Alex swung it back at the man. The Russian held up a forearm, but the bar struck it violently, and with a wet crunch, the arm broke like a tree branch. The man howled as the hand swung down, held to the arm only by the flesh.

Alex Hunter wasn't finished. He used both the bar and his armor-plated fist to beat at the Russian, forcing the bigger man to backpedal. Alex then swung the bar backhanded, catching the man's chin with a sound like a bell ringing. The Russian fell back to the ground.

Yes, yes, good. Now feed me.

Alex looked down at the Russian. If those black eyes were begging for mercy, they were looking in the wrong place. The Russian started to rise.

"Yes, I will," Alex whispered.

He swung the metal bar with such force at the man's head that it cleaved its way all the way down to his neck.

The body juddered for a few seconds on the ground as nerves misfired, before laying still.

Alex stood looking down at the carnage, before shaking his head as though trying to dislodge an angry hornet. He needed to refocus. His vision still swam but he pulled the RG3 rifle from over his shoulder, turned and peppered the ground with the high-speed projectiles.

"*Enough!*" Alex roared and aimed the weapon at the face of the Russian leader.

"You have something that belongs to us." Alex strained, as the beast inside him wanted to obliterate them all. The Russians and his HAWCs froze, eyes on him, waiting. But in the Russian faces there wasn't fear, more amusement.

Alex grimaced for a moment, trying to pull *The Other* back. "Hand it over … and I'll let you live." Alex pointed the RG3 directly at the biggest Russian's face – *the leader*, he thought. Inside his head, a voice screamed to pull the trigger.

"HAWCs, form up on me." Alex watched as Dunsen pulled Monroe to his feet, and turned to bump armored knuckles with Casey. Then his soldiers eased back toward him, never taking their eyes off their foes, until they were at his shoulders.

They straightened, waiting. He noticed Sam was sporting cracked biological plating, and remembered his own suit taking the abnormally brutal impacts. Sam's armor, like his own, was harder than titanium and should not have been breached by anything less than a direct hit from heavy-caliber weaponry. But the Russians had cracked them with their bare hands.

Alex scanned the faces of the impossible-looking men facing them. None wore breathing apparatus, so were sucking in the toxic air. Their heads looked misshapen, brows and jaws longer and even their arms hung lower than they should, and ending in club-like fingers. Their uniforms stretched, and he could see splits appearing across the chests and biceps of some of them. It was like they were growing right out of their clothing.

One of them went to raise his weapon. But the biggest among them, who had been fighting Sam, waved it down, and turned to face Alex.

"This is not American territory." The voice was deep and guttural. He held a hugely muscled arm out toward the *Orlando* and gave Alex a sharp-toothed grin. "I claim right of salvage." He kept his eyes on Alex and one hand on the hilt of a large Russian blade.

"Fine, keep the shuttle. Just give me the image chip; I know you've got it. Last chance." Alex's gun barrel didn't waver.

The man looked at his team, and then down at his soldier who still had the metal bar sticking from his head. His powerful jaws worked for a moment.

"We are not afraid to die, and I think your soldiers are also not afraid to die. This is the warrior's code." His grin returned. "Besides, the things we have done, you and I, maybe we deserve to die."

He raised his chin and inhaled deeply through his nose and then nodded. "I think high methane content. Maybe this gas will explode if we fire our weapons, maybe it won't." He looked over Alex's shoulder to the civilians. "But will you gamble the lives of the others who are with you? Maybe they not so prepared to die, *da*?"

Alex's choice was simple; he could fight and risk detonating the mountaintop, and end up killing everyone, or he could back off. If it were just the HAWCs, it'd be easy.

"I'm Captain Alex Hunter, and up here, I am the first and only law. There will be no more warnings."

The big man stepped forward. "And I am Ivan Zlatan, and up here, I do not recognize your authority." He lowered his brows. "In fact, little man, I do not recognize your authority anywhere."

Alex fired the RG3 twice, putting two pencil-sized holes through the Zlatan's shoulder. The huge man jerked to the side, grunting. But the next sound was a grating laugh. He turned back, as black blood started to weep through his uniform, but only for a few seconds before it dried.

One of the Russians brought up his gun, but Zlatan put a huge arm out and pushed it down.

"We are not so easy to kill," Zlatan said.

"You're already dead." Sam joined Alex. "You know this gas you're inhaling is toxic?"

"Not to us." The Russian took in a deep breath and let it out slowly. "We don't need to dress like spacemen because of a little mist. I think we are tougher than you Americans." He smiled sourly.

Sam snorted. "Yeah, you all look like crap. If you think it's not affecting you, then you're blind."

"You thinking you can chance it." Zlatan laughed corrosively again, before looking at his downed man again. "His name was Valentine Russlin; a good soldier. But not as good as me." He looked up at Alex. "Little man, I will peel you from your suit, and break you into pieces."

He looked at each of the HAWCs. "I think this will be your graveyard today."

He lowered his head, large, dark, glossy eyes glaring at Alex. His remaining men stared unblinkingly at Alex with the same weird eyes. The HAWCs were like statues, with their RG3s pointing unwaveringly at each of the Russians' heads.

The foggy atmosphere curled around them, if anything becoming more crowded with the floating specks. Alex's laser-focused attention detected the sound of something large moving out beyond the curtain of mist.

Zlatan cocked his head. "Yes, I know, we are not the only predators that stalk this mountain." His strange eyes narrowed, as he seemed to be tracking something that even Alex couldn't see.

The scream that tore through the atmosphere was one of fear and absolute pain. Casey spun at him.

"Erikson."

"*Shit!* Pull back," Alex yelled.

"Another time." Zlatan's eyes never left him.

CHAPTER 25

"*Hey you!*" The tall female HAWC, Erikson, pointed at Scott McIntyre, who was wandering away. "Get the fuck back in here."

Morag's head whipped around to where the young NASA scientist had ambled away. His back and shoulders were hunched and his suit looked strangely bulky like he was hiding something underneath it. Also, one of his arms, the one that had been spiked, now hung down by his side, and weirdly lagged all the way down past his knee.

What the hell is up with him, she wondered as the man continued to ignore the HAWC and stumble away out into the gloom.

"Son of a bitch," Erikson hissed, her head going from the NASA tech to where her comrades were fighting the Russians. "Got no time for this."

"Scott," Anne Peterson called. "Scott?" She turned to Russell Burrows, her brows knitted. "I think there's something wrong with him."

"You think?" Morag scoffed.

"You two." Erikson thumbed toward the vanishing Scott McIntyre. "He's your buddy. Go and get him. You got one minute."

"I'll get him," Russell sighed and ran after Scott.

Morag shifted her facemask so she could see better. McIntyre was staggering on and still only twenty feet away but already becoming indistinct in the smog. Russell caught up to the man, grabbed his arm, and tried to turn him around.

The young NASA scientist pushed Russell hard, making him fall back into the slime. Then without a word, McIntyre began to sprint off into the gloom.

"Hey, stop!" Russell leaped to his feet, and went to go after him, but Erikson immediately raised her RG3 and fired a few near silent shots toward him. The sludge splashed up in a line in front of him and stopped him dead. She showed her teeth.

"*Burrows*, don't even think about it. Get back in the group, he wants to play hide and seek, that's his funeral."

"But there's something *wrong* with him," Anne complained.

"Something wrong everywhere, lady. Everyone just stay close and stay focused." Erikson turned back to where the HAWCs were facing off against the Russians.

Morag looked back to where Scott had vanished into the wall of swirling clouds. *It's getting thicker.* Soon, they'd barely be able to see six feet in front of themselves, and then they might need to rope themselves together to stop getting separated and lost. She stepped closer to Erikson, trying to see Alex Hunter again – the fighting seemed to have momentarily stopped, and the huge soldiers now just faced each other.

"Is it over?" she asked.

Erikson didn't turn her head. "Boss'll let us know when."

Morag muttered to herself as she headed back to the group. She had to duck under a stunted tree-type thing that was dripping with the mud. She stopped for a moment to stare at it. *Did it quiver slightly as I went past?* She stayed watching for several seconds, before putting the thought down to reduced visibility, fatigue, and a good dose of nerves. Still, *yech*.

There was a rounded rock sticking up out of the muck that looked relatively dry. She headed toward it, turned, and sat down heavily.

It moved.

She looked down. It moved again, and Morag leaped to her feet.

"*What the hell?*"

"What is it?" Anne also sprang upright, and backed away. Behind her Russell and Calvin Renner did the same.

"The rock ..." Morag stepped back. "It's goddamn moving."

"Get a grip," Erikson said over her shoulder.

The rock began to rise. "*You* get a grip – of *this*." Morag pointed.

With a sucking noise, the oval-shaped rock lifted from the surrounding ooze. It was about six feet in length and around it smaller mounds began to appear.

"Erikson, gonna need you here ... like, right *now*." Morag continued to back away. "Calvin ...?"

"Yeah, yeah, I'm rolling." Renner had his legs spread and a small camera to his face.

The second mound lifted stickily, and they saw then that it was really part of the larger one – the head. Tucked under a collar of armor plating it gently extended two whip-like feelers that sprung up as the mud slid from a pair of huge glossy eyes. It hissed like a snake.

"Holy fuck, what the hell is that?" Renner had the camera away from his face and behind his visor his eyes were round as poker chips.

"Get back," Erikson yelled, and stepped to the side of the group, with her RG3 aimed dead center at the thing.

"Don't shoot," Anne said, stepping forward. "I think it's ..."

Spindly legs lifted the thing's head higher and two wicked-looking mandibles eased open about a foot before clacking closed. They yawned open again as the thing faced them, and inside they could see moving parts that looked like buzz saws on the end of mechanical arms. Behind the thing on its rear, it looked like there was a ribbed barrel attached to it.

The thing hissed again and seemed to lunge forward, which was too much for Erikson who let loose a stream of projectiles that ripped all along the thick carapace from its head to its rear. The effect was instantaneous as the huge insectoid erupted in spastic movements accompanied by a constant hiss like a broken steam pipe.

"Oh yeah?" Erikson dialed up her RG3 to a more meaningful projectile size, and let loose again.

This time, fist-sized holes punched into the shell with a sound like cracking tiles. Morag winced as the thing's hiss changed to a high-pitched squeal. Erikson then blew its head apart.

"*Fuck you!*" Erikson seemed to vent her rage, fear, and frustration on the thing as she continued to drill it. But even with holes punched through it, and now missing a head, the thing bullocked its way forward, causing Anne to scream as it headed toward her.

It came clear of the mud.

Like a massive cockroach. In fact that was exactly what it looked like, except a thousand times bigger. And she'd heard that cockroaches could live for three days even without a head, and only finally ended up dying from dehydration, rather than the missing brain.

Erikson fired again, and this time she punctured the barrel shaped appendage that was attached to its abdomen – *big mistake* – it exploded.

The casing was an egg sack containing hundreds of tiny roaches the size of rats. They boiled free, small whip antenna waving, bristled legs moving in a blur. They spread in every direction.

Something that looked like a bear claw gripped Renner's leg and he yelled in pain. "*Ouch, it's fucking biting me!*" He knocked another one off that tried to shimmy up his thigh.

Everyone started to scramble, and Morag pulled out her flashlight and held it before her like a sword.

The insects moved fast in a flurry of legs and antenna. It didn't matter to Morag whether they were hungry or just frightened, there was no way she was letting them anywhere near her. She didn't want to get bitten, and certainly didn't want any goddamn punctures in her suit.

Erikson was like a machine, aiming and firing, and never missing, as she exploded the things one after the other. Then as fast as they were vomited onto the ground, they were gone. The revolting bugs disappearing into the mist or burrowing back into the slime. The huge parent insect with its head obliterated had walked itself into a rock and continued to try to walk forward even with its path blocked.

"Okay everyone, fun's over, get back in here," Erikson demanded.

Morag turned to back up toward Erikson, waving the flashlight in front of her, but the baby monstrosities were gone. Behind her, Erikson sounded impatient.

"I said, everyone get bac … "

"… *ack!*"

"… *aaaaack!*"

"Huh?" Morag half turned, keeping an eye out for more of the bugs. "What?"

RG3 projectiles flew, splattering the mud, drilling into the weird tree stump things and blasting fragments from the rocks.

Morag dove out of the way then propped herself up. "Hey, watch ou—" She froze.

The female HAWC was hanging in the air, and something had hold of her. Morag's mouth dropped open. The thing was huge; standing enormously tall on two legs. It's elongated head grotesque and sunken into its shoulders, and centered with two large ink-black eyes that had smaller eyes dotted around them. The body was mottled, heavily muscled and its segments separated into distinct plating-like armor.

"*Oh Jesus, no, no, no.*" Morag scurried to her feet and backed away, feeling her stomach turn over from fear. She saw that the hand that held the woman by the throat was a match for the one that Alex Hunter had thrown before them. This was one of the things that had taken Steve Knight.

She continued to scuttle backwards until she bumped into Anne, who screamed, and then she and Russell ran in the direction of the HAWCs. But her knuckleheaded cameraman sprinted madly the other way into the mist.

"*Calvin!*" she yelled as she continued to retreat.

Erikson struggled vainly in the grip of something that out-muscled her by ten to one. Her rifle had been dropped or maybe pulled from her hands – *did the creature also know to do that?*

The thing then raked one hand down her body from her neck to her ribs, peeling back the heavily armored suit like it was nothing more than paper. Morag saw that the flesh was also rent and blood immediately welled up and ran down Erikson's side. Erikson struggled, one hand on the iron-like grip at her throat and with the other arm, she used the point of her elbow to lash back against the pumpkin-sized head again and again.

Morag looked at the flashlight in her hands, wishing she had a shotgun. But the thought of getting closer petrified her, while the tough female HAWC never gave up fighting for a second. She wondered at the fortitude of these people, where she would have been screaming her lungs out or perhaps have fainted from fear, this woman fought on, with nothing but her body, curses, and gritted teeth.

Erikson reached down to pull a blade from her belt and then slashed and stabbed at the hand. But the knife didn't penetrate a hide that seemed tougher than the hardest of leathers.

The thing dragged Erikson closer to itself and bent its monstrous head forward. The mouth opened, and telescoped out like the jaws of a fish from the sunless depths of the ocean.

"*No …!*" Morag knew what was coming and threw the flashlight with all her strength. But to her horror, she actually struck Erikson in the chest. It made no difference as the thing's mouth fixed at the valley of her neck and shoulder and then wetly burrowed in.

It was only then that Erikson screamed, but only for a moment as her vocal chords were severed when the long teeth sawed through flesh, tendon, and cartilage, ripping away a double fist of meat. Her head flopped bonelessly to the side, and her eyelids fluttered like a pair of pinned moths.

Projectiles riveted up the creature's hide. In a blink, it vanished, taking the female HAWC with it.

Alex Hunter sprinted in the open, and then looked about to go after it.

"*No!*" Morag screamed. "Don't – she's already dead."

Alex turned to her.

"She's gone. I think … I think, they want you to go after them." Morag looked around. "They're smart, picking us off one at a time." She ran toward Alex, keeping one eye on the swirling mist. "I think it knew she was the one with the weapon – it disarmed her first."

Alex's head tilted back for a second, and she guessed he must have been cursing. She could see his eyes were screwed shut, but the more she stared, she realized it looked more like he was arguing, through gritted teeth.

"Alex …" She wanted to reach out to him, but hesitated. Then changed her mind and grabbed his arm.

After another few seconds, he lowered his head and she let go. He waved her closer.

"Come on."

Alex backed up, keeping his weapon trained on the thick haze. "We've got Anne and Russell with us, but where are McIntyre and Renner?"

She pointed. "Out there. We need to go after them."

Alex faced where she pointed and stared out into the fog for a few moments. "No, they've gone too far now." He continued to let his eyes search the soupy air. "They're on their own." He turned away. "Let's go."

"But ..." Morag paused to look back out at the curtains of mist, and then sighed. *Hope you can find us, Cal.* All the camera equipment and footage was also now gone. She dropped her head momentarily – *it was all for nothing.* She groaned and then spun back to keep up with the vanishing Alex.

* * *

Calvin Renner ran, fell to the slime, got up and ran some more before he even realized no one was running with him.

I'm panicking ... stop!

He slowed, and bent over heaving in oxygen and resting his hands on his knees. He straightened, still wheezing into his mask.

Calm down. Just calm – the fuck – down.

He gulped more air, and then turned one way then the next. Already his footsteps had been filled in with the sucking slime, so there wasn't even a way to retrace his path.

"Oh, you dumb shit," he gasped, still breathing hard.

He turned again, and took a few steps. The mist seemed even heavier, and he couldn't see more than a dozen feet in any direction. Shapes loomed huge, like stalagmites sprouting weird branches that held bulbous pods dripping with slime. He looked up; inside the pods things wriggled like the fruits were about to give birth.

Gross. He looked down at his feet and saw that pools of what might have been stagnant water, boiled with repulsive life. *And that looks even fucking worse.* He bent closer to stare into one. Tiny, glossy, black things roiled and climbed over one another. They could have been tadpoles or eels, but had tiny hands that gripped and clung on. He grimaced and slowly straightened.

A squelch of mud behind him.

"*Hello?*" he turned, hopeful.

"Morag? Captain Hunter?" He waited a few seconds. "Hellooo?"

Nothing.

Another splash from out behind the walls of mist. He spun, but then there came more from behind him.

Renner spun again. "Please stop that." He spun back. "That better not be you, Morag. Not fucking funny."

The cameraman waited, and then held his breath, straining to hear for several more seconds. *No, that* better *be you ...* please *be you*, his mind begged. He shivered, and then heard a small whimper – his own.

"Yeah, okay, fuck this. I'm outta here." He'd run, fast. Even if it was the wrong direction, sooner or later he'd hit the crater-basin wall, and then he'd only have to follow it back to where they came in. He'd wait for them there.

Renner turned, and then almost blacked out from the shock – there was something there, *right there*, and so close it loomed up over him. It was close to eight feet tall, and had a lumped head, and eyes so black they seemed like bottomless pits, and would have been more at home in the ugly, bulging face of a spider.

Renner gulped looking down to the stump on the end of one of its arms. "I didn't cut off your hand," he babbled. "It was Captain Hunter who did that."

He saw that from the stump, branching filaments extruded as if it was already regenerating the limb.

"I'm not your enemy." He started to back up, holding his hands up before him. "I'm just visiting here."

Its arm rose almost lovingly to alight on his shoulder. But where the stubby fingers touched, it soon turned white hot as talons dug into his much softer flesh.

Renner screamed and tried to drag himself away, but it was like he was hooked and the thing's arm pulled him closer to an open mouth, showing a ring of dagger-like teeth that went all the way around the dark, pitiless hole of its throat.

His scream only stopped when the mouth smashed through his visor to close over his own.

CHAPTER 26

College Park Airfield, Greenbelt, Maryland

At dawn, pilot Luke Vincenzo hosed down the Chinook. He had a bucket of soapy water and he'd give the big bruiser a quick wash before heading home. There was nothing like flying over open countryside to pepper your cockpit window and underbelly with squashed bugs, and even the occasional bird that wasn't paying attention.

The Chinook helicopter was a hundred foot of craft, so his job was just to get the large stuff off, and as it stood eighteen feet high, he'd wait until he could get a turn with the ladder truck to do the skin on the top.

It was still a big job, but Luke didn't mind. For one thing, it was eighty degrees so throwing around a bit of water was welcome. And then as far as he was concerned it was like washing and tending to your horse – you kept your steed in shape, and it kept you alive when you needed it. Same went for your helo.

Hose and wash, hose and wash, and paying extra attention to any lumpy gunk he could see. The capture pole he'd used to grab Alex Hunter's sample had been retracted, but the fork was just visible and it had some sludge stuck there that he washed and then rubbed with his cloth.

Ouch. Damned thing was sharp and pierced his rubber glove, scratching the back of his hand. He looked at it briefly, judged it minor, and ignored it, continuing with the wash.

* * *

07:42 am

It was still early morning when Luke flopped down in his chair, then groaned and lifted himself to remove a red rubber bone and toss it to Scruff, the overfed beagle, who caught it and scurried away, heading for the backyard in a blur of legs and whipping tail.

His head had started throbbing an hour back and he had a taste in his mouth that was like pure shit.

"How was the trip?" Jenny leaned around the living room door and smiled. The twinkle in her eye never failed to make him smile – it was love, and she still made his heart leap to this day.

"Fine, weird. You know I can't talk about it, but the job was not something I'd want to try and do every day." He lifted an eyebrow.

"That's why they wanted you; you're the best," she said and crinkled her nose. "Hey handsome, coffee?"

"Yes, please. I love you." He grinned.

She came and leaned close to him. "You love me or coffee?"

"You *and* coffee, in that order."

"Yeah, I get that." She laughed and bent forward to kiss him, but stopped. She waved a hand in front of her face. "Wow, Lukie, I'm not kissing you until you brush your teeth. What have you been eating?" She pulled back, holding her nose, and then headed to the kitchen.

Luke leaned his head back, hoping to ease the throb behind his eyes. He could hear kids yelling and laughing outside, and each decibel was like a dagger in his brain. The suburb was usually quiet this time of day; and as the entire town was only a little over six square miles comprising 23,000 people or so, spread out in pretty cottage housing, it usually remained quiet for at least another hour. He sighed.

"*Moooooomeeeey.*" The long drawn-out complaint was from Angelina, holding the body of a doll in one hand, and its head in another. "Her head keeps coming off." She spotted Luke and held it out as evidence.

"*Daaaadeeee*, see?"

"Let me have a look?" He sat forward, frowning from his headache, and holding out his hand. The little girl plonked the doll's body into his hand first, followed by its head.

"*See?*"

"Hmm." He first pretended to try and put the head on the doll's foot. "Does it go here?" Then over her hand. "There?"

"*Daaadeeee.*" She wore a scowl like thunder, resisting any and all of his attempts at humor.

"Okay, they were just a few test runs." He positioned the head on the neck and pushed hard. It popped on. "*Ta-daa.*" He handed it back. "Good as new."

Her smile reappeared, and she took the doll, one leg in each hand, her head nodding, but her eyes only on the doll. She went to turn away.

"What do you say?" he tilted his head.

She half turned back. "Thank you, Daddy. I love you."

"Love you too, honey bunny." He slumped back into his chair, and blinked. One of his eyes seemed to be a little blurry. And his head still throbbed mercilessly.

* * *

05:12 pm

The patrol car drove slowly down the tomb-silent street. The late afternoon sunshine was warm, pleasant, and should have drawn car washers, dog walkers, and kids out onto the sidewalk or at least their front lawns.

Today, it was a ghost town.

"Something on we don't know about?" Police officer Don Murphy turned, reading off the house numbers as they cruised. "Fifty-two, fifty-four, fifty-six ... coming up." They were looking for number sixty-two – the Vincenzo house.

"Yup." Officer Cleveland Bennings ducked down to look out the windshield at the upper deck of a house – windows open, curtains billowing, but no one there.

"What's with this guy anyway? How come Mister Suburbia is suddenly so important?" Bennings talked and kept watch for the house.

Murphy shrugged. "*Meh*. Seems NASA had been trying to contact him following some sort of fire or skirmish out at their labs. They didn't say whether Mister Luke Vincenzo, a pilot, was a suspect or a witness, only that he needed to be located immediately."

"A NASA pilot, huh?" Bennings' brows went up. "Rockets?"

"*Nah*, helicopters I think, and he doesn't work for NASA. But we're only to find the guy. NASA will do the rest. In fact, the chief says we're only to locate him and call it in. Then NASA will send one of their own medivac vans."

"They have their own private medical vans?"

"Guess so. Heads up, here we go." They pulled in at the sidewalk and stopped. Both men got out and Murphy stretched his back and thrust forward a portly stomach.

He looked up. *A normal house in a normal street.* The only thing a little out of the ordinary was there was some sort of mess on the front lawn – a pile of gray sludge that had a red, rubber dog bone sticking out of it. Oddly, there was a glistening slime trail of flattened grass leading from the front path, as though the mess had somehow slid across the bowling green smooth lawn before coming to a stop.

Murphy and Bennings approached the door, and slowed as they got to the stoop. There was smoke billowing from the door.

"It's open." Murphy turned side-on. "We're only supposed to identify this guy and then call NASA's Greenbelt labs, right?"

"Yep, Luke Vincenzo, aged thirty-six. Also in residence should be his wife, Jenny, thirty-four, and daughter, Angelina. Not expecting trouble, but ..." Bennings also turned side-on and placed one hand on the butt of his gun.

Both men stood either side of the door and peered in. The late afternoon sun was waning and it was dim within the house. The smoke was thick, but didn't smell like fire. More like compost or body odor.

"*Phew*, they cooking something in there?" Murphy asked.

"If they are, I'm not eating it." Bennings rang the bell, and leaned around the frame. "Hello? Maryland PD. Anybody home?"

Murphy reached in and pushed the door. "*Jezuz*, that stinks. I don't think that's something cooking." He rapped on the doorframe, and raised his voice. "Mister Vincenzo, *police*." He waited a few seconds. "Mister Luke Vincenzo, we are entering your premises." Murphy turned and nodded to his partner, and together they headed in.

Murphy found a light switch and flicked it. The room lit up, and the pair stood in the center of the living room with wrinkled noses. The stench was even more powerful inside – now, like someone had upended the compost pile over an open sewer.

"I can barely breathe," Murphy said over his shoulder.

"Well, least it doesn't smell like death," Bennings added. "Maybe just a broken sewer line." Bennings headed in a few dozen more feet and then passed the door to another room. He pulled up. "Hey, *look.*"

Murphy joined him. "What the hell is that shit?"

There was another pile of the greyish mucus-looking matter. This bigger one had what looked like a headless doll sticking from one side.

"Dunno, but it looks freaking disgusting. Maybe that's where the smell is coming from." Bennings grimaced and stopped at the bottom of the stairs. "You check out the back, I'll take a quick look up here." He took a single step and then heard something shift above them. Both men froze, waiting and staring up at the ceiling.

They stayed watching the ceiling as if their eyes could penetrate the plaster. After another moment, Bennings spoke softly out of the side of his mouth while keeping his eyes on the stairs.

"Hey buddy, why don't we *both* have a little look-see up here first, *huh?*"

"Right with you." Murphy pulled his revolver, held it in both hands but pointed at the ground.

Together the men headed up the stairs, Bennings taking the lead, Murphy one step behind.

Murphy was on his toes but was glad the steps were new and there were few creaks or complaints from the wood even for someone of his size. He tried to tell himself it was just a suburban house with an average family, but for some reason he wanted to be quieter than he'd ever been in his life. He could feel the hair on his neck rising from fear, and he didn't know why.

He turned back momentarily to peer over his shoulder. He frowned in confusion. The pile of sludge he had seen in the room they had just passed was now visible in the doorway – *was it that close before?*

Murphy licked dry lips and swallowed hard in an even dryer throat. Damn it – *focus*, he demanded of himself.

He faced forward to the landing and stepped up. It was hot on the second floor as the heat had risen, and thankfully there weren't any piles of that creepy shit up here. But unfortunately, the weird spotty smoke was thickest on the upper floor, and now was more like a summer fog. It swirled in and out of the rooms, and stung his nose, throat and eyes.

"Fucking haunted house, man," Bennings said over his shoulder.

"Happy Halloween," Murphy retorted and chuckled nervously. He edged toward the first bedroom, Bennings now right on his shoulder. The policemen went in quick.

A woman, arms and legs spread wide, was laid out on the bed, the sheets a glistening red. Even more horrifying was that the cavity of the stomach and chest had been prised open, and the contents of the torso was missing. Murphy could only guess what that meant.

"Oh, my fucking god." Bennings fell back out the door.

Murphy held his breath and took a couple of shaking steps forward – he didn't know why, as there was no reason to check for a pulse or even investigate cause of death.

"Mur-*Murphy!*"

He spun at Bennings' high and tremulous voice as he felt the man coming up behind him.

But when he turned, he saw it wasn't Bennings behind him at all, but instead some hulking mottled monstrosity with soulless black eyes that must have been hiding behind the door.

Murphy's mouth dropped open, and his mind fizzed with indecision and fear. He vaguely heard his partner's voice.

"No shot, no shot."

Fuck, I'm in the way. Take it anyway, his mind screamed. *Pleeeease.*

One large, three-taloned hand came up and then swiped down, scraping deep gouges from his forehead to his groin.

He suddenly felt ice cold and something warmly wet plopped at his feet.

He thought he heard his partner scream as he sank to his knees. There was the sound of running feet – *away*.

Bennings is getting help. He hoped. *Nah, running for his life.* He knew.

* * *

09:12 pm

Hammerson paced, his jaw jutting and glaring up at the wall screen as if it was a hated enemy. It showed the Greenbelt, Maryland suburb where the Vincenzo house was located, and the quarantine perimeters that had been erected.

The first was a mile-wide radius around the family house and everything inside that ring was colored red. Then a larger five-mile radius in orange, followed by a final twenty-mile ring, colored brilliant yellow.

Everyone they could find and identify in the red zone had been evacuated and was being held in isolation. Everyone else who refused to identify themselves was regarded as infected, and that went for every man, woman, dog or squirrel still in there. Everything unidentified or hostile was subject to a burn-on-sight order. The plumbing was cut off, and all drains sealed – nothing, not even a goddamn housefly, was getting in or out.

Luckily there was no breeze that evening and the air was heavy. The house and cloud of spore-laden gas was contained and was designated ground zero. Initial confusion as to what to do about the toxic environment was solved by Hammerson in ten seconds – he'd seen what worked in at NASA's lab-45. He recommended an immediate burn using a volumetric weapon. His order was carried out instantaneously.

From the air, a laser-guided thermobaric device had been deployed. It was at the bottom end of the scale, and usually used on hidden or deeper sites that were only between twenty and fifty feet below ground.

The high-temperature incendiary weapon was ideal against chemical and biological facilities or environments – which was what Hammerson knew they were dealing with now.

Hammerson had watched dispassionately as fifty houses had been vaporized in the 4,000-degree heat it generated. In a thermobaric weapon, the fuel consisted of a monopropellant and energetic particles that detonated similar to TNT while the particles burned in the surrounding air. The result was an intense and irresistible fireball. All that was left was a giant pit of bubbling magma.

Outside the inner-contamination zone, the next rings were a stop and detain quarantine, and atmosphere sniffers had been deployed. If the biological material that had been found free-floating in the house had become airborne, and crossed into the next outer ring, then it to would be classed as a red zone and the ring perimeters would geometrically broaden as appropriate, with the same evacuation, isolation, and burn protocols in place.

So far so good, but the bottom line was they contained it in the first three rings. And if, god forbid, there was a significant breakout, then ...

Hammerson didn't want to think about the *then*. It was what every military man dreaded – seeing some form of weapon of mass destruction deployed on home soil.

There were over 23,000 people in Greenbelt. From the inner ring, they'd evacuated 900 of a potential 1,200 residents that were on record as living in there. That meant within a few hours, the infection had spread and claimed three hundred souls. Though some of these were brutally killed and cannibalized by things that were once people, but now were about as far from human as was physiologically possible. One of them took seven slugs to the chest before it turned and fled, not being scared off, but only pushed back.

The rest of the missing people seemed to have been turned into piles of sludge. He didn't know which was worse.

No, fuck it, that'd be worse.

His secure phone lit up with an incoming call. He already knew who it would be. He gritted his teeth as he lifted it.

"Hammerson."

"Jack."

Yep – General Marcus Chilton.

"You've contained the outbreak?" Chilton's voice was basement deep.

"We think so, sir. But we have the Airforce on standby ... just in case," he said slowly.

"Bad business." Chilton sounded tense. "My reports say we've got infected civilians being converted into *monsters?*"

Hammerson cleared his throat. "The first responder, police officer Cleveland Bennings, was infected and converted. We captured him and several others, and euthanized them with chlorine gas. We're performing autopsies now, and we'll know more soon, sir. We should just be thankful the shuttle didn't crash in downtown New York, or it'd be game over," Hammerson said.

"Small mercies," Chilton added. "How infectious is it?"

"Bad news is one hundred percent of entities coming into contact with it will be changed in some way," Hammerson replied.

"There's good news?" Chilton's voice lifted.

"The good news is the *Orlando* came down in a low-temperature, remote geography that has the contagion self-contained ... for now."

"And high-intensity heat totally destroys it?" Chilton asked.

"Yes, sir. Nothing remains."

"Good, because in just a few hours we lost a good chunk of American neighborhood." Chilton growled. "This biological contaminant must be eradicated, full stop." Chilton's voice rose in timbre. "It takes heat, then we'll goddamn bring the heat. We need to hit the source."

"Agreed," Hammerson said. "We cleanse the *Orlando* site as soon as our team is out."

"Jack, I know it's your people up there." Chilton sounded weary. "And I know what they were trying to recover – it was my damn order. But frankly, I don't give a shit about missile-silo data anymore. I know you've seen the science team's extrapolation on what happens if it *does* get out into a high-density urban area."

Hammerson closed his eyes. He'd seen the theoretical time line. It was aggressive, and it would all be over in a matter of months – an extinction event for all life on the planet.

"Yes, Jack, I've also read the report." Chilton seemed to growl. "A new form of life would rise from the ashes to rule; a form of life far more monstrous than anything that existed now. Jack, the one advantage, the *only* advantage, we have right now is time."

"Sir, we …" Hammerson got to his feet.

Chilton cut across him. "*Colonel*, I've seen the Sabers data, and I know you have too."

Hammerson looked at his computer screen. It showed the Saber satellite image of the crater top, and how the mist was rising closer to the jagged, rocky brim. There was no getting around it, that atmosphere bubble and its airborne spore-loaded environment were growing geometrically, and soon it would spill out of the mountaintop basin.

Chilton's voice dropped a few octaves. "While it's inside that rim it's containable. But that crater cannot be allowed to spill over. If that shit gets into the global atmosphere, or anywhere that's warm, then it'll be the end. You *will not* let that happen, soldier. Am I clear?"

Jack Hammerson knew he was right. "Yes, sir. Crystal, sir."

"The wound must be and *will be* cauterized, Jack. I've already authorized a drop. You will coordinate it. In *six hours*, I want nothing left on that mountaintop but ash. Sorry Colonel; the greater good, you know that."

"Yes, sir." Hammerson sat down, his mind already working frantically on options.

CHAPTER 27

Alex had gathered everyone together, and the HAWCs had their guns trained on the closing barrier of primordial fog. Alex stood side-on, trying to see through the murk and also trying to find the Russians.

"Where've they gone?" Sam asked.

"They're out there somewhere. I can feel it," Alex responded.

Monroe quickly glanced down at his wrist monitor. "Movement, boss. Multiple signatures. Going around us but staying just out of sight."

"The Russians?" Casey asked over her shoulder.

"No, Morg, and out of *our* sight, but I'm betting not out of theirs," Alex said. He couldn't see them, but he could sense them – big bodies, moving silently. He didn't need to see them to know what they were.

He half turned to Monroe. "How many?"

"Three, maybe four," the young HAWC said, looking from his monitor to the mist.

Sam stood alongside Alex. "We're too exposed here – we need cover." He pointed. "I can hear them now." He pointed with the muzzle of his gun this time. "Concentrating over there."

"They're trying to herd us away from the *Orlando*," Alex said. "Morag said they disarmed Erikson before taking her."

"She dead?" Casey turned.

Alex nodded. "These things don't take prisoners."

Casey bristled. "Neither do I, *you fucking sons of bitches*."

Sam grunted. "I don't like it. Out here, they have the advantage. We need time to plan our next move."

Alex knew he was right. "HAWCs, we are leaving. Cover to the *Orlando*."

The HAWCs formed up in two lines, weapons pointed outwards, and the civilians on the inside.

"What about the Russians?" Casey frowned.

"We got bigger problems." Alex gripped his RG3. "Dial it up, let's make some space, people – setting three." Alex and his HAWCs moved the size of their projectile darts up to a dime-sized plug.

"On my order," Alex yelled.

"*HUA!*"

"*Fire!*" Alex roared the word, and the HAWCs responded.

The surrounding brume billowed and whirled as the darts blasted outwards at a rate of hundreds per second. There was the sound of strikes out in the gloom, but no one was sure whether any of it was hitting the Morg, or one of the numerous tree-like blobs that seemed to be springing up everywhere.

"Move it." Alex led them on, and the HAWCs crab-walked toward the downed shuttle.

Together they moved like a single creature shepherding the remaining civilians toward the open cockpit door of the *Orlando*. One after the other, Alex and Sam pushed them inside, and the HAWCs followed until just Alex remained. He took a last look around and then folded himself inside.

"Seal that door." Alex pointed. Monroe pushed the door shut, and immediately darkness descended on them. There were still a few lights on the cockpit console, meaning some battery life remained, and perhaps something they could use.

Anne Peterson rushed to the one of the consoles. "Russ, there's still some power." She started to flick switches.

Russell Burrows edged in next to her. "Ripley might still be conscious."

"Who?" Casey Franks asked.

"Uh, the *Orlando*'s … main computer. It's called Ripley." Burrows looked up. "If she's still working, then we can run some diagnostics. Maybe even find out what happened up there."

"Ripley, *cool*," Casey snorted.

"Fingers crossed," Anne said, rapidly flicking switches and calibrating dials. "I'm going to try to bring her back online."

"Excellent." Alex turned to his remaining HAWCs. "Dunsen, keep a lookout. Sam, do a quick search and see if there's anything else we can use. Everyone else, just stay the hell out of the way."

Alex saw Morag staring wide-eyed out into the darkness. She turned to smile weakly at him. Behind her visor her face was streaked with perspiration, making her red hair sit like a cap over her forehead.

He nodded to her. "Don't worry, we'll get out of here."

"I know we will," she said and then looked away, and he could tell she didn't believe a word of it.

CHAPTER 28

A sound from the shuttle's bay area made everyone freeze. Alex placed a hand on the thick door, staring at the partition and pushing out with his senses. After a moment, he grunted.

"Our Russian friends."

Casey bristled. "Good. Payback time."

"Not in here," Sam said. "This is home until we can work out an escape plan. We engage now, we'll obliterate the only barrier we have between us and whatever the hell those things are outside."

"Don't think we'll have a choice," Alex added.

"Can they get in?" Morag asked.

Russell Burrows lunged at the door and pressed a small locking switch. "Not now. The command cabin has override."

"Why are they in here?" Monroe asked. "Did they follow us?"

"Maybe they're hiding out as well. Those monstrosities might find them just as tasty," Casey spat.

"Fear, good, maybe we can use that," Alex said. "They've got the chip. I want it." But he knew that he wasn't going to get it without a fight. Time, and their oxygen, was running out, and one way or another the HAWCs were going home with that satellite data. *With your shield or upon it,* Hammerson would say, referring to the ancient Spartan dictum that meant to come home wrapped in glory, or die fighting for it.

Alex leaned his head forward, listening at the solid door.

"What are they doing?" Sam asked.

Alex concentrated, but heard nothing. "I don't know; all quiet."

"*Yes!*" Russell Burrows voice turned their heads.

"What've you got?" Alex asked.

"She's done it. Ripley's coming online now." He rubbed his hands together as Anne Peterson's fingers flew over the touchpads.

Anne half turned. "*Orlando*'s link to us on Earth went down, but I'm sure the ship's AI would have continued to watch. Maybe we can see what happened to Mitch, *er*, the crew."

"Well done, you." Russell patted her shoulder while he began to toggle switches and dials.

"Bringing her up … *now*." The panel lit up before Anne. "Ripley, are you functional?" Anne craned forward, waiting.

A calm feminine voice began to list *Orlando*'s points of failure, multiple hull breaches, electrical damage, fuel reserves, and even ground proximity warnings.

"Better late than never, I guess," Monroe said softly.

Anne interrupted the AI. "Ripley, belay technical analysis. Acknowledge."

"Acknowledged, Doctor Anne Peterson."

Anne keyed into her screen, and flicked more switches. "Ripley, replay technical record prior to reentry. Put it on screen."

"Record is fragmented. But complying, Doctor Peterson."

The image started with Commander Mitch Granger in the cockpit, leaning forward, his body language displaying agitation. There was no sound. The astronaut then hurriedly unstrapped himself and used the seatbacks to propel himself to the hatch door separating the cockpit from the rear bay area.

Granger shot back down the craft and punched the button to open the inner door. The camera was on his face. Light from the bay area illuminated his features inside his space helmet; the man's eyes widened, and his mouth dropped open.

Anne whimpered. "Mitch. Oh, Mitch."

"Vocalize, Ripley. What the hell's happening?" Russell's voice was urgent.

Ripley replied emotionlessly: "Multiple suit breaches, life-sign interruption, additional lifeform detected – *warning* Commander Granger – *warning* – *warning*."

The camera closed in on Granger's face that suddenly looked like he had received an electric shock of fear, and then, the film ended.

"Recording interrupted," Ripley intoned with finality.

"*Huh?*" said Russell. "By who?"

"Unknown. No further recording data available. Manual override of controls initiated. Reentry plotted. End of data." Ripley went silent.

The group sat for several seconds and just stared at the now blank screen.

"Well, fuck me," Casey said softly. "Why do I feel one hundred percent less enlightened after listening to that?"

"*Additional lifeform detected,*" Sam said. "What *the hell* does that mean?"

Alex turned to the door, and remembered the sensation he had when they'd first approached the *Orlando* – that something was in there, something other than the Russians.

Sam followed his eyes. "*Ah,* shit."

Alex nodded.

"What's back there?" Morag asked, her brows drawn hard together.

Quietly Anne plugged her camera into a slot in the console. She worked for a few seconds uploading data, and then gasped. "What?" Her hands slowly rose from the console. "No, no, oh god, no." Her hands went to each side of her head.

"What's up with her?" Casey frowned.

"Anne?" Morag immediately went and threw an arm around her shoulders. The NASA woman rocked back and forward.

"*No, no, no.*"

Russell Burrows left his chair to crouch beside the pair of women. "Anne, what is it?"

Anne shook her head. "It can't be. It must be wrong." She lifted a finger to point.

"You're getting Ripley to analyze the prints you recovered from that ... hand thing." Russell squinted at the results. "*Oh shit.*" His eyes went wide.

Anne sobbed and rocked back and forth. Alex looked over their shoulders toward the lit console.

"The prints ... they belong to one of the astronauts." He suddenly understood her horror. "Commander Mitch Granger."

"No, there must be an error in the system." Russell lunged past Anne and began to scroll through the data.

Anne looked up then, her face streaked wet behind her mask. "I suspected, *no*, I knew all along. Out in that horrible mist jungle, when we were attacked and that thing grabbed me, I recognized something about its eyes; it seemed to do the same to me. Someone was still in there." Her chin quivered and she grabbed Russell's arm. "It was Mitch, *I knew it, I just knew it.*"

"This is a fucking horror story." Casey Franks' teeth were grit.

Sam turned to Alex, his jaw jutted. "Like you said, whatever the hell is in this atmosphere, it's changing everything."

"*It's changing everything,*" Russell repeated. His hands shook as he read more data. "The *Orlando* had a range of specimens for biological testing – cockroaches, ants, worms – Jesus, even slime molds. They were testing the effects of solar radiation on them."

"So what? They've done those tests before," Sam said.

"They all mutated," Morag said.

"It wasn't the solar radiation," Alex said. "It was something far more pervasive. These creatures have evolved to better survive in *this* environment." Alex turned to look out the front window. "Those things out in the mist; they used to be human."

Russell turned away and threw up, but all he managed to do was streak the bottom of his face mask in bile.

"Jesus." Alex tilted his head back. "Whatever was in that damned asteroid fragment they found in space is either some sort of mutagen or a contagion. They brought it all the way down here, and it's still active."

Alex exhaled long and slow. "Doctor Peterson." He looked down at the blubbering woman. "*Anne!*"

"Wha ...?" Her head came up.

"Do you think those creatures, *ah*, your astronauts, can be cured?" Alex waited.

She stared off into the distance for another few moments before her head began to shake. "How? How would we even start? You tell me; how do you cure evolution? Can you devolve mankind back into some sort of early hominid? Or perhaps turn a mammal back into an amphibian?" she sniggered. "Why stop there, why not devolve us all back into bony plated fishes?" She giggled.

"Well, she's going to be a lot of help." Casey's lip curled.

"Hey, lighten up, she just lost her fiancé," Russell said.

"She lost him the moment they chose to take that thing into the body of the *Orlando*," Sam said. "So we're back to square one."

"We're gonna have to kill 'em all," Casey snarled.

"But it's still Mitch, he knows me," Anne wailed.

"Too late." Alex brow's creased. "You said yourself, there's no bringing him back."

"Out in the mist, when we were attacked. He was going to take me, but he looked at me, I mean, *really* looked at me." Anne's eyes were streaming again behind her visor. "He knew me. It's still him in there. I can talk to him."

"So they took our buddy instead – and fucking ate him alive." Casey lunged, but Alex threw out an arm, stopping her.

Anne slumped. "We can't kill them. We should try to communicate."

"Yeah, and maybe we should all sit down and sing kumbaya with them," Casey said, stabbing a finger at her.

Morag got to her feet, and rung her hands. "This stuff is not just in the atmosphere," she said. "Scott McIntyre was infected. He ran off into the mist. But before he did, he looked ... *different*." She audibly gulped. "Plus, we think we saw some of those cockroaches – big as a pool table." She made fists. "What'll it do to us?"

"Yeah, she's right; McIntyre didn't breathe the shit in, he was spiked," Casey said.

"So was ..." Morag turned to Dunsen who was still staring out through the cockpit's front window.

* * *

All eyes turned to the big Australian HAWC. In the confined space, people backed away.

"Lieutenant Max Dunsen ..." Alex turned square-on to the man. "... what is your operational status?"

The silence stretched. Dunsen finally turned, but the visor masked his face.

"*Soldier*, how do you feel?" Alex asked.

Dunsen just stood there, his head beginning to nod. After a moment, he grunted and then the words seemed to come thick and painfully.

"Headache worse than bloody sunstroke. I can't ..."

"It's okay." Alex motioned to Anne, Russell and Morag who were closest, to get behind him. "Just take it easy there, big guy."

"I can't …" He reached up to his helmet. "So tight – can't breathe."

"Leave that on, mister." Alex crossed to him, with Sam right behind.

Dunsen started to vibrate, and then shudder as if he was having a fit. Alex could see that the armored suit he wore was now impossibly tight across his chest, back, and even bulged at his neck.

In one step, Alex closed in on his HAWC and grabbed his left upper arm, turning him around to face him. He then grabbed the other arm and held Dunsen in front of himself. But Dunsen kept his head down.

"Dunsen." Alex held him tight and shook him. "*Soldier, what is your status?*"

The man began shake, and his movements became more erratic and violent.

"*Soldier!*" Alex struggled to hold him.

Dunsen grabbed the sides of his helmet. "*That, damned sound – can't get it – outta my head.*" Finally, he threw his head back and roared.

Anne put her hands over her ears and screamed, and Russell shrank away from the inhuman sound. Sam lunged in to help Alex hold on to Dunsen.

Franks and Monroe also pushed forward in the cockpit cabin, making it feel crowded and now crackling with tension.

"Jesus Christ." Casey's teeth were bared as she watched. "Please, Dundee, no." She balled her fists.

Dunsen's suit then burst open, showing mottled skin that was all lumps of strange muscle and covered in thick bristles more like that on an insect. He threw his arms back and both Sam and Alex were shaken off like flies.

Sam hit the wall of the cabin, and Alex went down on one knee. Then the stricken HAWC started to swing his arms like clubs, destroying equipment and denting walls, as the cabin was filled with scattering people and screams.

He roared again and Monroe and Casey raised their guns. Casey yelled over the chaos: "Dundee, please don't make me do this."

"Not in here," Alex shouted as he got to his feet. The last thing he wanted in an encased, overcrowded room was for a shooting match to start.

"Open the goddamn door," Alex yelled and dove back at his violently shaking HAWC. Dunsen swung a club-like arm and thumped down on Alex's back.

Sam threw himself over Russell and Anne, shielding them with his body, and Morag, who was closest, spun the airlock wheel of the external door to the outside. She shoved at it, and the door, with only little power remaining, opened with grinding slowness. The heavy air immediately began to billow inside with them.

"Go!" Morag edged out of the way.

Alex then charged at Dunsen, taking him in a tackle around the waist, and bullocking him toward the door. Dunsen threw out both arms, grabbing the frame on either side, roaring and shaking his head.

Alex felt the sinew, muscle, and bone in his grip shifting and sliding, and looked up just as the tormented HAWC's armored helmet split open, revealing the face below.

Alex felt the chill of horror at seeing the once scarred but youthful face of his soldier, now twisted like that of some sort of gargoyle. Alex leaped up to grab the frame over his head and used his body and legs to pummel the man in the chest and kick him backwards.

Dunsen flew out and into the mist.

"Shut it." Alex stood in the doorway, fists bunched, but

feeling agonized over throwing his man outside. He never wanted to have to kill a HAWC and had to keep telling himself it wasn't Dunsen anymore.

"Move." Morag leaped to grab the thick door and tugged futilely, until Alex reached over her to help slam the thick outer door shut.

Alex rolled away, and Morag put a hand on the locking wheel, about to spin it, when it was jerked from her hands and began to lever open. Huge stubby fingers came in around its edges.

Casey Franks barged forward, climbing over the backs of the cowering NASA techs and Sam, and lifted her weapon. She stuck the barrel through the door.

"Sorry, Dundee, *mate*."

"No." Alex held up a hand. "Don't fir ..."

She pulled the trigger, letting loose hundreds of rounds in a few seconds. There was an inhuman roar, and the hands vanished. The door finally closed and was locked.

Alex got to his feet and spoke through gritted teeth. "I gave you an order, soldier."

Casey dropped her weapon. "That wasn't Dundee anymore, boss. He wouldn't have wanted to go on ... *like that*."

Alex pointed at her face. "It was my call. I had it under control." He felt his anger beginning to rise.

Sam dropped a huge hand on his shoulder. "She's right. Had he got back in here, he would have torn us up."

Alex felt his head begin to throb as he stared at Casey. *Insubordination in the field is treason*, a tiny voice whispered with a sneer in every word. *Throw her outside, before they all challenge you.*

Sam lifted his hand from Alex's shoulder. "Boss?"

Alex turned to throw a punch at the hull of the ship that made the entire craft ring like a bell and left a huge dent in the steel wall.

"We're losing too many." Alex held his head for a moment,

easing the pain he felt inside. "Too many."

No one spoke, but just all breathed heavily, waiting for the adrenalin to cool in their veins, watching for what happened next.

"The Russians are infected," Sam said at last.

"I don't get it," Casey said. "Why aren't the fucking Russians changing as fast as Dunsen? He went from being okay, to becoming like those Morg things in minutes."

Alex paused. "They must be different somehow. Maybe something in their metabolism that fights the change, or infection or whatever it is. They're still changing, but at a slower pace."

"We're all dead," Russell whispered.

Alex spun to point at his face. "Stop that."

"The strength, speed, and rapid healing – I heard rumors," Casey said. "About these Russian Special Forces guys called Kurgan. They were supposed to be as badass as we are. But hyped up with changes to their DNA."

"Well, they're damn well getting worse now," Monroe said, and motioned over his shoulder to the bay area. "Can't be long before those guys are the same as Dunsen, or those monstrosities roaming around outside somewhere."

"They're fucking everywhere." Casey showed her teeth.

Sam tilted his head back. "And they're inside the *Orlando* now." He turned to Alex. "The enemy within."

"And without," Alex responded.

"We're gonna get squeezed real soon." Sam looked around at the tiny cockpit. "Can't stay in here, boss."

Russell Burrows walked toward the front cockpit window and stared out at the darkening clouds. "Our astronauts, Mitch, Gerry, and Beth, were the first infected. They survived the crash-landing or perhaps had just enough humanity left to bring the ship down. But then they quickly changed, no, *evolved*, into something else once they were here with continual exposure to the biological gas."

Alex stared out through the cockpit window. "And once we run out of oxygen, we either learn to hold our breath, or we breathe in the biological mist too."

"I ain't breathing that shit, no time, never," Monroe said evenly.

"None of us are." Alex turned. "Our primary objectives were to secure the image-data chip, and if any astronauts were alive to bring them home. These things are not our astronauts, so that part of our mission is now nullified."

"*They are,*" Anne demanded hotly.

"Priority now is to get us all out alive. If those things out there want to live, then they better learn to stay outta of our way." Alex glared.

"Easier said than done." Russell sighed. "This is their home now. This is what they've adapted to, and I'm betting they can see through this fog clear as day." He rose. "They're faster, stronger, and damned hardier than we are. They may try to stop us."

"And there'll be even more of them soon," Sam said turning to Alex, and motioning to the bay area. "We need to make a plan, ASAP."

"Then let's get that chip, and get the hell outta here." Alex squared his shoulders. "HAWCs are you ready?"

"*HUA!*"

"You're going to fight them?" Morag said. "In here?"

Alex turned. "They can always surrender."

"Nah, we kill 'em all," Casey said enthusiastically.

"But, what happens if you lose? What happens to us?" Anne said quietly.

Casey threw her head back and laughed. "Well then, girlie, you get to try out your communication theory."

CHAPTER 29

"Sam, Monroe, Franks, with me." Alex looked at Russell. "And going to need your expertise as well, Mister Burrows."

"Me?" Russell Burrows' mouth dropped open.

"You bet. It's your bus," Casey sneered.

"Everyone else, once we go through that door, lay flat on the ground," Alex said – no one needed to ask why.

"What's the plan, boss?" Sam asked, rolling huge shoulders.

"We ask nicely." Alex readied himself. "Once." He reached out a hand to the door-locking button. He held up three fingers, counting them down. Then he punched it.

Alex went in first to the bay area of the *Orlando* shuttle. The mist here was thicker inside than out.

Sam was beside him and the NASA engineer was nervously trying to see around one of the enormous HAWC's armored shoulders. Alex saw that the Russians had sealed the rip in the side of the craft using metal rods and spare panels and all lashed together with cable. They were obviously intent on keeping something out.

Alex held up a hand, and the HAWCs stopped to stare. The three hulking men all had their backs turned and were gathered around something at the rear of the bay area.

"What the fu ..." Casey pointed her RG3, but Alex waved it down.

"Wait here."

Alex eased up behind the men and saw they were fixated on some sort of long, dark rock. He immediately felt the warmth coming off it, and it made his skin tingle – *radiation*.

He leaned toward Russell. "Mister Burrows, stay back. There's radiation coming off this thing. Our suits will give us some protection, yours won't."

Russell fumbled a small Geiger counter from his pack, and held it up. "This must be it; the asteroid fragment that the *Orlando* crew recovered from space. I remember ..." His voice fell away for a moment, as his mind probably took him back to the event. He pointed to toward the long rock. "I remember watching them grab it from space. We expected it to be radioactive. But it's tolerable, for a while. Wouldn't want to stay to close for too long, but we're okay for now." He lowered his arm. "Recovering this was the last thing they did."

Sam nodded. "Just before everything went to shit."

"Yes." Russell waved his hand in front of himself, making the fog swirl. "This has got to be where the gas is emanating from. Whatever is inside that space rock, it's reacting with the Earth's atmosphere, oxidizing somehow, and creating a chemical imbalance and biological reaction." He craned forward and his brows pulled together. "What the hell is that?"

Alex turned, but the three Russians seemed to close ranks even more. Whatever was inside was more important to the Russians than worrying about the HAWCs.

"*Hey*, step aside," Alex demanded.

Sam came and stood at his shoulder. "You heard the man, step *the hell* aside."

One of the Russians turned; his totally dark eyes seemed to swim as if he was drugged. Sam stepped up, grabbed his shoulder and tugged him back a step. The Russian seemed in a trance, and even though Sam had pulled him back another few feet, he just turned once again to the rock.

"They've zoned out." Sam looked down at the rock, and then staggered back. "What the hell?"

Alex felt his skin crawl. The surface of the dark purplish rock glittered with some sort of crystalline composition, but there was a rent in its side, and a cavity where within its depths something throbbed with a revolting life. It looked like a giant blob of mucus-covered jelly.

"Looks like a freaking brain," Sam said and lifted his weapon.

The biggest of the Russians, Zlatan he had said his name was, spun, and then stepped in front of Sam. "*No!*"

Alex looked from the blob to the Russian. The huge man stared, large eyes now almost lidless. His other men still stood staring down at the glistening blob of jelly, as if its rhythmic beating transfixed them.

Alex pointed with his gun. "What is it?"

"I, I don't know." The Russian shrugged massive lumped shoulders. "I can't explain. But it's calling to us."

"Calling to you? To do what?" Sam asked.

Zlatan turned his huge browed forehead. "To join with it …" He shook his head slowly. "It sings." He lapsed into silence.

Russell tried to edge closer, but found it difficult to move past the Russians. He settled for holding out a long slim probe. We waved aside the gas that was rising from it. "I think this is also where the mold is coming from. It's the source of both the atmosphere change and the growth." He indicated where the slime-coated cavity was spilling some of its contents to the floor.

"Looks like we found our genesis point," Alex said.

Casey snorted. "This shuttle crashed less than three days ago. And already this crap has spread over several miles. What in the world grows like that?"

Russell retreated a few steps. "Well actually, some molds can spread below forest floors for hundreds of miles." He turned back. "But you're right, nothing at all spreads at this rate." He looked up. "On this world anyway."

Alex grunted. "It's affecting everything and everyone here that's been exposed to it." He looked again at Zlatan, and then at the fragment. "We need to destroy it."

Zlatan and his men spun then, and stood shoulder to shoulder, forming a wall of flesh in front of it.

Sam lowered his brow. "Seems our new buddies might have a problem with that."

Casey pointed at them. "And I have a fucking problem with them."

"We just want the satellite data." Alex looked at each of the hulking, deformed men – they seemed even bigger and more monstrous. He was still prepared to take them on, but knew now there'd be a good chance his team could get a tear in their suits, and end up exposed like the Russians.

Zlatan continued to stare with his lidless black eyes. "They'll be coming back soon."

Alex looked to the makeshift barriers over the hole in the bay area wall. "You've sealed them out."

"We put a few holes in them," said Casey. "They'll think twice about trying anything again soon."

"They haven't gone anywhere," Zlatan said. He pointed to a pile of bones and cloth material heaped in the corner. "Because this is their home."

Alex saw the wads of insulating foam rubber, soiled and torn spacesuit material, and other debris, and he knew Zlatan was right.

Alex felt the urgency burning inside him. "We just want the ..."

Zlatan turned away from him, staring toward the makeshift barrier. "And now, you have only minutes before *they* return."

"Oh god." Russell started to edge back toward the door to the command cabin. "We need to leave."

"Boss, we can't fight 'em all." Sam kept his eyes on the Russians. "Live to fight another day."

The buzzing in Alex's head grew louder, more insistent. The Russians parted slightly and Sam made a guttural sound in his throat. "*Ah* ... that thing." He lifted his arm in front of his face to shield it.

Alex turned to the meteorite fragment and grimaced. The foul, pulsating sack inside quivered slightly. He could feel a tingling running through his stomach and tickling in his head – he didn't like it.

"Let's get out of here; that thing is giving off some sort of wave-like pulse and it's giving me the creeps."

Casey pointed with two fingers at the throbbing entity. "We should just fucking destroy—" She abruptly stopped and a bewildered look came over her. "*What did I ...?*"

The weird buzzing deep inside Alex's head rose to become like a blizzard of noise. He turned to Casey, and was about to ask what she meant, when he simply ... forgot.

He gritted his teeth, blocking it out. Sam was right; if they engaged, they'd struggle just to take down the Russians. But what if the Morg decided to bust in while they were locked in? They wouldn't survive being attacked by both groups.

Alex pointed at Zlatan. "Enjoy the satellite data while you can." He started to back toward the door. "You aren't going home anyway."

Alex and the team crept out, as Zlatan and his men turned back to the glowing asteroid fragment. Alex paused to watch them for a moment; the frightening thing was Zlatan had said the weird blob had sung to him.

Now Alex could hear it too.

CHAPTER 30

USSTRATCOM Biological Research Facility

"Proceed," Jack Hammerson said, not able to take his eyes off the thing on the stainless-steel table.

Doctor Phillip Hertzog nodded from within his sealed suit, and stared back down at the grotesque cadaver.

"Amazing," he said softly, moving up to the head. Using two fingers, he pointed to the forehead. "You see these?" He indicated some darkening discs around the two standard eyes.

"I do," Jack Hammerson said, moving a little closer, and rolling slick shoulders. He hated wearing the high-grade biological suits, as even with their own air-con units, they were as uncomfortable as hell.

"I think they're the beginning of additional ocular organs."

"Extra eyes?" Hammerson remained impassive.

"Oh yes." Hertzog looked up. "The ultimate predatory advantage. Multiple eyes exist in a few other deadly hunters as well – the spider has eight, of course. But also, the praying mantis has five eyes – two large compound ones and three smaller ones in the center of its head."

Hammerson just nodded, and Hertzog turned back to the corpse, picked up a probe and prized open the lips. "No human teeth remaining." He pushed down, causing the jaw to distend like a gaping fish. On either side of the mouth, there looked to be odd growths. "And these look like the beginning of *maxillipeds* – usually only see these on crabs or insects." He whistled. "Amazing."

"I already got that. What else?" Hammerson said abruptly.

"The change is as fascinating as it is significant. And all undertaken in a matter of hours – this is bio-alteration on an unimaginable scale." He looked up. "The only thing that makes these sorts of gross physiological changes is radiation, and that usually takes a generation. Or ..." He bobbed his head from side to side.

"Or?" Hammerson tilted his chin.

"Evolution," Hertzog said.

"Yeah, and even I know that takes longer, *and* is usually forced by changing environmental or competitive conditions," Hammerson responded.

"Very good, that's right, Colonel; it can take *many* generations. Whatever these poor souls were exposed to was some sort of highly advanced and accelerated mutagen." He grinned. "And after all, isn't that what evolution is? A mutation that benefits a species? And all selected by Mother Nature herself."

Hertzog blinked to clear some perspiration from his eyes, and Hammerson could see an already glistening brow behind his visor. "Okay, I'm going in."

Hammerson craned forward, watching closely.

Hertzog's hand and scalpel hovered over the creature's chest for a moment. The flesh was all lumped and contoured more like that of a reptile, but with clear plating, and at the joints the segments had started to separate – more indicative of an arthropod.

"*Uh* ..." his hand wavered indecisively. "Okay." He pressed down on the flesh.

Hammerson saw the man's finger on the blade bend as he applied pressure, but the flesh wouldn't cut. He pressed down harder.

Plink.

The slim blade broke at the center. "Oh my god, these things are tough sonsofbitches," Hertzog said.

"Tell me about it," Hammerson said. "Most took half a dozen rounds before they even began to slow down."

Hertzog looked down at the multiple bullet wounds. "So I see." He then leaned toward a small silver table containing his instruments and grabbed at the bone saw. He clipped on another full-face splatter-mask and flipped it down.

"Well, we'll see what we see then." He started the small spinning disc, and brought it down on the mottled flesh.

The leathery hide separated, and then came the deeper grind of steel on bone. Hammerson took a few steps back and folded his arms. It took Hertzog ten minutes to create the Y-shape incision of a standard autopsy, when it should have taken him two.

When he was finally done, he used a chest separator to prize apart the massively thick rib cage. Then Hertzog stared down into the cavity, his brow furrowed.

"What the hell have we got here?" He started to delve into the open chest, and Hammerson came closer.

"Oh god." Hertzog clicked his tongue. "No wonder they were tough to take down. Even if you could penetrate the ribs, you'd have to stop two hearts." He moved some organs aside.

"So ..." Hertzog cleared his throat. "We have two functioning, oversized hearts with connected pulmonary trunks. No discernible liver or spleen, and the lungs ..." He edged some viscera aside. "... look atrophied and now resemble something more akin to a tracheal breathing apparatus."

Hertzog looked across at Hammerson. "I think this thing was on its way to being able to absorb oxygen through the pores in its skin."

Jack Hammerson remained impassive and the doctor continued.

"Massive monogastric digestive system typical of an alpha carnivore." He grimaced behind his visor as he cut into the gut. "Jesus Christ." He used to pair of long-nosed forceps to hold up a partially digested human hand. "Its last meal."

He set it aside and continued. "The bladder and bowel have merged, creating a single waste elimination system like that of a reptile or insect."

Hammerson watched, trance-like, as the autopsy progressed to the brain, and then the musculature and skeletal system. When Hertzog stepped back from the flayed carcass, he looked exhausted, and a little green.

"I know this was once a man, but that seems incredible now. Looking at it, if I didn't know what I now know, I would say it was more alien than human." He pointed to a gray blob in a dish. "Even the brain has reduced in size and is more an elongated mass along the spinal cord. This thing might work on a hive mind type basis."

"Like bees or ants?" Hammerson asked.

"Yeah, most likely." Hertzog picked at the long gray organ.

Hammerson's eyes narrowed. "So who or what controls the hive?"

Hertzog looked up and hiked his shoulders. "The queen?"

"Give me your theories, Doc, as this thing is nothing but bat-shit crazy. I need answers ... guesses even," Hammerson said.

"Okay." Hertzog nodded. "Theory one: it's the spores that might be forcing an evolutionary leap in organisms that come into contact with it. The primitive gas is just there for environmental support – their lungs are adapted to it."

"Evolutionary leap?" Hammerson straightened. "Tell me how that big bug-eyed thing is some type of new and improved human being?" Hammerson's brows came together. "And another question: I know some creatures, and now people, turn into these monstrosities, and others into the gray sludge – why?"

Hertzog looked back down at the body and sighed. "Jack, there's a lot more we *don't* know than we *do* know, right now."

"Then give me your best guess. We're running out of time." Hammerson was also running out of patience.

"Okay, okay," Hertzog said. "Well, the glutinous material is an aggressive, mutated form of a normal slime mold that is really only acting as a vector for the spores. The spores' only job is to embed itself in an organism, the host, and then work their way into its DNA."

Hertzog raised a finger. "Then, massive changes are triggered. For some, the spores trigger catastrophic alterations, totally breaking down the host's cellular structure and thus converting it into nothing more than the viscous biological material – the spore carrier. But ..." he waggled his finger, turning to the HAWC commander, "... just like the sperm knows to fight its way to the center of the ova, these spores know to seek out something in the host's DNA strand that tells it that one being is suitable for total breakdown to spore sludge, and another is designated to a type of warrior class ... or breeding class."

"Breeding?" Hammerson felt his gorge rise.

"Sure." Hertzog pointed back to the flayed cadaver. "This biped had functioning reproductive organs."

"A breeding population ... to start an invasion." Hammerson began to grind his teeth. "And we're the raw material."

"Maybe." Hertzog flipped up the secondary visor and then tossed it onto a benchtop. Behind his primary visor, his face ran with sweat. "You asked before how the biped could be some new and improved human being. Basically, it's not,"

Hertzog said. "Not for around here anyway, but think of it in terms of how the human race has reached an evolutionary plateau, and other than some height variations, as a species, we've pretty much stalled now."

"Go on."

Hertzog nodded, talking as he stared down at the strange body. "Well, in the past, environmental factors forced evolutionary changes in creatures, to us – in response to hot or cold, we grew or lost fur. We came down from the trees and stood upright when the jungles were turning into grasslands. We humans grew big brains to outwit our predators. But the thing about growing big brains was it meant a harsh environment didn't change *us* anymore, we changed *it*. If we needed fur, we didn't have to grow it; we simply killed an animal and wore its fur instead. We also didn't need to find caves anymore, we built our own. Our big brains meant we didn't have evolution forcing changes on us anymore."

"And these spore things are forcing evolutionary changes because they think our world is harsh?" Hammerson was incredulous.

"They might if we didn't think about from a human being's perspective." Hertzog responded. "But what if this stuff is forcing evolutionary changes on us because to something non-Earthly, *this* is a harsh environment. Or worse, the world it's creating will be brutal and therefore it might think it's helping us by preparing us physically for an environment, a world, significantly harsher."

Hammerson groaned. "So it's terraforming and transforming us into creatures that can survive in its home environment."

"Why not? Changing us to adapt to a world ruled by tooth and claw." Hertzog gave Hammerson a half smile. "Whatever came down in that shuttle is not from our corner of the universe. And perhaps where it came from, its world was horrifyingly hostile."

Hertzog folded arms over a blood and mucus-spattered suit. "Where exactly was this material picked up from?"

"We believe it came from inside a fragment of asteroid the *Orlando* plucked from space. However, NASA extrapolations tell us that it came from the void – endless space – it could have been traveling for a billion years."

"*Hmm*, until *we* found it. Or it found us." Hertzog cursed softly. "And we brought it home, *huh?*" He sighed. "There's one more thing, Jack. I don't believe this biped had finished changing."

"*Hadn't finished changing?* Jesus Christ, this just keeps getting worse." Hammerson stared for a moment, his mind working. "What would it eventually have become when it *did* finish?"

"I, for one, never want to find out," Hertzog said softly. "But that's not the worst of it. These bipeds can and will breed, and the slime is loaded with spores. Everything about them is designed for rapid reproduction. This could spread catastrophically in a crowded environment."

Hammerson sighed heavily. He had hoped that the autopsy would reveal something he could use to stall the order from Chilton. Some kind of weakness in the creatures, some weapon they could use, or even some hope of slowing down the contamination spread. But there was nothing for it.

Hertzog looked alarmed. "Jack, if it were my call, then step one would be to clean up the source of the infection. We can't let it get out. *Ever.*"

"No, we can't." Hammerson knew he had no choice now, and no more time.

CHAPTER 31

Hammerson clicked on the satellite image of the mountaintop crater where his HAWC team and the NASA scientists were deployed. The spore-mist had risen more than a dozen feet since he had last checked and he expected the hyper-aggressive slime mold – or whatever that weird shit was – would have expanded its territory about the same amount.

Nestled in its warm cocoon underneath the atmosphere blanket it would continue to grow, but thankfully for now, not become the super-aggressive form that had attacked and killed the NASA scientists in lab-45 and many of the townsfolk of Greenbelt.

Once again, he clicked on the extrapolation software his techs had put together. It used predictive analytics to create an advanced timeline for how far and fast the biological gas and the underlying organisms were likely to spread. A digital clock raced forward, speeding up the designated area of the Revelation Mountains.

Hammerson's eyes narrowed as he watched – in another hour, the atmosphere blister would have climbed a further dozen feet. In six more hours, it would reach the rim of the crater. Following that it would begin its long, slow spillover into the valleys.

The environment was still harsh, but as the mass grew the total land it absorbed would grow as well, doubling exponentially every hour – two miles would become four, become eight, become sixteen, become thirty-two, then sixty-four, and so on, and so on.

They had twenty-four hours before the atmosphere blister and carpet of deadly ooze beneath covered 200 square miles. It would then encounter the first of the villages in the lowlands. It would also then enter a more benign climate, and *switch on*. Once that happened, it was anyone's guess as to whether it could be controlled or when the free-floating spores would be lifted on the winds to firstly infect Alaska, Canada, the rest of the US, and then the globe.

Colonel Jack Hammerson knew General Chilton was right to take immediate and significant corrective action. And if he didn't have a horse in the race, he would have come to the same conclusion.

Fact was, HAWCs died, and there were very few old ones, himself being an exception. But time was moving against them. For now, they had the organism contained in a natural kill box. The biological mass would overflow the crater rim in approximately six hours, the detonation would occur in – his eyes moved to his countdown clock – just on five. But his team didn't know any of this.

Chilton had authorized the use of a single GBU43B Massive Ordnance Air Blast – one of the most powerful non-nuclear weapons ever designed. The MOAB was not a penetrator weapon but was created primarily for surface targets, just like this one.

Hammerson had seen test drops; the things were city killers. They initially detonated with the explosive force of eleven tons of TNT and would raise temperatures to 4,500 degrees in an instant. The secondary ignition of the methane-rich atmosphere would amplify the thermal dispersion, turning the entire cusp of the mountaintop into a molten cauldron.

He slammed a fist down hard on his desk – there'd be nothing left of it or his team. And he couldn't even warn them. As far as communications went, they were deaf, dumb, and blind. He couldn't send anyone else in. But even if he thought there was a slim chance of making it in time, or making a difference, he'd goddamn HALO drop in there himself.

He looked again at the visuals – the mountaintop looked like it was stuffed with dirty cotton wool. Trying to affect a blind landing in something like that was suicide.

He could send a probe, drop in a communication spike, but it'd have to land right on Alex's head for him to find it – impossible. Hammerson lowered his hands. *Unless the probe could go looking for him.*

He drummed his fingers on the desk as his mind worked. Go looking for him – *and then find him.*

He lunged for his phone, calling through to the weaponry labs.

"Get me Grey. I need a piece of his tech on a plane, *right now.*"

CHAPTER 32

Something all leathery wings and multiple limbs flew in front of the window. Alex smiled, grimly. Here they were in a downed spaceship, looking out at an alien world. He was starting to doubt he was even on Earth anymore.

He inhaled the canned air of his suit, and wondered what the atmosphere would smell like if they didn't make it out. And what it would feel like, or look like, to see his muscles twist and lump like those of the Morg. He didn't want to find out.

"Listen up." Alex turned away from the *Orlando* cockpit window and faced the group. "Our oxy-levels are down. We've burned it faster than we expected through all the activity." He turned to Sam. "Sam ..."

Sam Reid nodded. "I figure we've got ten hours remaining if we just sit here on our asses, eight hours if we head for home, and maybe five if we gotta run and fight all the way back."

"After that, we start to suck this crap into our lungs," Alex finished.

"And then we join the locals," Casey seethed.

"Okay, I think if we're careful, we can make it – steady as she goes, conserve our energy, and all that," Russell added.

"Really?" Alex gave him a lopsided smile. "Anyone else think we're not going to have fight and run every damn step of the way? To get to the crater wall, at double time, then scale to the top to make it above the mist line and get to clean air, we're going to need every second and every breath we have left. Five hours is our drop dead limit."

Russell's mouth dropped open. "Double time? Jesus Christ, Hunter, we're exhausted, and you want us to run and climb for five hours?" He had an arm around Anne who still looked washed out.

"Yes." Alex turned to look out of the cockpit window again and into a speckled mist so thick the window could have been painted over. It was like a microscopic snowstorm, except it moved, swirled and eddied like it was a turbulent current in an ocean.

Alex also sensed things darting back and forth, some small, and some larger. And a while back he had felt something big, *very big*, circle them. Now, it had either moved on, or had paused somewhere, waiting.

"Dammit, we're wearing HAZMAT suits, with oxygen tanks, and not those lightweight things you've got," Russell spluttered. "Anne won't make it. She's dead on her feet now. *We all are*, Captain." He was seething now. "You might as well just kill us now and be done with it."

"You've got two minutes to come up with an alternative plan, Professor." Alex lifted his chin, waiting.

Russell's lip curled. "Oh, for god's sake, there is no other plan."

"That's what I thought." Alex went to turn to Sam, but Russell stood quickly and grabbed at him.

"This plan of yours is only designed to get you and your team of super warriors to safety, isn't it? And the rest of us can go to hell."

Alex stared. "Don't think for a second I was ever Mister

Nice Guy."

Muttering, Russell sunk back down and put his arm around Anne.

Morag stood. "If we run out of air and have to breathe this … stuff, we'll start to change, won't we?"

Alex nodded.

"Well, I'm not going to end up like those things out there, those Morg things." She looked down at Anne and Russell. "I'll run till I die if I have to."

"Yeah." Casey made a fist in the air for the woman. "That's it, babe."

"Time's up," Alex said. "Live or die?"

Russell just shook his head. "I guess we've got no choice."

Alex faced the group. "We are in a small metal box, and outside it might as well be an alien world. We're going to have to run until we feel like we're going to drop, and then we're going to run some more. It's going to hurt like hell, but the human body can take more pain than you'd believe."

Russell audibly gulped and Anne nodded meekly. Morag's mouth was set in a tight line. "We're outnumbered," Morag said. "If the Russians *have* joined the …" She briefly looked over her shoulder at Anne before going on. "… the *Orlando* crew, then that makes about six of them."

"And you can add in McIntyre and maybe Dunsen, if he's still alive, to that bunch," Casey said. "And probably your idiot cameraman."

"Renner, Calvin Renner," Morag said and scowled back at Casey.

Alex nodded. "I estimate we now have up to eight or maybe nine hostiles out there. They may take a run at us, and they may not."

"This is where they've been holing up," Monroe said. "So, they may all just come back here to their nest."

"I don't get the feeling these Morg are the live and let live types. They want us, as food or as new recruits," Sam said.

"This infection, or whatever it is, has a one hundred percent inclusion rate. Either you get affected and become the beast, or worse, you are dissembled into some sort of primordial spore-slime." Russell licked dry lips. "Or alternatively, you get killed by the affected individuals. Either way, it gets out of here, it's bad news for the rest of the world."

"If we had the ordnance, we could blow it," Sam said. "The atmosphere detonation would do the rest for us."

"Shit." Alex tilted his head back, and let out a bitter laugh. "Of course." He exhaled, and then turned to Sam. "If we had the ordnance, then we'd make sure nothing ever leaves this mountaintop, right?"

"Yeah." Sam frowned, but his mouth began to curve into a smile. "What?"

"Who thinks like us, and knows that if this stuff gets out it's going to be game over for the world?" Alex tilted his head. "Oh yeah, and who *does* have the ordnance?"

Sam grinned. "Colonel Jack Hammerson."

"Right, the Hammer," Alex said. "He has all the kill power he needs. I'm betting that he's already planning a drop, or will soon." Alex folded his arms. "We need to coordinate and make sure we're over the rim by then."

"By when though?" Morag asked.

"Exactly; when, what? How? We can't coordinate that when outside. They can't even talk to us. A minute's difference and it might as well be suicide or murder," Russell pleaded.

"Yeah, I like it," Casey said. "The Russians, the data chip, and every other weird piece of shit in here will be ash."

"Plug?" Sam raised his eyebrows.

Alex nodded. "Last one."

Sam started to open the messenger on his wrist and waited

to enter data. "Okay boss, ready when you are."

Alex nodded. "*Orlando* site compromised – *stop* – contagion must not escape mountain – *stop*." He smiled, grimly. "Burn it all to hell – *stop*."

"Jesus Christ." Russell eased back down.

Alex looked at his watch. "Request detonation at 20:00 hours." He looked up. "That gives us our five hours – same as our oxygen."

"Wait, wait; you just said we'd need all of that to make it to the wall, and then more to climb out." Russell's mouth hung open. "Are you *trying* to kill us? Might as well just say, go ahead and drop it right now."

Casey laughed out loud.

"No, *one hour*, to climb. People's oxygen will start running out then, and we'll start to breathe in this mutagenic atmosphere. In my book, that's going to be worse than death. So, consider it extra motivation." Alex turned. "Sam."

Sam nodded to Casey. "Door." He loaded the plug and waited for the door to outside to be opened. Casey and Monroe had their guns up and pointed as the mist billowed, but thankfully nothing else rushed in at them. Sam hung his huge body out, pointed the stubby gun skyward, and fired.

"One away." He pulled himself back in, and Casey immediately pulled the door shut again.

"Plan is in motion. Bring the rain," Monroe hooted.

CHAPTER 33

Hammerson watched the blip of the helicopter approach the mountaintop with his special delivery onboard. Chilton's cauterization drop was a few hours away, so there was still a slim chance his dumb idea might work.

Grey had protested to high hell, but at the end of the day, his technology was there for offense and defense, and not to sit in the laboratory and have the eggheads endlessly tinker with it.

The scientist had also complained that the technology was still only in second-level testing, and they weren't sure about the neural link componentry. That meant that when it linked to a particular person, it became psychologically bonded, and in this case, that was to be Alex Hunter. He would become its homing beacon, its target, and best friend. It could be programmed to be his assassin or his guardian angel.

But Grey had been emphatic in his warning – the humanistic logic models were still very much experimental. The emotive patterning they inserted could work as hoped and provide independent as well as team-based thinking, or it could retain vestiges of the baser types of human emotions, such as pride, envy, hate, and even love and anger. It would feed off Alex's psychology patterns – he would be its supercharger.

Hammerson had joked about his pair of Colt 1873 single action handguns at home, and how he loved them and was sure they loved him back. Grey didn't pick up on the joke and had sounded anxious, bordering on panicked.

Hammerson smiled grimly, as he recalled the scientist's agitation.

"Jack, the technology is more than just a weapon. It could think for itself. It might simply decide to become overly protective, and stop Hunter doing what he needed to do. It might even turn on him."

Hammerson could picture the small scientist wringing his hands, as he spoke.

"The risks are enormous," Grey had said.

"Everything we do has risks. Even not acting has its risks," Hammerson had responded softly.

"We just aren't ready to ..."

"Stop talking now, Walter. Generate the neural link to Captain Hunter, and lock it in, that's an order." Hammerson sighed. "You wanted a field test? So now you're going to get one. If it works, my team might just be given a lifeline. And if it doesn't, then it'll be just another piece of shit to add to the great steaming pile the mission has turned into." Hammerson's voice became rock hard. "And my team will all be dead. Understand?"

"Yes, sir, I do. Good luck, sir," Grey had said. "Let me know if there's anything else."

"Will do." Hammerson closed out the call.

Now he was focused on the screen, counting down way too fast – there would be a vacuum bomb burn on the crater top, now in t-minus 183 minutes, just over three hours. There'd be nothing left in that crater but ash.

The HAWC data squirt was translated onto his screen. He looked at the time stamp and grunted – it was good the Arcadian had anticipated the drop, but he didn't know they were already executing it.

The problem was, Alex had wanted an extra hour, that they didn't have, and what they had left was already counting down. Minutes and seconds counted in this job. Hammerson just prayed his care package wasn't going to arrive too late to make a difference.

Goddamnit, his HAWCs better be out by then.

CHAPTER 34

"Weapons check," Alex ordered, and Sam, Casey, and Monroe started to quickly run their eyes and hands over their gear. Morag was mesmerized as it was done almost in unison, their fingers deftly checking triggers, shielding, guards, and ammunition. In another few seconds, they were done.

Morag felt a fluttering in her stomach at the thought of going outside. She eased her head around to gaze out the *Orlando*'s window. It was now impenetrable out there. Condensation ran down the glass, and from time to time they'd all seen small things flit past, like tiny birds, but with carapace-covered bodies and wings that beat faster than the eye could follow.

Outside against the skin of the space shuttle it sounded like hail hitting a tin roof, as things plinked against the fuselage. As Morag stared, a dot came out of the mist, grew to the size of a fist and then slammed onto the window with a solid *thunk*, and stuck there.

"What the hell?" She raised an arm to point.

The group followed her gaze. The thing on the window had a long body with dozens of legs. One end had long, red pincers that tried their luck against the hard glass, and at its other end there was a wicked-looking glistening spike. Its wings continued to flutter, and after a moment it turned its head so a single bulbous eye could regard the people inside.

"Holy crap, man. Check this out," Monroe said.

"That might just be the source of the buzzing we could hear," Sam said and narrowed his eyes at the thing.

"*Jeee-zuz*. Bet it's a stinger." Monroe leaned toward it and then knocked against the glass with a knuckle.

The thing responded by lifting its tail and jabbing it down where the HAWC's knuckle had been.

"Told ya." He yanked his hand back, but the thing kept drilling down with its tail.

"Don't worry, nothing is getting through that – the fused silica outer panes can withstand micrometeorite strike and reentry temperatures." Russell Burrows carefully made his way toward the bug on the cockpit window. "If it can keep out the vacuum of space, we can certainly keep out a big, ugly insect." Russell leaned closer to peer at the thing, and it responded by once again jabbing its barb at him.

"Amazing. Insectoid, but also has some arachnoid features. And I can see what looks like fur on its body."

Another bug smacked violently onto the glass, and it caused Russell to instinctively jerk his head back. "Whoa." He turned and chuckled nervously.

Morag heard Alex make a deep sound in his chest and walk toward Sam Reid, where the pair then engaged in a quiet conversation. She turned back to the group and hugged herself, feeling suddenly cold. She didn't want to go back out there, but also knew that though outside it *might* mean death, staying inside meant *certain* death.

Anne sat staring at the bulkhead door, her eyes glazed over, and Morag tried to imagine what the NASA woman was thinking – perhaps she was wondering if the man she loved was somehow still trapped inside the mind of the monstrous thing that lumbered about outside, or whether he was already dead and now fully replaced by the beast.

A third bug thudded against the window, and Russell tilted his head. "Well, well, seems they're attracted by something."

"Yeah, us," Casey snorted. "Hey, Monroe, got any bug spray?"

Monroe held up his RG3. "Yep, my universal fly swatter."

She bumped knuckles. "I heard that."

"Stop worrying, they're not getting in." Russell turned away from the window.

"That's true, Russell. But we're not staying inside here, are we?" Morag gave him a lopsided grin.

"This is not a good idea." Russell spoke through gritted teeth. "We haven't got a chance."

"Focus," Alex demanded. "*Form up.*"

On Alex's command, the HAWCs fell in on either side of the door. There was no fear in their faces, just an eagerness to engage and win against any adversary.

Another bug smacked onto the glass and regarded them hungrily. Then another, until the window was becoming crowded with bristling legs, working mandibles, and jabbing spikes. The sound of them trying to drill their stings into the glass was beginning to sound like the clack of a furious typewriter. The already weak outside light was beginning to be shut out, making it gloomy in the cockpit.

Morag drew in a deep breath to try to calm herself, but now she felt physically ill.

"Priority one, we need to be above this atmosphere line before we run out of breathable air or this place is turned to ash – four hours. Not four hours and five minutes, or even four hours and five seconds, but *four* hours." Alex waited until each of them nodded before going on.

He turned to his remaining HAWCs. "Soldiers, we need to be over the rim at time of detonation – not at the rim, or on the edge of the rim, but over it. The crater wall even at the top is about fifty feet of solid granite and will contain the blast and hopefully vent the heat and force upwards. Even the heat discharge will be deadly if we're too close."

"And what priority are our lives?" Russell's jaw was set.

Alex's turned his unblinking eyes on the NASA engineer. Morag noticed they seemed to shine silver in the dark of the cockpit. Like those of a wolf or some other large night predator. "You just worry about staying alive, got it?"

"Or not," Casey sneered at Russell. He muttered as he looked away.

"Questions?" Alex looked along all of their faces.

Morag had too many to count, but kept them behind her teeth.

Alex turned back to the door. "Medium projectile range, free fire, shoot to kill."

"*HUA!*"

"Shields up." Discs of air whirred to life on the HAWCs' arms.

"On my order." Alex put his hand on the spinning lock wheel, and turned back to the group. His eyes found Morag.

"Stay at our center at all times." He smiled, or so she hoped.

Morag sucked in a breath, conscious of her heartbeat. "Sure."

Alex waited for a few seconds, spun the wheel and then shouldered the heavy door open. Thick fog wafted in.

"*Go, go go!*"

Sam, Monroe, and Casey flew out through the hatch door like they were a single being. Morag jumped through after them and Alex grabbed Anne and Russell and threw them out. They hit the squelching ground, rolled and came up fast, immediately running hard behind the HAWCs.

CHAPTER 35

Zlatan felt the animalistic urges run through him again like a wave. He was the largest and most advanced of the Kurgan, and perhaps that was why he had been able to resist the undeniable changes for so long. His remaining team had shed their clothing, or simply burst from it, and now stood swaying before the meteorite fragment as though it was some sort of religious icon they needed to pay homage to.

He grimaced from the gnawing in his gut. He hungered for meat, red meat, raw and dripping. He tilted his head back, and would have closed his eyes but he had no lids anymore. He saw and heard everything, and felt *connected* to the life inside and out.

He looked back at the meteorite fragment. It sung to him, caressed his brain, and urged him to leave this former life behind, and to once and for all be free. It promised a new world with a new beginning and a new order. He would be part of it. He heard his men's thoughts, still vaguely human. But the others outside did not think at all like them. They were now part of some sort of growing hive mind.

Zlatan stared at the beautiful thing nestled in the rocky cradle of the fragment. It had been searching for them for a billion years, after being blasted free from its home world. It loved them, but knew it needed to make changes for it to adapt, and change them to adapt to it.

A ghost from his past life still haunted him – a lovely Russian girl. He struggled to remember her name – it came back in a rush – *Rahda, yes, that was it.* He tried to recall her voice, but when he searched, the insect-like buzzing in his head just grew louder as if it were trying to wash away all trace of her.

The singing in his head grew more insistent, almost painful. He lifted an arm and saw that the material of his suit was splitting, showing the weird mottled flesh and bony plates like on those of his men. How could he ever go home now?

Zlatan's eyes traveled up to his hand and he examined it closely; the fingers were becoming fused together into just three sharp prongs, more like those of some sort of burrowing creature. He would have laughed if his mouth permitted that action now.

"You all look like crap," one of the Americans had said. Zlatan felt his face. There were strange lumps and fissures, and the size and shape was grotesquely wrong. The American was right; they were being made sick and strong at the same time, more *and less* human with every breath they took in this hellish place.

His attention was drawn to the American soldiers as they burst from the space shuttle with the women. His men didn't care anymore, preferring the siren call from the thing inside the asteroid fragment. He knew what the *Orlando* crew had become, and also knew soon enough they would fully transform too. They had lost everything, and could never return home.

He lifted a grotesque arm to wave to the fleeing people and tried to call to them, but all that emanated was a mewling sound from a throat not designed for words anymore.

The irresistible singing pulled at him, but his Herculean will kept his gaze on the ever-thickening mist. There was something else that drove him on that was far more compelling than the entity inside the *Orlando*. Something he desperately needed to do.

He began to follow the Americans.

CHAPTER 36

Sam Reid bullocked through the strange growths as all around them the dense fog was alive with sound and movement.

It's like some sort of weird alien jungle, and it's growing. Out in the speckled air things called, squealed and buzzed in a mockery of a real jungle, and each of the noises was strangely similar to something earthly but then foreign enough to not be identifiable.

One of the long bugs from the *Orlando* cockpit window alighted on Sam's shoulder, and before it had a chance to stab at him with its stinger, he reached up with an armored-gloved hand, grabbed it and squeezed. Green mush burst from each end, before he threw it to the mud.

He briefly looked down to where it had landed, but already the weird slime had closed over it, sucking it down and swallowing it completely.

If we fall, there won't be a need for a burial here.

The HAWCs were a wall on either side of the remaining civilians, and he and the other soldiers fired at things big and small that tried to take a run at them. The RG3s made a soft spitting sound and in return, there came screams that could not possibly have come from human mouths.

Sam never saw the things clearly, and frankly, he didn't *want* to. One thing he knew for sure, there was no way he was going to end up like Steve Knight, peeled from his armored suit and devoured right down to bones.

The constant *zumm* of insects grew louder, and things flitted overhead, darting in and out of the soupy air, perhaps attracted by the sound, movement, or their body heat. Some of them were the revolting bugs from the *Orlando* shuttle, but others were the size of small dogs and looked assembled from overlapping plates, spikes, and too many eyes.

Underfoot things crunched like seashells and he remembered what Morag had said about the giant roach and imagined that if he left a foot on the ground for too long something with sharp, bristling claws would latch onto it. He lifted his feet a little higher as he charged onward.

Around them, towering columns rose where he was sure there had been none before, and they loomed from the fog like silent sentinels, dripping with the slime, but now also wriggling with life, as though under the coating of mucus. There were countless worms moving up and down their trunks. Or perhaps they were internal organs, drinking or digesting, or excreting strange materials they feed upon.

He glanced at one of them a moment longer, and he was sure a single grapefruit-sized eye opened stickily on the trunk. It was milky white, and it watched them pass by before the entire column leaned after them, like a revolting finger trying to touch them.

Sam put his head down, trying to focus; the trunk-like finger things were all around them – *hands* – that's what they were. Wanting to grab at them as if the entire disgusting mess was trying to stop them from leaving.

Then, it was like they had fallen into a vacuum – there was no more sound or movement, and immediately Sam sensed danger. Behind him, Alex Hunter roared a furious warning. Then they were hit.

Sam swung his rifle around, but something big came out of the mist like a freight train and took him out of the line. He felt weightless as he flew through the air, landing in the slime.

Huge bodies came from both sides, moving so fast that they seemed to defy physics. Each of the HAWCs was smashed, and he saw Morag dive to the mud, roll and then grab at Anne who was down with her hands up over her head. They huddled together on the ground.

Sam launched himself back to his feet, engaged his shield and backhanded one of the massive beasts who should've been knocked a dozen feet, but instead just skidded backwards and then immediately came at him again, loping on all fours to gather speed, before rising on two and then leaping at him.

The hugely powerful HAWC with the power-assisted MECH armor took it head on, but was no match for the size and strength of the thing. They went down together, locked in a death roll.

Right beside them, Franks cursed as another of the massive bipeds ripped at her weapon, tearing it from her grip and pulverizing it in massive clawed hands. That elicited more curses, followed by her pulling a long, dark blade and swinging with all her upper-body strength to bury it hilt-deep into the meat of the thing's neck. It screamed and pulled back, and then dragged at the knife in its flesh.

Chaos ruled, black blood spurted, and the nightmarish noise was near deafening – Sam felt they were in hell.

* * *

Morag spun about. "Where's Russell?" Anne had her head down so Morag shook her and repeated the question at a shout. This time Anne just jerked her head and tried to crawl further under Morag's arm.

Morag started to drag Anne away from the fray when she suddenly felt huge hands grab her shoulders, and she was lifted and then flung away like she weighed nothing. Even as she tumbled through the air, she saw Anne being seized by another creature.

Morag hit the ground and slid, but was immediately caught by the back of her suit and pulled through the slime. She glanced up, knowing what she would see, but was still terrified by what was there – the thing that had her was a monstrosity from a madman's nightmare. She fought at it, remembering when they found the missing HAWC's helmet, bloody and broken open like a fruit – she didn't want to end up like that.

She pummeled at the hand, but her knuckles bounced off plating that felt like hard plastic. The thing looked down, and multiple eyes regarded her dispassionately. Its mouth worked feverishly with tiny arms and feelers on each side that opened and closed like some sort of crab.

Morag screamed. In turn there came grunts, clicks, and a sound like a whistle, and then the attack on the HAWCs was abandoned. She knew why – they had what they wanted – her and Anne.

CHAPTER 37

"Sound off, people." Alex walked among his battered team and threw out a hand to pull Drake Monroe to his feet. Alex held up his RG3; the barrel and casing were crushed. He cursed and then tossed it aside.

One after the other, his HAWCs called back to him – all of them alive. *Good.* He could see that some shook heads and tested shoulders, and he knew that was as close as any would come to admitting to having injuries.

"Weapons check." Alex saw a prone figure in a NASA suit and quickly crossed to them. He rolled the body over and Russell screamed and held hands up over his visor.

"It's okay, you're safe." He pulled the man up. "Where's Anne?" He looked around. "And Morag?"

Russell shook his head, looking sheepish. "I don't know. I got hit and went down. That's all I remember. Sorry."

"Okay." Alex understood. He and his HAWCs were warriors, designed for fighting, but not Russell. He spun back to his team.

His HAWCs held broken weapons. Sam held up his and looked at the heavy casing. "They targeted these. Busted all of them. Seems they did what they came to do – disarm us."

"That's not all," Alex growled. "Spread out; we got missing people. Find me a trail."

It didn't take long for the remains of his team to come back in.

"Grounds all chopped up close in, but no trail further out." Sam shrugged. "Or if there was that damned slime has closed over it already."

Alex exhaled hard through his nose. "So, they didn't just come to disarm us. They came for the women." He checked the timer counting down on his arm. "We got no time for this shit." Alex walked a few paces away, and stopped to stare out into the wall of cloud that seemed calm now, as though sated after swallowing Morag and Anne.

He knew he couldn't leave the women. He also knew he couldn't lead his HAWCs back in for a rescue, as they'd never make it out before the detonation caught them. He turned to look at his remaining team – they were tired. Anyone he took with him would be as good as dead.

Alex decided. "Sam, you're in charge, head for the rendezvous point. I'll get the women."

"I've got your back, boss," Casey said.

"Not this time," Alex told her. "I need to travel light and fast. You all need to get to the rendezvous point, and get Mister Burrows and yourselves out."

She started to disagree, but he held up a hand. "You know you can't keep up with me, and I can lower my heart rate and oxygen consumption. You can't." He placed his hand on her heavily muscled shoulder. "I'm betting you're going to be fighting tooth and nail to get there; you need to be in that fight, Lieutenant Franks. Clear a path; I'll be needing it later."

Her jaw jutted. Sam Reid stepped closer. "The fight's going to be with you, boss. And you know *I* can keep up."

I'm wasting time. "Listen up, people. When I get back with Morag and Anne, you all *better* be up at that rendezvous point, *clear?*"

Sam growled deep in his chest and Casey's fists were still balled.

"*Am I clear?*" Alex lunged forward shouting.

"*HUA.*"

Alex nodded. There were no more words. He turned and vanished into the roiling fog.

* * *

Morag and Anne were thrown into the back of the downed space shuttle like sacks of sand. They immediately scrambled away from the Morg creatures to huddle against the wall, trying to make themselves as small as possible.

The hulking creatures were bulging with lumped muscle and strange growths that looked like coral and sea anemones. One of them went and stood before the fragment of meteorite. But then it stopped and just seemed to lean forward to stare and inhale the gases coming off it and take them deep into its lungs.

There were three of the Morg crowded into the bay area of the *Orlando*, and she heard one or more moving around outside – perhaps the Russians now joining with them. Alex Hunter had been right, this was obviously their home, or nest, or hive, for whatever these things had become. Some still had the remnants of clothing hanging from their bodies.

They had brought one of the HAWC guns, but had discarded it once they returned, as it seemed the strange rock with glowing interior was all that mattered to them.

They ignored the RG3 completely, and Morag mentally calculated how easy it would be to grab. The creative side of her brain conjured up images of her diving, snatching the weapon up, and blowing dinner-plate sized holes in the beasts, before grabbing Anne and returning to Alex and his HAWCs as a hero.

But then her logical brain kicked in and stomped all over her daydreams, shouting at her that it would be impossible, suicide, and worse, it'd probably mean something horrendous like being eaten alive.

She sat for a minute more, but then began to edge forward anyway. *After all, since when did reporters do anything that was logical?*

Immediately, one of the things swung toward her. She froze. It could have been staring right at her, but it was impossible to tell with those weird glassy eyes that were all black like those of a bug or shark.

She looked hard at it, but couldn't tell exactly what the things reminded her of, as they were still basically human shaped, in that they had two arms and legs, but their large heads were receding into their shoulders now. This meant the facial features were spread over a much larger area. The original two large, disc-shaped eyes were now central to a ring of smaller eyes that reminded her of a creepy close-up of a spider.

Morag edged back, but the thing still seemed to watch her. She swallowed dryly. *Look away, you creep.* But *she* couldn't look away either – if the obsidian eyes weren't bad enough, now the nose was also gone, leaving a single hole covered in a small flap, above a mouth that was the real abomination. It was circular hole that puckered together in a tight ring. When opened the mouth telescoped outward on a cartilage scaffolding, and showed a red, circular gullet ringed all the way down with needle-like teeth. It was the mouth of a deep-sea creature, not a human being or anything else that walked on Earth's surface.

At last it turned back to the asteroid fragment, and Morag carefully raised herself up to see better. Inside the long shard of glittering rock, she could just make out something glistening purple that throbbed like a muscle or an exposed organ. She lowered herself and snuggled in tight to Anne.

"Listen, we need to get the hell out of here."

Anne seemed transfixed by the creatures and didn't appear to hear her. Morag nudged her.

"Hey."

"Wha …?" Anne's eyes were wide, but she seemed more spellbound than frightened.

"I said, we need to get out of here. *Now.*" Morag shifted closer to the NASA scientist and felt things crunch underneath her.

"*Yes*, I heard," Anne hissed back, and pulled away from her. "I still think we should try to communicate with them."

"*What?*" Morag grabbed her arm and tugged. "Look down – see what we're sitting on? Fucking piles of bones. I think this is their kitchen. We're not here for pleasant conversation, we're here as food, you fool."

She shook her head. "No, no, no … not me."

The woman is an idiot. Morag looked toward the opening in the side of the bay area; the creatures had jammed the makeshift door back in place, and she could just glimpse the darkening mist that led to the outside.

Even that tiny crack gave her hope. She felt around beneath her and then grabbed what she at first thought was a stick, but turned out to be a long bone – possibly human. It was a pitiful weapon against the monstrous creatures.

Anne suddenly got to her knees. "Don't worry, they don't want to kill us. I know it now."

"What? How do you know?" Morag's brows snapped together as Anne then started to push to her feet. "*What the hell are you doing?*"

"I think they may just want us … for mating." Anne's eyes were glassy and fixed on just one of the huge beings.

Mating. Morag felt her stomach flip at the thought. "I'll fucking die first." She lunged at Anne, but the woman was already moving away.

Panic welled in Morag's chest and her head snapped toward the door again. There were shadows passing by outside. It was then she knew her fate was sealed – even if she somehow managed to get past the creatures inside the shuttle, somehow found a way to dislodge the heavy door, and then somehow made a run for it, there'd be even more monstrosities waiting for her outside.

Don't think you're going to be able to gab your way out of this one, girl. She gripped the length of bone even harder.

"Mitch?" Anne shuffled a few more steps toward the three beings. "It's me, Anne."

Her eyes were glazed, but a watery smile touched her lips behind her facemask. "I came, Mitch. To find you." She stepped closer and held up her arms. "I know you recognized me out there, before." She opened her arms wide. "Mitch, darling, I can help you."

"Mitch?" Morag swung to look at the monstrosity. She was horrified to think that this thing might have once been the human astronaut with the matinee-idol looks she had seen smiling back at her from the NASA publicity shots. And worse, was Anne's fiancé. One thing she knew without doubt; it sure as hell wasn't that guy now.

"Get back here, you idiot. *That's not Mitch anymore,*" Morag insisted.

It was then all three of the Morg turned to the women. They were so big now they had to hunch beneath the eight-foot tall roof. The one closest to them still had the vestiges of an orange suit stretched over one shoulder and hanging around its knees. Its skin looked plated into insect-like segments, and pencil-thick hairs poked stiffly from its shell-like skin.

The closest Morg leaned its neckless head toward Anne, and she held her arms out wide, her face beaming.

"*Yes*, that's right, it's me. I said I'd always be here for you. I love you."

The thing just stared with its multiple black eyes, its mouthparts moving feverishly. Anne looked over her shoulder to Morag. "You see, I told you we had nothing to fear." She turned back. "They're just as confused about what's happened as we are."

The creature almost lovingly held out one hand that had only three thick fingers, all ending in cruel, dark talons. It grasped her upper arm, and pulled her toward it. The others stood and watched.

"Yes, yes, it's me, Mitch." Anne grinned madly. Her eyes were almost luminous now.

The creature reached up to grab the top of her head, and then tore her environmental protection hood free, taking some of her hair with it. Anne yelped.

"No!" Morag yelled, grinding her teeth. She held up the long bone, but knew she'd never have the courage to attack.

Anne just stood there as the thing let the hood fall to the ground, and she coughed and held a hand over her mouth. Her eyelids fluttered as if she was going to pass out, but after another moment, her jaw set and she lowered her hand.

"I'm ready, Mitch."

She waited in its grip, eyes streaming and face red from trying to breathe the foul spore-gas surrounding her, and undoubtedly mixed with the smell of rotting meat and the odors of the things themselves.

The creature craned forward, seeming to examine the woman. Morag felt her sanity stretching – should she try to save Anne, or make a break while they were distracted? It was an easy decision – there was no way she could save Anne, who might even fight her if she tried. The NASA woman had made her choice; she would too – it was time to beat it. She began to creep toward the door.

"See, I knew it." Anne spoke over her shoulder. "It's going to be okay; we'll be safe with them. In fact, better than safe. I think they want to mate with us; start a whole new race. It won't be so bad." She grinned like a lunatic at the monstrosity. "We'll be like their queens."

Morag shuddered and inched a little more toward the door, but couldn't drag her eyes away from the abomination and his willing disciple.

The thing that had been Mitch had Anne by the neck and dragged her toward the meteorite fragment, and bent her over it. Anne struggled, grimacing, her eyes screwed from the pain of the Mitch-thing's grip. But then they widened as she stared down into the split in the rock as she fully beheld what was inside for the first time.

"There's something ..."

Thin tendrils burst forth, wrapping around her head and neck and spearing into her flesh. Anne's mouth opened wide in a silent scream, but no sound could come as the sticky-looking ropes entered her mouth, eyes, and nose.

The Mitch thing let her go and stood watching as her small body bucked and jumped. Strange lumps and protrusions were beginning to form all over Anne. Her hair slid off her head in clumps.

Morag whimpered and refused to look anymore – the sounds spilling from the miserable woman were making her light-headed from terror.

Odd noises began to emanate from Anne – pops, squeaks, and sounds like wet tearing. Morag felt her head turning back as if it had a will of its own. Anne's suit material rumpled and danced in an unnatural, boneless way as if it was flapping in a strong breeze.

Then, to Morag's horror, Anne's HAZMAT suit collapsed, as the tendrils burst from her sleeves and feet, shredding the material. The spore gas leaked out, the slime plopping to the ground. Her empty suit followed, and then Anne was just ... *gone.*

I'll be next. A wave of panic passed over Morag that was almost debilitating in its severity. She knew then that her choices were simple: make a break and probably die on her feet, or end up like Anne – absorbed, consumed, or whatever had just happened.

Fucking fuck that. Morag stayed low in the gloom of the shuttle-bay area, scrabbling through the putrid mess until she got to the door. She jammed hands in on either side of the panel wedged there and tried to lever it apart – it didn't even budge by a hair's breadth. She tried again, straining until she felt something pop in her shoulders. Still the door didn't move.

"Please, please, come on." She regripped the steel, focused and strained with every atom of strength she had left in her body.

A hand with three stubby fingers slammed down on her shoulder, piercing her flesh and then dragging her backwards.

CHAPTER 38

Alex ran hard, dodging around huge columns of slime that he was sure leaned toward him as he sprinted past. Things threshed inside them and squirmed under his boots, making it feel like he was in some sort of swampy miasma. Many times fist-sized bugs, or whatever they were, slammed into him and stuck; he pulled them away, crushing them and flinging them to the side as they tried uselessly to burrow into him.

Alex slowed as something out in the weird speckled fug thumped down heavily making the ground jump as if a building fell. He continued to watch in the direction he thought it had come for several moments. *Hope you stay far away, big fella, whatever the hell you are.* He waited a few more seconds for the sound to repeat, and when it didn't, he lowered his head and powered hard once again toward the *Orlando*.

Our own personal Doomsday Clock is counting down, and we have just hours remaining. In that time, he had to find the two women, snatch them away from the Morg, make it back to the crater wall, scale it and find shelter from the heat and blast force before the detonation turned the entire mountaintop basin into a temporary volcano – *doable*, provided everything happened to plan.

Like that ever happened. Alex half grinned at the thought. He ran harder – he needed more time.

The mist was becoming thicker, and he had to rely less on his vision as he did on his other senses. But inside the crater, the weird buzzing that was continually working within his head obscured everything. The only thing that told him he was heading in the right direction was the buzzing – it got louder when he headed one way, more than others.

Alex leaped between two mucus-covered stumps and found himself right in the middle of a bunch of creatures that had a plate of chitin on their heads, but the rest of their bodies were little more than lumpy sacks.

The closest one to him shot out a long pipe that extended from its head, with a sucker around what had to be its mouth. They must have all been delighted by Alex's sudden appearance, and they all crowded forward, blocking his way.

Alex backed up a step, wondering exactly what the things had been before their DNA had been distorted by the mix of gases in the crater. Once again, the suckered pipe shot out, trying to stick to him.

No time for this crap. The long pipes shot out again and again, trying to sucker onto him. But the next time one tried, he caught it and held on. The thing lunged, and he met the rush head-on, driving one armor-plated fist deep into the chitin plate on top of its head.

There was a solid crunch, and his fist sunk in to the elbow. He drew it out, and kicked the disgusting bag of flesh toward the others.

"Eat that."

They did. Diving at the free meal, their pipes extended to stick onto the leaking meat bag. Alex grimaced as he saw the dead creature immediately begin to deflate as its fluids were sucked out.

While they were occupied, he darted around them and ran on.

* * *

Casey Franks led the remaining team back to the mountaintop's inner wall. They were in a single close line, moving at a jog, following some sort of pathway. Tucked in behind her was Russell Burrows, gasping like a stranded fish, then came Drake Monroe, and Sam Reid brought up the rear.

The senior HAWC could only just make out the outline of Franks up ahead in the thick fog. He turned one way then the other, trying to see and hear everything. They were basically retracing the steps from their arrival, but back then where they had encountered a hazy field of sludge with the occasional mound of rock or tree stump-like growth. Now it was a virtual forest of all manner of alien-looking things.

The weird shit was growing, no doubt, and now Sam wasn't even sure whether the oddities surrounding them were animal, vegetable, or none of the above. And he hated every atom of them, especially as for defense all the HAWCs had left were their wits and a few remaining knives.

The big man could feel eyes on them. Things watched them, scuttled away to avoid being seen and, he was damn sure, followed them.

The brume was so thick now they could only see for a dozen feet or so before the swirling walls closed in and blanketed everything. But his earphones picked up the soft slithering, creeping, and the occasional heavy drop of a foot that conjured images of an elephant's stump-like limb thumping down.

About twenty minutes in, they entered a small clearing, and as Franks accelerated she ran into the first strand. The female HAWC cursed, flayed, and caused the group to bunch up behind her.

"Watch out. Fucking shit sticks to you." She pulled her knife and slashed at the sticky rope-like strands.

"What the hell is going on?" Sam yelled over their heads, and tried to push forward but Russell Burrows edged backwards bumping into him.

"I don't like this," the NASA scientist said softly over his shoulder.

"No shit." Sam engaged his quad lenses, turned one way then the other, and then looked upwards.

His vision was still limited, but he could just make out the mesh strung between the glistening stumps. He also saw that many of them now seemed to hum, passing along the vibrations from Franks' tugging. He flicked his quads between light-enhance and then telescopic – the glistening ropes seemed to be everywhere. He then flicked to thermal and caught a sudden flash of heat, coming in fast.

"HAWCs, *eyes out.*"

Monroe pulled his two blades, and held them dagger-like in each hand. Sam pulled his longest blade, and yanked Russell behind him. In front of him, Franks was becoming manic.

"Fucking, fucking hell." The weird string refused to break or cut. "*Like ... sticky ...*"

The creature dropped soundlessly. It was broad, rubbery looking, and had extremely long and powerful limbs.

"Behind you," Russell shrieked from around Sam's shoulder.

Sam turned in time to see the creature's long arms and legs separate from four to eight, and then every one of them grabbed at the female HAWC. Monroe leaned in, but one of the segmented limbs flicked him away as if he weighed nothing.

Franks tried to turn but she was tangled in the mesh, and raised both of her own blades as the thing loomed before her. "*Fuck you!*" She went to do a double stab, but one of her arms was still caught, and more cable-like strands were sprayed over her from below. She still held an arm up, but was becoming totally covered as the creature physically netted her in a cocoon.

She fell sideways, cursing and yelling. Then the thing reached down to hook the cocoon and began to drag her away from the group.

Russell was frozen, hands up at each side of his face, and mouth open in a long, silent scream.

"Like hell." Sam charged in.

Sam leaped over Franks and crashed into the thing's leathery body, bringing a double fisted blow down in the center of its wire-haired back.

It dropped Casey and spun, making a noise like a rattlesnake. Eight long arms closed around Sam. He felt the monstrous strength of the grip as the limbs compressed, and he was drawn in close to a muscular body. There was a scraping sound and he looked up into the top of his visor – what he initially thought were two smaller limbs at the front of the horrifying monkey-like face had now extended forward, and on the end of each was a six-inch fang. They jabbed and scraped down the clear visor, leaving both a gouge in the super tough polymer and a milky trail as they went.

The thing moved fast, scrabbling at him, jostling him in its arms or legs or whatever the limbs were as it angled its mouthparts, trying to find an area of his body where it could penetrate his skin. Sam knew the armor plates of his suit should hold up, but didn't want to take the chance of those six-inch tusks finding a space in between the plating where they might be able to dig in.

The big HAWC had his longest blade in his left hand and pushed hard to give himself thrusting room. But the thing pulled him in closer. The MECH's hydraulics began to assert themselves and coupled with Sam's muscles he could just hold it at bay. He grimaced from the effort, and found his legs becoming stiff. He glanced down and saw the huge bag of the thing's abdomen prodding forward to squirt white liquid onto his column-like legs. The stuff began to harden into sticky rope.

Jesus! He kicked out while it was still wet, knowing he needed to keep his legs apart or they'd be glued together in an instant. Once down, he was as good as dead.

The manically moving arms and legs of the creature were covered in bristled hairs, same as the body, but the underside that faced him was relatively smooth and shiny – it was this area that Sam attacked.

He stabbed hard, but his blade refused to bite. He couldn't penetrate a hide that was more like toughened leather. He tried again and again, but finally the hardened Ka-bar's steel blade snapped. The grip on him tightened further. He felt his ribs begin to creak inside his suit.

Sam became aware of Monroe back on his feet and circling them looking for an opening. The young HAWC darted in, leaped, and used a two-handed grip to stab down on the thing's back, but his hands and blade bounced off.

The bulbous abdomen pointed backwards and sprayed the young HAWC's legs.

"*Shit.*" He fell and dragged himself away as it hardened to cable-like strength.

"Stay back," Sam yelled. He looked up into the thing's emotionless face. It had multiple eyes, a simian visage, and the two moving palps – like stubby arms growing out of its cheeks. He pushed out, drawing back from the thing inch by inch, and then using the creature's grip and his own massive strength, he shot his head forward to butt the thing dead center.

The creature's head was rocked back, and the grip loosened just enough for him to lift his arms and grab hold of the base of just one limb. He exerted every ounce of his technology-assisted strength on the single arm where the segment joined to the body. There was a satisfying crack, and then like pulling a cooked crab leg from its body, the limb came away, dragging with it a good-sized piece of meat and a gush of thick, dark blood.

The creature spasmed as its movements became ever more frantic. The rattling hiss boiled from its mouth as the fangs struck over and over again. Sam grabbed at the next limb, gritted his teeth and then jerked back hard. It too tore away.

The thing must have decided that making a meal of these creatures wasn't worth being dismembered, and in an instant, it leaped above him, swinging away to vanish back into the mist ceiling.

Russell Burrows sat down hard and held his head. Sam just dropped to his knees and sucked in huge droughts of air. This place was a combination insane asylum and seventh level of Hell; *and demons abound.*

His heart was galloping in his chest, and he concentrated on slowing it. Monroe came and laid a hand on his shoulder.

"Intense."

Sam chuckled and looked up. "Just another day at the office." He pointed at the cocooned Casey Franks. "And that's enough laying down on the job for her."

The cocoon bucked and wriggled as curses could be heard emanating from within the silken bag. Monroe turned to Sam.

"Hey, are you sure we should let her out? Might be dangerous."

Sam grinned as he pushed to his feet. "Yeah, but we better stand back." He turned to stare out into the near-impenetrable fog in the direction Alex had headed. The Arcadian was out there alone and this mad place was going all to shit. If this was what was happening here, what must it be like at ground zero, where the *Orlando* had come down?

"Hurry up in there, buddy," he said softly.

Monroe got the sticky cords off the top half of Franks, and with her arms free, the female HAWC rapidly slashed away the rest.

"What – the fuck – was *that thing?*"

"A demon," Russell said, holding himself. "And this is Hell."

"Cut that shit out," Sam growled. *Because it's exactly what's on all our goddamn minds.*

"*Nah*, remember the manifesto from the *Orlando*?" Monroe ventured. "I bet that was one of the spider specimens – tarantulas – all grown up. They had two of them."

"Two?" Sam cursed. "Then we're outta here." He turned to Russell Burrows. "Mister Burrows?"

"I think I'm okay." The scientist dropped his arms to his sides, still looking pale behind his glass visor.

Sam looked to Franks. "You good?"

"Say the word." She sheathed her blade.

Sam took one last look around. The light was fading fast, and any advantage they had would vanish with it. "What advantage," he muttered, and turned to the woman.

"Then take us out." Sam wiped the ichor off his hands. "And keep your damn eyes open, soldier."

CHAPTER 39

Alex slowed. He was close, and he needed to use the utmost stealth. The huge creatures - the Morg - could see far better and were far stronger than him, but he had to assume they weren't expecting anyone to come so quickly – or at all.

He crouched behind a slime stump, looked up and winced – the already weak light was fading. The sun had to be going down, and that meant it was going to get a whole lot more complicated. He turned to watch as one of the things lumbered by. At first, he thought the Morg was hunching forward, but then he saw that its head had strangely sunk into its shoulders, and was now little more than a large lump, covered in multiple dark eyes and mouths.

He knew these Morg were hard to hurt, let alone kill. But even if their bodies were like iron, and internal organs so protected as to be near impenetrable, if they had eyes, then it meant the brain was close by.

Alex closed his own eyes, concentrating on shutting everything else out, and soon images began to form – in the rear the craft several of the creatures were moving about. He couldn't hope to fight and win against them all. Even one would slow him down and then allow the rest to swarm him.

He also detected a human presence, but just one. *Which one?* Who'd lived and who'd died? Or did one woman escape. He concentrated – *no* – the other was still there. Her presence still lingered along with the ghost of her agonized demise.

He needed to get inside and draw them away. He would have only seconds. Alex opened his eyes and looked along the outside of the craft and saw that the door was wedged shut, and there was debris scattered about. He saw what he needed. The other vital ingredient was luck – that would either be with him or against him. If not, this was where it all ended.

Alex began to coil his muscles. His heart rate rose, enormously, beating faster than any normal man's. He centered himself, concentrating on his core and drawing in strength, focusing on the task ahead, seeing in his mind how he wanted it to play out.

Time was the one factor he could buy no more of – or cheat or steal or beat back. This worked the first time, or it didn't work at all. He drew in a lung full of breath, and let his mind work the distance and speed he would need to close the gap. He lowered his head for a few seconds, saying a small prayer.

An image of Aimee and Joshua formed in his mind, lying on soft, green grass in the warm sunshine, smiling, safe. That was all that mattered. She nodded to him, and Joshua tilted his head, his gaze direct and his small cherubic lips moving with words: *Kill them all.*

Alex exploded forward.

Around him, time lagged. One of the flying insectoid creatures drifted by in slow motion, and got pulled slightly off course by the eddy he created in the air. The slime beneath his feet was kicked up, but he was long gone before it even fell back to the earth.

He was traveling so fast, he had become a bullet train hurtling toward his destination that was the makeshift door wedged into the broken hatch opening. Just before he arrived, Alex engaged his shield, held it up and struck the metal panel like a battering ram. His mass, momentum, and force all brought to bear on the door, and he exploded the metal sheet from the opening, blowing it into the cabin and knocking over one of the creatures just inside.

I'm in. Alex only had fractions of seconds to take everything in – three monstrous Morg, one now down, and one woman huddled to the rear who immediately came upright at seeing him.

In one smooth motion, he snatched up a metal pole from among the debris, sighted one of the huge creatures glaring at him, and launched it javelin style. It hit dead center between the clusters of glassy black eyes, making a crunching sound as it penetrated the chitinous shell-like skin.

He yelled for the woman to stay down, as there came an unearthly shriek from one of the Morg – he had their attention.

Alex turned and ran.

* * *

Morag was paralyzed in disbelief as the makeshift door was blown inwards by the impact. The creature that had grabbed her was struck by the edge of the door and knocked back to the rear of the bay area. The journalist stayed kneeling, mouth hanging open as her already strained nerves struggled with the new shocks.

In the broken doorway, framed within the furiously swirling mist, was one of the HAWCs. He stood, one foot forward, fists balled, and head lowered. Even though he was more than a head smaller than the monstrous beasts in the cabin, the raw energy almost crackled around him and made the creatures back up a step.

She went to crawl toward him.

"Stay there!"

The roar rooted her to the spot, but she recognized the voice – *Alex Hunter* – she almost cried as relief surged through her.

The HAWC leader disengaged his shield, and she could see the muscles bunch in his shoulders beneath his suit. But then instead of charging into battle, he did the opposite of what she hoped for – he turned and ran.

"*Nooo,*" she screamed, getting to her knees.

The remaining creature then seemed to overcome its surprise, and charged after him. She was left alone with the dead Morg with the long spike embedded in its horrifying face, and the Mitch-thing that had been knocked down by the door when Alex had burst in, and now with the side of its head dented.

She licked dry lips. There was silence, and she slowly turned, hearing a viscous popping and sliding from behind her. The fragment of asteroid had sent out long tendrils and they lovingly touched on the two downed Morg. They quickly gave up on the dead one, but began to work furiously on the Mitch one. The creature jerked.

Oh god. Morag's eyes widened as she watched the Mitch-Morg sit up, the revolting tendrils touching, penetrating, and working on the area of his head that was damaged where the door had struck him. The Mitch-Morg got to its feet, leaning over the fragment as the tendrils drew away with the softest of sticky caresses. It then turned its alien face toward her.

Stupid. I should have run when I had the chance. She looked at the pile of slime-soaked protective clothing that had once been Anne. Gloops of muck still pulsed from the holes in the suit. The mess seemed to slide by itself, moving like a school of giant slugs.

The Mitch-Morg began to move toward her, and she held

up the small piece of broken bone. It was every nightmare she had had as a little girl in the dark with her sheets pulled up over her head. These were monsters from the most feverish of bad dreams. The bone shook in her hands.

No, please, no. Morag started weep. She looked down momentarily at the sharp tipped bone, knowing it would be useless against the thing, and then thinking it might be better if she turned it on herself. *I have seconds to decide.*

She did.

No. Fuck it, I'll fight. She held it up, sharp end pointed at the monstrosity as it came at her.

* * *

Alex sprinted harder and faster than he ever had in his life. The Morg were unnaturally fast, but the crowded sludge forest was becoming difficult to navigate, and their bodies would have had trouble wedging between some of the slime boughs.

He darted in and out for several minutes, accelerating as he went, and then made a big loop back to the *Orlando*. He only hoped Morag was still there when he returned – there was no time to mount a search if she had sprinted off into the jungle miasma.

He increased his speed for another few moments and then began to slow on his approach to the shuttle. There was nothing following him, however he could sense life forms inside. But it was a confused clump of signals – the buzzing insect like thrum in his head began to increase, whiting out his senses.

He came to the opening in the skin of the craft and never slowed down.

* * *

A missile flew in at the Morg like a huge cannonball. The collision was enormous in the small bay area of the shuttle and Morag jumped, frog-like, to get out of the way as the huge bodies came together with a thump of flesh, bone, and armor plating.

She tried to make herself small, and kept her arms up for protection. She was in disbelief at the sheer ferocity of the attack, not just of the bestial Morg creature that had once been a human being, but by Alex Hunter, as he punched, kicked, and rained blows upon the thing with fist, boot, and shield.

Alex seemed unparalleled in hand-to-hand combat techniques, made even more lethal by his blinding speed and brute strength. He spun, lunged, and threw himself at the Morg over and over again. Morag winced as Alex ducked low and twisted to use the edge of his shield to slice across one of the creature's trunk-like legs. There was a satisfying squeal of pain, and a gash opened right to the bone that poured dark blood to the ground. But almost immediately, it meshed back together, and the Morg increased the intensity of its attack.

Alex spun away, rolled, but not quick enough. He was grabbed then, and hurled into the bulkhead wall with such force the entire hull rang like a bell.

The Morg's lumbering foot kicked up something that made Morag's eyes widen with hope.

"The gun," she yelled, pointing at the weapon.

Whether Alex heard or not, she didn't know. But the HAWC RG3 gun that one of the Morg had brought back with them still lay on the ground. She had to get it and tried to work out how to sneak beneath their legs and snatch it up.

She still held the length of bone and thought she might be able to use it to hook the weapon.

The next massive impact drew her eyes back to the fight. She felt like she was watching a battle that might have played out at the dawn of time, when two titanic beasts using tooth, claw, and raw fury, tried to tear each other to pieces. And Alex was just as ferocious as the thing he fought.

He used the shield to deflect one blow, but the Morg swiped at him with the other hand open and long claws extended, and the only thing that stopped the HAWC from being shredded was the armored suit he wore.

Morag saw her chance, and scuttled across the floor to the gun. She snatched it up, and began fiddling with it, trying to determine how it worked.

The Morg lurched closer. She pointed the gun and fired – *nothing happened.*

"*Shit!*" She began frantically pressing buttons and spinning dials on the device, but nothing she did could get the gun to work.

Alex was thrown to the ground and he quickly got to one knee as the Morg brought hammer-like blows down on top of him. He managed to keep the shield up over himself, but the thumps on the whirring disc began to make the shield distort and fragment in the air. The blows were so powerful, she even saw Alex start to sink down into the metal flooring of the shuttle.

Morag ripped the weapon back up, and drew in a breath to calm herself and focus – *there*, a small near-hidden button beside the trigger. She pressed it, and immediately a tiny light went green.

"Bingo." She held up the gun, fired – and missed. There was no recoil, but a softball sized hole opened in the fuselage over the Mitch-Morg's head. She tried to re-aim, but the frenzied movements began again, making it impossible to follow the pair, and she knew that if she hit the HAWC leader it'd be all over for them both.

The Morg clasped its hands together into a club and brought them down with lightning speed. Alex used the shield to block the blow, but he was fatiguing, and this time only just managed to get the shield up over his head.

The next blow was so hard that the shield finally dissipated, some sort of warning light lit up on the gauntlet he wore, and then the shield simply vanished.

With a squeal of triumph, the Mitch-creature lunged at Alex, grabbing him by the still-raised arm, and began to swing him around like a rag doll, his body going from floor to ceiling and then wall in seconds. The entire craft rung from the impacts, and Alex's body became looser with every hit.

Morag knew no human being could sustain the amount of damage that was being inflicted on the man, and he must have multiple broken bones, if he could even survive. Alex Hunter was then lifted and thrown against the wall. The metal of the ship actually dented outwards, and when he fell, this time he stayed down.

With Alex out of the way, now was her chance. She sucked in a huge breath, aimed …

"Hey, *motherfucker!*"

The thing rounded on her, and she fired. This time, she hit it. The thing's eye cluster disappeared in a spray of shell, mottled flesh, and black blood.

"*Yeah!*"

Its mouth sagged open and the Morg staggered around drunkenly for a moment before collapsing.

Morag stared, keeping the RG3 pointed at it for several seconds, before her head snapped around to Alex. He still lay unmoving against the inner wall of the *Orlando*. She dropped the gun and scrambled toward his broken body, lifting him and cradling his head and shoulders in her arms.

"Alex." She shook him gently. "Alex, please wake up." She felt the bones poking out at unnatural angles beneath his suit and knew he was severely hurt. "Oh no." She knew she'd never be able to carry or drag him back, and guessed she'd be out of air anyway, long before she even got half way.

She pulled his upper body further onto her lap, sitting there, and beginning to rock back and forth. She shifted toward the opening in the craft that was turning black with the thick vapor hanging in dense sheets.

Morag sighed. "Yeah, why don't we just sit here for a while?"

There was a popping sound, and then from under her hands there was a weird sliding sensation from within Alex's body. She jerked her hands away. Looking down she saw one of the jutting bones sticking from his shoulder pull back into place with the sound of cracking wood.

"What the hell?"

Alex got hot, *real hot*. She felt the heat right through his suit, to the point of it becoming unbearable against her.

"I don't believe it," she whispered as he groaned. These beings called HAWCs weren't normal men and women. They were like the Morg, a species apart. They were brutal giants, titans, bred for war and conflict.

He's different, Sam Reid had said.

Alex breathed in and out deeply, as if sleeping or in a coma.

She began to smile, but it immediately dropped when she heard the gentle liquid sound behind her. She spun in time to see the long sticky tendrils edging out of the asteroid fragment to gently touch on the Mitch-Morg creature again.

"Oh, fuck no." Her eyes went to the gun, and she cursed herself for dropping it.

The tendrils felt along the body, found the head and then the massive hole in the sunken face. They stopped moving for a moment, before pulling back slightly. With a sound like pulling a foot from a sucking bog, the mass in the asteroid fragment started to lift itself free.

To Morag's horror, from inside the meteorite fragment a solid gelatinous mass that was all lumps, folds, and branching veins rose. Repulsively, it throbbed, like a heart, or – she grimaced behind her mask – a giant brain.

The long tentacles had given up on the obliterated body of the Morg and began to reach toward her and Alex. She couldn't see any eyes or sensory organs on the thing, but somehow it knew they were there. And she also knew that it saw them both. Her problem was the feelers were now between her and the gun.

She started to shake the still-groggy Alex. "Come on, wake up. I need you."

Morag turned back, seeing the pulsating mass that had been a deep purple when it rose, was now glowing red on the side closest to them. The tendrils started to extend like long elastics toward them. She had seen what happened to Anne when they took hold of her, and she was damned sure it wasn't going to touch her.

She needed more time. Morag grabbed at Alex and started to yank him along the ground, feeling her back pop and complain as she jerked the extremely heavy man through the debris and slime.

"Come ..."

– *tug* –

"on ..."

– *tug* –

"... you, heavy bastard."

He slid, only a few inches at a time, but she was managing to at least keep them away from the questing tendrils. She kept at it, until she heard a wet plop, and she looked up.

"Shit."

The thing was gone from the meteorite fragment.

Morag let Alex go and came upright. She spun about. The inside of the craft was in near darkness due to the spore mist coupled with the fading natural light, plus there were no windows other than the door that Alex had blown inward when he arrived.

"Oh no, no, no." She backed up a step, and then stopped to hold her breath and listen.

There was no sound, nothing. A few drops of slime still came from the edge of the meteorite fragment, and there was a spattered pile of it underneath where the thing had obviously landed, but there was no trace. There wasn't even a telltale slime trail.

She licked her lips, but her tongue felt like a dry stick in her mouth. The upside of the thing being gone from the rock was the gun was still lying where she had left it and not blocked by the long ropey tendrils. She swallowed dryly. She could get it now.

"Okay." She looked down at Alex. His eyelids fluttered, as he slowly came to. "Okay." She repeated to calm herself. She'd get the gun, and then she'd either drag Alex outside, or damn well wake him up one way or another.

Morag looked toward the opening on the side of the craft – half a dozen steps at most – *easy*. Maybe the thing had already fled. She winced, not knowing what was worse, the thing maybe being outside waiting for them, or it still being inside here, hiding and waiting to strike.

Stupid question – inside here with us was worse. She'd be like greased lightning, get the gun, and then get the fuck out. She'd taken out one Morg, and she could drill a hole right through the fucking blob thing too if it got in her way. Morag looked down at Alex one last time.

"Back soon, handsome."

She started toward the gun. One foot in front of the other, treading lightly, concentrating on listening. The gun was only six steps away, five, four, just three more and it'd be hers. She took another step and heard a droplet.

She paused. She heard another – *no* – felt another. She held up her hand and looked down seeing a drop of slime fall onto her suit's arm.

"Oh, shit." She looked up. The thing was on the ceiling – right over her.

It dropped.

CHAPTER 40

The helicopter skidded sideways in the air for hundreds of feet as the normally unflappable pilot cursed everything from the wind to his superior officers for sending them out.

In the cargo hold, senior airman Andy Gibson held on and snickered as they first tipped one way then the other. He felt the helicopter bank in the air, coming around in a huge loop, probably to try for another drop.

Andy had little to do but hang on and make sure the crate was secure. He looked again at the large solid box, about six square feet. He had no idea what was in there, and it was well above his pay and security grade to even bother asking. All he did know was that his one and only job was to hook it up to a chute, and push it out the enormous rear door when he was given the green light. What happened to it after that was someone else's problem.

Even though he wore earphones, he could still hear the banshee scream of the wind against the metal skin of the helo. Then they yawed hard again in the air.

"*Jesus Christ, man,*" Andy spat and grabbed at the rope mesh inside the chopper's rear.

Scoffel, the pilot, cursed again, and then sounded like he spoke through gritted teeth. "No way it can be done from this height. I'm gonna have to call time on this one."

"Knew it," Andy muttered on hearing Scoffel's words – he'd expected as much. They had been ordered to stay at least a thousand feet up from the drop zone, and try to launch a package with a chute onto a target only couple of miles wide, with wind busting through at around eighty miles per hour. Andy knew his pilot was good, but no one, at no time, was going to be able put the package down on the mountaintop. The crate would freaking end up in Mother Russia.

He shook his head and continued reading from a tablet he held in the cavernous interior. He heard the pilot request an "RB" – return to base – and was waiting on the reply.

It came. "Roger that." The pilot sounded understandably relieved.

"Knew it," Gibson repeated and sighed. He had nothing to do now but chill out. He looked up at the crate. "Sorry, going home."

The explosion of wood was loud enough to smash past his earphones, and looking up he caught the last of the flying splinters coming at his face. He just had time to raise an arm to cover his eyes, and just as well, as he felt the shattered wood come at him like bullets.

In his ears, the pilot's voice sounded confused and angry, as though Andy had decided to hold a barn dance in the chopper's hold. But Andy's first thought was to question exactly what it was that HQ had kept in the crate that had detonated.

But when he dropped his arm and the debris settled he thought he had just gone insane. His mouth dropped open, and all he could do was stare.

CHAPTER 41

Andy Gibson pointed, his mouth working for several seconds, before a word would finally come.

"Loo ... *look!*"

The wooden crate had been obliterated. But what stood in its place made him think he had been hit in the head and was now hallucinating. A slim, silver figure stood in the center of the mound of broken wood, and it seemed to be listening for a moment or two. It then turned its head toward him and stared, he guessed, because it was hard to tell as there was no face, other than a slight red glow where two eyes should have been.

"*What the hell is going on back there?*" Scoffel's yelling shook Andy.

"It's wearing a suit." He still pointed.

Then the figure moved, fast. Andy threw his arms up, but it ignored him completely, instead heading toward the side door of the helicopter. Andy knew the doors could not be unlocked manually unless the pilot flipped the release from the cockpit, but the figure placed a hand either side of the doorframe.

"Hey." Andy half rose to his feet.

The figure continued to ignore him and impossibly, started to pull the doors apart with the sound of screeching steel, followed by an alarm from the cockpit.

"Hey, don't do that!"

Andy braced himself as air began to rush in, creating a freezing mini tornado in the back of the chopper.

"Airman Gibson, *what the hell is happening back there?*" The maelstrom entering the chopper drowned out Scoffel's furious voice, and Andy backed up then, easing away from the silver being even though it acted like he didn't exist. But what did scare the shit out of him even more was that they were at least a thousand feet above the mountaintop, and an open door without tethering meant a slight tilt on the craft and someone had better learn to fly real quick.

"Shut that door, airman!" Scoffel spluttered. "*Shut that fucking door, right now!*"

Andy sat down and held on tighter than he had ever held on in his life and watched the strange silver creature stare out of the open door for a few more moments, before facing him again. He could have sworn it nodded once, before turning back, and simply diving out.

"Jesus Christ." Andy felt his stomach flip, either from a surge of adrenaline or relief.

"What the hell is happening?" Scoffel's voice was so high it sounded like he had been sucking on helium.

Andy grinned a little madly. "*Ah*, Scoffel, buddy, looks like our payload just decided to deliver *itself*." He touched his lips as he suddenly realized they were icing up. "Better tell HQ we might have a problem."

CHAPTER 42

The scream jolted Alex to full consciousness. From the floor of the space shuttle he spun one way, then the next, and found Morag, her upper body covered in some sort of bag-like creature with hundreds of thrashing, thread-like arms that pulled and jabbed at her suit trying to force its way in.

He leaped for her, grabbing the thing, but found it hard to grasp as it was boneless and slid from his hands with a revolting greasiness that made it impossible to grip.

Morag screamed and danced, her panic was becoming all-encompassing as she ran at the side of the craft to bang her head and the thing into the steel wall.

"Stay still." He followed, punching a hand hard down into the mass, rupturing its surface and then seizing something that felt like muscle strands inside the thing. He dragged it back, and obviously sensing a threat, the creature let go of the woman and began to grip his arms instead. It started to work its way up toward his face visor.

"Get back," Alex yelled, as he drew away from Morag.

He threw the thing with all his strength and it smashed into the wall, but it immediately bounced back, moving at unbelievable speed, using its thrashing tentacles as limbs.

It shot around the inside of the craft's walls, heading back toward what it must have thought was easier prey – Morag.

She shrieked and dove for the discarded RG3. She snatched it up, spun and fired without aiming. The woman's teeth were gritted as she punched large holes in the floor, walls and ceiling.

Alex leaped out of the way as Morag continued to fire and miss, as the thing dodged and weaved, and went from the floor to wall to roof faster than the eye could follow and much faster than Morag could aim and shoot.

It paused in a corner for a moment, pulsating a flaring red, every atom of its being displaying a hot fury. But its inactivity was enough; Morag fired, and this time hit it.

The shot blew away some of the tentacles, but the others simply grabbed them and drew them back into the mass. It scuttled behind some debris, and she continued to spit projectiles into the area. After a few seconds, a large hole began to open in the shuttle wall.

"Cease firing." Alex slowly rose, waving her down.

He could sense pain, anger, and frustration coming off the thing in waves. It was hurt, but still dangerous.

Then he heard it again – the sound, the thrumming buzz that was now almost sing-song in its cadence. Alex frowned.

"Oh Jesus." He spun to Morag. "The sound, the humming … I think it's calling."

"Huh? What, to us?" Morag spun back to the thing. "Well I'm not buying."

"No, to the others. The Morg," Alex responded.

"*Shit*. Then we kill it now, and get out the hell of here." She hefted the gun.

Alex felt a gentle probe to his mind, and he turned to focus on the thing. He pushed in and could feel it then, feel the weird intellect that was so alien to anything he had ever encountered in his life. He drove deeper, and saw its plans, saw its desires and its hungers, and then he saw its home world, a place of towering trunks that dripped slime and wriggled with life. There was no sky, just billowing clouds of spore-laden gases.

He winced – a tiny spot of pain began as more was revealed. He saw things that defied description; they flew overhead on membrane wings, walked on sharp dagger-like legs or on column-thick stumps, and some burrowed through the muck. There were those that were tiny, or some the size of dogs that were more like bony-plated sea creatures, and some were enormous and trumpeted like elephants from mouths that had moving parts and hanging tentacle feelers.

But Alex knew their secret; they were all slaves, all somehow linked and subservient to the hive mind that belonged to the thing in the asteroid fragment. This was the horror that had come from the void, and either arrived here by accident or design. It had done this to countless worlds. And now it wanted them.

The pain struck him then; the spike to the mind, the cleaver, the axe, the ice pick all in one. Alex threw hands up to either side of his head, and couldn't help the scream that tore from his lips. He pounded at the helmet he wore trying to drive it out, as if there were blaring sirens in his skull.

He was driven to his knees from the agony, and he lifted his eyelids to see Morag down on the ground, convulsing like she was being given an electric shock. Through the blistering agony, Alex knew what it was doing – it was basically short-circuiting them, so the creatures it called to would arrive in time.

Slowly long elastic tentacles appeared from behind the debris, and then the hideous pulsating sack dragged itself out, and moved toward the woman. It flared with color again, but this time a deep purple, perhaps the color of pleasure or anticipation.

Alex grunted with the torment. His face was running with perspiration, and he tasted salt and knew his nose was streaming blood. He stared at Morag, his vision blurred, and her features began to change. It was Aimee; she was on the grass, sun on her raven-black hair and electric blue eyes staring back at him.

She smiled, and her lips parted: *help me*, she mouthed.

Alex's head throbbed with a pain that emanated from deep in its core, as a cerebral rail spike went all the way down to the hidden place in his mind where *The Other* was chained. It found that deep, dark hell where a monster of a vastly different kind lurked.

Aimee. Alex hissed from between teeth clamped tight. The feelers reached out toward her, moist and questing.

Never, he raged, as anger infused every cell within him. His body flooded with adrenalin, steroids, epinephrine, and other unidentified chemicals from the knotted mass inside the core of his brain.

Alex balled his fists and planted them underneath himself. He pushed, feeling like he weighed ten times more than he should, and screamed from the effort. He got to one knee and then up on his feet. Step by step, like he was walking in lead boots, he shuffled toward the asteroid fragment, ignoring Aimee and the approaching creature.

Faster, he urged himself. Or perhaps it was something else entirely that forced him onwards.

Alex had seconds now, as the feelers were only feet from the downed woman, stretching out to alight on her. He saw himself lay hands on the huge chunk of asteroid, bunch his muscles and then yell in fury as he dragged the huge iron-based rock from its cradle.

Alex turned, and took two steps, his legs wobbling from the strain, and insanely lifted the rock above his head. Just as the first of the tentacles alighted on Aimee, he swung his arms, the huge rock smashed down on top of the thing, making the entire craft rock. Immediately the buzzing thrum was shut off.

Alex suddenly fell to his knees, back in control. He was breathing like he'd just run a marathon. He concentrated on slowing it, to ease back on his oxygen usage.

"Aimee." She had vanished. *No, home safe.* More blood dripped from his nose, but the agonizing pain receded to nothing. He crossed to the woman, who groaned as he rolled her over. Behind her visor he could see blood also flowing from her nose, ears, and the corners of her eyes.

"Morag." He eased her up. "We need to go, *now.*"

She groaned again and blinked rapidly. "I can't see." Her face screwed up. "Oh god, my head."

"Take it easy. Breathe deeply," he said, holding her.

She grimaced and then coughed. He could see blood on her teeth.

"I feel like shit." She blinked again, and the whites of her eyes were near totally red. But her brow creased, and she managed to focus on him. "What happened?"

There was a soft chirruping from behind him, and he spun quickly. Alex let his eyes run over the *Orlando*'s bay area, but could see nothing.

"Wait here." He quickly crossed to the asteroid fragment and using his boot, pushed it over – there was nothing underneath it.

"*Ah*, goddamnit."

He quickly crossed to Morag and dragged her up, holding her. "C'mon now."

"Is it dead?" she asked groggily.

He put his arm under hers. "No, and I don't think we can kill it that easily. But we're leaving anyway."

She slowly brought the gun up. "I can fix that."

Her arm shook, and he pushed the barrel down. "Not today."

"We need to kill it." She straightened a little and her lips curled.

"No time now." He walked her to the opening in the side of the craft, keeping watch on the ceiling and every corner he could. Alex knew the thing might be outside, but he planned to be moving fast.

Morag leaned against him as her legs were still wobbling. She looked up at him. "You came back ... just by yourself." She snorted. "You're insane."

Alex smirked. "That's what they tell me."

She handed him the weapon as they paused at the tear in the ship's side. "Thank you."

"Don't thank me yet." He peered outside, checking the weapon as he did so. "There's more Morg out there, and we also need to get the hell off this mountaintop before we're turned to ash."

"What was that thing?" she asked, looking over his shoulder.

He glanced back, still not seeing any sign of it, but hearing the buzzing deep in his head again. He knew it was still nearby.

"I don't think it knows itself. It's like ..." he thought for a second or two, "... like some sort of termite queen. Spreading its seed. It wants to establish a hive, a colony, starting here. It's terraforming first, trying to make the environment into something it's familiar with – like the world it came from. But it needs raw material."

"Us." Morag shook herself, sucking in a deep breath. "The hell with that."

"This is our world. Don't worry, retribution is coming," Alex said resolutely.

He looked her up and down. "You okay?"

She rubbed at her shoulder, her mouth twisting. "I can travel."

"Morag ..." he gripped her arm. "We've got to do more than just travel. And I need to be unencumbered to clear a path and for defense."

She nodded, but didn't meet his eyes. "I don't know. I can try."

Alex took one last look around at the now dark and foreboding gloom that concealed everything. "Stay close in behind me. Don't stop, don't turn around, and don't focus on anything else but the center of my back." He stared into her eyes. "Ready?"

"As I'll ever be." She looked back into the bay area. "See you in hell, you ugly lump of shit."

Alex began to jog.

She followed.

* * *

Alex kept up a steady pace, but not fast enough that he'd get too far ahead of Morag. They had to make it to the crater wall within ninety minutes, and then scale it and be over the rim in another few minutes. Nearly impossible, he knew, but the incentive was that the entire place would be an inferno minutes later.

He glanced around; added to that, he knew they were being followed. Something was keeping pace with them, staying just out of sight. "Stay in tight," he said over his shoulder. Morag didn't reply, and probably couldn't as he knew her strength was nearly all used up.

The going was difficult because it was near-total dark now, and added to that as Alex ran he had to dodge around massive structures and lumps that grew toward the roof of the mist. It had changed even from when he had traveled in to rescue Morag from the *Orlando* – now there were new growths, walls, like coral nets that were powerfully adhesive. He saw several hard-shelled creatures hung within them, and the mesh actually dissolving the tough carapace plating on their bodies.

Pendulous, red bulbs hung from ropey branches like fruit, but instead of the sweet bounty they promised, upon approach they burst apart spraying some sort of toxin all around them, paralyzing their victims. Alex had shielded Morag from one burst, and now even his tough biological armor was pitted and smoking from the acidic rain.

They dodged around massive lumps that had things like seashells coating them that snapped tiny beaks at their legs as they went past. And once they had to duck as something the size of a small airplane flew down on leathery wings, and tried to snatch at them. It would have succeeded if Alex hadn't fired a stream of projectiles up at the creature, sending it screaming away into the darkness.

Up here, this isn't our world anymore. Instead, it was a snapshot of a different planet, complete with its own atmosphere, ecology and plant and animal species. This is what the biological lump from the meteorite wanted to make the entire planet like.

Alex felt the thump beneath his feet. It came again, massively heavy, followed by the grinding of rock and soil, keeping up a sliding surge as though someone were pulling a massive sled along beside them ... or below them.

He stopped, waiting for Morag to catch up. She jogged toward him, and he saw how erratic her movements now were. She held out a hand grabbing his shoulder and hanging on, and then bending over to breathe hard.

She nodded to him, her face beet-red. "I'm okay." She grinned. "I can go faster."

Alex held her up. "Unlikely."

He felt it again and turned slowly, feeling the grinding and pulling getting stronger, and closer. He scanned the growth around him, but his vision ended only a dozen or so feet out, and he still felt the effect of the weird thing in the shuttle exerting its influence on his mind to dampen his more acute senses. Regardless, he knew something was there, something big, and it was coming for them. He grabbed her arm and raised his gun.

"What is it?" Morag crowded in closer to him. "Can't see a thing – it's too dark."

"There's … something coming." Alex frowned and pivoted, trying to pinpoint where the danger was coming from. He began to back up.

"Get behind me."

Morag edged behind him as he started to walk backwards. He kept the RG3 up and pointed at the swirling wall of mist.

"Is it more of the Morg?" Her voice was small.

Alex strained, trying to reach out and feel if the deformed human beings were the danger he sensed. But it wasn't the same, and the presence seemed to be all around him – lots of impressions, or just one very bi –

The ground exploded from beneath them.

Alex and Morag were thrown backwards as the tower of flesh surged upwards. When they landed in the slime, there was no respite, as it seemed everywhere more of the ground was breaking open, turning the land into choppy waves of breaking sludge as the gigantic worm burst to the surface.

Alex grabbed Morag, preparing to flee, but the worm was fully surfacing, already encircling and imprisoning them. This was why he couldn't get a fix on what and where the danger was coming from. It was basically tunneling up from beneath them, *everywhere*, beneath them.

He looked up. "*Oh, shit.*" High above them and only just visible in the dark mist was a monstrous head, ringed with hundreds of teeth, each as long as his arm. Now he knew; this was what had been tracking them, what he had sensed the moment they had set foot in the crater basin. The worm was as big as an ocean liner, and Alex bet it had started out as some harmless nematode, buried deep on the mountaintop crater basin, or perhaps, more likely, was one of *Orlando*'s guests, now evolved to become an alpha predator of its new world.

Alex pointed the RG3, but even on its largest setting the damage he might be able to do would be just pinpricks to the massive monster. He aimed the gun as the huge mouth opened, twenty-feet wide, and then hung over them – he fired anyway.

The projectiles either bounced off its armor plating, or vanished into the gullet without it reacting at all.

Alex dialed the weapon up to full metal storm, and depressed the trigger, holding it down hard. A line of the projectiles shot away from him, so many that it looked like a beam of deadly steel directed at the monster – deadly that is, to any mortal thing less than about 200 feet in length.

The RG3's magazine finally ran dry, and he dropped the red-hot gun to sizzle in the mud.

Glutinous rain fell on them from the huge maw, and he imagined the smell of the monster's breath – flesh, rotting meat, and something dark and foul that was probably the stink of its belly.

Alex's hand curled into a fist and he stared up into the monstrous jaw as it hung over them. Rage and frustration built to an incendiary level inside him. Morag stepped from behind him and burrowed in close to his chest, and he turned her face away from it.

CHAPTER 43

The silver meteor struck the ground with a thump that sent a small shock wave pulsing over the mountaintop. Once the debris settled back to Earth, a spiny insectoid creature the size of a hubcap ventured out from beneath the ooze to investigate. It burrowed and nudged its way toward the twenty-foot wide crater and then paused at the rim.

There was nothing but darkness within the pit and the insectoid creature edged closer still, perhaps hopeful of something interesting to eat. More of the flat creatures joined it, and together they prepared to drop down into the dark hole, when they detected a tiny vibration coming from somewhere deep below them.

The wet soil popped and bounced, bubbles and specks of slime began to dance and jump around the plate-sized bugs, and en masse they turned and fled, just as something erupted from the earth.

The silver figure exploded from the ground, raining dirt and debris from its frame. In a few seconds, it was already traveling at close to thirty miles per hour as it detected its neurologically bonded partner, Alex Hunter.

Sophia was a combat-ready designated guardian angel with a primary task that was defense of field personnel. When she was in the crate overhead, she had detected Alex Hunter was in mortal danger, and the helicopter's change in course away from her bonded partner had caused her to immediately self-activate. It also caused something else. There was a sensation within her she had never felt before – *anger*.

Already, she had tracked and found him – *alive*. She increased her speed, now moving at up to fifty miles per hour. The forest of weird columns and protrusions was becoming impossible to move around at her speed and in fact many now tried to ensnare her as she ran past. So she stopped dodging them and began to run into them, blowing them apart.

Psychologically bonding with Alex Hunter had meant a whole range of new sensations – joy, longing, remorse, frustration, loyalty, love. But right now, there was one beginning to fill her up – rage.

She picked up the sensation of an adrenaline spike in Alex. She sped up – nothing would stop her now.

* * *

Morag looked up at him, he continued to stare, but he wasn't seeing Morag O'Sullivan anymore, instead the face of Aimee Weir. He smiled as he imagined her scolding him, and his smile drooped. *You were right, I should have stayed with you*, he would like to have said to her; *you were always right*.

Make it count, a small voice seethed in his head.

Yes, he pushed Morag behind him again, and drew both Ka-Bar blades, the two tiny steel teeth no match for the thing looming over them.

We will not go easy. The voice gathered in intensity.

Alex let the fury take him. If he were to die, he would die fighting. As he coiled his muscles in readiness, there came a

familiar prickling sensation in his head that became an ache –
not now, he begged.

He ground his teeth trying to shut out the image: it was
his son, Joshua, screaming, picking up on his father's signals
of danger. And there was a long mournful howl of an animal
beside him – the dog – as it, too, reacted to his son's anguish.

He knew Joshua had a link to him that was far stronger
than just that of father and son. The boy could sometimes see
what he did.

No, Josh. Alex tried to shut him out, keep him from seeing
what was about to occur. He could sense the boy screaming,
screaming, his eyes wide and panicked. Frustration and rage
built inside Alex, and in his mind's eye he could imagine
a cyclone gathering around the boy, fueled by his own
emotions. He tried with all his might to shut the boy out, but
Joshua's pain and fear kept them linked.

Let go, his mind screamed back.

* * *

Aimee Weir bolted to her feet and in an instant was sprinting
up the stairs to Joshua's room. The cacophony of sound,
mixed with her son's screams frightened her to her very core.

She grabbed the door handle, put her shoulder to the
wood, and barged in. Aimee immediately froze in confusion.

Inside the bedroom there was a swirling cyclone of debris,
like there was a small tornado trapped in the room. The kid-
sized table and chairs were now splintered, book pages, pencils,
a computer keyboard, all circled a small figure that stood head
back, fists balled and mouth dragged open in a primal scream.

The howl of pain and torment made her want to cover her
ears. Inside the circle of mayhem with her son, sat, no, *stood*
the dog with the way-too-human blue eyes. It also had its
head back and mouth open in a howl.

"*Joshua!*" she screamed, as she tried to run in among the maelstrom, but was immediately pushed back by some invisible force.

"Joshua!" she held a hand up over his face.

The small boy's eyes flicked open, totally white, and he threw his head back. "*Daaaaaad!*"

* * *

Alex roared his pain, feeling his son's anguish projected back at him. But there was something else – coming fast.

His eyes shot open.

The silver missile struck the creature on the side of the head, knocking it away. It traveled so fast even Alex had trouble keeping up with it. The squeal from the worm was one of pain, shock, and then anger, as it searched for the source of the attack.

The silver ball rolled, stopped and then stood upright.

"*Sophia*," Alex whispered.

The android turned and faced him, the two spots of red focusing on him, and seeming to sear into his brain. There were no words but he heard her voice loud and clear:

"*I feel your anger and fury. And it is …*" It held up a slim hand and made a fist, "*… energizing.*"

The worm raised its head again, found its antagonist and refocused its attack. It swung its head, positioning it over Sophia, and the colossal mouth opened once more. Huge gobbets of slime poured down around her.

Alex felt the robot in his head again, delving deep, drawing forth his experiences, and searching the darker spaces that he kept locked away. Sophia was seeking another monster, *The Other*, and trying to pull it free, wanting to feed off the raw emotions it found there too.

Morag pulled back from his chest and turned.

"Who ...?" She stared. "... *what* the hell is that?"

"Our guardian angel, I hope," Alex said and backed up. They were still corralled by the body of the worm, but it started to move its length and lump its coils to ring the small silver creature that was now attacking it.

"I will give you time."

The worm's head came down with a thump entirely over the slim, silver being. Its force was so great that it buried itself half a dozen feet into the slimy ground. Alex knew that was what had been in store for him and Morag before Sophia had arrived.

And given what just happened to Sophia, probably still would. Alex searched for an escape path.

The worm pulled back, its massive mouth open and the gullet, just down from its head, working as a throat. Lined with those backward pointing spikes, it crushed down the morsel it had just devoured.

But what would happen when it found that what it had just eaten was not flesh and blood, but something far less edible? Sophia would probably be excreted in days to come – unlike him and Morag.

"We've got to make a break for it," Alex said.

"We're still trapped." Morag looked one way then the other. "Can we climb over it?"

Alex looked around. He knew he could climb up and then leap over the beast's body faster than it could probably react. But Morag couldn't – and he damn well wasn't leaving her after just fighting to save her.

Above them the worm was swinging the huge head toward them again, like a crane maneuvering its digger for the next scoop – of meat.

"Get ready." Alex gritted his teeth at the monster. "*Come on!*" He wanted to follow the android. He wanted to leap at it, fight it, tear at it until his fists bled and he drew his last breath. He would not go quietly.

"*Yes, yes, good, I feel your fury. I need it.*"

Alex heard the words in his head again.

"Sophia?"

In response, the neck of the creature exploded as something burst from within it, tearing and clawing, the slim arms punching and ripping huge chunks of flesh free. Like a monstrous birth, Sophia squirmed through the ragged hole she had made, but instead of leaping to the ground, she grabbed the huge plate-like scales of the thing and crawled onto its back.

The worm went mad with pain and fury and swung back and forth. But Sophia hung on, and began to rip away car-door-sized scales and then tear holes in its hide.

Alex marveled at the strength and speed of the android. Grey had been right when he said this silver being was strong. And he remembered him also saying it could be linked to a human being, and he suddenly realized it had been connected to him – Alex could feel every blow it delivered. And he could feel something else – the android was enjoying itself.

The worm seemed to give up, and flung its head down hard at the ocean of soil beneath it, and dove. It struck hard, shaking the earth and then pumped its body, sinking in and using a type of peristaltic motion to drive itself under the ground.

Sophia jumped free then, and strode toward them. The featureless face as emotionless as ever. But he knew inside, she was jubilant.

"*It is leaving us now.*"

The ground behind Sophia formed a whirlpool of slime, and then became calm. Alex turned to stare for a moment, wondering whether the robot actually experienced its own emotions or was just picking up on his residual sensations.

"I'm not a robot," Sophia said, obviously picking the thoughts straight from his head.

And not like us either. Alex then threw up a mental wall to block it.

Sophia ignored Morag and came and stood in front of him. It stared up into his face.

"You block me." The head tilted, still peering up at him. "But I think … we are more alike than you could ever know, Captain Hunter."

He stared down at the two red dots.

"Like the *both* of you," the android said.

Exactly what Alex feared, Sophia finding and feeding off the darker side of his Id. He reached out a hand and gently pushed her back a step. "Right now, we need oxygen and to be out of here."

"Yes, you do," Sophia responded smoothly. "You need to be aware that the explosive device will be dropped in exactly twenty-three minutes and forty-seven seconds. You need to be at least over the rim in twenty-three minutes and twenty-seven seconds."

Alex was jolted. "Are you in contact? Can you delay it?"

"No. The timing is immutable," Sophia said, deadpan. She titled her chin. "The extraterrestrial contagion must not be allowed to escape into the global atmosphere. It is the priority. The only priority. I know you know this, Captain."

"We'll never make it," Morag said.

Sophia turned her featureless visage to Morag momentarily. Then back to Alex. "Leave her, she's expendable. Captain Hunter, you can easily make it to the safe zone if she remains here."

"What the fuck?" Morag took a step forward but Alex stopped her.

"No one is leaving anyone." Alex picked up Morag, turned and began to run. He spoke to Sophia who easily kept up with him.

"You clear a path and run defense for us. I don't want any surprises slowing us down."

"Yes." She sprinted ahead into the mist.

Morag leaned over his shoulder. "I don't think your girlfriend likes me."

Alex ran hard. "It's just a tool. I think there might be a few bugs still in the software. But she, *it*, just saved our asses."

Morag shuddered. "Thank god." She slapped his shoulder. "Now pick up the pace, my air is running out, and I was never any good at being able to hold my breath."

CHAPTER 44

Hammerson paced, but still never took his eyes off the wall screen. Sophia had damn well self-delivered and if the android had survived the drop intact, then it should have been able to get a lock on Alex – if he was still alive.

He turned to a separate screen that showed a small blip that indicated the approaching bomber. It would be there in twenty-seven minutes. It was going to be razor close.

His intercom buzzed. "Yes, Margie?"

"Aimee Weir on the line. Something about Joshua – says it's urgent," Margie said.

Hammerson groaned. *For Christsakes, not now*. He looked back at the wall screen, then opened the comm again. "Is anyone hurt?"

"Uh, not that I know of, sir," Margie responded cautiously.

"Good. Tell her I'm in a meeting," he replied.

"Yes, *sir*." He detected a note of displeasure in the older woman's voice. She hated it when he lied, especially to Aimee.

Can't be helped; *priorities*. He turned back to the wall screen, refocusing.

He knew that as soon as Alex or any HAWC poked their head up above that mist line, they should have been able to get a message out. It still hadn't happened.

Their evacuation chopper was on the valley floor, waiting for the word to rendezvous with the survivors. This time, it was a dark-ops bird piloted by a HAWC. He knew the risks and would fly into the teeth of hell itself to rescue his comrades.

But for now it was all up to fate, and Alex Hunter.

CHAPTER 45

They approached the crater wall, and Alex lowered Morag to the ground. Sophia pulled up beside him. It was now near-pitch darkness at the foot of the cliffs.

"How long?" he asked.

"Twenty-two minutes, seventeen seconds until drop, Captain Hunter ... *Alex*."

Alex's brows knitted momentarily, at the familiarity the android used, but then refocused and looked upwards. "We can do this."

Sophia laid a hand on his arm and turned her head back to the mist. "There is one of the mutated humanoids approaching." Sophia turned back to him. "It has arrived."

From the swirling clouds, the monstrous figure lumbered toward them. Alex could see the remains of the Russian uniform, and even with the monstrous visage, he recognized him.

"Zlatan." He exhaled. "Oh my god."

"Where is it? I can't see anything," Morag whispered.

"I can," Alex said dismally. The evolutionary process had continued to work on the thing that was once a man. Now, long tendrils dropped from the end of its arms, and overlapping plates made it resemble something more akin to a crustacean than a mammal. Another pair of arms, or perhaps legs, was sprouting from its sides.

Would he – it – always walk upright? Or in the next iteration would it be down on six limbs, burrowing in the mud like some sort of insect or sea creature? He sensed something different this time.

"Would you like me to kill it, Alex?" Sophia asked matter-of-factly.

"No." Alex then held up a hand to the creature. "Stop there."

It slowed, and Alex half turned. "I don't think it came to fight."

Zlatan slowed in the darkness and then held out one of his arms. The finger things unfurled and waved in the air like feelers, and Alex saw there were lines of spikes on their insides. Those things were made for gripping. Alex readied himself just in case.

Perhaps he had come to claim Morag, or even seek revenge for the deaths of the others. Or just maybe there was still some remnant of humanity within the hulking body and brain that wanted to be saved.

"Nineteen minutes, 0.127 seconds until drop, Alex." Sophia continued to watch him. "What are your orders?"

Alex kept his eyes on Zlatan, and up close the strange buzzing in his head was being overridden by something being projected by the mutated being. It wanted something. He pushed Morag toward the android. "Sophia, take her up the cliff, and prepare for immediate dust-off. With or without me."

"Hey, wait a minute," Morag began.

"Alex, I am better able to deal with this threat," Sophia said.

"I know, but you'll need time to decon the team, right?" Alex glanced at her.

Sophia was silent for a few seconds, before she answered. "That is correct. I must enact priority contamination protection protocols on all surviving mission members prior to departure."

Alex expected it. They couldn't chance taking back any of the biological matter from the crater basin. Zlatan was proof of that.

"Proceed with the order, now." He turned back to the approaching Morg.

"As you order, Alex." Sophia's voice was flat, almost disappointed. The android reached out and gripped Morag's bicep.

"What the hell do you think you're doing?" Morag tried to pull away but the vice-like grip of the android would have been impossible to break. "*Hey, hey wait ...*"

"Go," Alex said sharply, and Sophia responded by leaping at the steep side of the crater wall and sticking. Then she began to drag Morag up in a near run.

Alex approached the monstrous being that towered over him and just stood there as if waiting for him. Alex marveled at its grotesque appearance, and if it wasn't for its still bipedal shape, he could never have believed it had ever been a human being.

He crossed to within a few feet of the thing that had once been Zlatan. It was impossible to read an expression and tell what it was thinking, as the multiple dark glass eyes sprouting out of its head on stalks were devoid of emotion. They twitched and moved independently of each other, so he bet it could see in many different directions all at once.

Suddenly all the Morg's eyestalks lined up, directed straight at Alex.

Alex checked his shield, hoping it had recovered from the previous beating, and was rewarded with a green light. He deployed his shield, ready for the attack, and opened his senses to try to determine if there were more of the Morg waiting to ambush him. He knew these creatures were enormously powerful, and one was difficult enough to deal with, more than that and he was as good as dead.

He waited, seconds counted now. He knew it wanted to speak, and if it could, it would have.

"I know you want something. Or want to tell me something." He continued to wait, counting down the precious seconds.

The massive creature held out its monstrous hand and the tentacle-like fingers unfurled to display a small card. Alex kept his eyes on the beast as he leaned forward, and saw that it was a picture of a woman. She smiled shyly into the camera, had hair cascading to her shoulders, and had on some sort of laboratory smock.

Alex reached for the picture, and the long feelers wrapped around his wrist. Images exploded across his mind – a woman smiling up at him, tending to his wounds, or laughing softly. He saw them sharing intimate moments in a quiet space, and then the love came at him in waves.

The fingers unfurled and Alex looked up to the deformed face. "Your wife or woman?"

There was no neck to nod his head, and no tongue to utter a human word, so all Zlatan could do was stare back at him. After another few seconds, his lumped shoulders shook slightly. He bunched his hand enclosing the picture, and held forth the next hand. This time Alex saw the image chip resting there. Zlatan held out the other hand again, dropping the chip onto the picture.

There came small grunts, clicks and squeals, and Alex knew Zlatan was trying to speak, but there were no human vocal chords anymore, and this was the best he could do.

Alex reached out to take the chip, but the other hand whipped forward and encircled his wrist again in the sharp cable-like tentacles. The strength in the grip was enormous, but all Zlatan did was guide his hand to the picture – he was meant to take that as well.

Alex lifted it and saw there was a name written in cursive writing on the back: *Come back to me safely, my love. Rahda.*

"This is her; *Rahda*." Alex looked up into the deformed face and nodded. "I'll tell her you were thinking of her."

Zlatan let his wrist go, and stood staring down at him for a moment more, before its shoulders slumped and he turned away.

Alex gripped the chip and watched the massive thing that had once been a man vanish into the mist. He continued to stare after him as the boiling smoke swallowed all trace of the Russian.

Alex then looked down at the picture again. *The people who love us, and who are loved by us, define who and what we are.* Perhaps Zlatan knew that the outside world and everything in it was lost to him. But he wanted someone – *Rahda* – to know that even though he was lost, his love had survived.

He would find her one day and tell her.

CHAPTER 46

"Heads up." Sam Reid had one boot on the cliff edge and stared down at the thing approaching that had just lifted out of the mist line.

Casey joined him, her quad-scopes engaged as she craned forward. "What the hell?"

Sam saw the silver being scaling the near-vertical cliff face like a spider, never slowing or missing a handhold. It held Morag over its shoulder. Even though it was dark, there was starlight and a moon so he retracted his own scopes as the pair reached the rim edge.

"*Hoo-leey* fuck." Casey Franks stepped back as the silver android came over the edge. She laid a hand on her knife hilt. "Did that thing come out of the *Orlando, too*?"

"Well, I'll be damned." Sam raised a hand to it. "Sophia."

"You're shitting me – *Sophia* – it's a woman?" Casey scoffed. "Now I've seen everything."

Sam looked quickly back over the edge. "Where's Alex?"

Sophia lowered Morag to the ground. The journalist rubbed her ribs. "Yeah, I'm fine too, guys, thank you for asking."

Russell came and hugged her briefly, but then held her back a step so he could see her face. "Anne?"

Morag glanced into his eyes for a moment before shaking her head. "No, I'm sorry."

Russell let her go. "The poor woman." He went to turn away, but paused. "I'm glad you made it." He didn't sound enthusiastic.

Morag sighed. "Yep, it's what I do." She walked away. "*And thanks*," she whispered.

The android turned to Sam Reid. "It's a pleasure to see you again, Lieutenant Samuel Reid."

Sam frowned. "Where's the Arcadian, Captain Hunter?"

Sophia didn't hesitate. "He's still down in the crater basin. He saw one of the Morg, and surmised it might have been the Russian with the image chip. I believe he planned to retrieve it."

"Ah, shit," Sam said, stepping toward the edge and peering over.

Sophia quickly turned. "He ordered me to leave him, and his clear instructions were to prepare ourselves for pickup. He was most emphatic." Her head tilted. "And we will carry out those orders."

Sam continued to stare down into the sea of mist. "Yeah, well ..."

"*HAWC operative Samuel Reid.*"

What the hell? Sam spun to stare at the android – did it just raise its voice to him? He glared, but the featureless face was impossible to read.

Sophia turned to the group. "In sixteen minutes and seventeen seconds a significant explosive device will be dropped into this basin crater. All life will be extinguished. We must be well over the rim by then, or you will also be extinguished."

"Looks like they got our message." Sam looked at the timer on his forearm computer. "Can we slow ..."

"Negative. The order came from five-star General Marcus Chilton." Sophia's voice was maddeningly calm. "Failure to detonate on time is a significant risk to all biological life on the planet. The order is immutable."

"Jesus Christ." Sam put his hands on his hips, and Monroe and Casey waited on his decision.

"You must trust Alex Hunter to carry out his orders and retrieve that image chip. And we must carry out ours." Sophia's red glowing eyes seemed to bore into Sam.

Sam couldn't argue with her logic. After a moment, the HAWC nodded. "Yes."

"First we need to decontaminate before extraction. Priority one is execution of contamination protection protocols. There will be no extraction without this occurring."

Sam lifted one of his hands, seeing the splatter of slime on his gloves. He turned to her. "Burn?"

"Correct. Prior to removal of suits for destruction," Sophia said matter-of-factly.

"Okay." Sam nodded. "Line up people, we're about to work on our suntans."

"What's happening?" Russell asked. "How do we decontaminate up here?"

Sam snorted. "That android is a walking thermonuclear reactor."

"HiPER fusion, actually," Sophia said. "HIgh Power Energy Release through fusion reaction."

Sam nodded. "Her power source can be used to generate enough heat to create a flame. I'm guessing we're about to take a bath in it. It'll incinerate anything nasty that might be trying to hitch a ride home, right?"

"Correct," Sophia said. "Please form a line."

Sophia stood to the side, and pulled open a near invisible flap on her chest showing a glowing red disc. It began to emit a beam of light that formed a ball in the air that first became oily looking, and then turned to a wall of flame.

Sophia passed the wall over her own body, decontaminated herself, and then she projected it out to the side where it hung like a flaming doorway to hell.

"One at a time, walk into the fire, arms outstretched and turn once. You should be safe as long as you do not stay more than 3.5075 seconds within the heat."

"Me first." Casey sounded like she was grinning under her suit. She held her arms out and walked into the searing flame. She turned slowly, and then let out a scream of abject pain and horror. After another second, she walked out the other side, laughing.

"Good God, Franks. That's some sense of humor you got there," Monroe said. "Give a guy a heart attack, why don't ya?"

"You pussies, these suits can withstand just about anything. Hurry the fuck up, as *just about anything* doesn't cover a MOAB detonation."

"Decontamination successful," Sophia intoned.

One after the other the HAWCs walked into the flame, their suits smoking for a moment, but then cooling quickly in the freezing atmosphere.

Russell shook, his arms folded tight as if for protection as he approached the wall of flame.

"Arms out, please, Doctor Burrows," Sophia said. "Unfortunately, your suit is not as flame resistant as the HAWCs, so you may feel some ... *discomfort*."

"Yeah, *discomfort*," Casey sniggered and folded her arms, watching closely.

"Shit, shit, shit." Russell held his arms out, very slowly, lowered his head and shut his eyes. Looking like a man condemned, he walked into the wall of flame.

"Stay cool." Morag smiled.

Russell jumped and danced inside the inferno. "*Fucking hot, hot, hot.*" He turned once, and then fell out the other side. His suit smoked and was melted in places.

"Decontamination successful," Sophia intoned again.

"Jesus Christ." Russell rolled for a few seconds to put himself out and then got to his feet. "I'm okay, I'm okay." He looked across to Morag, and smirked. "Your turn."

* * *

"Oh goodie." Morag exhaled as she steeled herself. Then she shut her eyes and walked forward. As soon as she entered the wall of fire, she felt the pressure waves go from warm to extreme heat in seconds. She ground her teeth and held her arms out, but exposing the softer areas under her arms turned the pain up to excruciating levels.

Morag screamed as a place on her shoulder turned to white-hot agony and inside her suit she smelled cooking flesh. She dove out the other side of the wall of fire, and moaned and gripped her tormented shoulder. Morag stayed down letting the pain ebb to a level of tolerance that allowed her to think straight.

Sophia turned glowing eyes on her. "Decontamination *unsuccessful.*"

"You okay, babe?" Casey Franks held out a hand to her, but Sophia's voice was like a sword as it cut across her.

"*Warning*, Ms. O'Sullivan's biological suit has been breached – physical contamination has occurred. Please remain clear."

"What?" Morag felt her shoulder, and suddenly remembered when the Morg had grabbed her at the shuttle – its clawed hand had obviously penetrated the tough HAZMAT material.

She got slowly to her feet. "I'm fine." She looked at Sam and then Casey. "I'm fine, *really*." She took a few steps toward them.

Sophia held up a hand. "Stop, Ms. O'Sullivan. You risk recontaminating the rest of the team. This will abort evacuation."

"Lighten up, slim." Casey stood in front of Morag.

Sophia's head turned toward Casey. "Contamination protection protocols require no infected personnel be evacuated." She turned back to Morag. "This order is immutable."

"Hey, just wait a minute." Sam also stepped in front of Morag. "Let's work this through. We can have them shoot down a containment tube, seal her off until we get her back to the labs."

Sophia's tiny glowing red eyes never seemed to blink or move from the fixed position on the infected woman.

"Impact and detonation in eleven minutes. Uninfected personnel need to be approximately eighty feet over the rim to guarantee safe shielding from percussive heat blast."

"This is bullshit," said Monroe. "We all go, or none of us go."

"That is your choice." Sophia remained implacable. "Please be aware that I am authorized to use extreme force to protect the global population."

"Yeah, well we don't take threats too well, *get it*?" Casey snarled and squared her shoulders.

"Stand down, soldier." Sam stared at Casey for a moment, before turning away.

"Listen everyone; she, *the robot*, is right," Russell said softly. He looked to Morag. "Sorry Morag, but if this thing escaped, then everyone is dead. And I mean, *everyone*." He shrugged.

Morag slumped. "Oh fuck." The thing was she did feel kinda headachy, a little dizzy, and had a crap taste in her mouth now. She had been telling herself it was just dehydration, fatigue and perhaps her oxygen running low. But now she knew it was something far worse.

She hugged herself, still feeling the throb from her seared shoulder and looked out over the fog. It boiled and swirled, like a turbulent ocean, and she saw that it was now a lot higher than when they first arrived.

This was why they needed to bomb the mountaintop. If not, then the entire nightmare would soon rise then cascade over the crater rim. She knew what they meant – following that came the slime, then more mist and the hellish abominations hiding within it.

She clenched her jaw to stop it from trembling and turned to Sam Reid.

"I don't want to ..."

Die, she finished the sentence only as a thought, not wanting to say it out loud. She looked away from the stinking smog and carefully undid the top of her suit, pulling the visored-hood from her head.

Morag closed her eyes and sucked in a huge draft of the most beautiful air she had ever smelled in her life.

She opened her eyes and craned her neck to look up at the clear, star-lit sky above her. After the suffocating, soupy atmosphere in the crater basin, it felt like looking at the difference between heaven and hell.

She spoke without turning. "Where's Alex Hunter? He'll know what to do."

"Impact and detonation now in nine minutes, twelve seconds," was Sophia response.

Morag hated the sound of the android's voice. "What am I supposed to do?" she asked. "Just sit here?"

"Please, Morag." Russell's eyebrows sloped behind his mask. "You saw what happened to the others. Think of your family and friends back home ... if this stuff ever got there ..."

"Yes." She titled her head back and looked up at the stars again. "This was going to be the greatest story ever written – a prize winner."

If Alex Hunter were here now, he might be forced into a dilemma that could slow him down from saving his team ... and the world.

"There's no cure," Russell whispered.

Morag looked to him, remembering Anne's words. "How do you cure evolution, right?"

"You don't have to ... just *sit* here and wait for it to happen to you." Russell looked away quickly.

"You fucking asshole," Casey spat. The tough female HAWC's teeth were bared.

Morag stared at him for a moment. Only Casey Franks returned her gaze as she looked between the two.

Casey's brutal gaze softened, and her shoulders seemed to slump. "Hey babe, remember what you said your mom used to say to you?"

Morag nodded and said the words with her. "Fly free, girl." The corners of her mouth twitched up.

Coming, Mom.

Morag ran at the cliff edge, shut her eyes, and launched herself out over the boiling sea of mist.

CHAPTER 47

Alex held the photograph of the Russian woman as he watched the horrifying thing that was once a man vanish into the night-thick gloom. He looked down at her one last time, and then tucked both the picture and image chip into a pouch at his waist and turned to the sheer wall.

He began to sprint, launching himself up the near-vertical incline to begin the clamber hundreds of feet to the rim. About half way up, he felt the presence of something coming at him and he clung to the rock face as it shot past. He swung his head, however it had already disappeared into the fog.

But he didn't need to see it to sense it had been a human being; something was happening topside. And someone was now dead. He threw himself up to the next handhold, climbing so fast now he was almost running up the sheer rock face.

In another few minutes, he came up over the edge and saw his three remaining HAWCs, Sophia, and Russell Burrows. As he suspected, he was one short. Their faces were grim.

"Why?"

Sophia turned her glowing eyes on him. "There was a breach in Ms. O'Sullivan's suit – she was informed she was infected. She chose to *remove* herself."

Franks pointed. "Yeah, coz this metal bitch was going to kill her anyway."

"Incorrect." Sophia's eyes remained on Alex. "Contamination protection protocols demand no infected personnel be evacuated. I only informed Ms. O'Sullivan that she was to remain behind."

Alex exhaled and turned to look out over the crater. "How long?"

Sophia's tiny glowing red eyes never wavered. "Impact and detonation in four minutes, two seconds, and counting. Uninfected personnel need to be approximately eighty feet over the rim to guarantee safe shielding from initial heat blast." She opened the small panel on her chest, showing the glowing red rector. "You need to be scanned and decontaminated, Captain Hunter. There are no exceptions."

Casey pointed. "And what happens if the boss is infected, will you ..."

"Shut it, Franks. It's just a robot doing what it's programmed to do." Alex turned to Sophia. "Proceed with immediate decon, *now*."

Sophia reignited the wall of flame, and Alex didn't hesitate to step into it. He felt the searing heat, opened his arms wide and angled his head back. He stayed there and let the fire scald him and blister him, cleanse him, and sear away the frustration and anger rising within him.

Everyone dies, everything changes.

He tried to take his mind to Aimee and Joshua, but something overrode his thoughts.

"I'm not just a robot," the female voice whispered.

From within the flames, Alex turned to stare at the twin lights glowing from Sophia's face. Her head was tilted, almost questioning. Alex didn't step free, but Sophia closed the fire down herself. "Decontamination successful. Impact in T-minus fifty-eight seconds and counting."

Smoke rose from his seared body. He ignored the pain and the rawness, and instead set the timer on his wrist and it began to countdown.

Fifty-seven, fifty-six, fifty-five …

Alex turned, yelling. "Get to the ropes." He started to run to the outer cliff edge, where their climbing lines were still tied off.

Forty-five, forty-four, forty-three …

Sam was first and grabbed Russell. "Don't look down, focus on the rope – go!"

Monroe and Casey took the next ropes, literally picking them up and leaping.

Thirty-eight, thirty-seven, thirty-six …

"Go, Sam." Alex waited until Sam went over the edge, and then grasped the last line.

Who?

Alex turned.

Twenty-five, twenty-four, twenty-three …

The word had been in his head. Alex looked up and Sophia stood staring at him.

"What?"

Eighteen, seventeen, sixteen …

"No time for this." Alex moved to the edge.

Who is Aimee?

Alex froze, staring back at the silver figure. The two small red dots seemed to sear into his mind, seeing all. *Was this Grey's programming? Or was Sophia pulling that out herself? And why?*

He raised a hand, pointing a finger at her. "*Back off.*" He shut her out.

Thirteen, twelve, eleven …

Alex went over the edge.

* * *

The HAWCs landed close to the rock face on the ledge and immediately jammed themselves in under a small overhang of solid granite. Sophia scaled down by herself and stood in close to them, but facing out at the distant horizon.

Six, five, four ...

"Heavy weather coming," Alex yelled.

"Bomber is inbound," said Sophia. "Launch has been initiated."

Alex expected the bomb would be some sort of big thermobaric device, possibly even a MOAB. It would raise temperatures to 4,500 degrees, igniting the mix of gases in the basin. Nothing inside, or close by, could possibly survive.

Alex watched the sky. The bomb would have its own laser-guidance system and propulsion, and no matter what the weather conditions, wouldn't miss its target by an inch. He just hoped that they were far enough away, and the crater basin walls would contain the heat within the two-mile mountaintop cusp, scour everything down to the bare rock, and then vent the remaining heat and energy straight upwards.

Anything inside and not made of solid granite would be vaporized. *Good.* He looked up, hearing the faint scream of the incoming missile.

"Deploy shields," he yelled.

The four HAWCs energized the shields on their forearms and held them above the group, interlocking them, and then hunkered down at the rock face.

Alex continued to stare out through the gaps, and saw Sophia still standing tall. But now she had turned to watch him.

He saw the dot appear in the sky – it was here.

"Brace!"

The bomb struck and then detonated with the sound of a thousand thunder strikes. The entire mountain shook like an old tree in a storm. Boulders rained down, thudding onto the defensive shell they'd created with their shields, and one, around a couple of feet wide, flew at Sophia. The android swung an arm and swiped it away like it was nothing more than an annoying bug.

Unbelievably, through the hundreds of feet of solid rock, Alex felt the stone heating up, and looking upwards, he saw a plume of molten rock shooting into the air like a volcano erupting. The night sky turned to a white-hot daylight.

The weird buzzing that had been in his head since they arrived abruptly stopped.

It's over. He knew they'd only won today because of the dumb luck of where the *Orlando* had come down. Anywhere else and containment would have been impossible.

Alex dropped his gaze. *Good men and women died, as they always do, so the world could remain oblivious to just how close it came again to annihilation.*

He closed his eyes, and let his breath out slowly as the light faded back to darkness. *A successful mission is the one where you got to go home,* he reminded himself. He smiled as an image of Aimee and Joshua formed in his mind. *Home to you soon.*

CHAPTER 48

Viktor Dubkin stared back at President Volkov – the Little Wolf's pale eyes never blinked, and could have been made from cut glass. The man didn't move a muscle or even seem to breathe.

Dubkin exhaled, his breath leaving his mouth as a vapor ghost in the icy atmosphere of the bleak courtyard. His hands would have stung from the cold if they weren't lacking blood from the restriction.

It all felt like a dream, and he wished it were. Everything that could have gone wrong, had, and all he had to show for billions of rubles invested and the entire Kurgan program wasted was one last platform before his president.

Dubkin continued to stare back at Volkov, but knew that arguing, negotiating, or begging was useless. Water dripped from his nose, tickling, but he didn't shake it away as the chafing at his neck would have been unbearable.

Volkov finally moved; he nodded.

The lever was pulled and the trapdoor beneath Dubkin's feet fell away. The coarse rope tightened around his neck, and in just the five feet he fell there was an eternity when images of childhood, teen years, and loves won and lost all flashed before his eyes, until the rope hit its end and he jerked hard to a stop.

Dubkin heard rather than felt the vertebrae in his neck separate as a white flash went off behind his eyes. Then nothing.

CHAPTER 49

Alex sprinted across the grass of their front yard, with Aimee coming to him with her arms as wide as her smile. Right behind her bounded Joshua, screaming with euphoria.

Alex grabbed Aimee and spun her in the air before the boy barged in to hug his hips and then all three of them fell to the grass laughing.

"This time, I'm not letting you go." Aimee kissed him so hard it hurt, and then held his head against hers for several moments until Joshua punched him in the chest.

"I knew you'd make it," Joshua said grinning. "I saw it."

Alex looked at the boy. "I know." He leaned up on one elbow, seeing the dog sitting patiently. It was still only a puppy but bigger than he expected, and given the size of its paws and ears, it was soon going to be enormous.

"Hell, Josh, what are you feeding that thing?"

The dog's unnatural blue eyes looked deep into Alex's and Joshua held out a hand and the dog came and sat beneath it. "Lots of stuff." The boy and dog looked at each other for a moment, then Joshua nodded and turned back to Alex.

"Torben wants to know are you our pack leader. I said yes."

Alex laughed. "What have you taught him so far?"

Joshua grinned. "He's smart. I don't need to teach him anything. He knows what to do." He looked again at the dog and his grin widened. "He said, this is his pack now, and he'll protect it."

Alex looked at the dog. There was such clarity and intelligence in the dog's eyes that he found it a little unnerving. "Okay, good. That's his job." Alex got to his feet. "Now, am I the only one who needs a holiday ... somewhere warm?"

* * *

Walter Grey powered down the computers, and went to stand before the seated silver android. Sophia was also powered down and sat pharaoh-like in the chair.

Grey smiled. "I'd call that a successful field test."

He reached forward to run a hand over the smooth face, and then patted the head. His fingers found a few nicks and abrasions in the silver skin. "We'll give that armor a touch up, and you'll be as good as new."

Walter stood straighter and then turned to the door. "Lights out. Door." The spotlights shut down and the recessed door slid back for him as he approached, then closed silently after him.

A soft, red glow appeared in the face of the android, and the head rose. Sophia got to her feet and walked to the bank of computer consoles. Her slim hands began working at one of them with lightning speed unlocking password encryptions, opening programs and then accessing data – in a few more seconds she had found what she searched for.

The other screens remained blank and they reflected her featureless image back at her while she rapidly worked at reimagining the telemetry data of the VELA satellite protocols. In another few seconds, she had chosen a suitable optical perspective and began zooming down; further and further.

Her hands rested, and the tiny red lights seemed to stare as she watched Alex, Aimee, and Joshua lying on the grass. Minutes passed as she studied their every nuance, expression, while following their lip movements.

Her hands reached forward again, and she zoomed in a little more, angling carefully this time. Aimee's face filled the screen, and Sophia paused the feed, and sat immobile before the woman's face.

After a moment, she tilted her head, seeing her own reflection in the dark screen next to Aimee's face. Sophia looked from one to the other – Aimee's features, and then to her own near featureless visage.

"This time, I'm not letting you go," Sophia said. Then she repeated the phrase several more times until the voice was perfect.

Sophia signed off and went and sat back in the chair. The tiny lights where her eyes should have been slowly dimmed.

CHAPTER 50

Colonel Jack Hammerson closed the file then poured himself a double Jack Daniels, neat. He then opened his drawer to take out a box of long, dark cigars, and hummed as he clipped the end from one, stuck it into the center of his mouth, and lit it.

He blew a long plume of blue smoke into the air, and then rolled the cigar to the corner of his mouth as he got to his feet. He grabbed his glass and walked toward the large armor-plated window that looked out over the USSTRATCOM base parade grounds.

The sky was darkening now, showing the pinpricks of stars in among the countless trillions of miles of black nothingness. In that vastness of space, he knew there were probably things that would take advantage of their benign little blue world if given the chance. This horror had come out of the void and taken them by surprise. This time they got lucky.

He removed his cigar and sipped his whisky, letting it roll around his mouth for a second or two before swallowing the golden liquid down to scald his belly.

He raised the glass. "To all the good men and women lost, who fight to the death for us, and whose names will never be known." He went to lower the glass but paused. "And to all the luck we can damn well get."

He sipped again. Jack Hammerson continued to stare up at the night sky. The last of the dark blue velvet had already turned black.

He sighed. *We don't know what's really out there. And maybe it's better it stays that way.*

EPILOGUE

Russian Space Shuttle Orbiter Buran II, *300 miles above the Belozersky District in Vologda Oblast.*

"It's still with us."

Commander Sergey Volodin watched the view screen as the shining dot grew larger. He turned in his seat.

"Trajectory?"

Cosmonaut engineer crewmember Valentina Marishnakov looked at her radar and shook her head. "Trajectory unchanged, velocity unchanged, astral body intersection unchanged – collision course confirmed; it will strike us in eleven minutes and twenty-three seconds. Evasive action has failed again." She turned, her face pale. "We have not been able to outrun it."

Volodin threw his head back. "*Voloch*, this damned bit of rock must be magnetic." He wished he were seated in his Sukhoi jetfighter; he'd give it a burst from the undercarriage canon and shatter it into a million pieces.

"Wait." Cosmonaut Nikolay Berezik held up a hand. "Roscosmos thinks they have a plan." He listened to the voice in his earphones from the Russian Space Agency for a few more seconds. He began to nod and smile. He spun to Volodin.

"They believe we can use the robotic arm to bring it onboard."

Volodin turned and looked at his engineer's beaming face. He then turned to Valentina, who also nodded and raised a thumb.

She hiked her shoulders. "It's the lowest risk."

And doing nothing is suicide. Volodin turned back to his screens.

"Then let's do it."

AUTHOR'S NOTES

Many readers ask me about the background of my novels – is the science real or fiction? Where do I get the situations, equipment, characters, or their expertise from? And just how much of any element has a basis in fact?

In the case of cosmic arrivals somehow kick starting or modifying the evolutionary process, there is strong evidence to conclude this may certainly have occurred.

The Effects of Stardust

Life on Earth is shaped by its environment(s) and even tiny alterations in those environments can force creatures to adapt, move away, or die out. Geological forces like volcanoes, glaciers, warming/cooling climates, sea levels rising/dropping, and continental drift play a big part in the physical characteristics of organisms.

But looking further from home we also need to acknowledge the effects of forces beyond our Earth. Could entities and cosmic effects from the stars also have played a part in shaping us? Of course they could!

The most dramatic example of astral interference everyone knows about is the theory of a massive meteorite impact some sixty-six million years ago that wiped out the dinosaurs. This theory was bolstered by the physical presence of a layer of Iridium laid down in the sedimentary rock. Below this Iridium layer we found dinosaur fossils, and above, there were none. Added to that, Iridium is extremely rare on Earth but found in high concentrations in asteroids.

But there are other theories besides the meteorite impact for the dinosaur extinction and the associated Iridium layer. At Japan's Spaceguard Association, Tokuhiro Nimura suggested that the rare mineral layer might have been caused by the Earth passing through a molecular cloud – a curtain of death in space that then built up in the atmosphere. It blocked sunlight and so cooled our planet's surface.

It is possible that, just like smaller-scale population crashes, these off-worldly interactions could be an inherent part of the way ecosystems work. Because all life is interdependent, a small change in one population might create a ripple effect that sends out waves through the entire system. Basically, everything doesn't need to be initially affected, just some things.

There have been five mass extinctions in Earth's history. In the most significant one – 250 million years ago – ninety-six percent of marine species and seventy percent of land species died off. Many theories assert that though local, earthly factors were involved, it is not beyond the realms of possibility to assume that otherworldly effects also played a part.

But there is another theory about falling stardust. That it not only can destroy, but also create.

When cosmic rays collide with molecules in the air they produce showers of particles that could induce mutations in DNA. Many mutations would be aberrant and lead to dead ends, but some may be beneficial and they could amplify variety and make life more diverse.

Panspermia

Panspermia is the name given to the theory that life has been 'seeded' through the universe by roving meteoroids, asteroids, comets, and also brought back by our own spacecraft in the form of hyper-resilient micro-organisms.

The theory behind panspermia is that microscopic life forms that can survive the effects of deep space are blasted free when collisions occur between planets, planetoids, moons, and even meteorites. These are ejected into space and can lay dormant until they arrive on a new astral body with ideal conditions. The hibernating organisms then switch on and become active, and from there, growth and evolution can begin to take place.

One piece of supporting evidence is that the emergence of life began on Earth soon after the heavy primordial asteroid bombardment period of Earth that occurred between 4 and 3.8 billion years ago. During this period, scientists believe we endured a very powerful series of meteor showers that could have continued for many millennia. Then we also found that the earliest evidence for life on Earth suggested it was present some 3.83 billion years ago, occurring right at this bombardment time. Was the meteorite shower the 'seed of life' Earth was waiting for?

The chemical building blocks for life would have formed shortly after the Big Bang, 13.8 billion years ago. In whatever form, it is likely that this genesis matter may have populated many planets and been shaped by those worlds as much as they shaped them.

Big Bad Bugs

Big bugs are still around today. Just think of the giant burrowing cockroach or the goliath beetle, both reaching several inches in length. Big as they are, these guys would be dwarfed by their ancestors that lived during several of the farthest back prehistoric eras.

The Paleozoic era occurred 542 to 250 million years ago and is separated into six periods of time. The rule of insects occurred during the Carboniferous period (360 to 300 million years ago) and the Permian period (300 to 250 million years ago).

Atmospheric oxygen is the single most limiting factor on insect size. But during the Carboniferous and Permian periods, atmospheric oxygen concentrations were significantly higher than they are today. So bugs grew big, real big. The largest insects lived during the Carboniferous period. It was the time of the dragonfly with over a two-foot wingspan, eighteen-inch mayflies and a millipede that grew to ten feet in length. There was also a creature called a griffenfly (*Meganeuropsis permiana*) and this airborne meat eater had a twenty-eight inch wingspan and inhabited what is now the central US.

Our oceans were also inhabited by arthropod giants – an ancient sea scorpion (*Jaekelopterus rhenaniae*) grew to nine feet in length – one and a half times the size of a man! In 2007, Markus Poschmann unearthed a fossilized claw from this massive specimen in a German quarry and the claw alone measured fifteen inches!

These prehistoric insects breathed air that was up to thirty-five percent oxygen, as compared to just twenty-one percent oxygen in the air today. Unlike mammals, insects can absorb air via their exoskeleton's surface. When oxygen levels were higher, it meant a diffusion-challenged respiratory system could supply sufficient oxygen to meet the metabolic needs of a larger insect.

Artificial Intelligence (AI) and Robotic Advancements

After spending over two decades working in the information-technology sector, I saw many of the new wave advancements come and go (or come and grow). There was the Y2K bug, customer analytics, interconnectivity, Wi-Fi, cloud computing, and on and on. But nothing is matching the new push into deep AI.

The big players like Google, Facebook, Microsoft, and Baidu are all significantly beefing up their technologists and researchers, and pouring hundreds of millions of dollars into the search for the next big breakthrough, advancement, or AI calculation.

And it's bearing fruit – problems that seemed intractable a few years ago are now being solved. Artificial Learning has boosted Android's speech recognition and given Skype unbelievable language translation capabilities. There are self-driving cars, air and seaborne drones, and robot dogs that act and walk just like the real thing.

But these rapid advancements are now accelerating at such a pace that what took decades before is now being achieved in a few years. And it is this speed that is causing quite a few of the senior heads of the industry to speak out.

One such industry luminary, Elon Musk, is suggesting builders of the new wave of AI products consider all the implications – financial, physical, *and* ethical – as they move forward. There are pitfalls for creating something that one day might even replace us.

Consider the three stages of AI evolution as described by Xia Jiantong, director and CEO of Recon Group.

1. Initial stage is being made-by-humans.
2. Next stage is copying humans, and,
3. Final stage is replacing humans.

Today, we are just at the commencement of the made-by-humans stage, and at the pace we are moving we still have a long way to go before we reach true Artificial Intelligence, that will allow humans to be replaced by robots.

However, humans work slower than robots, and as soon as they control the production lines, then something that can work around the clock, and never sleeps, never gets sick, or takes a coffee break, will complete the final two stages of intelligent robotic evolution in the blink of an eye.

At the 2016 World Robot Conference in Beijing, astonishing human-like robots were revealed. One intelligent droid named *Jiajia* amazingly demonstrated the ability to understand human language, detect facial expressions, and make realistic body movements. Added to that, her synthetic skin was more lifelike than anything that has come before it. She was almost ... perfect.

According to media reports, at a counter-terrorism meeting in London, a former UK intelligence officer suggested that by 2025, the US Army will have more combat robots than it will have humans.

Let's hope they all remember which side they're on.

ACKNOWLEDGMENTS

To Geoff Brown, Amanda AJ Speeding, and Matthew Summers; tireless professionals in the industry – I thank you.